TAKEN BY TOUCH AND TORMENT

MAGGIE SUNSERI

Copyright © 2024 by Maggie Sunseri.

All rights reserved. No part of this publication may be reproduced, distributed or transmitted in any form or by any means, including photocopying, recording, or other electronic or mechanical methods, without the prior written permission of the publisher, except in the case of brief quotations embodied in critical reviews and certain other noncommercial uses permitted by copyright law. For permission requests, write to the publisher, addressed "Attention: Permissions Coordinator," at the address below.

Maggie Sunseri
PO Box 1264
Versailles, Kentucky 40383
https://maggiesunseri.com

Publisher's Note: This is a work of fiction. Names, characters, places, and incidents are a product of the author's imagination. Locales and public names are sometimes used for atmospheric purposes. Any resemblance to actual people, living or dead, or to businesses, companies, events, institutions, or locales is completely coincidental.

Cover Design by Story Wrappers — storywrappers.com

TAKEN BY TOUCH AND TORMENT/Maggie Sunseri 1st ed.

CONTENT WARNINGS

For a list of content warnings please visit Maggie Sunseri's website: maggiesunseri.com.

For self-love, the love that matters most—from which all other love ripples.

1

SCARLETT

Rune had once told me he called me Little Flame because I had a fire inside of me that refused to die. He'd said that no matter how many times I'd been betrayed, abused, demeaned, and violated, I possessed a blinding hope that I tended to devotedly, never allowing it to fizzle out. He'd said it was the most beautiful thing about me—this *radical choice to stay open and warm in a world that was overwhelmingly cold and brutal.*

Then he'd told me everything he'd ever said to me was a result of my succubus magick. My parasitic manipulation. He'd said that I meant nothing to him—that I'd *never meant anything to him at all.* Everything he'd ever felt for me was nothing more than smoke rising from my dead embers.

With an inflexible, thick collar locked around my throat, Rune's lyrical spoken poetry billowed further and further out of my reach. My kidnapper, the leader of the born vampires, hoisted me to my feet and pushed me forward.

My head spun, my empty stomach rumbling. Flickering crimson candles illuminated the golden designs on the dark walls and ceiling, the onyx statues of Lillian and her consorts, and the burgundy and black furniture.

"Go to the door," Durian commanded. His tone was forceful and cold. I flinched instinctively.

I'd been fighting for so long. To keep my head lifted, my steps light, my hope in a better tomorrow vibrant and within reach. I'd been absorbing every blow, transforming each crucifixion into sublimity.

But too many wounds had been dug into my flesh—my *demon* flesh. I no longer reached to close the cuts, to clot the blood. I poured, and I leaked. My head dipped. Each step forward was labored with the weight of my heaving limbs.

In Durian's palace, surrounded by Lillian's psychopathic spawn, I was hemorrhaging. And I was lucid enough to understand that made me marked for death.

My head pounded as I moved forward, my gaze trained on the heavy, ornate door that was left open just a crack. Liza must have delivered a brutal blow to my skull when she rendered me unconscious and dragged me onto her firebird. Not to mention I'd barely slept, ate, or drank water in days. Nor had I *fed*. Because apparently, I needed to be around others in order to survive—to siphon desire from surrounding people.

I'd been on my way to see Rune. To stupidly fight for *us* one more time, even if it killed me. Clearly, fate had much worse plans.

"No, no, no."

Durian's condescending voice raised the hairs on the back of my neck.

"Crawl, pet. You have not yet earned your walking privileges."

My face heated. I froze.

And in that sliver of hesitation, I heard a *whoosh* before a loud *crack*. An excruciating burst of pain erupted on the backs of my thighs. I cried out, tears immediately pooling in my eyes as I fell to my hands and knees. A shiver rolled through me as the biting sting continued to assail my nerves in aftershock waves. Whatever he'd hit me with had been long and thin, rigid like wood.

Durian clicked his tongue on the roof of his mouth, and I moved, unable to endure another blow. I reached my hands out. And I crawled.

"I'm not surprised you lack proper training, my dear," Durian said, a deceptive note of paternal warmth in his tone.

Now that I was aware of what I was—a sex demon, born of a human and a born vampire, descended from the Dark Goddess Lillian—it was as though a dam had crumbled. I understood now that if I reached toward Durian, following the threads of his mind that leaked out as energy into the stifling air, I could read the nature of his desires.

I tasted bitter, dry thirst on my tongue as dark splotches invaded my vision. My stomach twisted with nausea. Durian wanted me humiliated. He wanted me under his complete control, with no thoughts or will of my own. He wanted to feast on my pain, get drunk off my fear and my absolute submission.

He desired for me to no longer exist as anything more than as an extension of him. But he didn't want it to come easily. No, he wanted to break me slowly, agonizingly, meticulously.

I'd never felt such ice in my veins. I'd never glimpsed such dark, unending, cruel desires.

The marble was cool and hard underneath my trembling knees. I welcomed the reprieve of the soft carpet once I reached it. I tried not to think about how much of myself was on display underneath my sweaterdress with my ass in the air.

At the cool breeze on my backside, I knew Durian was following me as I crawled toward the door and the sliver of light beyond.

"The bastard *lord* did you no favors with his weak style of rule. You, a poorly behaved human servant, are but a microcosm of his grander failures, his inability to wield true, goddess-blessed power."

I gritted my teeth, and Durian somehow knew it. Another blow hit the back of my thighs and knocked the air from my lungs. I screamed, and Durian's sickening desire only flared brighter. When I sunk to my forearms, I was struck again.

"*Up*," he said, his tone as biting as whatever cruel implement he was beating me with. "You will not falter when you're given an order, no matter how much pain and discomfort you are receiving."

My tears fell, and worse than the watery blur was the wave of light-headedness that threatened to pull me under.

And yet, there was this one tiny burst of relief—a collection of threads that tethered me to this cruel vampire that grew stronger with every crack of agony.

Durian *desired* me.

I drew in his impulses, his wants and fantasies, and through the crushing heartbreak, hopelessness, and physical torture—I was at least able to breathe again.

DURIAN WALKED me like a dog through the palace. I'd been commanded to crawl at his heel, and on several occasions, I'd been beaten with what I now knew to be a cane for falling out of pace.

Several born were milling about the halls. They all stopped to watch the show with gleaming eyes and aching fangs. I felt their eyes on my ass and what they could glimpse underneath my far too transparent lace panties.

My skin burned. My knees ached as they treaded over

marble, and my thighs scabbed with blood blisters from the cane. The only thing keeping me from falling unconscious again was the fear that doing so would leave me even more vulnerable. The idea of not knowing what was done to me while I was asleep made me violently ill, pumping just enough adrenaline into my blood to keep me awake.

Warm witch light reflected off the marble floor, tiny sparks of magick crackling through the specks of gold. The magick in this place was different from what I sensed surrounded by Rune's turned vampires. Born vampire magick was more ancient, more animalistic. It was the cyclone of a natural storm; predators feasting on weaker prey; wild, brutal sex; vengeful spirits rising from the grave. This was Lillian's magick. Dark, mysterious, sensual, and brutal.

The same magick inside of me.

When I glanced up, meeting the eyes of two born men across the hall, Durian halted. I flinched, quickly averting my eyes to his sleek black shoes.

I assumed I was about to be punished again for taking a wrong step or lifting my head.

Durian yanked me up to my knees by my collar, forcing me to sit back and look out at the gathered crowd that continued to pour out from some large room.

I caught a glimpse of Liza with a couple of other born women. I homed in on the triumphant gleam in her amber eyes, the slow spread of a vicious smile.

And despite my brokenness, a glimmer of something downright feral rushed up from my feet to my burning face. When Durian's hand clamped down on my shoulder, it grew like the hiss of a spitting snake.

"Please welcome our newest member of court—my human pet, an innocent child of Helia, born and raised on dry lands," Durian said.

My eyes darted around, noticing several intakes of breath and crazed looks. The born prized humans from dry lands—mortal lands that were protected, vampire-free safe zones established after the war—above all others. Because the sick fucks wanted us childlike, frightened, and naive when they enslaved and abused us.

"Our lost little lamb found herself serving the godless bastard, Rune." Durian paused, and the crowd echoed back vitriol until he spoke again. "But I have reclaimed her for Lillian. Just as I will reclaim everything else the turned have stolen through blasphemy and the perversion of the Dark Goddess's natural order."

I wanted to lash out. I fought to keep my face neutral, even as my thighs screamed as they leaned back against my calves and vertigo tilted my world on a spinning axis. All I could do was grab ahold of the threads of desire lancing into my skin, twirl them around my knuckles, and *yank*.

Dark power erupted in the air, and several vampires rushed toward me from the crowd.

Rabid, hungry, and desperate, they slammed up against Durian's guards. I met the gazes of the vampires in bloodlust, and I played as dumb, frightened, and innocent as they believed I was. This only drove them wilder.

Durian's grip on my shoulder tightened as he had the unruly vampires subdued and dragged away. He looked down at me, and his satisfaction was a palpable flood of warmth.

"It would appear my pet attracts quite the attention. To keep her safe and pure, I will need to employ the strictest of slave protocol."

When he grabbed my chin, the flare of power slithered out of my reach. My heart sunk. He shoved me back down on all fours.

I thought of Snow. Of Penn. Jaxon. Eli, Winnifred, Tera, and the other witches of Lumina.

Their faces disappeared the moment the cane struck again, this time on my bare ass, the fabric of my sweaterdress clenched in Durian's fist.

"I said, *heel,* you stupid whore," he hissed.

I watched my tears fall freely to the beautiful marble floors all the way to my new home.

2

SCARLETT

"Remove all blemishes from her skin except the marks of my divine correction," Durian instructed an older witch dressed in simple black. Her long, black hair was streaked with silver, fashioned into twists.

The tip of his cane was underneath my chin as I stayed rigid and still on the floor.

"And you," he spat at me, "will take care of my property. You will eat, drink, and sleep. I will not have a weak, useless, ugly little girl for a pet."

"Yes, Master." I knew the words came from my lips, but my voice sounded foreign to my own ears.

"If she steps out of line, I will be notified," he barked at the witch.

"Of course, my lord." She nodded and bowed her head. The light from the nearby fire illuminated the warm tones in her light brown skin.

Durian left, and my posture sunk an inch, more pitiful tears leaking from my eyes now that I wouldn't be punished for them.

The witch worked in silence to remove Liza's damage to my

skull and Rune's fang marks from my skin until the only marks of ownership I bore were Durian's.

When she left, my heart shattered all over again. I frantically searched my body for a mark she missed—any evidence at all of Rune's love.

∼

As I lay on what was essentially a literal dog bed by my new fireplace, an untouched platter of fruit, bread, and meat with a cup of water sat at my feet. I stared up at the intricately painted ceiling. It was a scene of Lillian seducing human men in a dark forest, the moon big and orange in the distance.

What fitting art for a succubus slave's locked and guarded chambers, just down the hall from her new vampire Master.

Durian hadn't let me be fed from when I provoked the desire of his clan. As his pet, I was—at least in his presence—safe from the masses. My new reality had one silver lining.

In fact, there were three. Though the third one was not something I was yet willing to accept and understand in its totality.

The second silver lining was that although I was now a living blood bag and probable sex slave, I was apparently a high-value one. So at least I would be raped and tortured in luxury.

I laughed, the sound a strangled, hysterical noise. I fell in and out of the empty place as I curled up on my side, staring into the flames. Laying on my back was impossible, as I was unable to tolerate the excruciating sting on my ass and the backs of my legs.

In the empty place, there was nothing. No yearning. No reaching, laughing, crying, hoping, running. There was no life, and there was no death. It was the void, the utter darkness that came before all of our infinitesimal souls and their silly dreams.

This might not have sounded very comforting to the average

person, but for me, it was quite the warm and fuzzy alternative. Because when I slipped out of the empty place, I was crawling down the halls as vampires talked loudly about my body, as they laughed and leaped for a taste before being halted by Durian's guards.

I was with Trevin out back behind the bakery, where my body slid back and forth on the damp earth. The smell of burned bread wafted through the air, and rain poured from a dark gray sky. Then I was in the cemetery, my dress torn open. I was in the alley, razor sharp fangs slicing into my wrists and neck.

Into the void I went, whenever I could manage it, where nothingness was the most tender embrace.

I didn't know what it was inside of me that allowed me to sit up and finally eat the food I was commanded to eat. I could lie and say that it was the threat of more punishment if I didn't take care of my body, of Durian's *property,* as he had put it.

But that wasn't it.

It might've been that third silver lining.

The born thought I was human. But that was far from the truth. No matter how much I hated it, hated myself, I was half *them*.

I was not born to be Lillian's slave. I was her daughter.

I shoved food into my mouth on autopilot and washed it down with water. Maybe it was the Dark Goddess herself who'd imbued me with this lingering will to survive, despite every fiber of my body and heart yearning to succumb and try again next life.

After the word *succubus* had rattled around in my mind for so long that it lost all meaning and recognition, the ache in my brutalized thighs returned in full force.

Rune's face entered my mind, and I flinched as if someone had hit me. But in this luxurious slave's quarters, I was all alone.

Suddenly my collar was far too tight, and Rune's face was

back, impossible to shake. My chest heaved as I gasped for air, clawing at the leather, yanking it until my skin was chafed and raw.

I sobbed as the vampire lord of Aristelle haunted me, tormented me. Not with his cruel words, those final crumbling moments—but with his praise, his gentle touch, and his achingly beautiful sentences.

When Rune entered my chambers, my haze of sleep and possible head injury had me crying out in utter relief. I scrambled off my soft, cushioned pet bed by the fading fireplace and ran toward him. I didn't think about how he was here or anything that had happened between this moment and when we'd first met. My brain was too fuzzy, my body too heavy, the relief so palpable that it became a thick blanket of warmth over every inch of my skin.

Just before I fell into his arms, he grabbed me by the throat. His dark eyes were cold and mean, and before I could utter a sound, he threw me roughly to the floor. The cane wounds scraped against the carpet, making me cry out.

"Rune?" I asked, my eyes welling up.

He didn't say a word. His thorny branches trembled with dark power as he stalked toward me. I should've run, but I couldn't. It didn't matter how much violence was in his eyes, how much hatred was baked into the brutally beautiful planes of his face.

I loved him, and I missed him. I'd never yearned for anything more.

"Rune," I said again, breathy, desperate, heartbroken.

His hands once again wrapped around my throat, and this time, they squeezed. His shadows crawled all over me in a tight, painful embrace. They slid over my mouth and nose, digging into my hips and stomach and screaming thighs.

And I let them. My body lurched instinctively, fighting for air. But I stayed silent, staring into Rune's irises as he killed me.

He didn't have to say anything—I could hear his words in my mind clearly. *Soulless, duplicitous demon. Parasite.*

Nothing.

As I fell away, I saw Helia's radiant light above and Lillian's cruel beauty below. The sun and the dark moon. The two halves of my soul.

Then I saw Durian's face as I gasped for air. His beady black eyes and strong nose, his straight blond hair. He lifted me and placed me back on my bed by the fire, his ice-cold hand petting the side of my head like I was a skittish firebird.

"There, there, pet. You have more sleeping to do if you have any hope of attaining perfection. Tomorrow is your first day at court."

3

SCARLETT

The same witch who'd erased Rune's fang marks from my skin was my alarm clock the next morning.

"Up," was all she said, loudly and perfectly annunciated.

Every morning since Rune had told me I was unclaimed, it took me several agonizing seconds to remember I was no longer *his*. To remember I was a succubus, instead.

This morning, I had even more to remember. For starters, I was now a slave, just like Isabella—my cruel sister who was not actually my sister. I still didn't know what to think or feel about her, and to be honest, I didn't care to try to remedy that confusion when I had far more pressing concerns.

I bit back tears as I moved to my feet, my gaze lowered to the burgundy carpet.

"Today's uniform," the witch said.

She placed a flowing, translucent black gown on a rack by the window—the window with iron bars outside to prevent me, presumably, from leaping to my death. At least the second hanger included opaque golden undergarments, as skimpy as they were.

She turned back toward me and gestured to the impeccable, luxurious vanity and rose-colored stool. "You will sit there and do your hair and makeup in a way that is pleasing to your Master. You will wear the perfume in the silver bottle. If you feel you lack any of the necessary tools to attend to your beauty needs, then you will ring the bell." She pointed to a shiny bell on the vanity counter, and I could sense a charge of magick forged into its metal.

Her eyes narrowed. "You will refer to me as Aunt Carol. And I expect to hear confirmation that you comprehend my instructions, just as you would give your Master."

Aunt? As if she were my new family? And why the hell was a witch this high in Durian's ranks, anyway? The born saw all mortals as lesser-than, even witches. That was why mortals united with the turned to defeat the born during the war.

At the first sign of her hand twitch, I said, "Yes, Aunt Carol. I understand."

Besides the pet bed and vanity, there wasn't much else in my quarters in terms of furniture. There was a single plush black chair with a high back. There was a bathroom, too, though I'd barely glanced around its decadent surroundings the single time I'd used it.

Aunt Carol followed my gaze to the porcelain sitting tub with golden feet that I could glimpse beyond the open door.

She took a step toward me and wrinkled her nose. "You'd better bathe first."

MY HUMAN BODY might've been merely a deceptive glamour, but it sure as hell didn't feel like one right now. My knees were screaming. I'd never before been so grateful for the presence of carpet, so heartbroken when the patches of soft cushioning came to an end.

I crawled all the way to my Master, much to his delight. The sheer black gown hid absolutely nothing from the dozens of prying gazes. My golden, jewel-encrusted underwear shimmered under the witch lights. They offered little relief from my immodesty.

"What a good little human," Liza cooed.

Durian allowed me to sit back on bent knees in a kneeling position. He stroked my head as I glanced around, my witch handler curtsying before taking her leave.

I was in a throne room, sitting atop a dais overlooking the most violent display of mass hedonism I'd ever seen. Vampires below were drinking elixir, feasting on humans, dancing to strange, archaic music, and openly indulging in all manner of sensual acts. When I saw a human on some kind of ritualistic altar, pleading and writhing as vampires holding daggers encircled her, my stomach sunk. I looked back at my immediate surroundings.

Durian stood before a flashy throne of black crystal that swirled with flickering magick. Surrounding him were who I assumed were his inner circle, Liza included, along with mostly born men with rigid postures and unfeeling, severe demeanors.

I kept my face neutral, delirious with pain from the crawling. Next to Liza was a born woman with the creepiest, fake-looking smile, tall with black hair and a thin, pointy nose. Like all born, she possessed an innate, otherworldly beauty. But the cruel ice she radiated was nearly enough to overshadow her natural good looks.

"I must admit, I thought you'd been exaggerating, Liza," the creepy woman said, her voice deceptively high-pitched and sweet-sounding. "She's simply exquisite."

"She was made to serve Durian," Liza said. "More evidence Lillian has blessed him with his divine mission."

Being treated like a docile animal as I listened to them speak about me in third person had a way of making me want to go fucking rabid.

Durian's eyes were cold, calculating, even as he smiled. "I have no need for *more evidence.*"

Liza straightened. "No, of course, I—"

"Evangeline. Liza," a man barked, making a beckoning motion with his hand. The two women followed him off the dais without another word.

"Pet, how badly do you want to walk? This is a victorious day of celebration, after all," Durian said. Several of his men chuckled and watched me with cruel smiles.

Their desire radiated from them in a strong current. I pulled it toward me, using it to soothe my aching knees, to quiet my racing heart.

Victorious day of celebration. What the hell did that mean? Oh gods, what had happened? My panic surged. I might've been condemned to a fate worse than death, but I still cared what happened to my friends—to Aristelle and all of Valentin. The faith that Rune and the turned would at least one day annihilate the born and dismantle the slave trade was one of the few reliefs I still harbored.

Durian yanked me up to my feet and slapped me.

A gasp left my lips, and I saw stars.

"Pets don't think," he snarled in my face, his breath reeking of copper. "Your only purpose now is to serve. And I asked you a *fucking* question."

All of my unhealed wounds opened up, demanding my attention. I wanted to shut down, to recede into the empty place. My mind grew fuzzy, and I no longer felt any sensation in my body.

Five things you see, Rune's voice echoed from my memories, the only thing in my mind that wasn't violent and hollow. *List them, Little Flame.*

Durian's blond hair, straight and unmoving. His jet-black

eyes. His pale pink lips twisted into a snarl. The light of the grand chandelier above. The men in my periphery, tonguing their throbbing fangs.

"I would like to walk very badly, Master. If you will allow it," I managed to say. The cool air had bumps rising on my skin, my nipples hardening. And they could all see it—they could see every bit of me.

Durian nodded. "I will allow you to earn walking privileges, if you can prove to me your obedience."

I wanted to float away. I didn't want to be here any longer. What had I done to deserve this? My only crime was ever being born at all.

Something you can touch?

The floor. My bare feet touched the cool marble. "Yes, Master," I whispered, even as it killed me. I may have wanted to give up. But whether it was Lillian's spite, or sheer dumb stubbornness, the tiniest part of me wanted to go down kicking and screaming.

Rune might've called it my spark—before he had forsaken me.

What are three things you can hear?

Durian's hum of approval. The blood rushing in my ears. One of the born men behind me saying, *now that's an ass I'd like to sink my teeth into.*

"Listen carefully, human," Durian said, as if he were speaking to a child. "Any hesitation will cost you. More than three instances, and you lose. You will crawl for weeks until you can try again."

I couldn't crawl any longer, and it had been less than a day of it. My knees would give out.

"Bark like a dog," Durian said.

I hesitated. And it cost me.

Durian moved quicker than my eyes could follow. He lifted me and shoved me toward his throne. He manhandled me like I was nothing more than a doll until my hands were on either arm rest, my legs were spread, and my back was arched. My back was to the room.

I had become the throne room's centerpiece, and I could sense without turning that over one hundred pairs of eyes were trained on me. Or on my biteable ass, if we wanted to be specific.

Durian's cane came down over the bruises and scabs from last night, and my scream pierced through the hall.

With it, a wave of desire from the crowd. Powerful desire from powerful men and women, and it sunk into my skin like silk, fanning my spark with new air. I heard moans and screams echo back to me. I was in a room full of nothing but violence and sex. And whether I liked it or not, it was an energy that felt like home.

But then Durian struck again, and my knees buckled.

"If you fall, you lose," Durian said, his voice the crack of a whip.

I lost my ability to feel my magick and its threads of connection to the surrounding vampires. Humiliation, shame, and agony snuffed out my tiny, stubborn flame.

I cried, and the vampires laughed, making mocking noises of faux pity.

"Aw, poor thing," someone said, laughter in his voice.

"She'll learn," another said, throaty and lustful.

After three more blows, Durian grabbed me and pulled me up to rest against his chest. His grip was tight, his thumb fingering the O-ring of my collar. "Are you willfully disobedient, or are you just stupid?"

I didn't hesitate this time. "I'm just stupid."

He spun me around, wiping the tears from my cheeks as if they were mold on a piece of bread. "Bark."

I barked.

"Louder."

I trembled, my cheeks flushing even more than they already had been. I barked louder.

Durian grinned. "Good pet."

Cruel laughter billowed toward me. I breathed in deeply. I smelled hints of jasmine and florals from my perfume. I smelled copper and the crisp sweetness of elixir.

I wiggled my toes, rooting myself to my body. I pretended I wasn't one wrong move away from breaking irreparably.

"Now I'm going to give you a proper inspection. You will not move or make a sound."

My trembling didn't cease as Durian circled me. When his long, cold fingers trailed down my spine, I shivered.

Please stop touching me, I begged internally. But no one was listening. The gods had abandoned me the same as Rune.

"That flinch counted as movement," Durian said. "One more misstep and you fail."

He didn't punish me this time. But the threat of failing was enough to have me stock still, my heart pumping hard. I had the intuition that weeks of crawling wouldn't be my only punishment for failing my first test.

His fingers trailed around my torso to my hip bone, where he poked painfully. I didn't make a sound.

Then his fingers moved lower as he stared hard into my eyes. And I wanted to run. I wanted to *break*.

They halted an inch above my pussy. He grinned. "Bad pets don't get to be played with."

Was his lack of assault supposed to be a punishment? I stayed perfectly neutral, even as relief flooded through me.

He grabbed my throat and squeezed over the collar. As my oxygen depleted, I prayed once again for this to be over.

But prayer wasn't giving me shit. If the gods didn't care, then the only person who could save me was *me*.

I wasn't a defenseless human. I had claws, even if I didn't quite know how to use them.

I followed the threads of energy that connected me to Durian. Flashes of impulses and intuitions flitted through my mind. I thought of Snow, telling me she could see my magick bursting from my aura.

Right now, your powers are all gunked up, she'd said after she'd learned more about my succubus nature. *Sometimes they're blocked, and other times, your emotions are causing them to leak out all over the place. You're operating off pure instincts. Imagine being completely in control of who you are influencing and how.*

At the time, I'd told her I didn't want to learn how to control my powers. I'd wanted her to cut them out of me instead. And though that was still what I wanted, wielding this parasitic curse might've been the only agency I still had.

You want to be done with this, I whispered to Durian's mind as his other hand inched toward my breasts. I could sense that though he'd left my genitals alone, he still wanted to grope me—to show me how little control over my body I still had. He wanted this court to see I belonged to him. He wanted to mortify me, to see even more tears fall from my bright blue eyes. He wanted their brightness to dim.

But I knew he also had other desires, ones that had nothing to do with me. If this was some sort of celebration, that meant the rumored impending war had, in fact, begun. His desire for me was nothing compared to his desire for conquest. His desire to defeat Rune and rule all of Valentin.

You have much more important things to do. You want to torment your new toy later. She's nothing. Nothing at all in the face of everything you've ever wanted.

I repeated the sentiment over and over.

Durian froze, a flicker of momentary confusion in his eyes before his fingers halted before the curve of my right breast. I fought to keep my breathing even, to appear only humiliated and frightened as he watched me.

He needed to feel triumphant. Even if I had won.

He removed his hands from my body. "You may walk, pet. Go play with the other servants. No one is to feed from you."

I concealed my overwhelming relief.

He grinned, his dark eyes flashing. "Except your Master, of course."

4

SCARLETT

The other slaves, or at least the ones not currently *in use,* were gathered on the carpet in a plush nook in the far corner. Couches, chairs, and loveseats surrounded us. It was as though we were in an invisible cage, on display for hungry vampires to snatch us at any moment.

Except for me. And I learned quickly that while my position kept me safe from Durian's court feeding from me at will, it earned me no favor in the group of my peers.

Once again, I found myself surrounded by glaring humans.

"I heard she has her own room," one girl said, lifting her chin as she looked at everyone but me. She had copper hair, freckles, and moss green eyes. She had to be no older than nineteen, and her youth broke my heart.

"Obviously," a woman closer to my age retorted, staring at me unabashedly with captivating hazel-green eyes. She brushed an unruly black curl behind her ear. "She's serving *Durian*. The future born king."

A vampire cackling like a hyena suddenly leaped onto the carpet. She licked her black lips as she stared at me, but she grabbed the man sitting to my left instead. She dragged him away, sinking her teeth into his neck. His eyes rolled back, from dissociation or bliss, I wasn't sure. Probably both. With the glazed-over look in most of these slaves' eyes, I could see clearly they were drugged. Or self-medicated, perhaps.

I didn't want to ever get to that point. I'd rather be dead.

Our babysitters watched us like hawks, listening to our every word. A couple were stoic guards, and a few were so-called *aunts*. Which I now understood were trafficking handlers charged with training us to be the best slaves we could be for our vampire overlords.

The woman my age sighed. "Fine, I'll *bite*. What's your name?"

I didn't feel like talking, especially not to people who clearly already hated me without even giving me a chance. But I was worn down, and I'd rather not *give* them a reason to despise me. Better their ire be baseless.

"Scarlett." I glanced around at them, waiting for someone to introduce themselves in return.

Just when I thought they were all going to leave me hanging, the woman who'd asked me for my name finally spoke.

"Lana," she offered, even as she appeared utterly disinterested. Still, her eyes traced over my nearly nude form before looking away.

I looked at the young girl, lifting a brow. They were the two out of the bunch that seemed the most coherent and present, at least. Most others looked very much like their lights were on, but no one was home.

She stared back, her eyes narrowing. "I can't wait for Rosalind to show up. I wonder if one of her little birds has chirped about *Scarlett* and her flawless performance up on the dais."

At the reminder that the whole room had seen Durian beat, inspect, and chastise me like a wild animal he wanted to domesticate, I flushed with shame.

Lana watched me, her gaze cool. "Toughen up, buttercup. If Rosalind won't eat you alive, then one of the masters will. This is no place for weakness."

Fine. Lana's friend would go by *bitch* until she gave me her name. I knew I should've had compassion for her position, especially given her age. But I wasn't my best self right now. Maybe I *was* just a cornered, untamed animal, two seconds away from snapping my jaws. Having my entire reality and sense of self obliterated, my heart broken, and my body damned to slavery was more than enough to give me a free pass for general bitchiness, right?

I didn't acknowledge Lana's condescending warnings. But who was Rosalind? I refused to give them the satisfaction of my interest, so I'd have to wait to find out.

"Girls and boys," one of the aunts said. Her voice was strangely sweet, the cadence of a schoolteacher's. I didn't miss the way several slaves flinched.

All the aunts were witches. It was still baffling to me that mortals had been conned by Durian and the born, willingly engaging in such evil.

"I think it's time to recite one of your prayers. Our new servant of Lillian needs our help in repenting for her old ways and stepping into the Dark Goddess's will for her."

That didn't sound great. I braced myself for the worst.

Amid the chaos of bloodthirsty, celebrating born, the slaves knelt in a circle, their eyes closed and hands clasped. Even the ones who were barely conscious.

I followed suit, especially when I caught sight of several cruel implements sitting on a table next to the other two aunts. I didn't know what half of them were, and that greatly terrified me.

I closed my eyes, my shoulders brushing the two slaves on either side of me. One of them, a woman with a blonde bob, pinched me hard in the side.

I gasped, quickly shifting so that I no longer touched her. I bit down hard on my lip before I did or said something stupid that got us both in trouble.

"Lillian, we live to serve thee," the aunt said.

The slaves began speaking as one.

"Lillian, we live to serve thee. We are Helia's perfect children, born to serve. Let our blood be as pure as our hearts. Let us always strive for perfection, to be dutiful, obedient, and pious in our every action, word, and thought."

Oh, Helia. Sickness churned in my gut, rivaled by my growing anger. I suddenly remembered the way I'd been able to wield my power, to stop Durian from groping me. These young humans didn't have that asset. Of course, they hated me. I had my own room. I was protected from vampires in bloodlust. From my short time observing the dynamics at play, I could see clearly that most slaves were not serving one master. They were serving whoever grabbed them. They had no safety, no reprieve, not a single bit of agency.

I was the only one of us with any fighting chance. Of doing *anything* that could help us. Yet here I was, two seconds away from giving up and sinking into the void forever.

Torn between fighting and succumbing, I clenched my fists hard. I might've been hemorrhaging, dealt the cruelest of fates. I might've been confused and aimless. But there was one single thing I knew for certain. One spark that was here to stay, no matter what happened to my violated flesh and my crushed, shattered heart.

These men and women were not born to serve. And whether they hated me or not, I would use my last remaining days to do whatever I could to use my power for *them*. Because I was all they had.

A rich, beautiful voice cascaded over us.

"Hello, aunties dearest."

I opened my eyes, as did most other slaves. The woman

who'd stepped into the space commanded all attention, several vampires stopping whatever vile acts they'd been performing to gaze at her.

The aunt who'd instructed us to pray shot the woman a glare.

My heart slammed against my ribs, and I could no longer hear the vicious chastisement of the aunts or the moaning vampires and screaming mortals. My eyes were locked on the woman with full waves of blonde hair, a tiny mole just above her full lips and her eyes strikingly molten brown. But I wasn't staring at her because of her beauty, her curves on full display in a decadent pink gown with sparkling diamonds around her neck.

No. I was staring at her in *recognition.*

She was not human. Nor was she vampire.

"Rosalind," the young, freckled girl said, smiling genuinely for the first time. Even after one of the aunts hit her over the head with a holy book, the hint of her grin remained.

Rosalind was staring at me as intently as I was staring at her.

It was game over. I was done for.

Because if I knew what she was immediately, then she must've known the same about me.

"You must be Scarlett," she said, her red lips curving.

I wasn't the only succubus in Durian's palace.

5

RUNE

"I come bearing gifts," Uriah said.

I turned. A cold gust of wind lifted Uriah's blond hair. He grinned, lifting two severed heads into the air. He sent them rolling across the dead grass toward me.

Venn and Lorelei. Notorious born twins that had escaped execution during the war. Cruel, vicious fighters. No doubt connected to the slave trade and in Durian's favor.

Or, *were*.

These gifts would've pleased me. If I was still capable of experiencing pleasure.

I wouldn't feel any semblance of gratification until Scarlett was safe and back where she belonged. And even then, I might torture myself forever for what I'd allowed to happen to her. I'd broken all of my promises. To protect her, to keep her safe from even one more violation of her body and mind. To never let her go.

This was by far my greatest failure in my everlasting life. And I would never forgive myself.

I checked my invisible leash for her life force every couple minutes. It was the only thing keeping me from exploding and damning the entire realm. When her pulse was rapid and erratic, I had to fight the immeasurable urge to go straight to the border and rip apart every single born on my path to her.

I eyed the severed heads for one more second before silently walking past Uriah and toward the back castle doors. His smile had long fallen. When his hand closed over my shoulder, I paused, going rigid.

"We'll get her back, Rune." He lowered his voice. "Remember she's not defenseless. She's more than human."

My fists clenched. My shadows threatened to leak. "Barely. She has no idea how to wield her magick, and her body remains completely vulnerable."

"You've always told me how resourceful she is. Intelligent. Cunning. She's a survivor, just like you."

Speaking about her was doing little to calm me. Yet, I didn't want to talk about anything else. Save for how to best wipe the born from the face of the fucking earth.

Scarlett was everywhere, inescapable. Her soft laughter carried in the wind, and her piercing blue eyes overpowered my vision every time I glanced at one of my paintings and sculptures. Sometimes I heard her whispering something witty or bratty or hauntingly profound as if she were still beside me—as if she'd never left.

Though I refused to go anywhere near my library, I'd already ordered my attendants to rebuild the room of music. I needed everything to be perfect for Scarlett when I brought her home.

Uriah and I didn't exchange another word all the way to the deliberation room, where I stepped onto the small dais overlooking my inner circle. Light trickled through tall windows behind me, warm on the back of my neck. On the grand oval table sat chalices of blood, maps, and war plans.

Mason was no longer standing with me and Uriah. She was lost in the crowd. I couldn't stand to look at her right now. She'd not only been dead wrong about Scarlett, but she'd also still pressed the witnesses of Scarlett's kidnapping for evidence that Scarlett had gone willingly. I knew Mason had only been trying to protect me—to protect the clan. But presently, I didn't give a shit. Whether or not it was rational, I couldn't help but charge her with partial blame for allowing the other half of my soul to be ripped away from me.

"The kingdom has gone silent," I said. "The dignitaries were supposed to arrive this weekend, but now that they're meeting with Durian, we're not sure if the timing remains the same. Last we heard, clans of turned in Ravenia have risen from the underground. Uprisings are occurring all over the realm, and King Earle is losing his mind even more rapidly now that he's declared war on them all. Dissenters in his court and on his council have scattered."

I didn't let them see my brokenness. Not a single crack. I spoke to my inner circle as if nothing had happened. As if nothing mattered to me more than keeping Valentin firmly under our jurisdiction and obliterating the born.

"Doesn't the kingdom need us now more than ever?" one of my younger commanders asked, referring to our weapons and magickal goods exports. He'd arrived from the front lines hours ago and would be returning soon. "They're jeopardizing one of their greatest assets. What could Durian have possibly said to change Earle's mind?"

"When I faced Durian in Hatham, he was cocky. Calculated. I suspect he's been in communication with Earle for months now, whispering in his ear and feeding his madness. By virtue of being born, he has comradery with Earle that no turned will ever attain."

No matter how many centuries I ruled Valentin, infinitely better than any born king ever had, Earle would still only ever consider me a bastard. In Earle's ancient age, it wouldn't have surprised me if Durian had managed to radicalize him to his religious fanaticism with ease. Earle had a legacy to uphold, and he was likely more paranoid than ever with his own turning against him.

"We must turn our attention to the mortals and turned clans in greater Ravenia now. If we've lost the kingdom, then we need strong allyship elsewhere," I said.

Gina stepped forward, cloaked in black. She corresponded with my eyes and kept tabs on the kingdom through her vast network of connections. Her shadow magick was a great asset to the clan. She was able to charge her shadows with following and listening to unsuspecting enemies. The other eyes had similarly useful gifts for spying and subterfuge.

"I'm already in contact with rising leaders in Ravenia's turned clans," Gina said. "As well as a key informant formerly in Earle's court. Durian's religious resurgence is a plague, and it's been spreading rapidly among the born. Protections for mortals are diminishing in all of Ravenia. The slave trade only grows. But we are not alone in our fight—the other turned clans are not merely the criminals and anarchists that Earle has made them out to be. They are more like us than not. They want the born out of power and the mortals to be able to live freely."

I watched as the mood of the crowd shifted, eyes lighting up. I let them have this morsel of hope. Even if the unspoken truth at our throats was that the most powerful force in the realm was Earle and his army. If they were against us… well, it was best not to imagine that outcome. It was wise to soothe ourselves with the knowledge that at least Earle would prioritize his numbers and strength in his own kingdom. We technically didn't know for *certain* he was going to send a legion of born to fight with Durian to take back Valentin.

It helped no one to say the worst-case scenario out loud, not now that the war had begun. It was better to be prepared for anything, but still teeming with hope. Our once-human hearts depended on it.

After another long hour of updates from the border districts and doling out new directives, it was time to discuss what I wanted to address more than anything else.

"Have we uncovered Durian's gifts?" I asked. A few of the clan's eyes stepped forward, none with the correct answer on their lips.

"All we know is that he is said to be born from an ancient, powerful bloodline that fell out of favor during the war," Gerrie, my impossibly pale all-seeing eye said. "And this lineage has always had strong mental magick, often kept secret and not written in history books. His father was a rumored memory reader by touch."

Mental powers made sense, given Durian had spent his whole life influencing the born through his religious persona, speech, and propaganda. I'd long suspected magick had to do with how rapidly he rose to power and altered Valentin's trajectory.

When Mason stepped forward, the energy of the crowd shifted. Everyone watched us both carefully. Though my men and women would never question me and served me with the utmost respect, Sadie and I had also trained them well. They were primed to scan for weakness, to assess threats. And it was clear Mason had fallen out of favor.

Her strong physique was in a tight black uniform, her features unreadable. But I knew her well enough to catch the briefest flicker of regret in her dark eyes.

"Given Durian's probable mental abilities, is there anything we should be worried about with Scarlett in his grasp?" She cleared her throat, adding quickly, "She might not have control over what is revealed, no matter how loyal she is."

No one knew what had truly happened between Scarlett and me but Mason and Uriah. No one else knew she was a succubus, or that I'd unclaimed her. To this room, she was merely mine.

Even if the truth was that I didn't know if Scarlett would still be loyal to me after what I put her through. They'd said she'd been on her way to see me, but I didn't know what she was planning to say. It had all happened so quickly. Sadie showed me I couldn't be influenced by succubus magick, not since she'd finely tuned me into a being of perfect control, with no desire but my own. Then Snow had let me read Isabella's diary, all the cruel words about Little Flame and the horrors her sister had allowed to happen to her even when Scarlett was a child. Scarlett had discovered her true nature at the same time I had. Which meant our powerful, inexplicable connection was pure, our love the realest thing I'd felt in my long life.

But Scarlett didn't know that. Scarlett likely thought it had all been a lie. That I'd only been drawn to her because of *what* she was, not *who* she was. She thought I'd abandoned her, that she was nothing to me but a liability to dispose of.

Worse, I didn't know exactly what she thought or how she felt—about any of it. I hadn't given her the chance.

And now she was gone.

My shadows darkened the room a few shades, my unholy power sending everyone's eyes to the floor in subservience.

"My Scarlett has nothing to offer Durian. I shielded her from sensitive information that may put her in danger." The words scraped out of my throat like knives. "I will stop at nothing to ensure she is returned to me as soon as possible. And neither will any of you."

The unspoken message was clear. Anyone who brought useful information about saving Scarlett would be in my favor, forever. This was not the time for rash actions. If I had no duty to Valentin or ability to foresee the consequences of impulsive moves, I would've gone on a warpath to Scarlett immediately.

But I would never risk her life with my blinding wrath, nor would I risk everyone and everything she'd ever loved to save her. No matter my own obsessive, rageful desires.

"You have your orders. Soon, Durian's head will be in my fucking grip, and his palace will be burned to the ground," I said. "The born have dug their own graves. No mercy, no more compromises. They will bend to our will or be eradicated from this great island forever."

While the room erupted into battle cries and comradery, I scanned for those I needed to speak to one-on-one about Durian. There was no time to rest, no time to celebrate our recent wins. Not for me.

Not until Scarlett was back on my arm, her small hand wrapped around my forearm and those big blue eyes staring up at me like I was her whole world.

∼

URIAH'S EYES lit up the way they did every time Snow came around. After she'd fought for Scarlett more valiantly than a seasoned warrior, I finally learned her name.

She was out front on the castle lawn, bundled in a white scarf and long lavender coat. It didn't surprise me in the least that the weather had taken a turn the moment Scarlett had been taken.

When Snow met my eyes, she must've seen my state of mind plainly. Because she swallowed and lowered her intensity, shifting on her feet. Her green irises mirrored my own grief.

The world was colder without Scarlett's fire.

"Aren't vampires banned from care centers?" she asked.

"We won't be seen by anyone but Isabella," I assured her.

I still didn't know if this was right. No matter how horrible Isabella was as a human and a sister, she'd endured the unspeakable. And it had only been a few days since she'd been rescued.

Nevertheless, the three of us were on our way to see her. And to our utter shock, the healers who ran the center notified us that Isabella had agreed to the meeting.

I wouldn't have cared either way, but at least now I didn't have to advertise that fact to anyone.

Scarlett was the entire reason Isabella had been saved at all. In my eyes, Isabella owed Scarlett her life whether she would ever admit it or not. And we needed information about Evangeline, the born woman who had been keeping slaves in her depraved dungeon. She was high in Durian's pecking order, just as she and her deceased psychopathic partner had been during the war. No one had forgotten how many innocents he'd had slaughtered—even children. He was one of our first assassinations. We would also want to hear about any other notable figures and events Isabella witnessed or heard about.

We had no time to waste, not for Valentin and not for Scarlett. I saw no reason to give Isabella a grace period when she'd refused to give the same to Scarlett after her numerous assaults.

Humans, witches, and shifters looked at us with respect as we passed through Nyx. That was the thing about mortals—their allegiances and moods were frighteningly changeable. That was why I didn't much care when I'd fallen out of favor. This generation had no idea of the horrors my clan had saved them from, as most hadn't been alive during the war. Certainly, none of the humans or shifters. Now that we'd rescued not only Isabella's cell of slaves but also three others as we withdrew from the born districts, it didn't surprise me in the least we were back to being the good guys. Especially with the way the born had treated mortals on their way out of our own districts, going on slaughtering rampages in the name of Lillian.

"How's William, Blondie?" Uriah asked as we turned down another cobblestone street.

Snow's head swiveled in his direction, shock and then anger in her eyes. "First of all, as if I've had any time for or interest in *men* since Scarlett fell apart and then was kidnapped."

Uriah's smirk fell, but his cockiness hadn't left him completely.

"Second, how do you even know about that? My—my sex life is none of your concern." Her cheeks flushed, which made her angrier. "You vampires are so intrusive. And you're *way* too close with each other. You're like a weird fanatical cult."

I lifted a brow at her. "Don't you belong to a coven, witch?" I may have learned her name, but she didn't need to know that.

Uriah laughed, shifting closer to Snow.

Flustered, she crossed her arms and evaded both of our gazes.

"I was just curious, sheesh," Uriah said, as painfully transparent as ever. He watched her face, his satisfied grin slowly spreading.

My flicker of amusement in irritating Snow and watching Uriah pine over her was short-lived. Because I couldn't be close to Scarlett's friend without obsessing over the little seductress. And if my obsessions were unhealthy before, they were downright sinister now.

I wasn't merely missing Scarlett, haunted by her beauty, her vulnerable heart and her dangerous mind; I was also imagining all the ways they were harming her—hurting her even worse than I had before they stole her. And every time I imagined Durian or one of his men touching her, I immediately fantasized about all the ways I would rip them limb from limb. I envisioned how I would tear skin from flesh, invent new ways of torture never before seen in even the depths of Lillian's underworld.

"This way," a human healer said to us at the back of the building. Her lips were tight, eyeing our clan tattoos with severe trepidation. Still, she allowed us to pass through the quiet halls, checking at each turn for traumatized humans.

I didn't want to harm any of these mortals either. I was fully prepared to hide myself and Uriah in my shadows if worse came to worse.

Soft laughter floated from a nearby room. It sounded like a group of rescued women were playing a card game. One of them was encouraging another, speaking to her like Snow used to speak to Scarlett when she needed to be reminded of her own worth. I'd witnessed it at least a dozen times when I'd been following Little Flame.

There was another burst of hesitant laughter.

Even in my single-minded focus, I was shocked at the depth of feeling sprouting from my icy heart. Warmth spread from my invisible wounds, even as they pulsed and ached. I imagined Scarlett laughing and playing with them, finally healing the trauma she hadn't yet integrated.

The trauma that was now being multiplied exponentially.

The witch lights above flickered, and the human shot me a glare as if she knew I was responsible. I quickly reined in my power, clenching my fists and studying the soothing light blue walls as Uriah and Snow half-heartedly bickered.

"I'll be right outside," the healer said, lifting her chin and allowing us to enter a room to her left.

The three of us entered the space. Light beamed through tall windows. They were open, the pink curtains softly billowing in the frigid air.

A blonde woman sat in a wooden chair, unmoving. She was dressed for the outdoors in a puffy blue coat, the sun illuminating her solemn features.

Her eyes flew open when we moved closer, and she was quick to rise to her feet, her features twisting into disdain.

"Are you here to apologize for being a spineless, incompetent ruler, Rune the Ruthless?"

6

SCARLETT

When the door to my chambers flew open that evening, I was sure it was Durian or one of his guards sent to kill me. Rosalind might not have said what I was as soon as she saw me, but that didn't mean she hadn't alerted someone after I'd been ordered back to my room.

I couldn't make sense of any of it. The way she'd moved about the throne room without an ounce of fear. The only ones who appeared to hate her outwardly were a few of the born women and the aunts. Most of the mortals genuinely seemed pleased to see her—especially the young girl I'd learned was named Mairin. Mairin idolized Rosalind as if she were an older sister. She didn't scorn her for being an attention-hungry, evil harlot.

But they knew what she was—I'd heard one of the aunts say it under her breath. *Wicked demoness, a horrible influence on Lillian's servants.*

Rosalind had watched me just as closely as I her, and I hadn't gained an inch. I couldn't read her desires, ascertain her true feelings or motives. She was a wild card, and it was driving me even more insane than I'd already become.

I stopped pacing as my witch handler entered, my shoulders aching from how tightly they'd been tensed.

"Come with me, girl," Aunt Carol said, her tone clipped.

"Yes, Aunt Carol." I scanned her face for clues but came up empty. She was as cold and detached as usual.

She looked me up and down, a deep frown setting in before her lip curled.

She slapped me across the cheek, and I recoiled as the air left my lungs.

"You stupid girl. Why aren't you in your evening attire?" She pointed to the clothing rack by the vanity. It was dark outside the window, only the flickering lights of Hatham in the distance.

"I—no one told me—" I stammered, trying to stay present in my body as tears sprung to my eyes from the impact.

"Don't you dare make excuses. You exist for one single purpose. To serve Lillian by pleasing your Master."

"I'm sorry," I said quickly, before she could hit me again.

She pointed again as she glared down at me, and I was quick to strip out of my clothing. Modesty no longer existed for me, apparently. And these tiny, repeated violations did excruciatingly little to preserve my sense of self, to see my body as my own. It was frightening how quickly I started to see myself through the eyes of these hungry sociopaths—a mere object, disposable, replaceable, with no mind of her own.

My evening attire was a full white lace set of lingerie, delicate and innocent. A lamb being dressed for slaughter. Overtop was a matching white gown with wide slits, barely covering anything more than the under garments.

I wasn't allowed to wear shoes. But at least I was allowed to walk.

Out in the hall, vampires leered but didn't touch. Again, I thought of Rosalind. She hadn't been grabbed once. She wasn't a slave at all. Which made sense, considering she wasn't a child of Helia.

My head spun in circles, perhaps distracting me from the sinking fear that I was being led to my death. The world had taught me that most women saw me as a threat, competition to be eliminated. And with the way Rosalind commanded that room, I could only imagine she wouldn't want me to get in her way. That had to be what Mairin had been hinting at, when she said she couldn't wait for Rosalind to show up and hear about my *performance* on the dais. She must've thought Rosalind wouldn't care for me either.

Even in the chilly evening air, I was hot and itchy as we entered Durian's chambers down the hall from mine. I fiddled with the silk straps of my garter as my heart hammered. Every time I thought about what had happened in front of Durian's throne, I wanted to throw up.

I *did* throw up as soon as I was alone this afternoon.

Stay with me, Little Flame. Come back to me.

It was cruel that Rune's voice was the only voice my subconscious wanted to listen to. The only thing that was saving me, keeping me on my feet and not in a crumpled heap on the floor.

"Oh, pet," Durian said, rising from a grand desk, placed in front of ginormous bookcases. He set down his pen as he scanned the length of my body and waved Aunt Carol away.

The door closed behind me.

We were alone.

"I was worried white wouldn't suit your fair complexion," he said, moving before me in a quick flash of vampire speed. A long finger trailed across my chest. "But I knew my obedient little servant would make sure she looked perfect in whatever her Master gave her."

I gasped when his hands tore through my gown quicker than I could track, letting it fall to the floor in a pile of ripped fabric.

He drank my fear, sharply inhaling as his beady black eyes went wild.

That wasn't the only thing he wanted to drink. And his desire to drain my blood was so strong it overwhelmed me, just as it overpowered all of his other wants.

"Lay down on the altar, child of Helia," Durian said with a sick smile.

I followed his gaze. My stomach turned over. In the middle of the living area was a dark slab of onyx, red sigils carved over every inch of it. I could sense some kind of sinister, stifling magick from its stone.

No. This isn't what you—

I frantically begun to speak to his mind, to influence him as I had in the throne room, but his desire was too potent. I couldn't wrestle it still, turn it around in my palms. This was the moment I'd fled with past marks.

But I had nowhere to run.

Durian gripped my throat hard. "Now," he hissed. His moods were volatile, untethered. They could hardly be called emotions. I didn't think Durian *felt* much of anything besides the unending desire to destroy his enemies and rule above all the rest.

He thrust me forward, his vampire strength sending me to the floor. I landed on my arm strangely, my ligaments screaming in pain at the impact.

"Pitifully frail. I forget my own strength sometimes," Durian sighed. "Knowing that, it would be prudent for you to follow instructions without hesitation, no? How hard could it possibly be to fulfill your one purpose in this life, pet? All you have to do, for the rest of your short existence, is *obey*."

He spoke to me like I was stupid and worthless, as stinging as any slap. I pushed up and silently walked to the altar.

That third silver lining was still alive and well. He might've been about to torture me, but it was at least for sport and not because he'd discovered I was a succubus.

Rosalind had kept my identity to herself. *Why* was another matter entirely. And not my most immediate concern.

I shook with terror as my back hit the hard, cool stone. And when I went to wiggle my legs, I realized my body was being held down by invisible magick.

Panic surged. I couldn't get enough air into my lungs. I feared I might hyperventilate before Durian had gotten so much as a taste.

But then he was beside me, his fingers trailing from my neck down the center of my body to my navel. When he smiled, it wasn't robotic. It was as though he were smiling genuinely for the first time.

"Lillian, I pray you find this offering pleasing. I pray I consume this blood—the purest, sweetest I've ever scented—in a way that honors you. It was a grave injustice this being of light was in the bastard Rune's grasp. Let me reclaim her for Lillian now. Show her how it feels to be consumed by a true vampire descended from the Dark Goddess. She who reigns above all other lesser deities."

At the mention of Rune, a tear slid down my cheek—a gesture that no doubt had Durian's cock hardening in his pants. I wondered if Rune would care that this was happening to me. If he had known the truth—that I wasn't an enemy plant, and I was taken against my will—would that have changed how he felt about me?

It was all still a lie. He'd only ever been drawn to me because of *what* I was. Not *who*. Just like all the rest of them. I was a fool for running to him, for hoping and yearning and pining after him like a lovesick girl. In kidnapping me, Liza had likely saved me from getting my heart demolished all over again.

Durian bore his fangs. He lifted a dagger with an ornate black crystal hilt. When I shut my eyes tight, he growled.

"Look at me, pet. Or you will not enjoy how I force your eyes open."

I didn't even want to imagine what that meant. As I drowned in fear and pain, staring up at the glint of a sharp blade, I realized I now had new voices in my mind.

I wasn't sure when it had happened, but Isabella's voice that had once been so loud and cruel in my ear had faded.

It was Snow's I heard now. Her mother, Penn's, too. The voices of all my friends in Aristelle. And Rune's, before he'd broken me.

They argued with me, telling me I still meant something—that I still mattered to them. That I was still worthy of love and care. That I was perfect just how I was.

The tears flowed freely now.

The knife cut into my stomach as I was held still by magick. All I could do was scream as Durian carved into me. What was he digging for?

Perhaps it was that tiny spark that came and went, refusing to die completely. Or maybe it was the parts of me that still belonged to Rune, or the ones that still belonged to *me*.

The blood flowed from my torso, hot and slick, running off to the sides of the altar to be collected in grooves that led to a chalice at my feet. The whole thing was fucking disgusting.

I'd never burned with such hatred.

That was, until Durian held up a mirror, so I could gaze at what he'd carved into my stomach.

Durian.

He watched my face as I bled and cried. Then he moved the mirror and forced me to stare into my own frightened eyes, the disgust that had twisted up my features.

"Poor pet. Do you think so little of me that you thought I wouldn't notice your defiance? Your refusal to break completely? The ties you won't sever that still connect you to the abomination in Lillian's once great Nyx?"

My eyes were piercingly blue when I cried. I thought of my mother's painting of the sea in the upstairs bathroom of our cottage. I wondered if Jaxon had made it to Valentin's shore, if he'd seen those strokes of clear blue we'd always dreamed of. I hoped he had.

I wanted my mother, now, even if she wasn't my mother. Even if she hadn't been capable of giving me the same love I'd seen Penn give Snow. I wanted her love all the same, just as I'd always yearned for Isabella's.

I wanted Rune's too, as silly as that was.

It was all forever out of my grasp. Maybe that said something about who I was, at my core. A primordial wound that wept and wept, the same story repeated over and over until one of these monsters finally put me out of my misery.

The mirror was cast aside, and Durian's tongue grazed my navel. He sharply inhaled. His desire flooded me, and its corresponding strength only made me more angry, more violently sick.

How cruel was it that I was forced to feed off my own suffering? That what made me prey, in turn, made me a huntress?

"No wonder Rune wanted to keep you after centuries alone," he moaned with delight. "What enrapturing blood my pet has."

Again, his tongue lapped up the blood on my stomach, wet and warm against my skin. I swallowed down bile as I stared up at the sculpted ceiling accented with gold—the gaudy display of wealth gleaned from brutality.

His tongue trailed over the grooves of his knife marks, clotting the bleeding. Which would've been a positive if it didn't mean his saliva was now entering my bloodstream.

Against my will, pleasurable tingles spread from my wounds outward like ripples in a stream. The sharpness of the pain reduced, and my body surged with warmth.

Durian raised up and stared hard into my eyes, his mouth

covered with my blood. When he clamped down on my neck, I didn't scream. I didn't writhe. I let it happen, wrapped in a blanket of unwanted pleasure.

I wanted to go back to the pain. The agony was what made sense. That was what I should've felt. Not these swells of ecstasy. My mind filled with sweet numbness, far better than the empty place.

Though I had the thought that I wanted—*needed*—him to stop, I no longer experienced the visceral disgust, the discomfort, the fear.

Durian moaned as he fed, his hands holding my body down roughly, even though it was unnecessary in the face of the altar's bondage magick. I didn't feel any of his bruising touch.

In this delirious, uncontrollable rapture, the only thought I had was *him*. Not the man whose name was carved into my flesh, but the man whose name was carved into my soul. I saw Rune's smile, heard the deep rumble of his laughter—fell into it like the warmest, most decadent bath. I inhaled his woodsy, clean masculine scent, felt his shadows curl around me.

I didn't want to be anywhere else but with him. To *be* anything else but his.

Rune's.

Rune, Rune, Rune.

Rune!

"You stupid fucking cunt."

I was yanked out of my state of peaceful bliss harshly. I woke up on the floor, covered in blood. My neck was sore and searing with heat, the pain still eclipsed by pleasure.

Disoriented, I attempted to stand, but immediately fell back down.

I saw double. Two royally pissed off Durians were looming over me, the coldest fury in their pitch-black eyes.

"How dare you say his name when your Master feeds from you, when you're being reclaimed for Lillian's glory!"

When power flooded the room, his wrath cutting through my haze sharply, I didn't think. I scrambled, this time managing to stay on my feet as I ran.

Durian laughed. I didn't make it far before I was back on the ground, held down with a boot on my back.

"Running won't get you back in my favor, you useless whore," he spat. "No matter how much it excites me."

He flipped me over and straddled me, his eyes wild. I'd awakened his predator instincts. And even though thinking was more than difficult right now, I still managed to understand that I was losing far, far too much blood.

When he went in for my neck again, I hoped he was going to clot the open wound. But that hope was soon squashed as Durian sank his teeth into my skin and continued to steal my life away.

This time, locked in bliss and quickly fading, I only saw Rune's face twisted in wrath, in disgust.

I stared into his ice-cold eyes until I saw nothing at all.

7

RUNE

"Are you here to apologize for being a spineless, incompetent ruler, Rune the Ruthless?"

The room was dead silent as Isabella faced me down, not a hint of fear in her feral alley cat eyes.

Never in my *life* had I been spoken to this brazenly, let alone by a human.

I raised my brows. "No."

Uriah made a low whistle, and Snow peered at Isabella curiously—as if she were searching for Scarlett. I'd done the same.

We wouldn't find her.

"I am sorry for what you've endured," I said. "We've come to ask you about Evangeline Naya."

Though she fought to conceal it, not a single one of us missed her flinch. She swallowed, crossing her arms and holding tight to indignation.

"Who are *you*?" she snapped at Snow.

Snow glanced at me, and I shook my head slightly.

"We'll get to that," I said. "Help us bring your born captors to justice."

Isabella shrugged, putting on a look of boredom to pair with her contempt. "Justice," she scoffed with a roll of her eyes.

I had a feeling being helpful wouldn't be much of a motivator. "You could also frame it as revenge, if that helps." My veins hummed with power, but Isabella only reacted with more vitriol. "I assure you the born will suffer."

She was unmoving, waiting for more. I'd read her diary, so I already predicted this reaction. It was clear that Snow had naively hoped for better, as she stared at Isabella in shock.

"Don't you want to avenge the humans who were with you? Don't you want to help those who are still enslaved?" Snow asked incredulously.

"No. She wants money," I answered for Isabella.

Isabella shrugged a shoulder, defensiveness creeping into her vulture-like features. "You wealthy city folk don't know what it's like to have to fight to survive," she spat. "Don't you look down on *me* for ensuring I live to see tomorrow."

Snow took a step forward, raising her finger. She laughed bitterly. "*You* don't know what it means to survive. You're the parasite, you—"

Uriah moved to face Snow, cutting her off. He wrapped his hand around her forearm and softly brought it back down to her side. I'd never seen him work to calm someone down from a fight before. It was... eerie.

Isabella displayed confusion first before it quickly transformed back into spitting anger.

"You'll be paid handsomely for your cooperation," I said.

Snow made a soft noise of derision.

"Easy, Blondie," Uriah said, his voice laced with amusement as she glared at him and yanked her arm away. He only smiled, cautiously moving back to her side.

"And how can I trust—"

"A bloodsucking demon?" I finished for Isabella. "Can we skip ahead in the script, please? I'm growing impatient. Either you want more money than you've ever seen before, or you don't."

This was the first thing to make her lips twitch, her eyes glow. "I don't know much."

"How long were you kept with Evangeline?"

Again, a slight flinch. "Two weeks, I think. Time moved differently there."

"You're an intelligent girl. Far more than the others, I bet," I started, using the oldest trick in the narcissist handbook. On cue, her facial muscles relaxed, and she blew out a huff of air. "What did you overhear? What was your read on Evangeline and the other traffickers? What connections did you put together?"

As she went inward, I could clearly see the struggle on her face to remember any part of the last few months. I could also observe her fight against her own pain, using brute force to squash it back down and out of sight.

"Evangeline was a stone-cold bitch," she said.

"Yes. With a creepy-as-all-hell voice. Ugly as shit, too. Which I thought was an impossible feat for born vampires, but alas," Uriah said with a nod.

Isabella's lips quirked up briefly, but then she seemed to remember we were vampires she hated. "She was always making us say prayers to the demon goddess—her and the aunts both. They said they were preparing us for the new order, when the born took back their rightful place as rulers."

"Aunts?" Uriah asked.

"What they called the women who watched us, who told us how to behave and who to *serve*." An unconscious shudder rolled through Isabella, and her eyes dimmed.

Fire lit up my blood, and I fought to stay focused on the task at hand instead of letting myself become consumed with thoughts of Scarlett.

"The aunts weren't vampires. They were witches," Isabella said.

Uriah and I exchanged a glance. "It's that bloody *servants-of-Lillian* shit," he muttered.

Isabella shuddered again in confirmation.

There was a particularly nasty cult of chaos witches who shunned Selena and dedicated themselves to serving Lillian. They first popped up several centuries ago, rising in and out of popularity. Though they claimed to have been called to serve Lillian by way of mystical prophecies, the truth was that they'd been brainwashed by the born. It would appear that this ancient ideology was now being blended with Durian's religious and political ethos and the growing slave trade.

"That was what they called us," Isabella murmured. "Servants of Lillian."

My shadows were itching to escape my skin and go in search of *her*. To reach and claw and dig for her desperately, devotedly.

"They told us we wouldn't have to hide for much longer," Isabella said. "They said Lillian recognized no treaty, and that soon the turned would be wiped from Valentin and all of Ravenia, too."

"Did you catch any other names? Did you overhear any specifics?"

Isabella clenched and unclenched her hands at her side, looking away from us. "This other vampire woman was close with Evangeline. On one of her visits, she stormed in talking about how you killed her partner—Eric or something."

"Frederick," I offered.

"Yeah." She glared at the floor. "She was a nasty one, too."

Liza. We were getting closer to the unavoidable, the subject I knew needed to be reserved for last. So that Isabella would be as focused on remembering anything helpful for as long as possible.

"She was angry, but she was also excited about something.

She said she'd *figured it out*. She said she'd uncovered something valuable she could take from you before they took back everything else."

"That bit of intel is no longer relevant. Anything else?" I asked, and Isabella narrowed her eyes at my biting tone.

"Oh yeah, let me remember all the times they spilled their most valuable secrets to us *slaves*," she said sarcastically.

I ignored that comment. "Did you ever meet Durian?"

She shook her head. "And thank Helia I didn't. Because I've seen firsthand what he does to his slaves." She grimaced. "If they manage to survive him, they're all kinds of fucked in the head. I met one of his past *pets* in a club. She could barely string a sentence together. I couldn't tell if she was drugged out of her mind or just nuts, but I know for certain she wouldn't stop talking about seeing the future and hearing voices."

Isabella's eyes went dead again, and I knew we were reaching the end, at least for now. I ground my teeth together so violently I was afraid they'd crack. Isabella's words ran through my mind on repeat, interspersed with visions of Scarlett.

I managed to get the words out finally. "Did you ever hear any of them talk about Scarlett?"

Isabella snapped right out of her traumatized daze. Her eyes flitted between the three of us before landing heavily on me. "Scarlett Hale? From Crescent Haven?"

I nodded. "Yes. Your sister."

"She's not my sister," she snapped with a roll of her eyes. She returned her attention to me, drawing her brows together as she frowned. Then something clicked into place, and she suddenly smirked. "Oh. I see."

I stayed neutral, even as I felt anything but. Snow was having a similar reaction, and Uriah took a small step closer to her.

Isabella flung her head back in a cackle. "Leave it to my whore of a sister to seduce the vampire lord of Aristelle." She glanced at Snow with a sneer of utter condescension. "Let me guess, you're the replacement Jaxon?"

Snow exploded, throwing her hands up in frustration. "She's the reason you were saved! You owe her your *life*."

Isabella faltered. "She's the object of value that they took from you? Is that why you're really here?"

My silence was enough to answer her question.

"You're all fools," she said. "She is nothing more than a sex demon who jumps from man to man. Wherever she is now, I have full faith and confidence she's fucked her way to the top."

It was exceedingly rare I had to work this hard to keep my shadows from shredding a defenseless human woman to pieces. Actually, this was the first time.

Snow, on the other hand, had severed her last threads of self-restraint. Palms glowing with the soft moonlight of Selena, she ran at Isabella with nothing but fury in her eyes.

Uriah was slow to stop her, but he managed to grab Snow in time before she tackled Isabella to the ground.

Snow burned his arm with magick. He cursed, but he didn't let go as he dragged her backward.

"You're vile," Snow spat. "Scarlett never stopped fighting to save you, even when it put her in danger. And you deserved none of it." She wrestled out of Uriah's grasp and smoothed down her coat. "If you even *think* about telling anyone what she is or harming her any more than you already have, I swear to every deity above and below that I will destroy your miserable, spiteful ass. And I'll do it all over again in your next life, too."

I couldn't help but smile at Snow's declaration, but it was quick to turn into a snarl. "In case it needs to be said aloud," I said to Isabella. "I have eyes everywhere. You will stay here and write down everything important you can possibly remember, and we'll see how much it's all worth. You will be paid *after* Scarlett is home safe. Even a whisper that you've spilled her secrets and I'll let the witch punish you however she sees fit."

Snow nodded in solidarity. Uriah just looked... turned on. His pupils were wide as he stared at the witch.

I quickly focused back on Scarlett's pathetic excuse for a sister. When my shadows bled into the air, she finally nodded. Her infuriating smirk never moved an inch.

We left quickly, dodging glares from healers as they worked to ensure no humans stumbled upon us in the halls.

The sun was low in the sky, obscured by gray clouds.

"I'm a horrible person, aren't I?" Snow asked, wrapping her coat tight around her form. "I know she's been through hell and back. But I still want to slap that cruel smile right off her stupid face."

Uriah laughed. "You're too hard on yourself, Blondie."

"Stop calling me that!"

He threw her a suggestive side-eye. "If you ever need to unleash all that pent-up aggression, I'm here."

Snow glared at him.

"There's a sparring field back at the castle with your name on it," he finished.

She snorted, her anger melting slightly. It was just like Uriah to flirt by offering to fight a woman. Therapeutically.

Now that the care center was out of sight, and we were on a vacant side street, I stopped moving.

I've seen firsthand what he does to his slaves. If they manage to survive him, they're all kinds of fucked in the head.

My shadows finally leaped from my skin, crawling up the sides of buildings and shaking the earth with their wrath.

"Rune?" Uriah asked tentatively.

Snow moved to stand in front of me, looking up into my eyes. When she pulled me into her arms, I went rigid, my lips tugging down.

None of us spoke. I never relaxed fully into her hold, but my shadows slowly receded back to my skin the longer my pain found a home with hers.

That woman was vile. I'd be letting Scarlett decide Isabella's fate. But there was no way in hell she would harm my Little Flame with so much as another cruel word. Never again.

My thoughts spun in circles, each new one more terrible than the last. I had to get to her. She'd been with *him* for too long now. She didn't deserve to endure any more suffering than she already had in her short life.

"Rune," Snow said. "I'm sorry. I know that you love—"

Snow was cut off by a loud blast.

Uriah and I were quick to shield her, waiting for the rumbling to cease before searching for the source of the explosion.

"The care center?" Snow squeaked, panicked.

The smell of smoke filled the air. Distant screams floated through the streets. I called to my shadows, gathering power.

Shit.

My fangs ached, and I realized I was fucking *starving*.

8

SCARLETT

I slipped in and out of lucidity as I ran. Fear was a bitter taste on my tongue, and periodic shots of adrenaline were the only thing keeping me conscious. My vision was blurry, and my limbs barely worked anymore. My legs were heavy, my arms too clunky. I couldn't fight him off, couldn't stop him.

Rune.

He was chasing me, toying with me. Not in the way he used to. This wasn't a game.

Rune hated me. He wanted me to suffer. He wanted to crush me absolutely. I kicked at him, but he grabbed my ankle easily, pulling me toward him before he ripped into my flesh with his razor-sharp fangs.

He was going to kill me. I felt death's cold grip reaching, Lillian's fingertips brushing against my spine, her voice calling me back home.

Just like before, Rune didn't speak. He tormented me in a dead silence. Though he appeared as the man I loved on the surface, he didn't *feel* like him. Not anymore. It was as though his hatred had killed all of his humanity, drained him of everything I'd fallen in love with.

I blinked, and suddenly my hand was in Rune's, his other gripping a knife. As soon as I realized what was happening, I screamed bloody murder.

He brought the knife to my fingers. He was on top of me, pinning my other arm down.

"Please don't," I wailed. *"Please."*

The knife met my fingers. I blacked out again.

Where was I? The room spun. In and out I went. All I saw was Rune's frigid glare and his sadistic grin as he refused all of my pleas for mercy, all of my attempts to stop him from hurting me, to *talk to me.*

Say something. Please, just say something.

My hands left bloody marks on the beautiful walls. The ceiling became the floor; the floor became the ceiling. I ran even when I could no longer use my eyes. Had Rune removed them from my skull?

At some point, I must have collapsed for good. Because everything was deafeningly dark. In the cruelest twist of fate, the darkness erupted into a field of stars. I thought of the room of music, and my flame snuffed out.

∼

"Up," Aunt Carol barked.

I sat straight up, and I regretted the sudden movement. My head pounded, and my throat was dry and raw. But at least she'd woken me from a nightmare in which Rune was surgically removing my vocal cords and whispering in my ear that I'd *never sing again.*

I looked down at my body, covered in dried blood and bruises and fang marks. I'd never been more confused. I knew the nightmare I'd had was a dream, not reality. But I also had all these real *memories* from last night—visions of running from Rune, of him hurting me. I knew they weren't dreams. But I also knew Rune wasn't here.

I'd been with Durian.

A lump lodged in my throat. I was suddenly catastrophically numb and hollow. I had too much shit to shove under my mental floorboards. Too many open, leaking wounds. I feared what would happen if my sturdy wall of denial and avoidance finally crumbled. Durian might get his wish sooner rather than later.

I was on the verge of breaking.

I could feel it.

And Lana was right—I knew if I did break, my Master would eat me alive. Literally.

Aunt Carol had been screaming at me, but I'd hardly heard a word of it. I got up and stared at her, unblinking, not even when she slapped me. It gave me a sick sense of satisfaction to hear her yell at and hit me to no avail, unable to penetrate my dissociation.

I was barely present for the shower where my blood washed down the drain. Nor for the prayers recited on my knees by the window. I didn't feel a thing when food, water, and a blood replenishing tonic was forced down my throat.

I only started to feel something when I realized where Aunt Carol was taking me. Not to the dining hall or the throne room to see the other slaves.

No.

Right back to Durian's chambers. Where my own personal hell repeated all over again. This time, I learned not to say Rune's name.

In fact, I no longer wanted to think of him at all.

∽

I wasn't sure how many hours, or days, had passed when I heard a perfect, sensual giggle outside my door. Curled into myself, eyes shut tight, I wasn't even sure if I'd even been asleep or merely catatonic.

"You've been working so hard lately, Igor." The voice was the softest caress against my eardrums. "You deserve to rest your eyes. I won't tell anyone."

Then there were whispers, too low for me to hear, before they faded to silence.

At the sound of a click and the front door slowly creeping open, I jolted.

"Well, it's certainly better than the shared slaves' quarters. But not by much."

Rosalind. Her bouncy blonde curls cascaded perfectly past her shoulders, and not a single long black eyelash was out of place. She was in a glamorous pink robe of tulle and feathers. Underneath, a gown skimmed the floor.

She lifted a brow. "Those curtains are a *crime*."

I tried to stand, but spots swam in my vision. Rosalind noticed me falter and reached out, but I managed to catch myself.

"Careful," she said.

I tried to read her tone and her features for threats, but not only was she immune to my magick and perfectly unreadable, but my head was also impossibly cloudy.

"How have they not noticed that you've healed way faster than a human? Vampires are so silly. I bet if you *were* human, you'd be dead already."

Was she here to eliminate her competition?

"You haven't been at court," she said. "So I came to fetch you."

She offered me a hand.

"Fetch me? Or murder me in cold blood?" I croaked.

"If I wanted you dead, you'd be dead." She smiled, and I couldn't at all tell if it was genuine.

I hadn't realized how much I relied upon my gift to read others' intentions until now.

She gave her wrist a little twirl, still holding her hand out in the air between us.

What the hell did I have to lose? I only existed for Durian to drain me slowly of my blood and will to live. I'd been tortured endlessly for days now—I wasn't sure how many. Beaten, broken down. Plagued with visions and nightmares.

There was no way in Helia's green earth that Rosalind could be any *worse*. Plus, this was my first opportunity to learn more about what I was—what *we* were. I was only alive because I was a succubus. I had powers that I didn't know how to use, gifts that might help me survive Durian. I was failing miserably without an understanding of my magick. I was scrambling in the dark, and I had an intuition that my sheer dumb luck wasn't endless. If I kept going like this, he was going to kill me.

I took Rosalind's hand.

9

RUNE

Thankfully, it wasn't the care center that had been reduced to rubble. But it wasn't much better.

Rage was a boiling current in my veins. Like they'd been doing for weeks now, the born had targeted a blood café—one of the safe havens vampires could go if they were in or on the verge of bloodlust and didn't want to harm anyone. Instead of courtesans, healers and paid volunteers worked at these centers. Not everyone could afford to pay for blood or had willing mortals at their beck and call. Accidents happened, and this was one of the initiatives we'd taken after the war to maintain order.

We'd forced Snow to leave the premises with an assigned bodyguard. She'd wanted to help, but I refused to put Scarlett's best friend in danger. Besides, I'd be making short work of the born that remained.

"I need to feed," I hissed to Uriah as we faced down the destruction, lingering born fighting with patrolling turned.

Uriah shot me an incredulous look. It was beyond uncharacteristic of me to act so irresponsibly by leaving myself weakened.

"I know," I said. "It's been fucking impossible since she's been gone." All other blood was watered down piss compared to hers. And feeding from others felt disloyal, like yet another way I'd hurt her.

He nodded in understanding. "Never again, Rune. You cannot deplete yourself. Not now. Not fucking now."

"*I know.*"

Uriah pointed to a female witch reciting prayers to Lillian as she spread creeping black flames.

I didn't want to feed from another woman, especially not straight from the tap. But the fact that she was repulsive and also in league with the people hurting Scarlett was more than enough justification for me.

Fuel, not pleasure. Not by a longshot.

Uriah's shadows leaped from his skin as we joined the fray. They sliced through a born's neck. Blood sprayed. The born choked on his own blood.

I wasted no time grabbing the witch, my shadows locking around her. With a gasp, her black flames snuffed out.

"I wonder how Selena and Helia will treat you after you forsook them to spit at their feet," I whispered in her ear as she suffocated. "Guess you're about to find out."

I sunk my teeth into her neck. I choked down her unsavory blood, made even more rancid by her soul's putrid essence.

I took no care in throwing her body to the scorched street.

Mortals were wailing, dragging away the injured and slaughtered from the café that had collapsed on itself. One of my women with water magick was putting out lingering flames.

These born vampires and allied mortals must've never left our territory, living in hiding until their suicide mission. We had our own special forces still on born lands. They weren't this fucking stupid, though.

Finally, I had an excuse to unleash the wrath in my blood.

The born knew they were in trouble when my own

fighters suddenly receded. The sky went dark. The born turned toward me, hatred burning in their bloodthirsty eyes.

I thought of Scarlett.

A feral roar escaped my throat. My shadows exploded in all directions. They impaled each born, gutted them, destroyed them from the inside out. And it wasn't enough.

Mortals watched me in petrified terror. I wondered what they must've seen—a towering figure in all black, blood dripping down his chin, unholy shadows tearing through his rippling form and annihilating a dozen enemies in the blink of an eye.

I wondered if they saw my torment. My fucking *agony*.

Kicking a severed born's arm out of my way, I surveyed the mangled bodies before me. It wasn't nearly enough relief.

I couldn't act on my true desires. I couldn't destroy everything in my path on my way to her. I couldn't damn Valentin, sacrifice my clan and my city and all other mortals. She would never forgive me if I chose to save her and doom her whole world.

But that's what I desired.

Her.

Fuck everything and everyone else.

I wiped the blood from my mouth. My shadows slithered back to me, vengeful and devastated.

~

EVERY DAY that passed without my Little Flame I bought her a dozen new gifts. Clothing, new music she'd love, rare magickal objects and art. I wanted the castle to be perfect upon her return. I wanted it to feel safe—to feel like *home.*

I ensured the witches in Lumina were taken care of and watched over. Anyone Scarlett had ever loved was protected. I'd even corresponded with wolf shifters in dry lands to find her friend Jaxon.

At my desk, I drafted plans for defending against our worst-case scenario—a legion sent from the kingdom to take back Valentin for the born.

When Mason entered, I doled out a familiar coldness. She'd been working endlessly to overcompensate, to weasel her way into relaying messages to have an excuse to see me and prove her usefulness.

"The kingdom is sending Kole. He'll arrive in Hatham in a few weeks," she said.

"And no one has responded to any of our messages?"

"No."

Kole Tefar was a known adversary of my clan. That was the bad news about the council's chosen dignitary. He'd originally opposed the treaty that had ended the war, instated me as lord of Aristelle, and established the dry lands. But the good news was that there was a reason Kole had shut the fuck up about his bigotry at key moments during the war, allowing the treaty to pass and the kingdom to turn its attention away from Valentin.

A reason that involved lethally tall heels, the cruelest viper tongue, and a wicked backhand.

"I'll write to Sadie," I said.

Mason opened and then closed her mouth.

She would never apologize for what she did. Not when she still believed it was justified. And the frustrating truth was—her doubt *had* been justified. Given the information she'd had at her disposal, the truth of Scarlett's nature, and the gravity of what was at stake, Mason had done what she'd been trained to do. She hadn't once acted outside my orders. She hadn't betrayed my loyalty.

Call it the weaker, human side of me, but I still wanted to punish her all the same.

"One of the most powerful turned clans in Ravenia has

reached out. They wish to send their own dignitary to speak with us," Mason said. "Their leader's name is Kylo. They call themselves the Hekate clan."

"He'd better watch his back on the way over," I murmured. "This is a dangerous game we're playing."

"It's justified," Mason said, her familiar resoluteness admittedly soothing. "We will take care that this meeting occurs under the table. But even if we're discovered, we need only to point to the kingdom's initial act of aggression and subsequent silence. We are both rational powers merely acting in our own best interest."

Annoyingly eloquent and well-reasoned as always. She could've at least said something uncharacteristically asinine to give me good reason to continue icing her out. Intelligent but inconsiderate—an irritating mix of traits.

Mason glanced down at my plans. She frowned but didn't say anything.

"Out with it."

She sighed. "We need to start working with the mortals on the coast sooner rather than later. We're going to need numbers. Geographically, we have the upper hand. That needs to be leveraged as much as possible. In the sky and on land."

I gestured for her to take a seat.

We did nothing but work until sundown. Not a word about Scarlett was mentioned, and that was best for both of us. I needed all the distraction from my obsessions I could get, and I soaked up these moments of uninterrupted focus.

Because when I found my opportunity to rescue my Little Flame, I knew it would be difficult to do anything else besides tend to her devotedly until she felt whole again.

10

SCARLETT

Rosalind lived in chambers fit for a princess. We'd managed to sneak to her rooms undetected. It was the middle of the night, and Rosalind knew this castle like the back of her hand. She'd made our journey feel like it was the harmless fun of children playing make-believe, her energy soothing my terror until it was a dull hum. She giggled the whole way as she checked each hall, hid me in alcoves, and ushered me forward when the coast was clear.

Stranger than her childlike awe in a castle full of demons were the instances I'd caught myself nearly smiling back at her. She'd painted the world in colors again, and I understood clearly why she was beloved among the slaves.

With Rosalind, I forgot about my own dismal reality. The illusions she spun were so innocent and beautiful that I couldn't help but cling to them instead.

I reached for a billowing translucent curtain hanging from the ceiling, pulling the smooth pink fabric between my fingers before letting it go. Through a door on the far left side of her chambers I peeked into a beautifully feminine bedroom. I spotted a plush bed filled with blankets and decorative pillows, a canopy with tiny string lights draped above.

I recognized a white marble sculpture here in the main room, between decorative pillars and tall windows. The curvy, breathtaking figure was Heraphane, the first succubus.

Amid more billowing drapes and hanging lanterns in the shape of stars, was a cozy living area to our right. Nestled on a collection of cushions, a nude human man.

I jumped, casting a concerned glance at Rosalind when the man slowly opened his eyes like a sleepy kitten.

She was beaming at me, watching me appreciate her space. She quickly moved to the man, a gleeful bounce to her step.

Her hand softly grasped his chin. He stared up at her as if she were the sun itself.

"Cassius, baby," she crooned. "You may not speak a word of my friend coming to visit us, understood?"

He didn't even glance at me. He only nodded. "Of course, Rosalind. Never."

"Good boy," she praised, pouting her lip like she was speaking to a toddler.

But he ate it up, his chiseled, handsome face melting as if she'd given him everything he'd ever wanted. She whispered something in his ear, and he left. I noticed a white slave collar around his neck, bite marks on his tanned wrists.

When we were alone, she gestured for me to sit on a white couch beside her. She offered me lavender and chamomile tea in a delicate floral teacup with a rose gold handle.

I was at a loss for words. She glanced at my neck, and it took me a moment to realize she was staring at my own bulky black collar. Then her eyes trailed down to my exposed stomach, where the name *Durian* was splayed in ugly red knife marks. Every morning, Aunt Carol healed them, and every night, Durian cut into me all over again.

I pulled my black robe closed. I'd forgotten I wasn't in

anything more than a bralette and panties. Modesty didn't mean anything to me anymore.

Rosalind didn't offer me pity. Only confusion etched into her features.

"You know what you are," she said. "That's why you were terrified when we first met. Why you thought I'd come to kill you."

"I didn't realize succubi could recognize each other," I said, taking a tentative sip of tea. It didn't smell like elixir, nor could I read any magick in its warm depths. Like Rosalind had said, if she'd wanted me dead, she could've done it while I was sleeping.

"You know what you are," she repeated, her brows drawn. She stared at my neck again. "Yet you've allowed yourself to become a *human* slave."

"*Allowed* is an interesting choice of words," I muttered. "I didn't volunteer. I was kidnapped. The same as that man you were... entertaining."

She watched my face closely. "Why do you assume bad intentions on my part?"

I opened my mouth and then closed it. She had a human slave in her rooms. And she was a succubus. She was living in luxury in Durian's palace. The reasons to assume she was the worst kind of person were endless.

"Fine. You clearly don't want to answer any of my questions. That's fair," she said, her tone even as she lounged back on her couch. Her white silk gown bunched around her, her gorgeous legs peeking through the ample slits. "So ask yours."

"Will you answer them?"

She smiled, twirling a blonde lock around her finger. "I don't know yet."

"Is it as irritating to you as it is to me that we can't read each other?"

Her smile widened. "No. I find it exhilarating."

I let out a long breath.

"But I'm not the one with everything to lose," she said, and it wasn't in a cruel or sinister way. Only honest.

With a nod, I proceeded. "Why are you here?"

"If you mean in Hatham, I was born here, to a vampire woman," she said. "She's dead now. A good thing too, considering she tried to end me more than a handful of times." She studied her impeccably manicured nails, picking at a cuticle as she spoke. "Some children get bedtime stories, others nearly get drowned in the bathtub."

She laughed softly. And though her words made my heart sink, they equally made me lean forward—recognizing more of myself in Rosalind than just our succubus nature. I, too, had a penchant for using humor to cope with the overwhelmingly shit hand I'd been dealt in this life.

"I think my sister would've preferred if I'd been drowned in the tub," I said with a smirk. "She might've done it herself if she'd had the grit. And, of course, if she didn't need to use me to survive."

Rosalind relaxed, mirroring my small smile. "Cowardly. They're always so cowardly, aren't they?"

I assumed she meant the people who'd hurt us. It was strange to attack Isabella openly, to no longer be blindly loyal to my abuser. I still had a tinge of guilt. But I had a lot more anger now. It was getting easier and easier to see the situation for what it was and not for what I'd hoped it would be.

I nodded.

"But you didn't mean Hatham, when you asked why I was here. You meant this palace," Rosalind said, bringing us back to my original inquiry. "And the answer to that question is a very long story that I do not care to tell in its entirety. You're smart enough to ascertain the basic facts: I'm here because I'm an asset. I stay out of the way, and I do what is required of me to remain in the good graces of those who matter. Running from who I was didn't work. I think you may know something about *that*." She paused, and I made no reaction. "So I leaned in. I came home. I carved out a little nook for myself where I wouldn't be killed. At least not yet."

The most important question was on my lips, ready to hit its mark. *Are you going to tell anyone what I am?*

But when I spoke, those weren't the words that escaped.

"How does it make you feel? To know that true love is for other people and not for us?" I blurted, my heart pounding.

Rosalind's surprise was brief. She clicked her tongue against the roof of her mouth and stretched out her arms like a cat before relaxing deeper into the corner of the couch.

"Such a human question, Scarlett," she said with a smile that would've brought any man to his knees.

I scanned her face for evidence of heartbreak, of crushing loneliness. But despite all the horrors I could tell she'd been through, despite the knowledge of her own true nature, Rosalind hadn't lost a glimmer of her lightness or radiance.

"All love is manipulation, darling. Succubi are just better at it."

11

SCARLETT

Rosalind had sensed something off in the palace's web of desires, so she'd ended our midnight chat before I could ask any of my burning, important questions. She'd snuck me back to my room and promised to fetch me again tonight.

In the grand dining hall, Durian yanked me into his lap. We sat at a long table with only born men, and I could read easily that they were all immensely powerful in both magick and rank.

The ceiling above was another depiction of the underworld, full of minor deities, bloodthirsty, beautiful creatures, and vampires serving their Dark Mother. Gold and crimson were the primary accents, the gold accents shimmering as they reflected witch light.

Durian's cruel, cold hands held me tightly against him. Today I was in the barest of black lingerie sets, even as all the born were fully clothed and covered. My brutalized stomach was on full display.

"Didn't your father ever teach you not to play with your food, Durian?" one of the men joked with an eerie smile, his eyes on my marks.

I fought the urge to puke all over their barely touched plates of food. Half because I feared what Durian and these men would do to me if I did, and half because I didn't want it to splatter on Mairin, who was the table's centerpiece. She was nude and trembling, her strawberry blonde hair in a halo of curls around her head.

A born man leaned forward and fed from her calf roughly. Her eyes fluttered before closing.

Durian traced over his name that he'd carved again last night. "Oh, she hasn't earned playtime yet. We're still working on basic training, aren't we, pet?"

"Yes, Master," I said, in the exact cadence he preferred. Demure, frightened, and subservient. But never too weak, never too broken. Then I wouldn't be a fun toy to play with.

I sharply inhaled when he clawed into the wounds. I'd been wondering why Aunt Carol hadn't healed them today.

Durian's desires were getting easier and easier to understand. His most potent desire was always dominion over Valentin, and, eventually, over the entire realm. When it came to me, his desire lay in humiliation and pain.

He hadn't even sexually assaulted me, at least not in a clearly sexual manner. Sex didn't really interest him.

He violated me all the same. He especially enjoyed it when it was in front of all his men, whom he knew desired me.

On cue, Durian surveyed the table as he gripped me. "How about I let my pet off the leash for the night? The dutiful, rightful lords of Valentin deserve to taste the purest blood in the realm." He grabbed my throat, and the men's eyes went wild. "She would make a far more appetizing centerpiece."

"Agreed," Brennan said. He was Durian's second in command. He appeared deceptively youthful and handsome, his evilness hidden under effortless charm. He raked a hand over his strong jaw and sculpted lips. His short chestnut hair was impeccably groomed, flashing wealth with his archaic, aristocratic clothing that matched the others.

I was certain that he would've harmed me in altogether different ways if Durian wasn't so possessive.

I'd also come to learn that Durian's possessiveness was rooted more in control than it was in giving a shit what his men did to me. He wanted to deprive me of all touch but his, all pleasure but the unwanted waves of rapture from his venom. He also enjoyed showing off what he'd stolen from Rune, building up my value in the eyes of his men by keeping me as *pure* as possible.

"You would service my men without question, wouldn't you, pet?" he asked me.

I clenched my fists. "Yes, Master." I tried not to squirm, not to react at all, as every cock at the table twitched with interest.

"How would Rune react to learning you'd become nothing more than a used-up whore for his enemies?"

I hesitated, and Durian's nails opened up one of my cuts. I gasped, feeding off the heightened desire of the table until I didn't feel the sting anymore. "It would crush him."

It was a lie, I was sure. Rune didn't care what happened to me.

But it was what Durian wanted to hear, and I fed off his delight. I soaked it all up, even if I still didn't know how to use all this power stored inside of me. It was nearly bursting, begging to be transformed into influence.

At the thought of Rune, I winced, remembering all the times he'd hurt me this past week—in even worse ways than Durian.

Rune isn't here, I told myself again. *Dreams. They're all just... strange dreams.*

Oh gods, was I going insane?

I focused back on Durian. My stomach twisted up when I realized the desire to share me was no longer a tiny drop in his subconscious waters—it had grown into its own current, a viable impulse to act upon.

You don't want that, I whispered to Durian's mind, borrowing from my wells of stored magick.

The force inside of me was volatile, built from the strength of powerful vampires. The more desperate I became, the more my influence over Durian's mind spun out of my control.

"Remove the current slave from the table," Durian said flippantly, flicking his wrist.

I panicked, and Durian sensed it, his cock swelling beneath me.

One of the men slid the girl off the table and into his lap. She was barely conscious and limp, more doll than human.

After a day of religious sermons in the streets, rallying the born to fight a war, all these men wanted to do was torture mortals—mostly human women.

Was that truly the will of the gods? The will of the Dark Goddess? It couldn't have been. Because I was half born, half Lillian's daughter, and I still had a soul. I was born immortal, and I still wanted the same things humans did—connection, serenity, beauty, and love.

I was *immortal*. It was a reality I hadn't given nearly enough thought to. I hadn't had the opportunity. It wasn't like I'd live long enough for my immortality to matter. Though I would stop aging in my prime—if I hadn't already—my human body was still vulnerable. My only assets were my succubus powers and ability to heal more efficiently than a human.

At a soft click, I looked down at Durian gripping a leather leash attached to my collar's O-ring. My heart sunk.

I was not what Rune believed I was. I was not like *them*— these vile sociopaths.

"Up on the table. Now," Durian commanded. "And don't you *dare* spill a single drop of our drinks or knock anything over."

That wasn't an easy feat when the table was a minefield of chalices, platters of food, and multi-tiered serving dishes.

And the distraction of crawling around the obstacles to get to the cleared center of the table meant I couldn't focus on stopping what was about to happen.

Durian was about to throw me to the wolves.

My leash dragged behind me, clinking as it skated across the table.

At a prickle of heightened desire down my neck, I paused. I turned to see that the leash had somehow looped around a tall pitcher. I frowned. One of them must've used magick. They wanted me to fail.

When I delicately pulled the leash free, the whole table glared, looking to Durian. He stared at me, perplexed.

I played dumb, even as my heart slammed against my ribs. I turned back around, crawling to the safe zone and letting out a quiet sigh of relief. Then my leash pulled taut, and I made a strangled gasp as I clawed at my collar and moved into a kneeling position.

"Brennan," Durian said, holding tight to the handle of my leash.

No. Not him.

"Remove her clothes."

I froze. I still hadn't had to bare myself to these men—not like the other slaves. Durian was changing the game. He knew he had so much more room to break me.

What about my purity? I whispered to his mind. *This isn't what you want.*

I was yanking and yanking on those threads of desire, but my influence was too cloudy, too muddled with my own distress.

"Gladly," Brennan said with a dark chuckle.

Leashed to Durian and on my knees, strong hands yanked

me to my right. Platters of food lurched to the side, and a chalice toppled. The scent of copper filled the air.

"Your pet has made a mess," Brennan said, tearing through the last of my lacy black dignity as I swallowed down a sob.

"Perhaps a group punishment is in order," Durian murmured. "Then we could send an update across the border to Rune telling him what has become of his poor little human."

I was thrown back to the center of the table, my right leg covered in someone else's blood from the spilled cup.

I lay on my back, now fully naked, and I did everything in my power to clear my mind. I was out of time. I had one last chance to escape this.

"What a pristine little creature," a man said to my right.

"Her blood smells divine," another said. "I fear she won't have nearly enough for all of us to take what we want."

Cruel laughter and more crude remarks about my body filled the space.

I thought of Rosalind—how easy it was for her to spin her web at will. I remembered all the times I'd been able to match her skill without even trying, before I'd become uselessly fearful and blocked. All of those simultaneous games of chess in Noel's and then at Odessa, bending men to my will.

"No, she won't," Durian agreed. "Her blood is better than the finest elixir. And it's all *mine*."

I pretended the stakes were lower. Like I was merely working a room for tips, safe and protected by Odessa's bouncers. This time, when I spoke to Durian's mind, I erased the desperation and the fear. I painted my reality, and I charged my words with magick.

This was my world, and these men were merely side characters in my story.

What did Durian want? I'd been studying him, soaking in his expressions, his patterns, all the bits of his mind he'd inadvertently revealed.

I stepped into his mental field, and I held the reins of his desires with a loose, confident grip.

These men want to take as much as they can from you. You are right to be paranoid. They want what you have. Don't let them have it, I whispered to his psyche.

Durian paused. All men looked to him for direction. I pulled from their hunger. *They* were the ones who were desperate. They were the ones out of control, their minds ruled by fleeting whims and hedonistic impulses.

I took a deep breath. I slowed my heart.

I was the puppet master here.

You want to show them you hold all the power. They don't get to play with your toys. If they touch your pet, they'll respect you less. She will lose her purity and her value. And what if this is what she wanted all along? She's a dumb human in search of pleasure and touch. You want to deny her. You want to break her.

You want to remain strong and in control of everyone in this room, everyone in this realm. You aren't like them. *You're above all the rest.*

You want to preserve that.

That's what you truly desire.

My leash pulled tighter. I remained still, calm. I removed all of my visible fear, playing into Durian's paranoia that I *wanted* him to share me.

After an agonizing pause, he finally spoke.

"Did you really think I would share my pet with all of you?" Durian asked, a note of disgust in his voice. "This innocent lamb of Helia, gifted to the future ruler of all born vampires?" He stared at me angrily as he looped my leash around his wrist.

All. He'd said *all.* My ears perked up at his admission of treason. Pleasurable tingles erupted on my skin as my field of influence radiated from my aura outward.

Magick. I was using my magick. And it was *divine.*

It was as though my brain had rebooted after days of

numbness, thoughtlessness. I was *listening* again. I was processing. Remembering.

What would King Earle think of Durian's traitorous declarations?

The table was silent. And I could feel their frustration heating up the surrounding air, thickening it like blood.

None more so than the space around Durian's second, Brennan.

"No, my lord," Brennan said. "Of course you wouldn't. As enticing as her beauty is, we know she belongs to you."

There was something there, in the threads that connected me to Durian—Durian to Brennan—Brennan to me. I had entered this table's constellation of desires, their web of power. And they had no idea. I was a wolf in innocent lamb's clothing.

Even when I was wearing nothing at all.

Tonight, when Rosalind came to rescue me for our midnight chat, I would ask everything I could about how to control and wield my powers. She'd been right. Running from what I was had never worked. If I wanted to live, to make my last remaining days *mean something*, I'd have to lean all the way in.

12

RUNE

Past

The day my twin sisters were slaughtered by a group of born, they'd been playing in the woods on the outskirts of our neighborhood. They were eleven.

I was eighteen. It had been two years since I'd killed my father and my mother had shunned me.

You're dead to me.

Those were the last words she'd spoken to me. Even at my sisters' funeral, she'd pretended I wasn't even there.

I thought of the day my sisters were murdered nine years later, as I was strung up from the ceiling in Sadie's dungeon. Blood flowed freely from the gashes in my chest, pooling on the dark floor below.

The torture inflicted by my wicked mentor was nothing compared to the devastation I'd experienced when I saw my sisters' brutalized bodies on the forest floor. They'd been cast aside, drained of blood, amid dead leaves and huge, aboveground tree roots.

Crescent Haven had always been the most beautiful in early autumn.

The born had stolen that simple pleasure from me. They'd stolen my whole world.

I'd dedicated my life to protecting my sisters since they were first born. Helia knew my mother wasn't going to defend them. It was up to me. I was their hero—deflecting all of my drunk father's anger, drawing it away from the girls and toward me. I'd taught them how to read, how to escape our grim existence and dream of a better tomorrow.

Jesalynn and Lizbeth had been late to our secret meeting, the one we had every week without our mother's knowledge. I'd been making them a warm meal, preparing tea and setting out new clothes and books I could finally afford to buy them. I wanted them to have everything our parents could never provide. I sought to preserve as much of their childhood as I could. I didn't want them to grow up as quickly as I had.

The food and tea had been getting cold, and I'd grown worried. I'd gone in search of them.

I was the first to find their bodies.

Dead. Because the born could do anything they wanted, anywhere in Valentin, and mortals were powerless to stop them.

I had been powerless to stop them. Until I'd met Sadie, and I became the first human to be reborn a vampire by her cunning hands.

She'd saved me. She'd transformed my aimless vengeance into focused precision. She'd seen my potential, hidden underneath useless, weak human flesh, and she'd made my exterior match the darkness that already resided in my soul.

You will be the strongest of them all, Rune, she'd promised me. *And it will have nothing to do with me and my magick. The spell to* turn a human into a vampire pulls from the power a person already possesses.

The more powerful the man, the more powerful the monster.

The room was dimly lit and bare, designed to deprive me of all comfort, all beauty. Only pain. Only denial.

I spit blood on the floor, and Sadie had a dagger at my throat. Her sharp nails gripped my face before I could blink.

"Naughty Rune," she said with a sigh. "Has my schooling in manners truly fallen on deaf ears? Or was that your way of begging for more?" She released me, dragging the poisoned dagger down my chest before taking a step back.

I grinned at her, blood dribbling down my chin and staining my teeth. "My apologies, Mistress," I drawled. "My mouth was full."

I knew I was in trouble when she only smiled right back.

"Come on in, dear," Sadie said.

When a small human woman entered the room, an unconscious growl escaped my throat. Her cheeks were rosy, her copper hair long and straight. She wore a short white dress in the style of some quaint farming village.

"Cindy is going to free you and lead you upstairs," Sadie said.

I stared at her in horror, already writhing against the magickal bindings, my fangs aching so badly they were like knife wounds in my gums.

I had never been more starved. Physically, magickally, sexually, emotionally… for weeks now, I had known nothing but deprivation.

"You don't want to hurt Cindy, do you, Rune?" she asked, backing away as the human stepped forward.

"Get the fuck away from me!" I roared.

The girl trembled, pausing to glance back at Sadie. When Sadie nodded, she proceeded.

No. She had to stay away. I wasn't in control right now. The familiar tide of bloodlust arose, a wave of uncontrollable desire blurring my vision, rooting in my limbs, clouding my mind.

"Fight it, Rune," Sadie said. "I told you to think about the day you found your sisters."

My gaze snagged on the human's pulse. The scent of her fear filled the air, and I could do nothing but groan and shut my eyes.

"Open," Sadie snapped.

I obeyed, prying my eyes open. My breathing was short and shallow. I wrestled with the impending bloodlust—the disgusting side-effect of vampirism that I *needed* to eradicate, at all costs. Sadie had started her work right away.

I'd entered bloodlust every single day since she'd turned me.

It had been sixty-two.

I'd fed only in small amounts since my first feed, enough to sustain me and keep me from mummifying. But never enough—and never straight from the tap. The memory of drinking human blood for the first time was all I could think about some days. It had been so warm, so sweet, so beautifully powerful. I'd never felt stronger. I'd never felt more *alive*.

Sadie had been working meticulously, in ways I hardly understood in my delirious daze, to drain every last drop of uncontrolled desire from my veins. She dangled humans in front of me regularly, preying on my fear of hurting them.

She carved into my mind far more often than she carved into my flesh. She dug out truths I hadn't admitted to anyone. Desires dark, unfathomable, and depraved. Fears I'd buried and had never wanted to face. She yanked them all out of me and rubbed my face in each and every one.

"What did they look like, when you found them?"

The human paused right in front of me. I'd halted the process, my vision only half darkened, my body only partially outside of my control. I was so tired of entering into the mindless craze of hunger, only to wind up with scraps. I held onto myself harder than I'd ever clutched anything before.

For the first couple weeks, I'd done nothing but fight Sadie at every turn. I'd succumbed to bloodlust at the drop of a dime. I'd been *the worst brat of her entire career,* in her words.

I'd taken pride in that.

At first.

Now, I was finally beginning to recognize the cold, unappetizing truth that Sadie's methods were *working.* Sometimes slowly, always painfully, but gods above they were working. But only when I let them.

"They were bruised and bitten all over," I said, caught in the excruciating, shameful middle-ground between lust and denial, hunger and disgust. "They were only children."

The human before me was close enough to reach if my hands weren't bound above my head. She watched me with wide, pale green eyes. I recognized the pain in their depths. Empathy.

"The born didn't care. They'd…" I described details I'd never spoken before, and as I spoke, the human woman's eyes welled with tears.

A fat tear slid down her cheek. "You aren't like them," she said, a hardness to her tone that I didn't expect. "Mistress says you're hungry. I don't know what that feels like to you, but I remember when I was a child, that gnawing emptiness was frequent in my home."

She smelled of wildflowers and rain. I knew that her blood would feel like silk as it cascaded down my throat.

"If you want to be someone who *matters* in this life, you have to lean into the hunger. You have to sit with it. You have to feel it so viscerally that you no longer feel it at all. It's the fighting that makes it painful. The yearning, the wishing for something more than you currently have. Victory is for those who play the long game. For those who choose lasting fulfillment over fleeting pleasures. Victory is for *us*. Not them."

I tongued my fangs, but somehow, I was still in control. For the first time since we'd been playing these games, I saw the vision I'd had before I was turned. I saw myself uniting the mortals against the born. I saw myself leading an army of people like me—vampires who were once human, who'd had enough of the borns' incompetent, soulless rule and wanted to build a new world from scratch. A legion of protectors, fighters, and dreamers reborn from blood and magick.

"What do you desire, Rune?" Sadie asked.

Blood! my depleted, desperate body screamed.

"Valentin," I said.

When I was released, I immediately entered bloodlust. Sadie quickly subdued me with blood onyx poison and restrained me again before I could hurt the girl.

That was the farthest I'd ever made it, and I was rewarded with a small cup of blood. And though on the surface it had felt like I'd failed again, something inside my subconscious depths had shifted irreversibly. I was not the same as I was before. Slowly but surely, my shadow side was being integrated into my whole being.

Sadie was freeing me from the tyranny of the corporeal so that one day my fingers might brush the sublime.

∼

"How long did it take for the human to rehearse that little speech about hunger before she had it memorized, oh, wise one?" I asked Sadie about it a year later. I hadn't experienced bloodlust in months, and that session had marked the beginning of my true progress.

Sadie laughed. "Far too long. She was rewarded handsomely

for the feat, don't you worry." She winked, a filthy smirk on her lips.

"I knew as soon as the words left her lips that they had *you* written all over them."

We watched the sunset on the balcony. The spring air was fresh and full of promise as we listened to the sound of newly turned vampires sparring below.

"It's hardly my fault no one is as hauntingly profound as I." She waved a hand, taking a draw of her cigarillo.

I chuckled and dragged a hand over my mouth. The woman had *scripted* entire conversations—rewritten actual people as if they were mere performers in her grand production. How could I do anything but adore her?

"You were an awful sub," Sadie said dryly, and I laughed harder.

"Imagine that."

She sighed dramatically. "Yeah, yeah, you're *not a sub*."

"And you don't sound bitter about it at all."

Her green eyes went snake-like, but her lips still curved. "The best dominants have served as a submissive at least once in their lives. So I'd like to think that in addition to saving your life and guiding you into becoming the best person and leader you could be, I have also made you a stellar dom. *You're welcome*, all of Rune's future lovers."

I whistled, shaking my head and leaning back in my chair as I gazed on the horizon. "There is no one else like you in this hopeless, unchanging world, Sadie."

"And that is precisely the reason it's so hopeless."

13

SCARLETT

Every day that passed was a day that Rosalind kept my secret. I was thankful, but I certainly wasn't fully at ease. I wasn't stupid, no matter how many times Durian told me I was.

Tonight, I needed to learn how to lean in. The time for running had passed.

"And what do I get in exchange for helping you?" Rosalind asked.

We sat in her living area, where I gorged myself with chocolate and other sweet treats. My slave meals were clearly for fuel rather than enjoyment. On the other hand, it appeared as though Rosalind was given anything that she could desire.

"What do you want?" I asked her. I studied her flawless face, infuriated as always that I couldn't read her true motives.

She smiled. "Let's start with your secrets."

My stomach twisted. At first, I thought of Rune, before I remembered that was no longer a secret of value. Everyone here already knew of our involvement. It was the entire reason I was a slave.

There wasn't any information of value I had left to offer.

"Fine," I said. "How will you know if I'm telling the truth?"

Rosalind grinned. "That's part of the fun! Don't you see how great of practice this is? To use our skills on each other without the help of our magick?"

There was this infectious childlike enthusiasm in her voice that seemed so genuine, so pure. Yet I knew that was what made succubi so tricky—we were literally designed to manipulate, to draw sympathy, to appear humanlike, charming, and innocent. Everything about Rosalind drew me in. Her beauty, the light in her eyes, the softness in her features, her impeccable taste. But she could end my life at any moment, and it was downright *terrifying*.

She studied me, slowly exhaling. "You're still here, aren't you? Doesn't that count for something?"

I didn't—*couldn't*—trust her. No matter how badly I wanted to. No matter how much I craved for some semblance of warmth in this brutal, soul-crushing palace.

I nodded. I should've at least pretended to trust her. It could help lower her guard, make her more useful.

"Today, I used my powers," I began. "But only after trying and failing a bunch of times. It was like fear and desperation were stopping the magick from flowing."

"Yeah, that happens," Rosalind said with a shudder, as if remembering something unsavory. "How I see it, a great speaker is only effective if he projects authority to his audience. It isn't enough to *have* a voice—or to have power. You have to be able to wield it, and it has to be as effortless and natural as breathing. A speaker who appears weak and desperate will never win the minds of his crowd. To get what he wants, he must carry himself as if he already possesses it. The truth matters very little." She took a deep breath, twirling a curl around her finger as her brows drew together pensively. "Do you understand what I'm trying to say?"

"Mostly."

"Succubi who project victimhood will be treated like victims. That's just how it is," Rosalind said bluntly, lifting her chin.

"A bit harsh, no?" I murmured, my lips tugging down. Emptiness reached for me with cold, invisible hands.

"Don't misunderstand." She softened her tone and sipped her drink. "We are not to blame for the misdeeds of others. We can only draw out desires that are already present. We can't force anyone to harm us who didn't already desire to do so. That is a stain on their souls they will bear before Lillian in the afterlife, and she will decide their fate."

I looked away, my fists slowly unclenching.

"*But,*" she said, drawing me back to her eyes. "We are only powerless when we believe that we are. The first lesson in using succubus magick is that it will only be effective if we stand firmly in our power. When you used your magick today, what was the story you told about yourself?"

I faltered, a strange sort of embarrassment crawling up my spine. I'd never truly vocalized to anyone my exact thoughts when I wielded my weapons of desire. They seemed cringeworthy outside my own mind. Rune had come close when he was peering inside my depths, watching me up close and from afar. But even he hadn't understood the full extent of what I was. And when he came close, he'd fallen out of love with me.

I swallowed, quickly casting all thoughts of him away. I couldn't think of him anymore without at once thinking of his brutal torture of my body and mind. Torment that had now persisted intermittently for days.

"It's okay, Scarlett," Rosalind said. For a moment, her defenses dropped, revealing something more strikingly vulnerable. "I'll understand—the only person you've ever met who could truly say that and mean it."

I *had* promised Rosalind my secrets. I inhaled deeply. "I told myself that I was the puppet master, that I was the only one truly in control." I cringed hard as I spoke my next words. "I had the thought that they were merely side characters in my story."

Rosalind laughed, delight lifting her features. "That's fucking gooood."

I smiled shyly. "You don't think I'm a raging narcissist?"

Rosalind lifted a brow, waving her hands dismissively. "Pshhh. These men get to treat everyone like pawns in their game and they're applauded for being strong leaders, but we do it, and we're scorned as evil bitches." She rolled her neck. "They can call us whatever they want. They're still the ones on their knees."

I bit down on my growing smile. I wished Rosalind wasn't so damn likable.

"Okay, so fear, panic, and doubt dry up our powers. And calm confidence and unflinching self-belief make them flow," I summarized.

She nodded, giving me a double thumbs up. "Easy enough, right?"

"Yeah, sure, I'll just *not* be terrified when I'm being cut open on demonic altars and threatened with gang rape," I said bitterly, before I could stop myself.

Rosalind's smile fell, and she suddenly looked painfully uncomfortable.

Good. Maybe she deserved to feel uncomfortable living as a spoiled princess in Durian's evil palace. Something inside me soured. It didn't matter how likable Rosalind was, because as the slaves and I were being tortured, she was living in peaceful luxury.

She and I were *not* the same.

"It *is* more complicated than that, of course," Rosalind murmured. She cleared her throat, no longer meeting my eyes. "There's a flow to it. And it takes practice. You've survived this long, so I know you must be at least somewhat familiar with your own abilities. Even if it has only ever been intuitive and subconscious. We deal with powers of the mind—and minds are complicated. No two are the same. The key to our magick lies in treating each person as the individual that they are. When you speak to someone's mind, you *must* use their own voice. Any slips, and you risk not only losing control of your subject but also ripping tears in your glamour."

"As in, they might see that I'm a succubus?"

"They could come to suspect it, eventually, or if it's suggested to them by a third party. They won't see through you completely unless you're extremely weak, which is rare—that would require you to have not fed off desire for an extraordinarily long period, or exhausted your powers without any replacement energy. Tears in our glamour will usually only evoke suspicion, distrust, or general dislike without the mark understanding why. They will see through our illusion, our allure. They will become closed off to influence, the spell broken. This happens to us all the time—I'm sure you can think of plenty of examples of those who have become resistant to your influence, who don't care for you."

I could think of plenty, but I didn't need to vocalize that.

"Well, that's not ordinarily dangerous. But if you're in the middle of some kind of big play—with someone powerful, perhaps—it could create a very sticky situation."

I nodded. I shut out thoughts of Rune before they could root.

"You must mirror their inner voice. You must only wield desires that they truly harbor, and for the love of our Dark Mother, you *must* ensure you are strong enough to wield them. How much power you need to exert influence is dependent on how much the mark truly desires what you wish to happen. And that requires knowing, *deeply knowing,* your mark's mind. Especially a forceful one." She regarded me pointedly, and I knew she was warning me to be careful with Durian.

"Thank you," I said. I felt so torn—between anger and

gratitude, hatred and hope. But gods above, I was here. I was still alive. I wasn't broken.

I was *fighting*. I thought of Snow and my other friends, and my small spark of hope flickered. Maybe I could do more than survive and escape the palace. What if I could use my manipulative, beautiful weapons of destruction to enact vengeance for every act of brutality against my body and soul?

The parts of myself that had remained opaque and mysterious my whole life had finally been illuminated. I understood now how I'd been unconsciously pulling the strings for years—why sometimes an entire room mirrored my emotions, and other times people had been entirely repulsed by me. It was more than mere jealousy and attraction. I was the wolf caught in the henhouse; I was the spider casting inescapable webs.

Rosalind set her drink down and popped a small pastry in her mouth. "Your introductory lesson at the School of Rosalind has concluded." She eyed me as she chewed and then swallowed. "Your turn."

I fiddled with the hem of my black robe. I wondered if she was going to ask about *him*.

"What do you want to know?"

She studied me. "I want to know who you are."

"As would I," I whispered.

I made a quick calculation: Rosalind was freely helping me, and I knew that so far, she had been nothing but truthful. I also couldn't imagine a way that anything I said about my past could be used against me.

I relaxed. "I thought I was human until a few days before I was kidnapped by Liza and given to Durian."

Rosalind leaned in. "Because you were Rune's."

I winced, and Rosalind didn't miss the move. "I wasn't—it was more—" I shook my head. It didn't matter. There was no need to correct her. Two weeks ago, I would've said that Rune felt like the other half of my soul—always fated to reunite with me in any lifetime, in any body, even when we were merely specks of stardust up in the great expanse of the cosmos.

But I knew the truth now, what the old village witch Beatrice had warned me about before I left Crescent Haven. Falling in love had only made me feel emptier and lonelier than I'd ever thought possible.

"Yes, I was taken because I was Rune's," I managed through the sharp stabs of my crumpled heart.

"Who did you *think* you were?" Rosalind asked. Her eyes were probing, her voice soft.

I was grateful she'd left the subject of Rune alone. "I thought I was a human from some nowhere village. I was raised by human parents—someone left me at Helia's feet in the local temple. I didn't know that I wasn't my parents' child by blood. I didn't know I wasn't *human*. My friend—" I faltered, Snow's warm, understanding face bringing tears to my eyes. "She helped me understand that I'd been using my powers instinctively for years, but I've never truly been in control. They've ruled me more than I've ruled them. And that's why I need your help. I want my last remaining days to matter."

Rosalind's eyes flashed, but she didn't speak at first. She took a sip of her drink, gazing at the fireplace and the pink roses and vines that hung off the white mantel above. It looked like she wanted to say something but couldn't find the right words.

Then, in a flash, her features returned to their graceful nonchalance.

"You discovered your nature, but you don't know anything about your parentage?"

I shook my head, frowning. "Not a clue." Nor had I even had the time to consider it. Did it matter? Whoever my biological parents were, they clearly wanted nothing to do with me. But why hadn't they just killed me? Why put me in Crescent Haven, of all places?

As much as it pained me to think about it, I had to admit that I understood why Rune would think I was a plant. It was what made the most sense, given Crescent Haven was Rune's birthplace. But no one had ever told me what I was. If I'd been a hidden weapon, then my handler had been incompetent at best.

I was interrupted from my spinning thoughts by the sound of Rosalind's voice. She was back to looking uncharacteristically pensive.

"Do you think I truly understand you, now that I know the basic facts about your life story, Scarlett?"

My answer was quick. "No."

Her eyes flitted to mine.

"Then do not presume the same about me."

Her words struck me, and I realized that we'd gone somewhere deeper—Rosalind was offering me a peek under her flawless mask. Unless, of course, it was a tactful ruse. There was no way to tell.

"Who taught you about your powers, Rosalind?"

"No one. I taught myself," she said. She frowned then glanced away again, toward the statue of Heraphane. She surveyed the space—the beautiful art and décor, piles of unopened gifts, and platters of decadent food.

Finally, the pain and loneliness I'd been searching for entered her warm brown irises. She looked back to me.

"I was alone until I met you."

14

SCARLETT

"Position four," Durian said.

I quickly fell to my knees and opened my hips, tilted my head to stare at the floor, and placed my hands palm-up on my thighs.

"Good pet."

I couldn't dissociate in Durian's chambers tonight. I had to be fully present, fully alert. It was the only way I could survive his grueling tests and inspections. My mind flitted to the dungeons of Odessa, where I'd witnessed dominants and their submissives performing similar protocol. The difference was that those subs had consensually yielded their power.

I had once given someone my power. And it was nothing like this. Even if Durian and I acted out the same scenes I'd done with Rune, they would never compare. Bile churned in my stomach.

At the sink of my heart and the surge of fear in my veins, I quickly erased Rune's beautiful face from my mind.

Durian circled me. Straight blond hair brushed his shoulders, and razor-sharp eyes flashed ire. "Position seven."

I started to move, but then my face fell. Panic rose in my chest. "Master, there is no position seven."

He yanked me up by my hair, and I screamed. This elicited a deep moan from him. "My apologies, pet. We haven't learned that one yet. Why don't I just show you?"

Durian dragged me over to one of the chairs in his living room and threw me to the ground. I let myself be moved as a mere object—allowing him to shove my arms and legs apart and arching my back when he slapped my ass. I winced at the impact but fought the urge to move.

"Position seven is called *table*."

Last night, he'd caned me until I was sobbing and bleeding and then he'd licked the blood from my thighs and tears from my cheeks. He still barely allowed me to interact with anyone but him. He told me I couldn't be trusted until I'd gone through *rigorous training*.

Durian sat in the chair. Then he rested his boots on my back as if I were a human stool.

"It doesn't have to be this way, pet," Durian said with a sigh. He crossed his feet, and my back ached from the weight of his legs and the unnatural position. "I know you're fighting me still, despite your perfect little acts of subservience. That is why I won't allow you off leash. You have not been sufficiently broken in, and since you only continue this willfulness, I am forced to employ more custom-tailored methods."

After several beats of silence, he slid his legs off my back.

There was the unmistakable prickle of warning curling around my spine. I broke out into a cold sweat along my temples.

Durian stood.

I knew the energy in the air. Anticipatory hunger. Power for the sake of power, control for the sake of control. My body just another patch of land for men to stick their flags in.

The cool touch of the void brushed my cheek, promising me the sweetest of escapes. I wanted to lean in. I didn't want to smell burned bread, feel my body slide along rain-soaked grass and mud as Trevin's face hovered above me. I didn't want to hear Isabella's voice saying, *Scarlett, I've seen you flirt with Trevin at least a dozen times. You're a manipulator, and sooner or later the allure will wear off and they'll come to collect what you've so freely offered.*

I wanted to fade away instead.

But the more expansive part of me—that stubborn woman who flew on a firebird to the city of vampires, fingers brushing the clouds—she felt the ground beneath her, smelled fire and leather, heard crackling flames and Durian's quickened breathing.

I kept my heart steady even when Durian's hand trailed down my back. Even when I saw clearly this thread of desire, a premonition of what he planned to do, I stayed inside my body. I stayed inside the only place that still had power.

I was not a victim.

"Whose cunt is this, pet?"

"Yours, Master," I said, my voice shaking.

I slithered inside Durian's mind like a snake in his garden, camouflaged to blend in with the scattered bones and rotted earth. I leaned into my intuition, this magick that demanded my acceptance if I ever wanted to transform from hunted to hunter.

I lifted his desires in my palms, gauging their weight against my own strength—and I searched for the path of least resistance.

When Durian's fingers skated over my pussy, I leaned into his feather-light touch. I moaned softly and then froze, as if the reaction had been entirely unconscious, born of desperation and need.

Durian froze too.

And that's when I unhinged my metaphorical jaw, and I *bit*.

She may fear you, but she also desires you as much as you desire her, I whispered to his mind. *She is desperate for your touch. She respects the mark of a true leader—everything that Rune was not. She only recoils from you because she knows you love pain, and you would never give her what she wants if she revealed it to you. But in the end, she's a weak human who slipped and showed her cards. This is the time to strike, to make her even more desperate for you. Soon she will be nothing but a puddle of need at your feet.*

"Oh, pet," Durian said, his voice sickly sweet as he withdrew his hand. "Did you really think you could manipulate me?"

I held my breath. My skin was ice where Durian's hand had brushed, however soft and brief. My heart hammered erratically.

"I hear your heart pumping with lust, you pitiful whore," he said. "You are my slave to use at will, not the other way around. The pleasure of my venom in your blood is all you get until your needy pussy is *aching* from neglect. If anyone catches you playing with yourself, I will cut off your hands."

I whimpered softly, as if torn to shreds by his words. But underneath the layers of deceit, buried somewhere Durian couldn't reach, I *smiled*.

I'd done something else, when I'd been projecting my magick. A sneaky little burst of inspiration that came from the part of my subconscious that was constantly scheming, building roadmaps for manipulation, and analyzing patterns of behavior.

"Yes, Master," I answered.

Durian delivered a mean blow to my ass with an open palm. Before he could earn another cry from my lips, heavy knocking sounded from the front door.

He didn't show any emotion as he left me bared and spread as a piece of human furniture in his living room. He merely answered the door as if I no longer existed.

"New word has arrived from the kingdom. The meeting location has changed," Brennan's strong voice echoed through the space.

As soon as he saw me, a room away, I felt it. I replenished my powers with his gaze on my nude form. This evening's attire—only my heavy black collar—was supposed to humiliate me.

I chose to leverage it for every advantage it gave.

When I'd influenced Durian, I had also cast out a line through an invisible thread that connected me to Brennan. My hook had already been buried in his back, the moment he'd first laid eyes on me. Since that dinner where Durian had dangled me in front of him, that thread had gotten stronger.

I'd lured him here after priming him for days. He likely wasn't the one originally charged with delivering this message.

As the men talked in hushed whispers, I shoved the new trauma in with the old and closed the hatch. It was getting crammed down there.

I used everything I'd overheard, every subtle cue and slip of the tongue, and I melded my observations with the intuition of my magick. I slid between the cracks of Brennan's psyche with ease, as if he'd left the door wide open for me.

You've found her. Durian might know how to rule Valentin, but he never learned how to deal with females, I whispered to Brennan's mind, digging and rooting deeper. *The poor girl needs a man like you to show her what being with a righteous son of Lillian is truly like. She would worship you. You only need to draw her away, carefully. Durian will grow bored as he always does. That doesn't mean this delicious plaything needs to go to waste.*

"Perfect," was all I heard Durian say, and another sharp burst of intuition heated my neck. This time, I couldn't be sure of what I was picking up on. I was too enmeshed in my current scheme to spread myself thinner.

"I can ensure that no one touches her," Brennan said. "You'd be humoring the aunts and their bloated egos. They want her to spend time with the other servants and *learn Lillian's will.*"

I reached out to both men at once, coaxing them each delicately, keeping a tight grip on both reins. Durian was far more difficult to influence, but in the end, he acquiesced. After all, he felt as though he'd won this round.

In reality, Durian had been relying on me more and more to relieve every ounce of his paranoia and stress. He may have been brutalizing me, but he was also hooked. More than he'd ever imagined. He feared how much he'd been thinking of me, thirsting for my blood, proving to me without words how much stronger and more powerful he was than Rune.

"Fine," Durian said, now speaking loudly enough for me to hear. "No one may feed from her or touch her sensually. Everything else is fair game. Any missteps on her part or others' gets reported to me."

He thought I was mesmerized by him, that I secretly wanted to spend time with him. Now he needed to put up distance to continue his deprivation tactics. He wanted me to feel *hurt* that he was suddenly allowing others to interact with me.

The leader of Valentin's born clan thought he was playing games with a naive, confused human. He had no idea that I had guided his hand to make each and every move.

I had the fleeting thought that Rune would've been proud, if he'd still loved me. If he'd still been rooting for me, whispering that I was *perfect* into my ear as his shadows held me close.

It wasn't difficult at all to appear stricken, deflated, as Durian passed me off to Brennan. That glimpse of real turmoil was exactly what this game needed to make the king finally fall.

15

SCARLETT

I'd been allowed to wear a black dress with a deep cut and slits that went higher than my hips. As usual, it left little to the imagination. As I walked behind Brennan through the halls, I was caught between two equally strong urges.

First, to shower and scrub and cry until Durian's touch had rinsed away and sunk into the drain.

Second, I wanted to fucking smirk.

Durian had lost. He might not have known it, but he'd lost. I'd completely altered the behavior of the two most powerful men on the born side of Aristelle. And this newfound power felt good—better than good—it was the sweetness of a peach in the summer heat, the widest of grins as fruit juice dribbled down my chin. It was the streak of a firebird against the night. It was the flame that refused to die.

For the first time since I'd become a slave, I saw a way out.

Rune's voice echoed in my mind before I could stop it.

A powerful, well-trained succubus isn't only capable of provoking and feeding off sexual compulsion. They're able to pinpoint deeper desires, perhaps even ones that contradict a person's duties and loyalties. The little urges we repress, a succubus can locate and coax out, make so much grander than they ever would've been on their own. Incubi and succubi have toppled entire regimes when they've gone undetected.

Toppled entire regimes.

Those three words repeated through my mind. They were the vengeful flames licking up the sides of my devastation, my grief, my utter humiliation. They were the fury at the end of a long, dark tunnel. Frightening, terrible, and divine.

I wanted to laugh. When passing vampires ogled me, I fought the urge to lick my lips.

In a rush of vampire speed, I found myself snatched and pushed up against a wall in a secluded alcove of the palace halls.

Brennan flashed his fangs, his handsome features carrying a much different allure than Durian's. Durian was charming in his resoluteness, his call to the sublime and goddess-blessed, his eloquent, moving speeches and cold, warlord-style leadership.

Brennan, on the other hand, was the warmth and humor Durian lacked. Still a bloodthirsty, born psychopath, but more personable. If Durian was the spiritual and political face of the born, Brennan was the sociable man of the people. Compared to the other lords, he was a teddy bear.

He leaned into my neck, inhaling deeply.

Emphasis on *compared to.*

As usual when a man was this close to me, I only thought of Rune. The sickest part of me wanted to lean into the fantasy, imagine it was truly him instead.

But the hours of torture the past two weeks by his hand quickly snapped me out of it.

Brennan pulled back, his hazel eyes darkening as his arrogant smirk spread. His short chestnut hair was perfectly placed, his suit finely tailored.

"Hello Scarlett," he said. "It's a shame we've had such little opportunity to get to know each other, isn't it?"

I'd nearly forgotten what my name sounded like. The only person who called me Scarlett anymore was Rosalind.

I kept my mouth glued shut, playing into my innocent, confused, and subservient role. "I would never question my Master's methods."

"Mm," Brennan said, low and gruff. He leaned in close, his breath warm against my cheek. "Of course you wouldn't." He studied me closely, and it reminded me of how Mason used to regard me. He was searching for clues, for defects.

But my glamour was impeccable. I knew because I'd furnished it with strength from Valentin's most powerful vampires.

"Durian said you held absolutely no information of value about the turned," Brennan said.

It sounded nearly accusatory, but he wasn't so bold as to question his superior's capacities to glean information. I barely remembered that session—it was a blur of scalding heat, venom drunkenness, blows of pain, a dagger carving into my flesh. I was fairly certain I'd cried in Durian's arms about Rune.

Thank all the gods that it was a faint, messy haze.

"Apparently not," I said, and Brennan's eyes flashed at the hint of true emotion leaking through.

Now that I thought about it, it was actually rather insulting I'd never earned a piece of top-secret intel. It was as though Rune had always planned to lose me. Even when he'd smuggled me to his castle from Odessa the *secret way*, he'd rendered me unconscious.

Over and over, my heart shattered. The night sky that had once been full of glimmering stars went deafeningly dark.

"You've settled remarkably well into your new home," Brennan continued. "Most of Durian's *pets* go insane within a week. If they survive that long."

My lips tipped up slightly, and Brennan's eyes flew to them

and lingered as I spoke. "If you and I *had* gotten to know each other, you might've realized that I'm not replaceable."

I leaned closer and mirrored him, my eyes on his lips. I pulled back my sexual allure and twisted it into playful innocence—imitating Rosalind's lighthearted, comforting seductiveness.

Brennan's arms shot out, his pulse quickening and his eyes alight. "I can *scent* that, tiny human."

Tiny? That was a bit dramatic. I was maybe two inches below average, and I was by no means stick thin. These sickos wanted to play into our weakness and innocence to a grossly perverse degree. I was tiny compared to Rune, maybe.

A shard of memory glimmered behind my eyes—Rune's grip on my throat, his silence no matter how much I begged him to speak.

I shuddered.

"Don't be frightened," Brennan said, misreading my reaction. "You may be a servant, but, believe it or not—I actually prefer my women willing and enthusiastic."

I chose *not* to believe that. But I rounded my eyes as I stared up at him as if he were the pinnacle of gentlemanly chivalry.

"Are you interrogating me or flirting with me, my lord?" I shifted on my feet like I was nervous, then created a seductive contradiction with my accompanying smile.

Predictably, Brennan was enthralled, his own desire now strengthening the same magick that would later be used against him.

"You're a little survivor, aren't you, Scarlett?" he drawled, again showing his fangs. He didn't answer my question. "Far, far more intelligent than you let on."

Um, rude. I might've been traumatized to hell and back, but I hadn't realized I'd been coming off as stupid. I supposed Durian hadn't given me a single opportunity to show anything more than my obedience. Of course, his men would only think of me as a human doll passed back and forth between warring clans.

That was precisely why I needed this time off leash.

And Brennan had now become yet another man secluding me from the rest of the world. Proximity was a killer to any seduction. It was time for space.

"I'm flirting with you," Brennan finally answered, choosing the classic bold move in our little dance. "Durian has certainly spent more time and energy on you than any of his previous slaves..." He backed away, letting his thoughts trail off. "Ready to play with the others?"

Yes, which was why I'd subtly nudged him in that direction. I nodded with a small smile. It was time to alter my image again. No more cowering. It was time to stand out.

"No need to fear. You won't ever leave my sight," he said with hooded eyes.

Again, I thought of Rune. And again, I wanted to cry in the shower. This time I would wash away the remnants of a vampire's unwanted touch without his attentive care.

I had been right all along. I was always meant to absorb these devastating blows alone.

16

SCARLETT

In one of the opulent lounge areas in a sprawling drawing room, group prayer time with my fellow slaves quickly became a spectacle. When the aunts had us reach our hands out in front of us before a statue of Lillian, I arched my back and lifted my ass high before lowering into the correct position.

This elicited several moans and crass comments from our growing audience.

I got whacked in the side of the head with a holy book.

"Mm, yes, harder please," I groaned dryly.

The room of vampires laughed.

I hated every single one of them. Durian's lingering touch between my thighs made me want to crawl out of my skin.

But my process of reinventing myself was off to a stellar start. It was like playing a part in a grand production. I could dissociate and slip out of Scarlett, the traumatized woman who wanted to sink into the dirt and become one with the mycelium, and embody Scarlett, the demoness who did more than *survive*.

She waged war. She sowed chaos. She raised Lillian's dark underworld.

"Naughty human," I heard someone purr from behind me as an aunt shoved my head further into the black carpet.

My fellow slaves had stared at me with nothing but hatred when I'd first joined them. Now, the energy was shifting. They were starting to relax. They looked at me with new eyes—curiosity, confusion.

Because *I* was the one taking the brunt of the aunts' disdain and punishment. *I* was the one drawing the vampires' attention away from them and onto me.

I was protecting them the only way I knew how. No one could feed from me nor rape me. I would take all the rest if it meant I could distract these psychopaths from the humans far more vulnerable than I was.

I took a nasty blast of ice magick from one of the aunts, my bones rattling as I recited sickening prayers to Lillian justifying slavery.

"I always knew she was far less innocent than she let on," Liza's recognizable voice commented.

Then, the sickly sweet voice of her friend Evangeline filled the room. "Mm. Curious little vixen, lapping up the attention. I wonder how her Master will feel about her behavior."

"Jealous, ladies?" Brennan asked, earning laughter from some of the other men.

I nearly smiled as I finished the prayer. Psycho born vampire or not, it would seem I'd crafted my first protector.

The slaves and I raised back to our knees to gaze up at Lillian, and the aunts watched me with the eyes of hawks. Suddenly, a human woman was pushed down on the ground next to me. She was shaking violently.

"All I'm saying is," Evangeline said, closer now. She must've been the one that had shoved the woman to her knees. "She'd better watch her mouth."

I stole a glance at the girl next to me. She turned her head toward me.

I screamed.

Her mouth had been sewn shut. Black thread and dried blood zigzagged over her lips. Her eyes were hauntingly dim.

I scrambled to my feet. An aunt rushed toward me, and I threw up all over her ugly black shoes.

My careful web of power spun out of my control. The aunt peered down at her bile-covered shoes, then back up at me, cold fury in her eyes.

That was when I noticed Rosalind in the corner of the room. She wasn't attracting any attention to herself. She was only watching me. She glanced briefly at the slave's brutalized face before looking away.

The other slaves were reacting similarly. One girl shrieked. Another joined me in puking on the carpet.

"You. Insolent. *Bitch.*"

I wasn't paying attention to the aunt yelling at me. My focus was behind her, on Evangeline. She was grinning in triumph, her arm in Liza's.

I committed their faces to memory, and I saw those tall, spitting flames crawling up palace walls.

The aunt grabbed my throat, her hands shooting more ice into my veins as I shivered violently. I clawed at her arm as she lifted me up off the ground. Who knew witches could be this strong?

My vision began to vignette, darkness spreading out from the corners. I thought of Rune's cloud of shadows as I faded.

In the void, there was no suffering. No pain. No confusion. Life's ever-shifting kaleidoscope of love and grief, pain and euphoria, striving and sinking, melted into an opaque formlessness. Here in the nothingness, I was no longer responsible for myself or others. I was released, caught in an endless exhale.

What was existence, if not a responsibility?

Just as I had before, I chose Helia's light. I swam for it, like a raven flying toward the sun's rays that trickled through the tree branches of Crescent Haven's forest.

～

I REGAINED CONSCIOUSNESS. Vampires surrounded me. I tried to move, but I was paralyzed by magick. The translucent hem of my dress brushed my ankles, and my eyes darted around the drawing room's dark decadence of which I had become the centerpiece.

Aunt Carol glared at me with disdain, placing a bowl in my right hand and a chalice in my left. "When I release you," she said, "you will maintain this position. A single movement, and Lillian's children will punish you however they see fit."

"Within Durian's parameters," Brennan said, at the front of the crowd.

Vampires glanced at him curiously, and I locked eyes with him, feeding him a steady stream of reinforcement.

She sees you now, I managed to whisper to his mind, allowing my magick to be a lifeline—the only thing keeping me afloat. *You are the only vampire she truly wants.*

Brennan's eyes flashed. His desire continued to bloom, now with more ferocity. I tasted jealousy on his thirsty tongue. Perfect.

Aunt Carol removed her paralysis spell without warning, and I would've lost immediately if I hadn't been expecting the move. I held tight to the objects in my hands and gave them my best impression of a living statue.

Statue, doll, pet, toy.

My heart bled endlessly. I wondered if I would ever again taste a semblance of peace, let alone joy, before my time on this plane was cut short.

A vampire woman to my right was feeding from Lana,

petting her curly black hair as she sunk her fangs into Lana's breasts.

"You, an ungrateful slut, serve our rightful king, he who was chosen by Lillian to restore the world to its natural order." Spit flew from Aunt Carol's mouth as she uttered the words at me. "How dare you dishonor him by interrupting Lillian's prayers, drawing away glory from her to call attention to yourself!"

"I'm sorry, Aunt Carol," I said robotically.

I wished my magick was as instant as the shadow magick of the turned, or the powers of witches and the born. I wished my fury could crumble this room to ash and slice through the throats of these merciless monsters.

But gods above and below, I would make do with what I had.

For the girl with her mouth sewn shut. For Lana, Mairin, and the rest of the men and women who'd been stolen from their homes.

I did not falter. I did not succumb.

"That's not enough."

Aunt Carol subtly flicked her wrist, and the objects in my hands became twice as heavy. My muscles twitched.

"Tell these masters that whatever methods they employ to make their servants perfect in the eyes of the Dark Mother are righteous and justified." She turned and gestured to the crowd of vampires, thirsty and unhinged as they fucked my body with their eyes.

I knew what the intelligent move was. I knew what would better help me in the long run, what would even help the other slaves.

I locked eyes with Rosalind, still hanging back, barely paying attention to the vampire man fawning over her to her left. She gave me a clear, pointed look.

She knew what the right move was, too.

But I couldn't do it.

I opened my mouth to tell them they were all disgusting. That I hated them, and I hoped they burned for an eternity.

Aunt Carol turned back to me, her lip curling.

I closed my mouth.

I wouldn't doom the others. But I also wouldn't disrespect that woman's suffering—they could never get me to say that brutalizing her had been anything less than demonic.

Aunt Carol repeated herself, and still I stayed silent.

She flicked her wrist again, increasing the weight of the bowl and chalice. My muscles trembled uncontrollably. I breathed shallowly, grinding my teeth together.

I kept my face utterly neutral. I did not show them my hatred or my pain. I gave the aunts nothing.

And just like Evangeline had said, I lapped up the vampires' attention as if it was the coldest glass of water on the hottest day of the year. And I finished by running my tongue over my supple lips to get every last drop.

On the outside, I was stoic.

I was stoic even when my arms gave out and the golden objects fell to the floor in a deafening clatter.

I looked to Aunt Carol, as if silently asking her, *What next?*

She only shook her head with faux, cruel pity before leaving me alone in the center of a room full of vampires.

Evangeline smiled. "Poor, weak thing," she said with a sigh. Her voice was creepily high, her beauty ruined by her cruelty. "Her silence was clear. Her time as Rune's whore has left her with disrespect for her rightful lords and ladies. She clearly still sees us as the enemy, no matter what act she puts on."

"Didn't realize silence could say all of that," I muttered, unable to bite my tongue—the tongue that repeatedly got me in trouble with beings far stronger than I was.

Brennan smiled, shaking his head as his eyes burned my skin. Someone chuckled, and Evangeline's pale face turned red, a vein protruding in her forehead.

I was getting punished either way. It was worth it to take a swing at Evangeline. It was also very revealing—to see that regardless of her clearly high position, she was not as respected as her male peers. It seemed as though the born clung to archaic misogyny, despite worshipping a female goddess.

Regardless, when Evangeline decided my fate, they happily agreed.

"The other servants will punish her for our enjoyment. Put her on the cross."

17

RUNE

I looked out at the sparkling lights of Aristelle. I clutched the railing of my balcony, my onyx tattoos vibrating with power. I imagined the cityscape from Scarlett's eyes. Every time she saw the city's expansive splendor, her whole face lit up with childlike enthusiasm. Sometimes I'd catch her smiling or laughing to herself, when she thought no one could see her. That was how beautiful her heart was; she was able to experience such heights of joy from simple things I'd taken for granted for centuries.

I heard distant voices and calls of beasts. Some of my inner circle had organized a sparring competition in the back of the castle grounds, before the thin layer of trees secluding the land from prying eyes.

Sadie brought a legion of newly turned vampires on shadowbirds when she arrived, along with her two current favorite subs—a shifter woman and an uninitiated turned man. The man, Cliff, had been her favorite for over a century. He worshipped the ground beneath her more vigorously than the most faithful high priest.

It was still only a drop compared to my sea of endless

devotion to my Little Flame. She was the last thing I thought about before sleep. She haunted every dream, and she was the only name on my lips as soon as I opened my eyes. Not that I was doing much sleeping.

I had too many plans in motion, too many executions, interrogations, and acts of retribution to oversee. The borders had been solidified. Any born caught in our territory was killed or taken prisoner, and ours were given the same courtesy. Fighting had been mostly relegated to the border, with a few stray guerrilla style acts of terror closer to home. We were certainly not in a ceasefire, but full-blown battles had yet to commence.

What happened next depended on the meeting with the kingdom's dignitary.

Scarlett had been with Durian for over two weeks now. I nearly convinced myself I could feel her brokenness through that invisible leash, the blood bond I checked compulsively every few minutes. Her heart still beat, but fuck was it sometimes erratic and much too fast, other times too achingly slow.

I'd once told her I would sever the heads of anyone who dared feed on her addictive blood. I planned to make good on that promise and so much more. The born had not a clue of the wrath they would soon face.

At a brush of perfumed air at my back and the clicking of heels on stone, I knew that Sadie had joined me.

"It's done," she said.

My hands tightened around the railing, thorny vines leaping from my skin to wrap around the columns.

"Good. Thank you," was all I could manage.

Sadie didn't criticize my uncharacteristic show of emotion. She merely stood by my side, placing her own hands on the marble and avoiding my thorny shadow vines.

"I figured it out. Durian's *gift*," I said gruffly, staring angrily at the horizon. "I've pieced it together. The descriptions of his followers' religious experiences, his lineage possessing powerful mental magick, his father a rumored memory reader..." My jaw ticked, hissing out my next words. "The fact that he drives his slaves to madness."

"If he were a mind reader, he'd be much more powerful than he currently is," Sadie thought aloud. "Yet his gift must give him some key advantage. He didn't get to where he is now by being a keen fighter and orator."

"Right."

I took a deep breath, and *she* was the only thing I saw. Her big blue eyes, her warmth in spite of all of life's cruelty—her long waves of brunette hair twirled around my fingers as I whispered soothing words in her ear. Her soft giggle, the second most beautiful sound I'd ever heard in my endless existence. Trumped only by her stomach-dropping voice that never failed to bring me to my knees in worship.

"He's an illusionist," I said. The air around us darkened.

There was a brief pause.

"Visions," Sadie echoed.

I nodded. "He's using them to gain support. From his band of trafficker witches, the brainwashed mortals in born districts, and of course, the born themselves. Who knows what he's been able to make people believe. We thought he'd merely been shrouded by propaganda, but it's far worse than that. He is making the propaganda *real*."

"And it's a gift that would naturally be glamoured, an easy asset to conceal for one's gain," Sadie said. "It's impossible to tell that one's sense of reality has been manipulated while it's happening. Similar to a succubus or incubus's desire magick. The spell would need to be broken, and even then, he could merely start a new illusion."

At the mention of Scarlett's true nature, I no longer

experienced any semblance of anger, paranoia, or disgust. I only felt burning shame, deep wells of regret and self-loathing.

"Which makes our seat at the table even more imperative," I said through a clenched jaw. "On all levels. For her. For this city, and for the whole of the realm."

"Soon, my protégé." Sadie closed her hand over mine, a rare show of the unspoken platonic affection between us. "It won't be long now before she's back by your side. And I cannot wait to meet her."

I laughed dryly. "The thought of you two being in the same room used to terrify me," I admitted, distracting myself from my surging intensity. Anticipation, and dare I say *hope*, warmed the cool winter air around us. "As much as it amused me endlessly."

She smiled and shrugged a shoulder. "Terror is to be expected. You're not the first man to fear leaving his woman around me unattended."

I shook my head. A sad smile tugged on my lips. "Now, the two of you meeting is one of the strongest desires I harbor. Because that would mean I get to see her again."

Sadie clicked her long burgundy nails against the marble and stared straight ahead. "Your desire for her outweighs your desire for Valentin."

It was nearly a question, but not quite.

"It doesn't matter," I said. "I will do what's right for them both, because there is no world without Scarlett. And Scarlett is in love with the world. I would sooner die than let anything she loves go up in flames."

18

SCARLETT

The crowd was impossibly big and rowdy now as vampires arrived back to the palace after long days of committing atrocities in the name of Lillian. I was in an adjacent, darker space that resembled a room in Odessa's sex dungeon, but far more archaic and colder. I glimpsed frightening tools hanging on the walls and strewn on black tables—contraptions I couldn't be sure were for torture or sex.

Brennan lifted me like I weighed nothing and placed me against the X-shaped cross. He insisted on being the one to fasten the cuffs around my ankles and wrists.

He stripped me of my gown, and I fought the urge to cover myself. Instead, I scanned the crowd, fanning the flames of their desire as they gazed at me. I encouraged the craze, the heightened emotions, the cruelty. Then, I trained it all back on *them*. Each other.

Paranoia, scarcity, fear, distrust. Jealousy and possessiveness. I watched as certain vampires looked from me to their fellow psychopaths, their minds churning. Some shot glares, eyes narrowing on unsuspecting comrades.

"You're a sensation, Scarlett," Brennan whispered to me, his voice shielded by the din of the gathered vampires. He pulled the strap tight on my right wrist and buckled it into place. "No one has encountered a human like you in centuries, if ever."

I nearly snorted at the astute observation. It was easy to be unlike any other human when you were a demon.

He fastened the left wrist. "Don't think of this as a punishment—it will be bringing your vampire masters endless pleasure. It will bring *me* endless pleasure to see your delicious body on display."

I wanted to take a chunk out of his arm. Instead, I filled my eyes with yearning the moment he met them.

I wish I was with you, not with all of them. I projected this thought outward, playing around with using my magick in the first person rather than his inner voice. It seemed to work similarly, Brennan's desire now churning molten heat.

He trailed his hands down my calves as he cuffed my spread ankles.

"Keep it moving, Brennan," a man barked. "We're here for our evening entertainment. That entertainment does not involve *you*."

I recognized him as one of the lords. Brennan gave me one last burning gaze before displaying a rakish smile and rejoining his fellow men.

The other slaves were shoved forward, some clearly drugged or loopy from blood loss and venom.

My chest rose and fell rapidly, my nude body on full display. This was another moment I was caught between the ugly truth and a beautiful lie. The traumatized, terrified victim and the cunning, fearless seductress.

The slaves formed a half-moon around me—six women and two men. Lana's eyes flashed pity, while a few of the women appeared to be looking forward to hurting me. Mairin seemed torn, slipping in and out of lucidity. One of the human men was Cassius, Rosalind's lover. He was another sympathetic one, though his eyes showed the telltale signs of elixir, glazed-over and pupils wide.

The vampires gave instructions, smiling and laughing and clinking drinks. I could see underneath their joviality to the churning darkness of their shadow selves, festering at my direction.

"Go on, Cassius," Evangeline purred.

At the sound of her voice, Cassius flinched and moved immediately. In his hands, a whip. I trembled; my entire body tensed.

The sound of the crack was like lightning to my ears, and my scream was soon to follow. A searing line bloomed across my thighs, the flesh I'd learned quickly was far more sensitive than my ass. Tears sprung to my eyes beyond my conscious control.

How was it that when Rune had inflicted pain, it had felt *good*? Was there something wrong with me that I'd once yearned for violence, for torment and denial?

With Rune, everything sinful had ascended to divine. But perhaps that had all been a delusion, the same as our love.

Tears slid down my cheeks as Cassius whipped me twice more. I felt small and stupid as I fought against the leather straps, any attempt to get away, to hide my thighs from this agony.

A woman was shoved forward.

"Hit higher!" someone snarled as the crowd leered.

One vampire became so overwhelmed with lust that she grabbed the second male slave and began to grope him, sinking her teeth into his neck.

The slave held a riding crop, and she, unfortunately, appeared to be one of the humans that still had it out for me. Her lips were turned up, her features smug and dark eyes frigid.

I thought I remembered her name being Harley. Her long black hair swayed as she approached.

Obeying instructions, she aimed higher than my thighs, smacking left of my belly button. I cried out, again attempting to curl in on myself, but halted by the cuffs. She quickly struck again on the exact same spot, a smirk forming as I cursed in my next outburst.

I couldn't have attempted to wield my weapons of desire now, no matter how powerful I'd become. The seeds that I'd already rooted were the only defenses at play, as sharp stabs of pain ricocheted beneath my skin.

"Hey," Brennan roared. "Not on the stomach, you dumb bitch."

The critical lord from before raised a black brow with a high arch.

Brennan crossed his arms. "Humans have sensitive organs that are not always mendable. I, for one, don't want to break our toy before she's been sufficiently played with."

Aw. How sweet.

It was abundantly heartwarming that my vampire overlords cared about sadomasochistic safety protocol after long days of slaughtering mortals for sport.

Harley was one of the few slaves still wearing more than lingerie, her red dress only slightly torn as it clung to her curves.

She grinned as she stepped forward and reared her arm back. The leather end of the crop fell hard against my right breast, and I screamed again as I writhed.

"Now make it even," a lord commanded.

She hit my left breast, and humiliation burned my cheeks from this public violation, pain lighting up my every nerve. I couldn't think straight, couldn't find my footing. I began to detach, my grip on desire's reins slipping.

"Draw blood, Lana," Liza said, licking her blood-red lips.

Lana appeared, a silent apology in her eyes as she took Harley's place. Her shoulders were sunken, her own breasts displaying dried blood and bite marks. Her purple lingerie was merely straps of fabric accentuating her breasts and pussy, not offering an inch of coverage.

In her hands, a paddle studded with tiny metal spikes. My head dropped, and I stared at the floor. I no longer saw opportunity in the eyes of the crowd, my seeds of destruction. I only saw shame and sick enjoyment, the eternal reminder that my body had never been my own.

She struck a thigh, and I shuddered, the harsh sting penetrating through my dissociative blur.

I remembered swinging out by the woods, gazing up at the stars. I held that image as I allowed all things buried to rise again, all wounds to reopen. I was swept away in a wave of numbness, unable to endure the crushing weight of every bad thing that had ever happened to me.

I barely felt the second blow of leather and spikes. My body was as numb and hollow as my brain.

"Again."

Warm liquid oozed down my legs. Fights broke out instantly. Lana's assault continued through it all until I was covered in a river of blood. I fell in a vat of the crimson ooze, drowned in it. I saw nothing but flowing red, burning shame.

I barely registered Harley lifting my head up by my hair, spitting in my face. One slave hit my right cheek, another my left. They were all beating me now, egged on by the crazed vampires. Someone must've been given a blade, because I felt slicing, saw Durian's face looming over me from memories that assaulted my mind's eye.

The room turned chaotic, the slaves themselves turning on each other. Lana hit Harley across the cheekbone with a mean backhand. Cassius pulled Lana away, and the vampires were screaming at them all to keep hurting me. The humans were covered in my blood, splattering it on each other as they fought.

Guards struggled against vampires in bloodlust. Humans were thrown at the crowd, used as distraction from me and my addictive blood.

Everything had backfired. All I'd done—all I'd ever done—was make everything about *me*. I knew some of these slaves wouldn't survive, not when they'd been thrown to the bloodlust-stricken born.

And it was my fault. In my attempts to pull attention away from the other humans and play with the court's desires, I'd only created an unquenchable wave of lust that put everyone except me at risk. Slaves like Harley had every reason to hate me. I would survive, and they would be tossed away as if they'd never meant anything to the world at all.

The room was a blur of movement, and there was only one pair of eyes I looked for. Warm brown, framed by flawless skin and full blonde curls. Rosalind was behind the chaotic tangle of vampires, by a tall window with crimson drapes and a large potted fern. She was staring at me, confusion, anger, and concern breaking through her usually light and impenetrable features. It was strange to see her frown.

A figure eclipsed my view. Tall with muscles forged into weapons, creeping shadow tattoos thrumming with potency. His eyes were ice-cold, roaming over my body as his mouth twisted with disgust.

He opened his mouth, and Rune finally spoke.

"You are the most pathetic, useless human I have ever wasted my time on. You deserve everything you've gotten. You belong here."

My vision blurred and tunneled. His words were more cutting than any of his tools of torture.

He laughed. "I'm glad you're with them. Look at you. Ruined. Used. Worthless."

His voice used to be what I craved above all others. I'd clung to his every beautiful word, dissected his achingly gorgeous sentences. He had once been a lifeline, the first person to pull me out of the empty place and make me feel safe.

The first man to truly see me—all of me—and love every facet.

Covered in blood, the world slipping further and further down a long, onyx tunnel, I opened my mouth.

"I still loved you even when you were cutting my fingers off," I whispered. Lights flickered, highlighting the sharp edges of Rune's cruel beauty. "I still loved you when you bled me dry. I still loved you when your hands were locked around my throat, and you were squeezing the life out of me."

My body was slick with blood, my tears staining my cheeks. My surroundings were spinning colors and blotches of black. The only thing I could see clearly was Rune and his hatred.

I tried to speak, but I couldn't muster the strength.

"You're dead to me."

He spoke the words for me. I only nodded in agreement.

I blinked, and the world tilted.

"Acting out, pet?" a different voice asked, laced with dry humor.

I fought my heavy eyelids, my gaze trained on Durian. His slender fingers trailed down my cheek. His cool blond hair was tucked behind his ears, and his arms were rigid as he held me against his chest.

I found myself grateful Durian was here, that he was carrying me through the fray. In his arms, I was untouchable. When he was near, Rune couldn't continue to shatter me.

"Do you see now why she cannot be fed from by anyone but me?" Durian hissed at Brennan, whose eyes burned into mine as I struggled to remain conscious. "She's a rare jewel. *My* rare jewel. I am not surprised in the least that chaos ensued the moment she left my sight. The poor little lamb needs her Master."

He stared down at me. When he bent his head, I nearly thought he was going to kiss me. Instead, his tongue found a trail of blood on my chest, following it to a wound and lightly sucking.

My eyes fluttered, soon overcome by the sweet waves of rapture that swallowed all agony.

"What do we say, pet?"

I sunk into Durian's hold. "Thank you, Master."

19

SCARLETT

They managed to save ten out of the twelve slaves present at my demented crucifixion. In driving vampires to bloodlust, I'd killed two humans. I'd never hated myself more.

Durian had decided I'd earned a real bed. But I didn't use it. I curled up on my pet bed by the fire instead, plagued by bouts of weeping followed by numbness. I'd begged Aunt Carol not to mend my wounds, to leave those ugly red lines and patches of spike marks branded on my skin. She'd refused, of course.

She'd not only mended me, she'd also given me better food, including four squares of chocolate. A gift from Durian, delighted that I was the most coveted jewel in the castle and belonged solely to him.

How did I ever think I'd be able to take control of this situation? How could I think it was a good idea to drive the born to the peaks of desire with humans around?

My power clouded my judgment. It made me as selfish and attention-hungry as Isabella always told me I was. She'd been more correct about my true nature than I'd wanted to admit.

Days had passed, and I'd only used my powers as self-defense. I was too deflated to spin new webs. Turned out, the seeds I'd already planted were strong enough to maintain themselves no matter how small I made myself. And being intensely powerful beyond my conscious effort only made me despise what I was more.

Rosalind no longer wanted to be around me. She hadn't once come to rescue me for a midnight chat.

I was staring up at the ceiling when Durian entered my room, puzzled when he saw me on the pet bed instead of the one above the ground.

He peered at me for three long beats.

I quickly sat up and moved to a kneeling position, averting my eyes to the floor. He patted my head in approval.

"You blame yourself for their deaths," he said.

My gaze traced the floral designs in the carpet, my lips pulling down.

"Yes, Master."

No reason to lie. His ability to understand my current state shocked me. Durian was as sociopathic as they came. Though I supposed his position as a powerful religious leader necessitated that he understood emotions like guilt, even if he himself couldn't feel them.

"You may look up at me."

I tilted my head up, staring into resolute coldness, the unbreakable, eerie calm of a man who cared for nothing but world domination.

"Lillian does not accept sacrifices of guilt." He held my chin firmly, but not painfully. "She does not encourage asceticism or self-flagellation. You are *mine* to punish, pet. You may not do it for me."

I nodded. "Yes, Master."

I no longer put up a fight against Durian. I didn't have the space for it. In a den of lions, he was the king stopping the pride from tearing me limb from limb. After Rune tortured me, he was the one who gave me the barest forms of comfort, the one who drove the cruel turned lord away.

I knew it was sick, but I was dependent on Durian. He was the sole arbiter of everything I did. Every piece of food I consumed, article of clothing I wore, word I spoke, relief from pain I earned. As the days passed and my fight dimmed, he'd become the only thing I lived for. The routines, the protocol, the feeding—it bonded me to him, forced my body to become nothing but an extension of his will, my mind on a constant search to please him and avoid punishment. Isolated and shattered, he was the only glue that held my jagged shards together.

"I have a gift for you, pet," he said.

"Thank you, Master."

Pleased, he made a silent motion for me to stand and follow him to my unused bed. It was a two-piece, vibrantly blue gown. Though it was as revealing as my other outfits, it was decadent and beautiful. The top was essentially a corset bra with translucent sleeves. The bottom was two pieces of fabric for the front and back, bound together by a jeweled belt to wrap around my waist. My sides would be completely exposed. I'd long forgotten what it was like to leave my body to the imagination.

"It's beautiful," I said. Sunlight streamed through my window, illuminating the wooden floors and dancing across the dark green bedding. Why was Durian here, rather than Aunt Carol? He almost never saw me during the day, time typically used for attending to clan matters—matters I'd been left almost completely in the dark about.

It was as though the palace existed completely outside the reality of whatever conflict bloomed in Aristelle. The only hints I'd uncovered were whispers that the turned had raided born territories for slaves, but that the born had triumphantly pushed them back behind the border.

The other humans and I existed in this palace purely as a form of stress-relief and status symbols for the wealthiest, most powerful born.

"I'm glad you like it, pet." He paused, considering me for a moment. "Pets who behave get pretty things and greater freedoms. You have pleased me this week."

He fingered the O-ring of my collar, pulling me toward him and tonguing his fangs.

"I told you that one day you would have no reason to live but for me. Every promise I made to you is coming true. I've seen the way you've finally allowed yourself to break, to submit everything to me. And that is the only reason I have kept you." He gripped my throat. "Never forget to be grateful."

"Yes, Master."

He leaned in close. "Now, does my pet want to be a good little slave and sit in her Master's lap during a very, very important meeting?"

He spoke to me like I was a child. In the past, it had made me feel feral. Now, it was the only source of warmth in the castle. The only freedom from my thoughts of self-loathing and disgust.

"If that would please you, Master."

He grinned wider than I'd ever seen before. The hairs on the back of my neck prickled in recognition. This was no sociopathic imitation of a smile. And I knew that when Durian's smiles were real, someone—usually me—was in dire peril.

Yet, I no longer feared the torment. There was no use. It would ensue no matter what I did, so it was better to be pliable, to let Durian bend and shape me into his idealized object of perfection.

"It would please me more than you know. You'll even get to leave the palace." He stroked my cheek as I struggled for air under his tight grip. "But not to fret, your Master will be there to keep you safe."

Durian and I flew on a firebird, flanked by Brennan, two other lords, and two guards. I was shit at geography, so which direction we were headed was extremely unclear. Hatham soon faded from view, and foreboding fog and dense clouds obscured my vision of the ground entirely.

The wind was deafening. I would've frozen to death if someone wasn't using heat magick to keep us warm. Durian's magick was still a mystery. No one discussed it. He was hailed as Lillian's chosen, born to secure the borns' rightful rule. I sensed immense power from him at all times, but it was obscure, shrouded just like the land below this rolling fog.

It was heartbreaking to soar through the sky and not experience an ounce of exhilaration. That was when I knew for certain a huge, crucial piece of my soul had died. With Durian's arms locked around me, I was merely sick to my stomach until I was back to feeling nothing at all.

My neck was bare. Durian hadn't placed my collar back on my neck after he'd dressed me. It was strange to be without it, as I wore it almost every minute of every day. Aunt Carol only removed it for bathing, and Durian only removed it to feed from my throat.

One of the guards shouted something I couldn't hear, and soon we were descending, breaching the fog. I furrowed my brows, attempting to make sense of the land reaching for us.

I jolted when our firebird roared. Durian's desire was stronger than ever—for me, for Aristelle, for the whole world. His greed slithered around his mental landscape, ever-expanding and volatile. There was a level of anticipation and smugness that broke through my numb, gray walls—sending me on high alert.

The land in front of us wasn't nearly as densely populated.

We were on the outskirts of the city, as if we'd just left Aristelle's border.

My vision suddenly went dark, and I sensed a charge of magick in the air. Was it Durian's doing? I couldn't be sure. Panic twisted my guts, and I leaned into Durian's strong hold.

From what I understood, there were smaller villages and settlements between the city and the dry lands. These lands belonged to both mortals and vampires, but they weren't as protected by the rule of the turned nor vulnerable to the whims of the born.

It was where people went who wanted to be left alone.

Understandable.

I bit down a scream as our firebird roughly skidded on flat earth. My vision was restored.

We'd landed in some kind of worn down military outpost, a wide open field for incoming firebirds surrounded by crumbling buildings and training grounds.

I heard the calls of distant firebirds belonging to a different faction, and they sounded angry. I couldn't see them. Who were we meeting with? And why the hell was *I* here?

Durian helped me off the beast, his genuine smile back and more eerie than ever. Before us was a tall building, half-crumbled. I thought I heard voices from inside.

This made Durian's face twist into wrath. "How did they beat us here?" he spat at his men.

My ears tingled, and my neck seared heat. My whole body began to tremble. I could no longer hear the voices around me, and Durian had to all but drag me forward until I regained control of my body.

The warning bells were screeching now, and I was worried my heart was going to leap from my ribcage at the rate it was pounding.

We weren't headed inside the mess of patchy stone and faulty foundation. No, we walked around the side of the building, where there was a long table set with food and chalices in the middle of the field.

The first thing I saw were giant, bat-like beasts resting in the distance, their wings webbed and skin black as night. Another lone firebird was nestled between trees separate from them.

Next, I noticed there were almost an equal number of people as the men Durian had brought gathered on one side of the long table. Their backs were to us, and they wore all black.

Across from those in black, a man sat in flamboyant attire—a white ruffled blouse, a golden and burnt orange suit over top. Though he appeared young by virtue of vampirism, I could read the ancientness in his features. He was born.

Directly across from the born vampire was a witch in a black dress. Her magick was strange and deathly potent. Her brunette hair was meticulously styled, and her laugh held the vampire across from her in a trance.

I couldn't feel my body. I was only aware of my uncontrollable shaking, no matter how much warmth magick radiated from Durian's guard.

My eyes were stuck on the creeping, thorny tattoos of the man in the center, his tall form rigid as he faced away from me.

"No," I heard myself breathe.

They all turned, but I only saw *him.*

Rune.

I screamed bloody murder.

20

RUNE

"The kingdom hadn't been receiving any of our recent messages," I explained to Mason and Uriah in the deliberation room between gritted teeth. Sadie stood by my side. "They thought we'd gone dark in support of the turned in Ravenia. They thought *we'd* been the ones who had declared war."

Mason frowned.

"Durian must have a greater network of support than we thought," Uriah said, glaring ahead as he processed. He always looked angry when he was deep in thought.

We spoke with the kingdom most often via correspondence journals linked by magick. Just like the one I had given Scarlett. Durian's own spies had to have gotten close enough to each member of the council with a book and replaced it with a decoy, or at least one in particular. There were technically three journals in the kingdom's government, but there was only one we'd used consistently for a century—a line to the council's head and King Earle's most trusted advisor, Xenith. This journal or one of the others would likely have been handed off to Kole for the duration of his time in Ravenia.

Earle almost never wrote to us himself. He'd never truly respected us.

I hadn't even considered our lines had been compromised. The timing had aligned perfectly with Durian's political moves and the impending war in Ravenia. Though it had been the most harrowing scenario, I had genuinely believed Durian somehow gained Earle's support through his ethos alone.

"Imagine if the born had pretended to be us…" Uriah said.

I shook my head. "They wouldn't have known our codes."

Sadie nodded. "Too risky. They don't have the intel for that. It would've been sloppy."

"Durian preyed on each faction's paranoia expertly, making his own moves at exactly the right time to affirm each of his marks' faulty sense of reality." I was infuriated by the intelligence and foresight exhibited by a man I'd written off for far too long as merely an arrogant pest.

Durian had been intentionally positioning himself as a man to underestimate, powerful only in his speech and wealth, the stirring up of hatred and disorganized acts of terror. But it had been a façade.

"Our spies were merely working with the information available to them, blinded by our lack of true understanding. They ended up inadvertently reinforcing Durian's scheme," I concluded.

Mason's tattoos vibrated, the waves and whorls of shadow softly churning. She looked at Sadie, who was smiling like a Cheshire cat. "I assume you've already remedied the situation?"

Sadie uncrossed her arms and rolled her neck. Calm and unperturbed as ever. "Of course I have," she drawled. "I gave dear Kole a nasty fright when I intercepted him flying over dry lands."

We'd been watching for him, of course. I sent Sadie as soon as I understood his flight path.

"He always did enjoy a well-timed surprise, the more sadistic the better," she said.

No one knew who Sadie was to the turned. To Kole, she was a renowned courtesan, one of the few mortals who served the born on her own terms and lived to tell the tale. He had no idea that she'd used her position as a sex worker to meticulously plan the downfall of the born and the creation of an entire new race of vampires.

For all he knew, we'd tracked Sadie down and bribed her to help us. She was a fierce defender of Valentin mortal interests, but, in Kole's eyes, she had only ever been a dominatrix. No matter how many times she'd managed to manipulate him and others into during her bidding for the benefit of the turned.

The born had a blind spot when it came to powerful women, and I could only hope that same weakness was what was keeping Scarlett alive.

"Kole was given a new journal—he'd had one of the three potential decoys—and he's already sent us a new date and time."

Mason's eyes glowed even if her form remained rigid, her features stone. "Good. Just as it always should've been."

"Not quite," I said. My chest was tight, my shadows heavy with need—for her, always for her. "The born will still be in attendance, on neutral meeting grounds with harsh rules instated by the kingdom. The council may be pissed they've been manipulated, but that doesn't mean there is enough evidence to pin it all on Durian."

"Despite it being dead fucking obvious," Uriah muttered.

"He's still gotten to them, even if it was under false pretenses. Earle more than anyone else, unfortunately. That much is clear," I continued.

"But the path isn't as set in stone as we'd thought," Mason summarized. "It's not great. But at least we have more time to prepare no matter what's coming."

"Rune," Uriah said, glancing around for a moment as if to

make sure it was still only the four of us. "I know it's been mentioned in passing, but now that we've reached this point…"

I sighed. "Out with it, friend."

"*Should* we still be considering keeping peace with the kingdom? After everything they've done, everything they've allowed? The whole reason more turned clans have risen up against them is because Earle and his lords have begun to resemble Ivan and Haemon and their demented court of the underworld."

Ivan and Haemon Ardente were born brothers who once ruled Valentin. The first batch of turned, the three of us included, had been turned using Haemon's blood. Now we used the powerful blood of the fallen born king himself, Ivan, who Sadie held captive in a magickal suspension in her dungeons.

"Ravenia's uprisings are a reaction to the slave trade and attacks on mortals. Aren't their turned just *us*, centuries apart?" Uriah finished.

We were all silent for a moment.

"No one could ever be *us*, darling," Sadie finally said.

I was only half in this conversation, a truth I kept to myself. Mason and Uriah had yet to connect the dots. The reason why I wouldn't be able to sleep until this meeting.

"We need more information," I said, shutting down Uriah's fanaticism. "We cannot help Ravenia without first securing Valentin."

Before Uriah could utter another syllable, I added, "We're keeping our meeting with Kylo, the Hekate clan leader. That is already risky enough of a move. While I'm with you idealistically, I cannot ignore what is at stake for our own people, including the defenseless humans who live under our rule."

Uriah raised his hands and sighed. "Just some food for thought."

Mason had been staring at me, scanning my features as her lips pursed and eyes narrowed.

It looked like someone had finally connected the damn dots.

"You think he's going to bring her, don't you? When he learns you'll be in attendance?"

An ocean of feeling roared through my veins. The lights flickered. A muscle in my jaw feathered as I wrestled with my shadows.

"He won't be able to resist," I growled. I knew his type. I'd met many Durians in my lifetimes, even if their ambitions weren't nearly as lofty. They operated extremely predictably once you understood what motivated them. "He's been dying for my attention, for my acknowledgment of what he's done. He wants me to barter, to beg, to show at least a drop of my wrath for taking Scarlett. He's infuriated by my silence."

The fireplaces on either wall hissed as they extinguished. The spacious room went dark save for flickering witch lights casting shadows on the bookcases and furniture.

"And there's one thing I know for certain about my Scarlett," I said, my every muscle straining. "If a man's attention is on her, he will have no choice but to become unfathomably, insatiably obsessed with her. And if I know that, then Durian must know it by now too."

I saw a vision of shadows crawling up palace walls, rotting the building's foundation and reducing every born to a pile of ash and mangled flesh.

"Durian will bring her. He wants me to finally lose control. He needs a win, and above all, he wants to show me that he's capable of taking what belongs to me."

∽

I WASN'T—COULDN'T pay attention to Sadie's flirting with Kole. Involving her was a risk, but so was every move we made now.

We pretended not to be close to her, as if she'd weaseled her way into this meeting of her own accord. We also subtly hinted that she was Uriah's domme, much to his chagrin.

Sadie sat to my left, with Uriah to the left of her. Mason was to my right, followed by Percy and Dev, two members of my inner circle. Percy was ancient, technically older than I was given he was turned early on and when he was already over fifty years old. His shadows were potent poison. Dev was a strong fighter, a wielder of air magick and glamours. He was also popular among women, which had gotten him in trouble on more than a few occasions.

Kole refused to talk business until the born arrived, and he said so in a tone that very much made me want to slice off his tongue with my shadows.

I had never been more on edge. Thank fuck Sadie was here, a constant reminder of the necessity of maintaining my tenuous control.

At the call of firebirds, Millie and her shadowbird brothers and sisters growled and called back ferociously.

Sadie glanced their way, admiring another of her darkly beautiful creations—blasphemes of Helia's natural order.

I, on the other hand, went perfectly still. I cast out my hearing, listening for her voice. I hadn't known it was possible to want anything this badly, especially not after Sadie had crafted me into a finely tuned weapon of restraint.

Scarlett was the only thing in this world that could melt steel into water, carve gaping crevices into my heart and soul.

Footsteps and hushed voices grew louder. I could barely focus on the content of their words, only that each tenor was masculine.

Yet I knew he'd brought her, because for the first time since she'd been stolen, Scarlett's location had shifted. She'd been heading straight for me, the invisible leash growing shorter and shorter.

Until she was right behind me.

Sadie laughed. Mason's foot brushed mine, perhaps the most comforting move she was capable of giving.

Scarlett's intoxicating scent filled the air. Summer heat, berries and sweetness, violent storms, and sex—all of it coated with the unmistakable fragrance of her terror.

My fangs ached despite the substantial amount of rancid blood I'd forced down my throat before we'd arrived.

"No."

It was just one single word. Yet it was enough to crumble me to my core, to rid my mind of every last thought but the sound of her raspy voice and her erratic, frightened heart.

I turned.

My gaze locked onto those piercing blue eyes, those pools of feelings as vast and beautiful as the sea.

Her pupils dilated, and she *screamed*.

If I'd been crumbled by her voice, her wail of utter horror fucking shattered me. I would've shot up from my chair if Sadie hadn't sent a burst of pain across my cheekbone to snap me the fuck out of it.

Durian didn't miss my flinch.

Scarlett backed up into him, away from *me*. He whispered something to her, and she went silent. He clutched her to his chest, his fingers brushing across her bare midriff as she shook with fear.

And that was when I saw it—the ugly red marks carved into Little Flame's stomach, as if by a blade.

Durian, the marks spelled.

He'd done more than hurt her. He'd fucking brutalized her.

If not for Sadie, I might've rotted every single person in this field, including Scarlett herself. That was how little control I had left.

But I was not just any man. I was not a man at all.

I was Scarlett's God and Valentin's ruler. And I refused to

give Durian what he wanted. He would not leave this plane a martyr, assuring a bloody war with both the born and the kingdom. Nor would he see me lose control of my emotions and gain even a semblance of satisfaction.

We knew that if Durian brought Scarlett, he wouldn't merely show me that she belonged to him. He would provoke me by any means necessary. I'd allowed Sadie to see into my mind, to help fortify my strength in acting intelligently and not out of rage and whim. We'd done mental training every day since Kole had given us a meeting location.

Watching Scarlett cower away from me in the flesh, evidence of egregious violations carved into her skin, was nothing like the exercises and possibilities Sadie had prepped me with.

The only strike against Durian I could make in this moment was to guard my features, keep my screaming, bloodthirsty shadows to myself, and turn back around in my seat. It was the most excruciating movement I'd ever made.

"Durian," Kole said, gracefully moving to the head of the table to my left—closest to Uriah and Sadie. "I hope your flight was a pleasant one despite the weather."

I bloody hated politics. Though my face was blank when I stared at Kole, I couldn't stop myself from raising a single condescending brow.

Kole cleared his throat and gestured to the unoccupied side of the table. "Please, sit with us and introduce your friends."

I smirked. It looked like no matter how far Durian had slithered inside Earle's psyche, the kingdom still wouldn't refer to the born using their made-up titles. At least not yet.

Durian sat directly across from me, revealing none of his simmering irritation at Kole's slight. He pulled Scarlett into his lap, where she perched silently even as she still trembled with fear, refusing to meet my eyes. My gaze fell to her exposed legs, the garments she wore barely covering her or shielding her from the cold. It was more lingerie than clothing.

My fists clenched so tight under the table I feared I'd split my own bones.

I moved my gaze to Durian's smug smile, his cold, beady black eyes.

"It's a pleasure to meet with you finally, Kole," Durian said. "Today I'm joined by Lord Brennan, Lord Christoph, and Lord Nereus."

There were two men he skipped, dressed differently than the tacky displays of wealth worn by the *lords*. I assumed they were lackeys of some sort, dressed in plain burgundy.

Kole's jaw ticked. "I believe men still need to be ordained by the king to ascend to lord status, my friend."

Ever the spineless courtier, Kole softened his slap on the wrist with pleasantries.

Now it was my turn to smirk at Durian. I fought my every aching urge to look at Scarlett instead—to drink up every inch of her skin, to search her eyes for the soul I loved more than my city and this entire damned world.

I pretended like she wasn't even here.

Even when her eyes found mine. Even when her beautiful features twisted with pain and confusion, pupils wide and searching.

Durian maintained his composure as he tilted his head toward Kole. "I meant no disrespect to the crown. I've enjoyed my long correspondences with King Earle immensely these past weeks." His fingers brushed through Scarlett's dark waves of hair before trailing down her bare skin to her waist.

His eyes darted to mine, and I gave him nothing. I'd already assumed he'd been in contact with Earle, my hunch strengthened by the intel of my eyes in Ravenia. Durian was weaseling his way into the psyche of a paranoid king obsessed with preserving his legacy.

"Though I honor the rule of the kingdom, I also know that Valentin has a long history of behaving autonomously in many areas." Durian looked at me pointedly. "I live to serve Lillian, and it is my view that Valentin has been in desperate need of the Dark Mother's divine will for centuries now. It is *she* who has ordained me and my men."

A bold fucking statement. I watched Kole process Durian's words, his eyes narrowing. He might've agreed with Durian on some level that Valentin belonged to the born, but Kole was still here on behalf of the kingdom. And Durian's words skated dangerously close to treason, no matter how independent we had become from greater Ravenia.

The man to Durian's left, the one who I'd identified as Brennan, was staring at Scarlett. I recognized the look in his eyes—the look that had been a death sentence for men on numerous occasions. The craze of a man under my Little Flame's beautiful spell.

He was going to get those crazed eyes shoved back down his undeserving throat.

"Might we address the human you've brought?" Kole asked, seeming to table the current subject of Durian's audacity. His brows lifted as short strands of light brown hair grew tousled in the wind. When Scarlett met his gaze, his amber eyes sparkled. "Safe to assume she isn't a gift… on account of the strict *treaty* of this great autonomous island."

There was a kind of mockery in his tone that pulled Durian's lips into a smile while mine tugged down.

I didn't find a joke about Scarlett being an object to bestow to politicians as hilarious as the born clearly did. Especially not when she was currently enslaved, a direct violation of the treaty that Kole had subtly mocked.

Mason nudged my foot again. Sadie covertly flooded my mind with clarity, enchanted grounding crystals in her pocket and mine.

"She didn't want to be separated from her Master today, you

see," Durian said calmly, looking down at Scarlett as she twisted in his arms to gaze up at him. "Isn't that right, pet?"

Scarlett nodded, and my heart fucking tore open. "Yes, Master," she murmured, still trembling slightly with fear.

My ears were tingling at the sound of her voice, my head yearning to crane forward, to draw more of it out of her. No matter her words' heartbreaking contents. I knew that none of Scarlett truly belonged to Durian. Not her body, not her beautiful mind, not her blinding soul. All of her was mine.

Forever.

"Despite our power exchange *relationship*," Durian said, staring into my eyes even as he spoke to Kole. "She's my good little pet of her own accord."

Scarlett didn't contradict him. And seeing what Durian had done to her stomach, it was clear why. I silently fumed, imagining all the ways I would make Durian suffer—for centuries, millennia, even—before even considering putting him out of his endless misery.

Kole clearly didn't give a damn either way if Scarlett was a slave. He didn't even question the jagged recent wounds on her skin. He'd merely glanced at them with distaste, as if they were a blemish on a piece of art.

Scarlett suddenly shifted and looked back toward Kole, and I recognized the wheels of her cunning mind churn for the first time. It mended something broken inside of me, if only an inch. Just to see her feel something other than fear.

What was she thinking?

"I wanted to make her willingness clear, since we've brought up Rune's little political magnum opus," Durian said. "Lillian may not recognize laws designed to neuter her children and keep the born in a position of subjugation, but abide we must by the *current* laws of the land."

I did not yield. I stayed neutral as Durian spun his lies about Scarlett, his attack on my rule. I did not give Durian what he wanted, and to my own satisfaction, a hint of frustration finally crossed his dark eyes.

Though I'd avoided looking at her at all costs, each time I did, I saw plainly my Scarlett's brokenness, her pain that went on and on. I'd fortified my mind against mental magick as a precaution, hoping it might help counter Durian's visions. Sadie had told me it would guard me from Scarlett too.

I needed to let down those walls, even if temporarily. I had to prove to Scarlett I still loved her. I had to reveal that this was all a show—that I loved her endlessly, devotedly, perilously. I demanded her to feel how desperately I needed her back, so I could mend her every last wound. Her terror when she saw me was clear evidence Durian had already poisoned her mind against me, traumatizing her into a sick bond with him.

I would never forgive myself for letting any of this happen. For letting her flame dim. She was already terribly wounded when she met me, and now—gods above and below, my heart was filled with nothing but piercing stabs—because she had never looked so hurt and afraid.

She needed hope, and she needed it right now.

Durian twirled a lock of Scarlett's hair around his finger, oblivious to the silent exchange between her and Kole. Sadie hadn't missed a thing, subtly shifting as her focus moved from Little Flame to the dignitary.

When Durian's hand skated high on Scarlett's thigh, I finally refocused on him. I opened my mouth to comment on his religious nonsense, the only attack I could make, despite wanting to send my shadows to decapitate him instead.

But he spoke again before I could.

"Was she willing when she was with you, Rune? Before she left you for a stronger ruler?"

21

SCARLETT

When I first saw Rune, every single act of torture he'd carried out on my body and mind came rushing forward. I thought for sure he was going to snatch me from Durian to cut off my fingers again or drain me dry.

Rune likely thought I'd run to Durian of my own free will. He thought I was a succubus plant, an evil demon who'd never truly loved him at all. It made sense that he despised me.

In his eyes, I was nothing more than the enemy.

The sickest part of me wished Rune would crush me with his words again—feed the mounting guilt over what I was and what I'd done to those humans.

Durian had whispered that I was safe, that Rune couldn't hurt me. He'd reminded me to behave, and I clung to him for stability amid the waves of confusion and heartbreak.

But there was something wrong, something I didn't understand. Rune didn't glare at me with hatred. He didn't look anything like the man who'd tortured me for weeks.

Yet he also avoided looking at me at all. His gaze wasn't icy, but it was empty, disinterested.

Or at least, I thought it had been. But I'd noticed the way his eyes had flashed ever-so-briefly when Durian touched me. I searched and searched, but he didn't reveal anything more.

"She's my good little pet of her own accord," Durian said.

Something inside me shriveled when I was forced to agree with Durian's lie. Because I knew I wouldn't be helped, and fighting him might take me out of the game for good. Though there were moments I thought I deserved to die, I didn't actually want to. Not yet.

Rune's desires were guarded, his mind opaque. He'd disowned me. His men and women also paid me no mind, save the witch, who was eyeing me very carefully at intermittent intervals.

Who was she? And why couldn't I read *her* desires?

I could sense Mason's and Uriah's motivations, predictably focused on annihilating Durian and swaying the mind of this man I'd understood was some kind of mediator sent by the kingdom.

But why was so much of their desire focused on Rune? On helping him, giving him strength? Rune didn't lose his cool, his perfectly steady exterior. The ripeness of emotions in the air, hidden and carefully tucked away, did nothing to quell my questions.

My shaking eased the more perplexed I became. My mind, once overcome by panic, cleared like a dissipating fog over Valentin's beautiful mountains. I found myself focused on Kole and his growing interest in me. I sunk inside his psyche, parsing through the energy he freely projected outward. Some of his desire was focused on the witch, but a great deal of it swam toward me.

The more I flexed my accursed magick, the more I came back into my body. The more I came back to *myself*.

"Was she willing when she was with you, Rune? Before she left you for a stronger ruler?"

My stomach dropped, and my eyes flashed to Rune, as if seeing him here for the very first time.

The man I'd once loved.

You're dead to me.

You are the most pathetic, useless human I have ever wasted my time on. You deserve everything you've gotten. You belong here.

I'm glad you're with them. Look at you. Ruined. Used. Worthless.

Consider yourself unclaimed. You are nothing to me. You never meant anything to me at all.

All the cruel words, all the heartbreak, all the torture and the anger and the betrayal and the crushing, ruthless depths of despair, and when I looked at Rune—all I saw were stars.

I was still that naive, lovesick girl, foolishly yearning for the man who'd forsaken her.

"She didn't leave me," Rune said calmly, leaning back in his chair.

Everyone at the table was silent. Kole's features flashed in surprise, looking at me with new eyes—even more interested than he'd been before.

I held my breath. Did Rune somehow know the truth? Did he know that I'd been taken against my will?

Say it. Please, someone say it. Stupid tears threatened to form, my stomach in knots. I wanted someone at this table to tell the truth, to acknowledge what had happened to me.

"I let her go," Rune finished, his features utterly bored. "Now, can we please return to discussing matters of substance?"

My heart shattered. Tears finally welled. I wanted to go back to feeling nothing. I wanted that ridiculous spark of hope to finally die for good.

"Such as your continued acts of treason and terrorism that threaten both Valentin and all of Ravenia," Mason said.

Rune's eyes fell to mine just one more time, for the briefest of seconds. His features were blank, and he looked away.

But before I could shut down completely and return to a

blissful numbness, a gate opened in the space between us. A familiar heat erupted on the back of my neck. A dam broke.

And I felt it *all*.

Rune's tsunami of desire slammed into me. I lost my ability to breathe. Never before had I felt such intensity, such yearning. He desired me like no one had ever desired another. He bled for me.

It wasn't lust. Sexual hunger was a faded hum in comparison to the symphony of craving that lit up my every nerve, squeezed my heart in the strongest shadowed grip. I was back in the room of music, laying side by side with Rune as we stared up at the cosmos. I was sitting outside a café reading his recommended poetry, or even better, his own achingly beautiful prose. I was in his arms, once the safest place I'd ever known.

Wave after wave racked against my psyche—brushstrokes of rich color, melodies that spanned centuries, and the indescribable, undeniable feeling of something that transcended desire itself.

I jolted as if I'd been slapped, audibly gasping.

Durian halted speaking. I hadn't heard a word anyone had said, nor did I understand how much time had passed. All I knew was that everyone at the table was now staring at me.

Durian's grip on me tightened, fingers digging into my wounds. I winced.

"I'm sorry," I whispered on instinct, even if I still couldn't focus, couldn't breathe.

My stomach seared as Durian dug deeper. I only stared at Rune.

"As I was saying," Durian said, a note of anger leaking into his voice for the first time during the meeting.

It had a cold chill traveling down my spine, knowing I was the cause.

Rune didn't dare look at me. The waves began to lull now

that I'd acknowledged and fed from them, their strength like no power that had ever surged in my veins.

"I did not direct any of my devotees to commit acts of terror in Aristelle," Durian said, his focus shifting from Rune to Kole. Kole finally pulled his perplexed gaze off me. "My people are starving, impoverished, and living as second-class citizens under the tyranny of the turned. It is not hard to understand why they may feel they have been pushed to their breaking points, forced to live in direct opposition with their true nature."

Kole scratched his chin, and Uriah rolled his eyes. The two turned men on the other side of Rune appeared equally irritated, though they concealed their emotions better.

"If the standard of living of the born is what you were truly concerned with," Mason said coldly. "Then maybe you and your *friends* should consider donating your exorbitant amounts of wealth to poverty relief efforts. Or educational programs. Or, even easier, simply stop burning down blood cafés."

Brennan too had been glancing at me every once in a while, and now I watched his lip curl, staring at Mason with unabashed hatred.

"The born in Aristelle are suffering because they still refuse to abide by the law, choosing to live lives of crime and poor impulse control over building lasting success as valuable members of society. Instead of helping your people, you have merely profited off their misplaced anger by encouraging them to sacrifice themselves in futile acts of violence."

Uriah seemed satisfied with Mason's words. Rune merely lifted a brow in thinly veiled amusement at the born's amassing anger.

And I... I was still reeling. I swallowed, taking one deep breath after another.

Rune still loved me.

Rune still loved me.

Rune. Still. Loved. Me.

It didn't feel real. Maybe it wasn't. I was in the process of losing my sanity, after all—plagued by visions and memories that didn't make sense, yet I perceived as solidly as my current lived experience.

How was it possible for Rune to feel anything other than hatred? Nothing had changed. I was still a succubus. He still didn't know the truth of my innocence.

My magick vibrated in my blood, whispering for me to lean back into my power. To stop being a victim, and use the only advantages at my disposal to figure out what the fuck was going on.

"Let us speak plainly, brother," Durian said to Kole, the term of endearment putting the turned side of the table on edge immediately. "What has happened in Valentin goes against the world's natural order. It goes against the Dark Mother's will. We were not meant to feed in moderation, with strict stipulations, like docile house pets. Children of Lillian were born to rule. You see what is happening in your own land—the humans that have blasphemed vampirism, unnaturally claiming immortality for themselves in order to overthrow the king, the council, and his ordained lords and ladies. Who do you think inspired such a treasonous, chaotic state of the world?"

Kole sighed. "I must admit, I am sympathetic to this logic."

I didn't miss the way the witch's green eyes went reptilian, narrow and cold, as they landed on Kole. Nor did I miss the way Kole swallowed when he met her gaze, his features twisting in a new direction—back toward neutrality.

"*However,* it is not up to you and your followers to decide what is best for Valentin, nor the rest of Ravenia. Rune was ordained as this territory's lord, and as it stands, acts against him are still acts against the kingdom." Kole met Durian's eyes. "You say you have not directly given orders to commit acts of terror against the mortals and turned, but everyone at this table knows that is a half-truth. Regardless of your intentional wording and clever puppeteering, you have *directly* initiated the closing of borders and have amassed an army that is currently maintaining that border and provoking more violence. Your religious movement has sowed seeds of chaos, but you have also made your own clear directives as if you are your own state power."

"Every direct action we have undertaken has been out of self-defense," Brennan said. "Lillian called us to protect the born. Our people were left without any semblance of power in this city gifted to us by Lillian herself thousands of years ago."

This was part of Durian's religious ethos—that Valentin was a holy land gifted to powerful born bloodlines by Lillian herself. I recognized it from a passage in his holy book, the *Book of Lillian,* the aunts had read us before one of our prayers. My mind churned and churned, making sense of the subtext of each word. I'd been thrown in the deep end of this political landscape head first.

I straightened, eyes flitting from vampire to vampire.

Here I sat—drowning in self-hatred, confusion, agony, and blinding, all-consuming love—at a meeting that I now understood could not only change the trajectory of my life but also the lives of everyone I'd ever known. Snow, Penn, and the witches, Jaxon, Reggie and the other turned who'd been kind to me, every mortal on this island and perhaps the ones beyond it.

I shoved all other thoughts away other than my own usefulness, my utility for the good of others. And the moment I did, something inside me loosened, the shroud of futile, selfish self-pity dissipating. The last time I'd tried to help, I'd failed. I understood that.

But all I could do now was either give up, or try to do better. All I could do was honor the humans who'd been slain by my actions.

"I would also be remiss if I didn't address the firebird in the room," Kole said. His face fell into something severe, losing the friendliness he'd been employing to soften tensions. "It would appear that our lines of communication with Rune and his clan have been compromised. This meeting is not as it was originally planned. The council feels as though we have been intentionally manipulated, used as pawns in Valentin's current conflicts. This is an egregious act of treason, especially in the face of what everyone at this table clearly already understands about our own state of affairs."

I quickly processed what I'd heard. The born must've employed spies to change the terms of this meeting, to pit the kingdom against the turned.

Durian was silent, as were his men.

I focused on Kole, reading what the rest of the table couldn't. I traced the edges of his desires, felt where they were rigid and where they were malleable. My teeth ground, anger and disbelief at what I uncovered.

Kole was only pretending to hear out the turned, to slap Durian on the wrist for the borns' behavior. And the turned had no idea—I could read it from them, their hope that they were making progress, their desire for Kole to put Durian in his place. They didn't realize how bound they were by Kole's opposing desires. The single place of wiggle room, strangely enough, was in the thread of desire between Kole and the brunette witch. Everything else leaned heavily toward the born, an unspoken vendetta closing up his ability to be swayed.

"As Valentin's ruler," Rune said. "I ask what the kingdom plans to do about this *egregious act of treason*. Considering it doesn't take a genius to connect this act to whom it most benefited."

"Not to mention the clear indications we are heading into another civil war," Mason said, her features as hard and immovable as ever.

She no longer regarded me with suspicion. It was

surprisingly the faintest tinges of guilt I tasted on my tongue when she glanced my way.

Lord Nereus began to defend the born again, but Kole raised his hand to silence the table.

"It is the kingdom's official decree that a ceasefire be instituted for both parties until further notice. More deliberations need to be had, and more information must be gathered. If Valentin wants to remain under its own rule, this demand will be obeyed."

There was something wrong—Durian and the born remained unchanged, their web of desire breathing in and out in the same rhythm and cadence as it had before. I glanced at Brennan, noting the smugness on his features. He met my eyes, his irises darkening and an overconfident smile forming.

Rune's eyes widened at Kole's words, his lips curling as he addressed him. "The turned *respectfully* requests that the kingdom take this time to consider what is best for its own interests in Ravenia. And to consider what is at stake if Valentin's exports dwindle or become unavailable entirely."

Kole flashed his fangs, his gaze icy. He leaned forward and placed his palms on the dark table. "Is this truly the threat you wish to pass along to King Earle and his council, Rune?"

"I heard no threat," the witch said, speaking for the first time. Her tone was sultry, neither threatening nor easy. When she looked at Kole, she held him in nothing short of a trance. "As the only party here representing mortal interests, I believe the leader of the turned is attempting to remind us of what happened during the war. Blood shortages and massacres significantly reduced the mortal population and subsequently curbed magickal goods production for decades. Do we really need to prove for a second time what happens when Valentin's born are free to act however they see fit?"

"An excellent reminder for those who weren't even alive

during the war," Uriah added, shooting a look at Durian and Brennan.

Kole spoke, but Durian boldly cut him off as he stroked my hair again like I was a lapdog. "I'm glad you brought that last detail to the table's attention. Though we honor the wisdom of our elders, my lords and I—protectors of Lillian's children and rightful heirs to Valentin—are overwhelmingly composed of vampires with new, fresh perspectives. We are different from the born leadership that fell during the war. We are *stronger*."

Durian relaxed, and I noticed the flair of approval coming from Kole. Every time the born made a point, I read clearly the ease at which they influenced him. Kole was *searching* for reasons to back the born, and he was doing the opposite for the turned, no matter what valid points they made.

"Now, who even are you?" Durian asked Sadie. "And why is an unnamed *witch* permitted at a meeting of vampires to hear sensitive information of this magnitude?"

"Same could be said of your pet human," Kole snapped, for the first time lashing out at Durian.

Circular arguments commenced, but Durian and Rune stayed silent as their counterparts acted as each side's mouthpieces. Mason and the two turned men I couldn't name lamented about everything the born had destroyed, all the ways they'd broken the treaty and harmed mortals. Brennan bit back with more religious arguments for why the turned shouldn't even exist, citing the *Book of Lillian* as evidence that Durian and his lords were always destined to rule. Nereus drove home points about self-defense and the born as an oppressed people. Uriah called the *Book of Lillian* a con and Durian a charlatan. On and on, every single point of tension was aired out, and no one but me could see why everything they said was futile.

Kole didn't care. He was here to deliver a message and *pretend* to give a shit. But he didn't, not at all. Kole was interested in Durian and the born. And more than even that, Kole was interested in *Kole*.

Swaying him to the side of the turned would take careful, concerted effort by someone who understood exactly what made his mind tick.

Say, perhaps, a succubus fueled by the desire of Valentin's most powerful.

Rune and I locked eyes, and it was as if I were descending on the back of a firebird, wings spread wide. We maintained this prolonged stare for what felt like hours, neither of us moving, neither of us expressing a single emotion.

Nothing was spoken. A million things were said.

Cool fingers moved my hair off my neck. Durian roughly grabbed me, locking me in his ironclad hold as he shoved my neck to the side.

I finally understood why I wasn't collared.

Rune's eyes didn't leave mine. Not when Durian's lips brushed my neck. Not when his fangs sunk in, and my essence flowed down his throat, my eyes fluttering with unwanted pleasure.

Still, I only gazed at Rune, and Rune gazed back.

His shadows finally leaked, darkening the surrounding air. I heard loud voices, felt Durian's bruising touch all over my body as he fed. For a moment, I saw the void. The deep dark canvas upon which the cosmos was painted.

And then I saw a field of luminescent stars: bright, eternal, sublime.

22

RUNE

What would *really* be the consequences if I were to rot every single born at this table?

If only I hadn't vowed to protect the world Scarlett loved despite every way it had shown her its indifference.

I held her eyes as Durian fed from her, as he guaranteed his head would be severed from his body. The scent of her blood had everyone at the table tense with instinctive need, eyes flashing to my Little Flame.

As her eyes fluttered, Durian grabbed her roughly enough to mark her with bruises—on her arms, her hips, her ribs.

My shadows leaked.

"Rune," Sadie snapped. "One of you, please get your lord in check," she said to my clan to keep up our charade.

Ordinarily, her voice would've brought me back down to earth. But not today. Not with another man's fangs in my soul, my heart, my unending obsession.

"This meeting has been a sham," I spat. The comment was directed toward Kole, but my eyes never left Scarlett's, even when they closed shut.

"Rune, I was very clear that no amount of magick would be tolerated at this meeting," Kole warned, his tone sharp.

Durian licked his wound shut, blood on his lips as he slowly lifted to stare at me. "You were putting on a good act, my bastard brother," Durian said, oozing with smug condescension as his eyes darkened, staring hard at my growing cloud of darkness. "But I know how addictive my pet's blood is. I bet she's ruined all others for you."

Durian's hand trailed from her neck lower. Her heart beat slow and hard. He'd taken too much, and now she was drained. All I saw behind my eyelids was darkness and fury, no matter how much clarity magick Sadie fed me.

I had planned to wait until we were in the air before I rescued Scarlett. There was no way in this gods' cursed realm that I was going to allow her to remain Durian's slave for another minute after this meeting. I was always going to take her back, to follow all the kingdom's rules *except* whatever it took to bring my Little Flame home.

Durian's fingers trailed lower, and I realized our meticulous plan was about to go up in shadows. Mason tensed. My clan knew it, too.

"She has earned the obsession of my *entire court*," he said, and Brennan grinned as he flashed his fangs. "I understand now why you valued her so highly." His hand passed her belly button, and I shot up from the table. "Her addictive blood is one thing, but her perfect, adorable little cunt..."

I submerged us in darkness.

I ignored Kole's cowardly shouts, warning us that harming him would be seen as an act of war. I didn't give a fuck about Kole, about his pandering to the born, his blatant disrespect for my rule. The kingdom had refused to act, to dole out even the barest of punishments to the born in order to protect Valentin and enforce her laws.

Taking back Scarlett wasn't going to change anyone's mind.

It would be an act of justice; I was this island's arbiter and executioner.

Everyone moved at once.

"No killing," I managed to bite out, against my true desires.

"Maiming?" Uriah asked.

"Permitted. No, *encouraged*."

Durian shoved Scarlett, limp and unconscious, behind him. My shadows leaped from my skin. Brennan enacted a shield, and Nereus wielded light to counteract my maddening shadows. They weren't quick enough to dodge Percy's poison, and Brennan hissed as his translucent shield wobbled and warped.

I forced my shadows through the cracks. They were aching, heavy with the indescribable need to finally reach for her—to touch her and hold her close.

Durian threw a dagger quicker than even the most trained eyes could track. Dev must've been watching him closely, as he deflected it with air magick before it could slice through my chest.

"Hey!" Kole shouted, dodging the deflected blade.

Oops.

The earth trembled as Kole's rage multiplied. "You are all in direct violation of the kingdom's decree. This is *treason!*"

Even as I dodged and struck, pulling weapons from hands with my shadows and shouting directions at my inner circle, *she* was all I could think about.

Scarlett. My Little Flame.

But I could no longer physically see her. I craned my head, my shadows skirting along the ground. At a blast of light from Nereus, I winced, my shadows recoiling.

"Please."

My head swiveled, and I couldn't breathe as I watched Scarlett shakily stand and approach Kole to our left. Durian halted too, unaware that she'd dragged herself away from him.

"Please help me," she whispered with a scratchy voice, faltering and nearly falling back to the ground.

Kole steadied her, the ground's quaking replaced by a subdued tremble. I gritted my teeth. At least she was no longer in the direct line of fire.

Dev took the opportunity to lift the table off the ground and send it flying into the born with a mean gust of wind.

Kole held Scarlett steady as the powerful air whipped about.

"Now. Let's *go*," I ordered.

Everyone wielded their gifts to maximize this short window of time. Born shields crumbled, skin was afflicted with poison, and Uriah sliced through flesh. My shadows darkened the air once more.

We wouldn't be able to use Dev's glamour for long, not on this many of us. Kole looked utterly mystified by our coordinated display. It was incredible—the kingdom's utter disbelief when faced with our power and skill, no matter how many times we reigned triumphant.

I moved with vampiric speed toward Kole, toward *her*.

Her scent overpowered my senses so undeniably that I had to hold my breath as my fingers brushed her trembling body. I snatched her away with lightning quickness, holding her tight to my chest.

My shadows rotted the land, turned the skies obsidian. It took considerable effort not to let them feast on flesh. I was not merely Scarlett's Dark God. I was Valentin's too.

Shouts of frustration followed us all the way to our shadowbirds, who had sensed us coming and were ready for flight. They met us halfway across the field. Strangely, Millie didn't so much as sniff the air when I hoisted Scarlett onto her back. She accepted her presence immediately. How could she not? When Scarlett was merely an extension of me, our souls forever intertwined.

"Up," I commanded.

And we were soaring. My heart was in my throat, fear and adrenaline affecting me in a way they hadn't done since I was human. I held Scarlett tight to my chest.

She didn't speak, only leaned back into me, breathing rapidly.

"Are you injured, baby?" was all I could manage as relief coursed through my veins the higher we soared. I was careful to keep my touch minimal, only keeping her close to me for her safety.

She still didn't speak. And I didn't force her.

"Scarlett I—" There was so much I needed to say, and none of it was appropriate to throw at her yet. "You're safe. I love you, and you're safe."

She twisted around in my arms. Fog obscured the ground below, the distance we were putting between us and Durian.

"Hi, sweet girl," I murmured, staring into her big blue eyes as my jaw trembled with raw emotion. I couldn't help but stroke the side of her face, trail her cheekbone with the faintest touch. "You're—"

My heart hammered. I blinked. My grip around Scarlett tightened, unable to make sense of what I was seeing.

Scarlett was fading.

She smiled. Her piercing eyes turned to onyx. I could no longer feel her skin underneath my fingertips.

I reached for the empty air in front of me. I peered over Millie. To my left, Mason and Uriah stared at me in horror.

I unleashed a feral, guttural roar.

Scarlett was gone.

I reached for that invisible leash that tethered her to me, and I realized instantly what had happened.

Scarlett had never been in my arms at all.

23

SCARLETT

I nestled into Rune's arms, his shadows wrapping around me as I listened to the steady beat of his heart.

"You still love me," I whispered.

I felt that steady river of deep, undeniable obsession course through my veins. Evidence that somehow, beyond all logic and reason, Rune hadn't forsaken me.

I cried into his chest, gripping him hard, praying he would never let me go again.

"Wake up, pet."

My eyes flew open as Durian yanked me out of my blissful dream and back into my nightmarish reality. Standing over me were three men. Durian, Brennan, and…

Kole.

"You must be quite the rarity, my dear," Kole said, desire bleeding from beneath his flashy clothes. "To be coveted greatly enough to provoke such violent, politically short-sighted incidents."

I looked to Durian, sensing brewing paranoia hiding underneath his overwhelming air of victory. Everything came back to me all at once. I realized I was missing a huge gap of time in between Durian feeding from me, Rune's shadows leaking, and my arrival back at the palace.

Rune still loved me. Which meant he'd likely fought for me.

But he'd somehow failed.

Panic seized me. Rune was the strongest vampire in Valentin. How could Durian have thwarted him?

And why was Durian's paranoia circling me like a viper?

"Did I behave to your standards, Master?" I asked quickly.

This halted Durian, his severe features relaxing an inch. "Yes, pet." He smiled at Kole as he spoke to me. "Kneel."

I knelt, understanding we were in one of Durian's studies—black walls and dark furniture accented with crimson and gold. Magick emanated from the bookshelves and several trinkets and antique weapons were strewn about.

Anger boiled in my blood, as ripe as my fear and disappointment. Somehow Rune hadn't saved me. Was he okay? Surely Durian would be in a much different mood if he'd actually harmed Rune in a lasting way.

I was still a slave. Yet everything had changed.

I fought the urge to glare at Kole, who clearly cared so little about true diplomacy, justice, and the well-being of Valentin that he'd ridden back with the born to Durian's palace.

My collar had been placed back on my neck.

But *Rune still loved me.* He'd committed violence in my name. I didn't know how it was possible; but it was real—I'd held his heart in my palms, examined it from every reality-shattering angle.

Nothing was solved. I had a wealth of unanswered questions. But Rune had given me a lifeline, and I clenched my exhausted fists tight around it.

The whole world is doomed, Little Flame. We live and love anyway.

I couldn't let the tears form. I couldn't show an ounce of my overwhelming grief that I still sat here, kneeling before men I hated.

Durian scanned my face for evidence, and I stayed demure, feeding him back delicate strokes of his ego.

When Lillian's vengeful spite lit up my nerves, I allowed it to break through my walls of shame.

I would fight. As I always had.

I had a home to go back to. I had friends who adored me. I saw Snow's face, felt her arms around me as she laughed. I had…

Rune.

"Drink," Durian commanded, bending down to shove a potion in my face. I recognized its blood replenishing magick immediately, an expensive and rare commodity.

Rune had once told me he would have to give me these so he could feed exclusively from me whenever possible.

I drank this potion for *him*. Rune's achingly beautiful face was all I could see, the tips of his thorny shadow vines creeping up his neck. That dark, nearly black hair that was feather soft to the touch.

I handed the glass bottle back to my captor. When he patted my head in approval, my mind was flooded with a stomach-churning mix of satisfaction and shame. I hated the hold he had over me, despite everything he'd done.

"You are going to spend the evening with Kole, pet," Durian said with a sigh, a dramatic air to his voice. As if he were emphasizing how difficult it would be for him to share.

I tensed. I searched his desires for wiggle room, areas for me to slither between cracks and exert my own will. But his decision had already been made. I wasn't stupid enough to ignore Rosalind's harsh warnings. I couldn't afford to break the spell, to ruin the tenuous control I had over Durian by aiming too high.

I gripped my lifeline, even as my lip trembled.

I would make it home.

Kole peered down at me with a smile, his eyes soft. "No need to worry, beautiful human. I am at *your* command."

Confusion rolled through me, and for the first time, I dug deeper into Kole's surface level lust for me.

Oh.

He didn't want to dominate me at all. It was really quite the opposite. Sure, I'd still be used by virtue of being a slave. But it would be an entirely different game than the one I played with Durian.

Kole wanted me to have the power, even if it was all pretend. He didn't understand that I already *did.* And the power I had was real and overflowing.

"You are not actually off leash, pet. Do not let my generosity give you any ideas," Durian said dryly. "You will serve Kole in whatever ways he desires, just as it will please your Master. Consider this a reward for your good behavior and a very successful day."

My heart twisted. What had happened? I wanted to ask, but I couldn't appear too eager.

"Stand," Durian said to me. He looked to Kole. "You will be the first born vampire to ever feed from her other than her Master. Feel free to pull any of the others into your fun. What's mine is yours, brother."

Kole appraised me. "An honor, truly."

Brennan's smile was tight and fake. I gazed at him, rounding my eyes and feigning innocence and nervousness.

It should be you who spends the night with me, I whispered to his mind. *Durian continues to take you for granted. He's willing to share, but not with you...*

I looked down at the ground.

It's you Scarlett wants, Brennan. It should be you.

Brennan swallowed, and a wave of desire soaked into my skin. Better yet, a tide of anger and envy.

I quickly shut down the accompanying wave of guilt, flashes of what had happened the night I sentenced two humans to death.

Forward. I couldn't look back.

"What beautiful chaos you have stirred, little human," Kole purred, offering me a hand.

I took it. I stepped back into my power, and I gave this life one last shot. I'd give it everything I had. Because that was who I was, no matter how severely I'd been beaten down into the dirt.

I smiled at him, allowing some of my genuine cunning to leak into my irises as if by accident. "I didn't mean to cause any trouble, my lord."

His gaze roamed my barely covered form, his lips quirking up as he stepped toward me. "Hmm. And yet trouble is exactly what you caused—what you *are*. Do you enjoy inducing such violent yearning in both of Valentin's most powerful vampire clans?"

Durian tensed, searching my face again. "Answer him, *pet*."

Kole was of short stature, only a few inches taller than me. I met his eyes, my smile fading an inch.

"It scares me." I looked at the floor, and then slowly back up, my gaze flitting between Durian, Brennan, and Kole. "But I know I chose the strongest side. I know my Master will keep me safe."

When Durian's eyes burned into mine, I shut my mouth quickly, as though I'd revealed too much. As if he were someone I more than respected, but genuinely *wanted*.

You have stolen her weak little human heart, I spoke to Durian's mind next. *She is putty in your hands. You've poisoned her against Rune—everything you witnessed between them was* his *doing, not hers. She wants* you, *Valentin's rightful ruler. Her silly human brain has latched onto you, recognizing that you are the one who controls everything she does. You are her whole world.*

I danced and spun, taking back the reins of my webs—adding to them, bolstering them with my newfound power.

The power of Rune's eternal devotion to a demon daughter of Lillian.

24

SCARLETT

The born congregated in the dungeons tonight, which were half entertainment lounges like Aristelle's feeding clubs and half literal dungeons, for torture of a non-sexual variety. I couldn't tell which screams belonged to prisoners, slaves, or consenting vampires.

It all melded together into a depraved underworld of sex and violence. I couldn't deny it was an energy that felt natural inside my veins.

I was my Dark Mother's daughter, after all.

"They envy you," I whispered to Kole as vampires watched us enter the space together.

Kole straightened. His eyes were alight as his ego puffed up. "I can see that."

Candles and witch lights flickered, the atmosphere dark, mysterious, and decadent. A statue of Lillian stood against a far wall, a human-sized altar before her. I quickly looked away.

Durian and Brennan were upstairs somewhere attending to clan matters. This was my chance to gain a foothold with someone who didn't belong to Durian's clan, despite his sympathy for their cause.

Kole could help me. He had the power to change my fate. And maybe I had the power to change everyone else's.

A blonde figure emerged from behind two vampires—one with a ball gag in his mouth, drool dribbling down his chin, and the other a woman in a shiny black miniskirt and corset.

At first, Kole's attention was on the submissive man and his domme, his desire predictably flaring. Then it landed on the blonde walking toward us, her hair in perfect loose curls, a beauty mark just above her full lips.

Her dress was tiny and made of white fur, a bold fashion choice that perhaps only Rosalind could pull off.

"Hello, Scarlett," she said.

She was oozing sultry allure, no doubt feeding off this room as much as I was. In her eyes, I detected a hint of relief, a flash of curiosity.

I'd thought she hated me after my night of chaos and destruction, but it seemed I was wrong about a lot of things lately.

If anything, she looked happy to see me. Her shoulders relaxed, and her smile appeared genuine.

"Hi, Rosalind," I said. "This is my new friend, Kole. He's traveled all the way from Ravenia." I pretended like that was the most fascinating fact I'd ever heard in my life.

Rosalind mirrored my enthusiasm, her whole face lighting up. "That's incredible! I've always wanted to visit."

Our shared spectacle nearly made me snort with inappropriate laughter.

I would take comedic relief wherever I could steal it, at this point.

Kole took Rosalind's outstretched hand and kissed it. A few things fell into place all at once, the background hum of my always-thinking, always-processing mind coming to a screeching halt.

During the meeting, I'd learned that the communication

between the kingdom and the turned had been compromised. Kole had said that the meeting wasn't as it was originally planned, and the turned had accused Durian of treason. I'd been working out what had happened based on all that had been said, and it seemed clear that Durian had almost pushed the turned out of the meeting entirely.

But he hadn't succeeded. The lines had been restored.

And that meant...

I looked at Rosalind and then at Kole. A scheme took shape. I smiled wide.

Kole had a way to communicate with Rune.

I had a way to communicate with Rune.

∼

ROSALIND and I giggled as we fawned over Kole in a secluded seating area, entertaining him as we fed off this powerful dignitary's desire. We sat on the wide arms of a spacious chair with Kole in between us.

Strangely, Rosalind was a comfort. It was nice to have backup, even if I wasn't exactly sure why she was helping me. It was soothing to be with someone who understood what I was—who saw me and accepted me for my true nature, when everything else about my existence was currently a lie.

So far we'd avoided being fed from, giving Kole a steady stream of blood and elixir from chalices instead.

We learned quickly that teasing, denial, and control were essential to Kole's custom-tailored seduction. He *wanted* us to stoke his desire and then stomp all over him.

On a small dais ahead, a man was being hit with a flogger on a spanking bench, displayed for all to see.

"You wish that was you, don't you, darling?" Rosalind said, her hand trailing Kole's arm.

He gazed at her hungrily and nodded, his eyes wide.

"You wish it was you on display, humiliated in front of everyone. A succubus and a human overpowering *you*—a powerful vampire—and giving you everything that you deserve." Rosalind stroked his chin, and I watched her in awe.

I pretended that I wasn't totally out of my element, following her impeccable lead. I channeled what I enjoyed in the bedroom, and I did the exact opposite, playing the opposing force. I asked myself, what would *Rune* do?

Kole nodded. "Yes, Mistresses."

The irony was glorious. This was my most bizarre game of chess yet.

But the prize of winning—nothing had ever compared.

Rune. *Freedom.*

Aunts cast us glares from the shadows. They hated Rosalind, and I thought they also hated that I, for once, was not having the absolute worst time of my life. But there was nothing they could do. I'd been made off limits while I served Kole on Durian's behalf. I was untouchable, and gods did it feel *good*.

I winked at Aunt Carol, and she glared back, quickly stomping away. I would pay for that later.

Rosalind followed my gaze and laughed softly.

"Would you like more elixir, Kole?" I asked. Then, in a burst of confidence, I changed my tune. "I think you *need* more elixir. You've been working so hard." I held his gaze, moving my foot to trail up his pants leg. I stopped just before his cock.

His eyes went wild, his chest rising and falling rapidly.

"And your Mistresses want you as vulnerable as possible for us tonight." I made my voice richer, deeper—removing all the purity and submissiveness I usually donned with the born. "Who knows what we might do to you."

He nodded enthusiastically. "Yes, Mistress."

Rosalind watched me, a small smile on her lips. Her eyes burned with questions. "Stay put," she commanded Kole. "Do not move. Do not speak. Do not even *think* until we return."

We moved through the space together, the born nearly frothing at the mouth all around us. To say we were a force to be reckoned with was an understatement. Yet, in their eyes, I was merely an innocent human—only by Rosalind's side because she was helping me service Kole.

Rosalind's arm brushed mine, and I looked at her.

She picked up the pace, expertly guiding me through a labyrinth of bodies, sex and kink contraptions, and lounge areas before suddenly pushing through a door and into an empty room.

It was pitch black, and Rosalind yanked me inside quickly before shutting the door behind us. The scent of damp earth and stone was mostly covered by Rosalind's perfume. The noise of the vampires drowning in debauchery faded to a hum, and the clearest sound in the room was our rapid breathing.

"Spill. Now."

I faltered, pulling my arm out of her grip as I stood in the darkness with her. "I can't."

She was silent for two beats. "But you'll freely take my help."

I laughed bitterly before I could stop it, and Rosalind harshly shushed me.

"It's the least you can do, Rosalind," I whispered.

"You think I'm no better than them."

I slowed my heart, trying to keep myself focused even when all I wanted to do was imagine I was submerged in Rune's shadows instead. That I was safe again.

Rune still loved me...

I clenched my fists and buried my yearning with all my unprocessed trauma. "I don't know what to think," I said honestly. "Why didn't you come for me? After I killed those humans?"

Rosalind fumbled over her first words. She inhaled deeply. "You didn't kill them, Scarlett. *They* did."

A voice grew louder beyond the door, and we both froze

until it faded again. We didn't have much time before our absence set off alarms.

"But you were reckless," she admitted. "And I have to look out for myself. It's the only way people like *us* can survive in this world."

I didn't need to read her desires. I heard the genuine loneliness in her voice. Because it was my loneliness, the deep sorrow of a child singing to the indifferent cosmos.

"You don't know what I've endured," Rosalind said. "You don't know what's been done to me, over and over, until I figured out how to use my magick and carve out a place for myself in this world."

I thought of Snow. I reached for Rosalind's hand, and she tensed, just as I had once recoiled when shown acts of tenderness and warmth.

"I don't think you're like them," I whispered. I closed my eyes, digging around for my own intuition, the only thing I had when I couldn't read Rosalind's psyche. "I'm resentful because while the slaves and I are trapped and brutalized, you are free."

"*I am not free*," Rosalind said harshly. Her hand slowly relaxed in mine, regaining her composure. "You were trying to help them. You were trying to help them, and you failed."

I nodded before remembering she couldn't see me. I slowly released her hand, brushing my thumb across her skin soothingly as I did. It wasn't at all a natural move like it was for Snow or Penn, but Rosalind needed the comfort as much as I did.

"Yes. I have power, and they have none. I wanted my life to mean something." I paused. I couldn't influence Rosalind with magick. I only had my words, my actions. My hope, blinding and enduring no matter how much I'd been hurt. "Don't you?"

She was silent for a three long exhales.

"It's not that simple. You see the world in terms of good guys and bad guys, and there might be some truth to that. For *mortals*. But for you and me..." she trailed off, speaking impossibly quiet now. "The turned killed a succubus just last month."

"She was a spy," I countered.

"We are *hated*, Scarlett. By everyone who sees us for what we are. But at least to the born, we are useful. We share half their blood. They give us a chance if we can prove our value. I'm guessing the turned had no idea what you were, or you wouldn't have made it within ten feet of Rune."

We needed to wrap this up. My muscles were growing more and more tense the longer we were gone.

"They didn't know before, but... they do now." I needed Rosalind. I had to trust my instincts. "Rune knows what I am, and he still tried to rescue me from Durian." I heard Rosalind shift slightly. "My friends know what I am too, and they still love me. They're witches. I didn't even know *how* to accept such warmth and care when I met them, but they showed me. And I miss them so badly my heart fucking aches. I miss it all. The beautiful streets of Lumina, Nyx, and River, my shitty little apartment, the freedom of every simple pleasure—choosing what I eat and what I wear, reading poetry, singing in the shower, sitting outside cafés watching people living and loving each other fiercely. I miss *myself*, most of all."

A half-truth, because I missed Rune just as much.

"You could have it too," I whispered. "You could be free of this place. Of *them*. You would be protected."

The unspoken caveat—*if you help me escape. If you help me get back to them.*

"This is bigger than us," I continued, trying not to sound as desperate as I felt. "I know it's not simple. I know there's nuance and complications. But only one side steals mortals, sometimes children, to serve as slaves. And the other side has done everything in their power to stop them. I want to use my magick to help those innocents, the mortals who deserve to taste that same freedom I miss dearly."

Rosalind sucked in a deep breath. The air was heavy, my chest tight.

Finally, she spoke. "I will *not* be reckless and aimless, as you were the night they put you on the cross."

My heart sunk.

In the dark, her hand brushed mine, ever-so-briefly.

"What do we need from the subby dignitary?"

25

SCARLETT

It was easy for Rosalind and me to seduce Kole, wrapping him snugly around our delicate fingers. The best seductions were about filling *unmet* desires, finding those gaping holes and positioning myself as the only thing in this world capable of fitting inside that void.

In the end, what we all wanted most was to feel whole.

The more unsatisfied I could make a mark, the easier it was to make him fall.

Luckily for us, Kole much preferred being on his knees.

"You work so hard," I murmured, stroking his arm as we lay on a fur rug by the fire in one of the less populated areas. Ogling vampires were shooed away by guards, understanding how important it was to keep Kole happy. "You deserve to indulge, to relax completely and let your Mistresses control your every thought."

Kole nodded, exhaling deeply. He wanted freedom from an overworked mind. We'd artfully uncovered that he was tired of being mistreated by superiors in Ravenia, of feeling cast aside, unheard, and undervalued. It was how many men felt, when you really dug into their psyches. Thus, Rosalind and I became the easiest relief, both boosting his ego and supplying him with the right forms of domination and humiliation to cater to his sexual fantasies.

Somewhere in the distance, a violently loud orgy was occurring.

Rosalind suddenly gripped Kole's chin and pushed my head down, so that my neck was under Kole's face. She was gentle about it, but still I frowned at being used as blood bait.

"How good does her blood smell, darling?"

Rosalind stroked my neck, pushing my hair to the side to show off my jugular.

"It's like no blood I've ever scented before," Kole said, his voice strained and raspy. "Please, Mistress, may I drink from her?"

"Maybe if you continue to be a good boy for us," Rosalind cooed.

I suppressed a burst of laughter. This was absolutely absurd.

"You know, I didn't realize how much I'd been craving all of this... praise," Kole said shyly as Rosalind slowly lifted me back up.

Our eyes locked across Kole's form, and we teased him by leaning forward, as close to kissing as we could get without meeting all the way.

Rosalind smiled and slowly recoiled, looking back at Kole.

"Good boys get rewarded," she said. "And you've been a *very* good boy."

Kole's lips tugged down. "I thought I wanted to spend time with Mistress Sadie after flying all the way here, and it had been so long," he drunkenly slurred. "But I don't think I'll ever be good enough in her eyes. I'll always be her disgusting little rat."

Rosalind's eyes widened, her cheeks puffing like she was as close to laughing as I was. The idea of an ancient born vampire going by *disgusting little rat* in the bedroom was peak comedy.

Somehow, we both managed to turn our heads and swallow down the fits of hysteria blooming. I, personally, did so by thinking of the slave with her mouth sewn shut.

That was more than enough to sober me.

"That's enough thinking," I snapped at him. Then, I softened my tone. "You've been such a good listener. Our perfect pet vampire."

Kole batted his eyes at me, drinking up my approval as he let his mind finally rest. He glanced at a vampire getting shooed away from us by guards, and I could sense the bad kind of shame creeping around the outskirts of his mind.

We had him fully intoxicated, teased, and enamored with us. It was time to strike.

"Would you like to go somewhere more private?" I asked. "Your Mistresses demand you relax, allow yourself to become merely a vessel for ecstasy."

Rosalind made a face that silently said, *ooh that was good*. I winked at her, an unspoken high-five.

Kole happily agreed.

He was barely able to walk in a straight line, leaning heavily on me and Rosalind as we climbed back up two flights of stairs and zigzagged through the palace. I wasn't even sure he noticed the guards trailing us. Just as we reached his guest chambers, Brennan stopped us.

Brennan lifted a single brow, smirking at me. Though his eyes danced with humor, I could sense that he, too, was experiencing feelings of being overused and undervalued. His shoulders were tight and rigid, in need of a soothing, coaxing massage.

I grinned at him, showing him unhindered joy for the first time since I'd arrived in Hatham. The act took him by surprise, his delight flaring and bolstering his desire.

Look how free and sexy she is when she's not with Durian, I whispered to his mind. *He's ruining her, and he's too arrogant to see it. Just like he's too arrogant to see your value, to see...*

I paused, weighing where my threads were strongest, where Brennan's mind was starting to become malleable. I decided to go for a bold move.

He's too arrogant to see his own shortcomings in all arenas. Scarlett is the least of your mounting concerns.

I drank from his energy, my cup of influence more than spilling over. The more I poked and prodded, the more I was beginning to understand that Brennan had more than a few hidden desires that were ripe to exploit. Desires that positioned him against Durian—desires that maybe, just maybe, could one day transform into a viable avenue to hurt the born from the inside.

"Rosalind," Brennan said as Kole fumbled with the doorknob. "Kole." He tipped his head. "I'm pleased to see you're enjoying your stay so far."

Kole grinned back, bashful red flushing his fair cheeks. "I appreciate my hosts' hospitality."

"Could I borrow her for a moment?" He asked Kole, looking toward me. "I promise I won't keep her long."

Kole waved a hand and stumbled into his room, barely cohesive. I didn't think I'd ever seen a vampire this intoxicated before. Thanks to mine and Rosalind's fine handiwork.

Rosalind gave Brennan a nonchalant wave. "Hurry back with her, Lord Brennan." Flirtation oozed from her lips as she followed Kole inside his rooms, but I knew she meant her words a lot more pointedly.

Brennan nodded to the guards and instructed them to stay put. Then he led me to a room down the hall.

Once alone, he was quick to pull me into an embrace that would've been quite romantic if even a sliver of me genuinely desired him.

Witch light illuminated the high, grand white ceilings with red and gold floral designs.

"You were almost taken from me today," he said, his cold fingers trailing my cheekbone.

I internally rolled my eyes.

I made my voice small, my features fearful. "What happened?" I finally found my opportunity to learn what had occurred when I'd been unconscious.

His face soured. "That bastard attacked us and *attempted* to steal you back."

I bristled at the way he talked about me like I was some inanimate token.

"He failed, of course," Brennan said with a twirl of his fingers, now staring at my lips. "He royally pissed off the kingdom for no reason and made himself look like a fool. I wish I could've seen his face when he flew off with his goons and realized…"

He bit his tongue, and the desire not to spill whatever he was about to reveal was not a malleable one. He refocused on me.

Isabella's voice hadn't been nearly as strong lately, aside from when I was drowning in self-hatred after failing to protect my fellow slaves. But it was clear as day in this moment.

Sooner or later, they'll come to collect…

I swallowed, my face in his palm and my body pulled flush against his. "We shouldn't," I said, and he put his fingers to my lips.

Shit.

"Has Kole even fed from you?" Brennan asked, scanning my body.

I shook my head. Thank gods.

Brennan flashed a mixture of relief and anger. "Ungrateful fool." He rested his forehead on mine, his desire reaching its peak. "He's so intoxicated that you could convince him of anything. Say it was he who fed from you, and no one will question it."

Brennan lightly grasped my neck, and I knew what was about to happen. What *had* to happen, in order to maintain my spell. In order to make Brennan addicted to me, willing to cross even more boundaries on my behalf...

I needed to let him feed from me, even if my body froze at the mere thought. Even as I heard Isabella calling me an easy whore in the back of my mind.

Even if I saw Rune's face, utterly devastated and betrayed.

With Brennan in my back pocket, I was that much closer to home. I knew that underneath my shame hid the truth: If Rune truly still loved me, he'd want me to do anything to make it back to him.

"I want you," I lied. "I've always wanted you. I know it's wrong."

Brennan smiled. "I know, little human."

"I've been watching you—the way the whole palace respects you, is utterly charmed by you... you're a force, Brennan," I said. I closed the loop on my subconscious poking and prodding and pulled it tight. "You're a true *leader*."

Brennan's eyes flashed, his grip on my throat tightening as he pressed his hard cock against my stomach.

"I haven't been able to be myself since I arrived here," I said, letting raw emotion shroud my features. I slowly dragged my gaze from the floor back up to his eyes. "But with you, I feel like I can be the woman I was before I was Durian's. And what I've truly been wanting to tell you, all this time, is that I *see you*, Brennan. I see how hard you work and how wickedly intelligent you are. I've always been drawn to powerful men. And I can see you're the most powerful kind there is."

I quickly covered my mouth, as if I was frightened by what I'd admitted aloud. "I'm sorry..." I trailed off.

Brennan forced his lips on mine, his wobbling tower of cards falling to the ground all at once.

These men were the ones who were too fucking easy.

I swallowed down my shame and disgust as I kissed him back, unable to stop the tear that slid down my cheek. Behind my eyelids, all I saw was Rune, all I felt was the love he'd shoved toward me while I sat captive in his enemy's lap.

After what seemed like seven agonizing years, Brennan pulled away, his brows drawn together with emotion and his body swimming with lust.

"You're crying," he whispered with a frown.

"I'm scared of what Durian will do to me if he finds out about us."

Brennan looked pleased with my use of the word *us*. Who knew born psychopaths could be secret romantics? The cognitive dissonance here was strong.

"I'll protect you, Scarlett," he vowed. "You deserve to be treated like a woman, not a *pet*."

I felt it, that growing seed of resentment, that burst of red that looked an awful lot like lust. Jealousy and desire, two sides of the same temperamental, explosive coin.

I'd created a rift. No—not *created*. Succubi could only nurture desires that people already harbored. I'd taken a sliver, and I'd transformed it into a crack. With enough care and direction, one day it might crumble into an unbridgeable valley.

"Doesn't the *Book of Lillian* say that we humans deserve to be pets?" I asked.

Brennan gripped my waist, frowning. "I—you're better than the rest, Scarlett. You're different. Lillian only makes it clear the born were meant to rule, and the humans born to serve. That doesn't mean you can't *enjoy* your service. I could make you happy. I could treat you like a princess."

He still defended Durian's fabricated holy book. But with my magick, I could see even his loyalty to Durian's religion had wiggle room if Brennan was given enough motivation to stray. Such as the growing idea that perhaps *he* was destined to rule instead. And if he believed that, he'd have to expose Durian as a liar and a fraud.

Brennan was nearly a puddle at my feet at this point. More pathetic than Kole. Of course, he justified his obsession with me by putting down other humans, continuing to justify trafficking and servitude.

These powerful men didn't really have a spine when it came down to it. When you illuminated their deepest insecurities and resentments, they crumbled like sand in the wind.

Not Rune. Rune was the only king I'd never made fall. The only man capable of seeing me for exactly who I was.

And he still loved me.

Brennan's attention was back to my neck, sidetracked for too long. "As I said, this will be easy to cover up. I know we don't have much time before you need to be back," he said bitterly, still staring at my throat.

So much for treating me like a human being.

"Do you want to feel what it's like to be fed from when you truly desire it?" he asked me, eyes hooded and growing more crazed by the minute.

I knew how that felt. I remembered when Rune claimed me like it was yesterday. More tears formed.

"Yes," I lied. "Feed from me."

I went somewhere empty and numb.

I wasn't sure where Brennan touched. I didn't want to know.

I looked forward. I looked to freedom. I sighed contentedly, letting the vampire venom carry me back to Rune's bedroom, when I'd worn a collar and loved every minute of it.

Because it had meant I belonged to someone, forever.

He'd discarded me right after like I'd meant nothing at all.

My eyes welled.

Then he'd shown me his love had never truly died. He'd fought for me.

I was floating in a sea of rocking waves, shoved this way and that. Every once in a while, I felt the ghost of Brennan's lips on mine, his hands on my breasts or cupping my ass, his moans in my ear.

When I saw splotches of darkness in my pleasurable haze, I knew I needed to swim back to shore.

"Hey," I murmured, my eyelids heavy as I tuned back in to my surroundings. "You're taking too much."

Could he hear me? I was fading. Rune was right—it was dangerous for me to be fed from when I caused such a frenzy. Like elixir addicts, these vampires didn't know when to stop.

I pushed against a wall of muscle, his lips on my neck as my essence flowed inside him.

"Brennan you're going to kill me," I said, weak and panicked. I let my heightened emotions snap a cord of desire, shocking Brennan out of his daze.

He cursed, begrudgingly licking my wound closed and dragging himself off me. "I'm sorry, Scarlett," he said, his eyes wide as he regarded me like I regarded ice cream. He wanted to go back for seconds. "So Durian wasn't exaggerating for effect," he said, still strained. "I understand why the whole world is fighting over you. Your blood would start wars."

I wasn't sure my blood was necessary to incite conflict at this point, but I would take that rather poetic compliment. I struggled to find my way back to my body. I wiggled one set of toes and then the other. I identified what I smelled, what I saw, what I heard, and what I felt.

"As much as I want to fuck you until you're screaming my name and coming all over my cock... I wasn't prepared for the amount of self-control that would require of me. I need you to leave now," he said. "We'll finish this later."

He looked like he wanted to reach out but couldn't, holding himself back and away from me.

I pretended to be disappointed, offering him an understanding smile. "Don't make me wait too long."

"Never," he growled.

I fought the urge to sprint out of his chambers. When I was in the halls, I rubbed my neck.

Well, hey. At least I hadn't been raped.

26

SCARLETT

"He's out cold," Rosalind said triumphantly. We stood in the bedroom of Kole's guest suite. Kole was passed out, pants-less yet still in his suit jacket on the plush golden comforter.

"You're welcome," she added.

"Thank you," I said, rolling my eyes. "I promise I paid my own dues." I pointed to the fang marks on my neck.

Rosalind grimaced, then shrugged. "As far as vamps go, Brennan's one of the better ones. At least he's super cute."

I snorted. "Super cute," I echoed sarcastically, shaking my head in disbelief. "Did you get to call this one a disgusting little rat?" I nodded toward Kole.

Rosalind tilted her head back with laughter. "I wanted to, but I think you could feel what I did—he needed softer domination tonight after his *very mean* vampire overlords ripped him a new one this week." She mocked him in a condescending tone, as if speaking about a toddler.

I wasn't sure how it was possible to smile at a time like this, after yet another violation. But smile I did, because fuck if my life wasn't funny on occasion in between horrifically traumatic events.

"We need to find—"

Rosalind grinned, crooking her finger and gesturing for me to follow her to a desk. It sat facing a window, the crimson curtains closed.

"Please tell me he didn't put it in the desk drawer," I said.

"It was locked, and I can sense low level magick as added protection against lock-picking. Does that make you feel better?" Rosalind asked, biting her lip as she dangled a brass key in front of me. "Was in his pants pocket."

She slid the drawer open, revealing several journals. She gracefully waved her palm at the array of leather as if she were a merchant revealing her fine jewelry at market.

"The hard part is figuring out which one is which. All the pages are blank, and the markings on the spines are gibberish."

I rolled my neck. Okay, so it would seem there were at least a couple barriers to compromising lines of communication between great powers. That was reassuring.

Lifting each journal, I confirmed what Rosalind had already told me. The markings were indeed indecipherable. The only differences between them all were variations in color and size.

I closed my eyes and cleared my mind.

"As exciting as this has been," Rosalind said. "I'd like to reiterate my desire *not* to be put to death. Remember that choosing the wrong one wouldn't just be a little oopsies. It would be a... very *big* oopsies."

"Rosalind," I snapped.

She huffed and stopped blabbing.

The lines had been tampered with and only recently restored. Rune would've been involved in the process.

What had *my* linked journal looked like? The book that revealed Rune's beautiful words. All his promises I thought he'd broken.

My eyes flew open. I scanned each journal in the row. Mine had been dark brown, and it had been light in my palm, not too wide or thick.

That eliminated all but two, if my hunch was solid. There was always a chance Rune would've given a different color to every recipient.

Oh shit, didn't that make *more* sense?

My hands were clammy as I lay the two notebooks on the desk. Loud stomping from the floor above nearly made me leap out of my skin.

The color variations were minuscule. One was darker than the other.

I scanned the others before shaking my head. I had to stick with my gut feeling. Otherwise, I'd be writing in all of them.

I pictured that journal in my mind's eye, but it was getting harder and harder to remember exactly what shade it had been the more nervous I grew. I looked again at the markings on each spine.

"Valentin has eight letters," I whispered, counting the symbols on each.

One had an eight-letter word and then two other smaller words. If, in fact, the symbols corresponded to letters. Oh, gods.

The other notebook had a single word, six letters.

I shook out my hands and released a breath. I glanced at Rosalind, who was staring at me as she chewed on her bottom lip furiously.

I snatched the notebook that most matched my memories, backed up by the idea that the eight-letter first word on its spine was code for Valentin.

Hopefully.

Rosalind appeared two seconds away from bolting out of the room. "You do not look confident at *all*."

I shot her a glare. Even though she was right.

My hands shook as I opened the journal to its blank

parchment paper, relaxing when their appearance matched my memories, too.

When I touched the paper, I jolted. A word appeared, sparked by magick.

Code?

I deflated. If this was an automatic message, did that mean nothing I wrote would make it to Rune without getting the code right first?

Or was it simply to guarantee I was who I was supposed to be—in this case, Kole?

Was anyone monitoring the journals for new messages? Would it be instant? If not, then I might not even see if Rune wrote me back. It wouldn't be safe for him to do so.

I had *not* thought this all the way through.

"Helia above."

"It's Lillian who answers our prayers, darling," Rosalind said softly.

I would take the help of anyone or anything at this point.

Fingers trembling, I lifted a silver pen from the mahogany desk. And I wrote.

I need to speak to Rune. Is anyone there?

I was hesitant to give my name. Not when there was still a chance I'd chosen the wrong journal.

Who is writing?

The handwriting was sloppy, different from the elegant script from the first message. Someone was there. My heart beat hard and fast. Rosalind's eyes were wide, looking from the paper to me.

"You can't say!" she squealed.

Kole snored loudly, and I shushed her, glancing back at his unmoving form. I rubbed my chest.

Could a succubus have a heart attack?

"I need to speak with him," I said. "It'll only be my neck on the line."

I cursed every curse in existence, staring up at the gods before looking back down at the blank page. I wrote my reply.

It's Scarlett. Tell him it's Scarlett.

If I wasn't speaking to the turned, at least I'd know quickly, depending on their reaction.

No reply. Every second that went by felt like a chunk of eternity.

Rosalind was now digging her pretty pink fingernails into my arm, and I leaned into her, the pain keeping me from drowning in a sea of adrenaline.

Kole's heavy breathing was my only marker of time passing. We stood in a terrified stupor, staring down at the parchment.

"How long has it been, do you think?" I asked, my voice shaking.

"Like, at least fifteen years."

"That sounds right."

Rosalind glanced back at Kole, which triggered me to glance at him. Still face-planted.

When we turned back, Rosalind's claws dug deeper.

I shoved her hand away. "Ow," I hissed. Someone was writing. "Oh, fuck."

It wasn't the message itself—merely two words—that had me tipping forward, clutching the desk for support.

Prove it.

It was the handwriting. *Rune's* handwriting.
I wrote the first thing that came to mind.

You are the only thing that feels different in a world that never changes.

He would recognize my handwriting, too. Was that enough? Technically Durian could be forcing my hand, but that could be true no matter what I said.

Scarlett, baby. Fuck. My Little Flame.

The words were messy and quick, and they tore through me like a thousand blades.

You're drained. Your heart was beating so slowly earlier. Now it's working too hard. Baby, please calm down for me.

I scribbled back just as quick.

Sure, I'll get right on that.

I'm sorry. Fuck, I'm just so sorry. I've almost damned Valentin dozens of times since you were taken, gone on rampages through the born districts until I found my way to you.

I was conflicted. I thought he hadn't saved me because he hadn't loved me anymore, and he believed I was here of my own accord. Anger sprouted now. I'd suffered for weeks while he'd loved me from afar.

I knew it was more complicated than that. I knew that despite the way I saw him—the way the whole island saw him—as a dark god, he was not unstoppable. He was protecting more than just me. I knew he had a duty to his people, to innocent mortals, to all other slaves. I knew that if he damned Valentin for me, I'd never forgive myself or him. And if he'd ever acted rashly and failed, he could've jeopardized my safety even more.

He *had* tried to save me. He'd broken orders from the kingdom to do so.

I knew that he must've hated himself right now. And I refused to add another morsel of hatred to his pile, to this world.

I know, Rune. I know you've been driving yourself insane.

There was a pause, then he started writing again, quicker than ever.

How do you have Kole's journal?

I imagined his wrathful eyes, his beautiful cruelty.

Durian gave me to Kole for the night. I got him elixir drunk and searched his room. He's asleep. Does it matter how? We're wasting time.

Kole is in the palace? Spineless fuck. You're right—it doesn't matter.

A brief pause.

I thought I had you today. You were in my arms. I thought I was taking you home.

I was barely cognizant of Rosalind's presence anymore. She was half watching Kole and half nosily peeking over my shoulder. The wound from Rune's knife in my heart tore open, his words dancing over my ribs.

Scarlett, Durian is an illusionist, if you don't already know. Visions. Distortions of reality.

The message slammed into me, and for a moment I couldn't catch my breath.

Breathe, sweet girl. Breathe.

My perception of recent events warped. I thought I'd been going insane. Durian had been *making* me feel like I was going insane.

Breathing...

Good girl. I would spend hours writing to you if I could. Begging for your forgiveness. Explaining everything. But I need you to put this journal back exactly where you found it as soon as possible. I will not risk your life more than it is already in peril.

This felt too good to be true. His words melted through my betrayal and my grief, inducing a state that was equal parts dubious and relieved. No matter how feverishly I'd tried to rid myself of Rune, I knew even when his hands were wrapped around my throat that I would die loving him.

Scarlett, I need you to make it to Black Sapphire, Durian's club in Hatham. Tell me if that is at all possible.

I looked back at Kole. Then I thought of Brennan, his venom still coursing through my veins and dulling my senses.

Yes. I—

I hesitated, my hand halting in place. I glanced at Rosalind, and I started writing again.

I have marks that could take me, under Durian's nose. I also have a friend that would come, and I need assurance she would have protection for helping me.

Scarlett, baby, I will give your friend anything she wants for all of eternity for helping you come home to me.

Rosalind lifted her brows. "Pretty sweet deal."

Though she masked it with humor, I could see hesitation and fear swimming in her warm brown eyes.

Who are these "marks?"

I could imagine the look on Rune's vengeful face as he wrote the words. I felt the phantom squeeze of his shadows wrapped around me.

Kole and/or Brennan. Depending on how it shakes out.

Brennan's head is going to make for prettier garden décor than Kole's.

I snorted, wiping at my tears. This was really happening. I was speaking to Rune, something I'd once thought might never happen again before I died.

Try to bring the least amount of protection possible. Have them disarmed and their guard lowered. I'll have eyes looking for you, but they will be witches or shifters given the borders are closed. Don't worry if you're disguised. My people will be watching for Brennan and Kole every single night.

I felt light-headed, overwhelmed by this sudden shift of luck.

Okay.

I wasn't safe yet. I had not a single clue how I was going to pull off what I was promising. It just didn't matter. It needed to happen, so it would.

There was one nagging thought, a tiny whisper, that I was quick to yank out before it could root. What about the others? Wasn't I supposed to be making my life mean something—for *them?*

But I knew that I couldn't help them here, and I wouldn't be able to stay this strong forever. I could only hope I could finish what I'd started once I was free. I couldn't stay here. I just couldn't.

You're okay, Little Flame. You're going to be okay. I only need you to stay strong for a little bit longer, and then you'll be safe to let it all go in my arms. Don't let that flame burn out.

Rosalind was silent as my tears slid down my cheeks faster now.

You're better than all of them. More cunning and wickedly clever. You can do this. I love you endlessly. Now put the journal back. Remember that every single person that has hurt you will one day meet my fucking wrath.

The words stopped. I stared at the page, hoping for more even if I knew it was over.

Rosalind shook her head. "Wow, I... he really does love you, Scar—"

Kole's voice had us both freezing.

He mumbled what sounded like a name, but it was

indecipherable. We spun around to see that he was grumbling in his sleep.

I snatched the two journals and quickly replaced them in the desk in their original order. I eased the drawer shut and locked it back. Rosalind swiped the key from my shaking hand and replaced it in Kole's pants pocket.

We turned back to Kole, who grumbled again as he tossed and turned. Rosalind turned off the desk lamp.

She took my hand and pulled me out of the bedroom. On a spacious black couch, we shared a blanket and spoke in soft whispers.

I told her about Rune and Snow, my beautiful life in Lumina.

She told me about her first love, Zachary. She'd met him when she'd been running from her true nature, attempting to live life as a human. Zachary beat her to a pulp when he found out what she was.

I held her as she cried in my arms.

27

SCARLETT

Despite Durian freely giving me to Kole, my Master did not delight in sharing me. Especially not when he'd confirmed how valuable I was, the addictive nature of my blood.

I should've predicted his reaction.

"That's a good pet," he said as I crawled to him in one of his upstairs drawing rooms, adjacent to the deliberations room. The room was full almost entirely of lords and the most powerful born men, save for Kole, Liza, and Evangeline.

I'd only been summoned after their important deliberations had concluded. I was entertainment, not a confidant. My collar was on too tight, my straps of blood-red lingerie more revealing than ever.

Despite my hard work and intricate webs, I still wasn't permitted anywhere important. I wished I had more information of value to report back to the turned, more than what scraps I'd gained by my eavesdropping and reading of desire.

Brennan was right. Kole had been so intoxicated that it was easy for him to convince himself that he'd fed from me and couldn't remember it. That, or he was too confused and embarrassed to say anything to the contrary.

I raised my gaze from Durian's sleek black boots to his beady black eyes. His blond hair was perfectly straight as it fell to his shoulders, his black and burgundy attire meticulous. Royal wealth with a flare of ancient holiness. His hands were tucked into his pockets as he stared down at me, cold and unflinching.

The sound of a woman screaming had me turning my head. I caught a glimpse of one of the lords hitting Mairin, tearing into her slim neck far too violently. He was imagining it was me.

At a harsh slap across my face, I realized I'd fucked up.

"Bad girl," Durian chided. "Did your time off leash undo my weeks of careful training?"

Panic bubbled in my chest, my throat tight. The blow had tears springing to my eyes unconsciously.

"No, Master. I'm sorry, Master," I said quickly.

I felt Brennan's eyes boring into me, though I didn't dare look. Nearby lords chuckled. Even the ones immersed in conversation and feeding still had half their attention on me, the talk of the palace.

"I'm afraid you've forgotten your fucking place, pet," Durian spat.

Paranoia clouded his desires. I had the sick urge to beg, to earn back his praise. It had been carved into me—this desire to please him, to earn my right to exist. I feared how deeply he'd dug himself into my brain with his magick, his mind games, and the pain and humiliation he'd steadily supplied.

"I'm sorry, Master," I repeated, knowing it was useless. His mind was made up. He needed to reclaim me. And I wouldn't waste my power trying to change his decision so close to freedom.

Stay in your body, Rune's phantom voice whispered to my mind.

Durian shoved me to the ground, his boot on my chest in a flash. He pulled out his favorite cane.

"Tell me, pet, are you really Lillian's purest, most innocent lamb?" he asked. He brought the black implement down across my upper thighs.

I screamed. The sting reverberated through my body in harsh waves.

"Or are you a worthless, filthy whore?"

I flinched as if he'd struck me again. When Durian called me a whore, it was the same as when Isabella had. He wanted me smaller. He wanted me to feel stupid, weak, and pathetic—wholly dependent on him to earn back my worth.

Rune had called me demeaning names before, but it hadn't provoked remotely the same feeling. It had never been a slap. Only a caress, a depraved game, or a wicked show of dominance. He'd fulfilled my every last desire, and I'd never once felt unsafe in his powerful grip. His cruelty was for *me*. It had never actually been cruelty at all.

"You know how much I hate when you don't answer me promptly, slut," Durian hissed. This time when he caned me, it wasn't just one, two, or three strikes. His desire spun out of my control. His pent-up aggression and need to own me multiplied like a disease.

In strengthening my threads to Brennan, Kole, and the palace at large, I'd neglected the one thread that controlled my fate above all others.

Durian beat me until I bled, and then he licked my bloody thighs. He flipped me over as I cried, eaten away by pain and shame.

"Position five."

My vision blurred. I lifted my ass in the air. Durian caned my flesh until it was raw, and my brain was melted by venom and endorphins.

He shoved me back down, just a heap of skin and bones and

dreams and stars, a weeping wound spread wide for demented vampires to covet and devour.

Durian turned me over and straddled me.

I fought to stay here, for him, always for *him*—the ruler of my dreams, no matter how often this psychopath infected me with nightmares.

Durian gripped my throat, clenching around the locked collar that would never make me his.

"Who do you live for?"

Myself. My friends. Lumina. The stolen humans whose screams echoed through the room.

Rune.

"You, Master."

I saw a field of stars, heard the collected songs of *Frida and Friends*, that twangy fiddle and haunting voice, the sound of stomping and clapping. Love. That was what bloomed in my chest, for the briefest of moments, underneath my spitting anger, twisting pain, and waves of venomous rapture.

"Who do you belong to?"

The cosmos. Myself.

Rune.

"You, Master."

Durian grabbed my right breast, and his other hand cupped my pussy. They were emotionless acts, done only to violate me, to stake his ownership in front of a crowd of vampires who wanted me more than they wanted any of the slaves they currently brutalized.

"Whose body is this?"

Mine. It's fucking mine.

I stayed limp, expressionless. I fought dissociation and stayed present out of spite. He wanted me broken, and I refused to break.

I had hope now. Blinding, unkillable hope.

"Yours, Master."

I acted like he'd won. I used his perverse, sadistic desire and spun it right back around to use against him. Behind my eyelids, I saw visions of violence. Durian's skin ruined with marks. Durian's blood splattered on the floor. Durian's shocked face twisted with pain.

He stood as if it was of his own accord and not mine. He yanked me up and pulled me close, my back against his chest and his hand around my neck.

"Aunt Carol," he called. She approached. "Clean her up. Spiritually and physically. If she behaves, perhaps she can earn back her ability to entertain our guest and the court."

"It will be my pleasure."

And I knew she meant it, her smile nothing short of evil.

Kole watched us carefully, and I could sense his disappointment in Durian's words—the insinuation that I might not be available to him for a while.

I slipped through this crack of vulnerability and spoke to his mind.

You have the power to bring her back. Durian and the born are beholden to you. Here, you are the most valuable man in the room. They will bend to your will, just as you've always deserved. Scarlett is clearly a slave in this place, and her true desires are obscured. She wants you, a distinguished man of the great kingdom, not these lowlife islanders. She wants to dominate you like you've never been dominated before. Just look at the wicked way she longs for you. That's why Durian is so angry...

From Durian's grip, I stared at Kole for two seconds. It was more than enough. Then I looked for Brennan, delighted by his blatant display of jealousy and disgust. His lip was curled, his hazel eyes burning.

Durian shoved me at Aunt Carol, who handled me roughly as she and the guards took me away.

My men would fight for me. They were flies tangled in my

web, deluded into thinking it had been their choice to sacrifice themselves at my altar.

∼

Kole and Brennan were quick to convince Durian to loosen his grip and allow me back at court, by means I didn't know nor care to learn.

I only cared that they'd been effective.

Unfortunately, this occurred after I'd been sufficiently tortured by Aunt Carol and forced to recite demented prayers for hours on end.

I paid for every minute I spent outside of my gilded cage. Each time I entertained Kole, Durian brutalized me harsher than ever. I didn't know what it was inside of me that had this capacity to *endure*. Maybe it was a product of childhood trauma—losing my neglectful parents so young and then being abused by my sister. Maybe it was the darkness inside my soul, the kiss of the Dark Goddess.

I'd never been more grateful for that darkness I'd detested for so long. It was the only thing keeping me alive. It was what would lead me to my freedom, bring me up from this deep, oppressive pit one fistful of dirt after the next.

Tonight, we were in the dungeons, though the attendees were fewer than usual. More esteemed, too. It was like one of Odessa's private parties for the turned in the restricted sections.

"They don't care," I overheard Brennan whisper harshly to Durian. "They see us as squabbling children, unworthy of even the mental energy, let alone resources, to deal with. We're on our own."

Durian shot him a pointed glare as Kole entered the dimly lit room. I sensed that the energy between Durian and Brennan was more heated and volatile than ever, and other lords were taking notice.

From the context clues provided, I was getting the picture that Durian arrogantly believed the kingdom was already in the Valentin borns' back pocket. And Brennan disagreed, pointing to the fact that Rune had faced zero consequences for his breeching of the kingdom's meeting terms.

Aunt Carol shoved me toward Kole, forcing me to my knees.

Kole quickly shook his head in disapproval, pulling me to my feet and dismissing Aunt Carol.

"Good boy," I whispered in Kole's ear. "You're the only one who truly sees me in this place."

Durian watched me so intensely that his gaze scorched my skin. He hated how attached to me Kole had become, and I knew he was starting to worry about the prospect of Kole asking to take me back to Ravenia with him.

And I truly didn't know how Durian would react to such a request. He'd be pissed off, that much was certain. But he wanted world domination more than anything else, including me. If he thought I could win him more favor in the kingdom, I found it hard to believe he wouldn't pawn me off without hesitation.

It was also clear that Durian hated Kole's reversal of my role as a submissive and a slave. Though he would never admit that to the dignitary out loud. His archaic religious bullshit was supremely misogynistic and oppressive toward human women. He also despised what the perceived sense of power might do to my puny little human brain, potentially unraveling his tight chains of control. He frequently reminded me that I was serving Kole only at his direction, that I still harbored no power and was merely following orders. That I was just his pretty doll to loan out at will.

I pulled Kole away, my tight black dress shifting high on my thighs. Brennan and Durian watched me leave with Kole, with thinly veiled irritation.

I giggled, delighting Kole even more.

"It's a crime they've caged such a vibrant creature," Kole whispered. "You would make for the most exquisite courtesan back in King Earle's castle. It makes this place look like servants' quarters."

I pretended to hang on his every word, gently stroking his arm.

"You'd be free, you know. Courtesans have *clients*, not masters. They are taken care of. You'd be spoiled like no other courtesan has before."

I looked around, showing him genuine fear at the prospect of being overheard.

Kole's features hardened with masculine bravado. "We'll go somewhere private, Mistress."

I rewarded him with a grin.

Inside his living room, I lounged back on his couch as Kole knelt on the floor below, holding my fizzy mocktail and a plate of grapes like a vampire corner table.

It was kind of awesome.

"As you were saying," I said, taking a sip of my drink. "These courtesans... they're not treated as slaves?"

Kole's brows scrunched. "Not at all. Engaging in that nasty slave business is low-class behavior. There's an *etiquette* at our court, for all things, including proper behavior of lords and ladies, council members and officials. This includes how courtesans are treated. What fun are games of seduction if they're guaranteed?"

I popped a grape in my mouth and nodded. "My thoughts exactly." I bit my lip, my mind churning. I didn't trust a word he said. "I guess I just assumed that the born here and the born in Ravenia were..."

"The same?" Kole made a face of distaste. "We call it island madness, you know. The sorry state of vampires here in Valentin. I pity them, truly." He leveled a look of amusement. "*I* know you're not a dress-up doll, dear. I know that based on everything you've heard and seen living with both vampire clans of Valentin, you've put together your own judgments. You think that because I'm here with the born, that means I condone all of their actions and buy into Durian's legitimacy myths and religious movement. But you're only seeing the surface level of my actions. I'm a courtier, darling. I know how to play the game. Just as you do, I'm starting to understand."

Kole handed me my drink with a small smile.

I swallowed, and for a panicked moment I realized I'd dropped my mask, revealing a glimmer of my real emotions. I decided to use the lapse as an opportunity for honesty.

"I'm just trying to survive. I've heard Durian's *pets* tend to have shortened lifespans." I handed him back the drink after taking a swig. The bubbles soothed my nervous stomach. We were entering dangerous territory—our game entering the realm of the *real*.

His smile fell. "I see." He paused. "I like you, Scarlett. You're perhaps the only person in this castle I can speak openly with."

"I feel the same," I lied, letting my nervousness make me appear vulnerable. "Why are you entertaining the born? Aren't you afraid how that will look to the turned?"

Kole's eyes flashed with amusement. "Ah, perhaps you could answer that—why would *I* be entertaining the born?"

"You have a vendetta against the turned."

Surprise shocked his features. "I am not ruled by my vendettas. If I were, I wouldn't be where I am today."

Not a denial, but also clearly not where he was leading me. I found it fascinating that I was so underestimated in this world of powerful men that I was able to speak plainly with Kole in a way that not even Durian could.

I thought about his question. I parsed through the words spoken at the meeting outside of Aristelle. Durian had said something like *I've enjoyed my long correspondences with King Earle these past weeks.* That had surprised me at the time, though it didn't look like it had surprised Rune.

I knew that Kole felt mistreated by his superiors. I knew that he was out for himself, above all others. But how did he feel about the king? I was missing something. And I wished Rune and I had discussed Ravenia's political landscape in greater detail.

I cocked my head. "You're entertaining the born because Durian has become close to Earle," I said. "And Durian is a new power. You already understand Rune and the turned. It's Durian and the new born lords that you have less information about."

Kole's lips quirked up, a silent approval of my interpretation. Then his eyes strayed to my body, and his desire flared.

I grabbed his chin. I'd gotten better at pretending to be dominant in the bedroom.

My secret?

My utter fucking hatred for these born psychos. My ever-building wrath. My thirst for retribution.

As my fingers dug into his cheeks, Kole looked up into my eyes as if he were head-over-heels in love with me.

"Pathetic," I spat. Then, I softened my facial expression, took another swig of my drink, and placed the glass back in his hand, before removing my touch. I sat up and spread my legs, placing my feet on either side of his kneeling form.

He fought the urge to glance between my thighs, keeping my gaze instead.

"This place is killing me," I began. "I think you can see that."

I turned my allure on full blast, sneaking between the cracks of Kole's psyche and capitalizing on his aching needs, his unmet fantasies, and his fragile male ego. I envisioned my magick wrapping around us, twisting our paths to the desired outcome.

"I want to do something naughty, and I need your help to do it." I traced his jawline with my fingernail. "I want a night out in Hatham with you."

He raised a brow with a sigh. "Scarlett," he said, breaking his use of kink honorifics—not a good sign. "I will not aid in any escape plot."

I remained calm. His words didn't match his overwhelming desire. He wanted to please me. He just needed more convincing.

"Escape?" I shook my head with an easy smile. "I want to go *out*. To Black Sapphire. I've never been, and I am so, terribly bored." I pouted dramatically.

He relaxed an inch, still skeptical as he leaned forward. I pulled my head back in response, going cold on him.

"Brennan has already agreed to take us," I lied. "He'll ensure Durian doesn't find out. He's necessary, but you're who I truly *desire*."

Desperate for my warmth, jealous of the prospect of me being alone with Brennan out in the city, yearning to taste my promise of naughty pleasure and dangerous games—Kole was quick to fall.

28

RUNE

"Mom wanted her to have cozy socks," Snow announced as she entered the secluded living room she, Uriah, Sadie, Mason, and I had inhabited every night since Scarlett made contact. We sat in wait for word from Hatham together. "Because cozy socks make everyone feel just a little bit better about life."

Snow held up two pairs of soft-looking socks—light gray and white—before slowly lowering them. She paced back and forth in front of the fire. Uriah watched her like a child seeing a kitten for the first time.

"That's very kind of her," he said with a smile.

This drew a bewildered look from Mason and an amused one from Sadie.

Mason had wormed her way back into my most favored. Her time on the outs had made her even more effective than she was already, which worked for Scarlett's benefit. And I cared far more about that than useless grudges that served no one.

"Whiskey on the rocks," Sadie said with a snap.

Oh yes, how could I have forgotten her lap dog Cliff—who'd

been resting his head on Sadie's thighs and staring up at her like she was the planet he orbited.

He was quick to rise and go fetch.

"Where's the other one?" I asked, rolling my neck and stretching out my feet on the black leather ottoman. Sadie had also brought a leopard shifter woman with her.

"Kitten is off playing, no doubt collecting kisses from scary vampire women." Sadie shrugged. "She's been good this week."

Mason swallowed, crossing her arms and looking away.

Before I could dissect *that* reaction, Snow stopped pacing and looked at me. "How are you doing, Rune?"

How was I *doing*?

I stared at her, bewildered as I always was when Snow directed her sentimentality toward me. Even if only my most trusted men and women sat in this room with me, I felt overwhelming discomfort at their prying gazes.

The truth was that ever since Scarlett had disappeared in my arms, I'd barely slept, plagued by visions of her with Durian and his men. Seeing her in the flesh had ruined me. I was a man destroyed, haunted by my glaring failure to protect what I loved most.

Just as I'd failed my sisters.

This was exactly why I'd maintained distance for centuries, refusing to get too close to anything or anyone that had the ability to break me.

Snow's eyes dropped to my tightened grip on the arms of my chair, my shadows trembling against the muscles of my forearms.

"When we receive word from Hatham, I'd appreciate if you could pick up her favorites from the bakery," I said to Snow instead of answering her question. "All that sugary nonsense she loves. And food with substance so she doesn't make herself sick."

Everyone stared at me, but I only thought of Scarlett. I

imagined her features lit up with pure, innocent delight. Her charming surprise and gratitude at even the smallest romantic gestures, the discomfort she displayed when I showered her with gifts—which was half the reason I spoiled her so exorbitantly.

I knew that she wasn't going to be able to give me that giggle I was insatiably obsessed with, nor her heart-melting smile. Not for a while. But she still deserved every single pleasure, big or small, until she felt safe again. Until she felt like *herself* again.

"I'll pay Penn double for every item," I added.

"Of course, Rune," Snow said quickly. "She'd do it for free. She loves Scarlett. We all do."

I nodded. "Thank you." My tight shoulders dropped an inch. "She's easy to love."

Sadie clicked her nails against her glass of whiskey, and Cliff settled back down into his position. She stroked his blond hair with her free hand.

"She's already won my favor," Sadie announced. "And that's hard to do even when I've known someone for years."

Uriah snorted. Sadie judged people at first glance, and as infuriating as that trait could be, I had to admit her instincts were never wrong.

She grinned. "She had Brennan hopelessly under her magick at that meeting. And she already has Kole in her back pocket after a matter of days? She's incredible, Rune. She's going to make for a *powerful* asset. If we could ensure this rescue goes smoothly, then perhaps she could retain her hold—"

"She's not an *asset*," I growled. My shadows leaped from my skin to crawl down the leather chair. "I don't give a single fuck how the rescue goes as long as she is back by my side by the end of it."

Sadie moved Cliff's head off her lap and stood. The lights flickered, and the floorboards rumbled. Uriah rose and moved closer to Snow.

"Do not speak to me like that, Rune," Sadie snarled. "Now is not the time for childish, short-sighted blunders. Every move has to count no matter how much of your humanity you've allowed to cloud your emotions."

I laughed bitterly as we moved toward each other. The room shook with dark power.

"Hungry? I know where they keep the snacks," Uriah said to Snow, tilting his head toward the doors.

"I'm not defenseless, you know," Snow said, crossing her arms and standing her ground.

"You wouldn't be nearly as hot if you were," he retorted.

Snow's lips parted as she glared at Uriah.

Sadie's focus had strayed to Snow and Uriah too, her anger melting as she watched Uriah flirt and Snow fluster.

I reeled my shadows back in, and Sadie's magick quelled in equal measure. Her heels clicked against the floorboards as she continued to approach me. Her hand softly rested on my bicep before falling back down.

"I push you because I care," she whispered, her voice covered by Snow and Uriah's bickering. "Yes, about Valentin and her future. But also, about *you*."

A muscle in my jaw ticked as I stared into those reptilian green eyes.

"And you know what my judgment of Scarlett was at first glance?" She grinned, that infuriating all-knowing wisdom in her features. "That she is far more than a survivor. She's a facet of the divine dark feminine. She's a powerful being with her own gravitational field. If she wants to fight, when the time comes, you need to let her."

I swallowed down my anger. The thought of putting Scarlett in harm's way ever again made me want to go on a born killing spree.

Sadie lifted her chin. "She *will* want to, eventually. And when she does, she's going to claim her own kind of vengeance."

My mentor acting as if she knew Scarlett better than I did pissed me off nearly as much as her desire to use Scarlett as a weapon. I'd watched my Little Flame her whole life. I knew more than what could be seen on the surface. I understood every facet of her perfect, fiery soul, because it was a part of me —it always had been.

As I had every few minutes since she'd been taken, I followed that invisible leash that tethered her to me. I remembered watching my blood slide down her throat like it was yesterday, marking her as mine before she'd consciously understood it.

I sucked in a breath, and all heads turned toward me.

"She's moving. She's left the palace."

29

SCARLETT

"Kole wants to go to Black Sapphire with you, Rosalind, and me," I told Brennan when he snuck me into his chambers later that night. "It would provide us an opportunity to be alone finally, away from *him*."

Brennan's eyes widened, looking down at the way I'd placed my hand on his chest as I stared up at him. I positioned myself as weak and fearful, an entirely different game than the one I played with Kole. Only the barest sexual undertones arose from my rapid breathing, my dilated pupils and flushed cheeks. Rosalind had been helping me master control of my body, training it to show physical signs of arousal or other emotions necessary for a proper seduction, even when I was feeling another thing entirely.

"He does?" Brennan asked, confusion twisting his features. "With me? And not Durian?"

"He doesn't want to offend Durian. But he sees what I see— that you're a formidable leader who warrants far more recognition than you've been given. He wants to spend time with you somewhere you can't be overshadowed."

Brennan tried to mask his satisfaction, but I homed in on the upward tick of his lips. The way he stood a little taller, lifted his chin an inch.

Another powerful tool of seduction—making sure I was consistently the bearer of good news, never bad. I'd not only been boosting Brennan's ego, but now I was providing him with tangible evidence of my version of reality. Nothing was more powerful. In his subconscious mind, it was *me* who was elevating him, not Kole. I was the one who made him feel like a big strong man. I was the one who made him feel like *more* than what he'd been before, who held the keys to his every last dream in my palms.

There was no stronger force when making a man a slave.

He kissed me, and I pretended not to be revolted by his soft lips and forceful tongue. Suddenly, he pulled back.

"He wants to bring *you*?" His brows furrowed. "Durian will never allow it."

I let my piercing blue eyes pin him with the deepest sorrow, my bottom lip trembling. "I know. That was what I told him. He hoped you could sneak me out, just for one night of fun. I told him that was too impossible of a task, even for you. I'd never want to put you in a position that might get you in trouble with Lillian and her chosen future king." I stepped away from him, slipping from his grip and letting my shoulders slump. "I should get back. I wouldn't want to raise suspicion." I smiled sadly, and Brennan huffed in frustration.

"Fuck this," he said angrily, grabbing my arm and pulling me back. "It's a crime that you only get to be your true self when you're with me. You're so much sexier when you're *free*."

I couldn't have agreed more, dickhead.

"I could get you out," he declared. "Durian may act like he's a god above the rest, but I'm not his foot servant. I'm the second highest ranking vampire in born territories. I have *actual* royal blood in my veins. I refuse to let his sexual perversions and arbitrary rules act as a law above my own will." He stared at me, his lip curling as he thumbed my collar. "How can you own something you didn't earn?"

Baby's first pseudo-intellectual philosophical question. Rune ran circles around these idiots.

I shook my head. "I'm scared, Brennan." I took a deep breath, trailing my eyes back up from the floor to his. "But I want to finally be alone with you, to know what it feels like to walk into a room on your arm. And I want to do... other things with you..."

I feigned shyness, and it melted him even more. He was my knight in shining armor, the valiant conqueror winning my virginity with honor and virtue.

"It's a miracle you don't hate us all," Brennan said, his voice low and gruff.

I tried not to laugh.

"You deserve to see what true vampires are like, as opposed to Rune's uptight abominations. It's a shame you've only seen us through the lens of Durian's court, as his locked-away slave. The born territories are where all the best fun is had." His eyes lit up, stroking my cheek as if coaxing me into believing him. "Black Sapphire is the greatest den of ecstasy Valentin has ever seen—makes Odessa look like a Helianic nunnery. You deserve to experience that, especially before our descension into war."

I showed him my newfound strength, as if motivated by his speech. I returned to my easygoing, flirtatious demeanor.

"I believe you, Brennan. I want to see Hatham through your eyes." My smile faltered. "This is real, you and I. I can't help but feel as though Lillian has predestined our union herself. And nothing holy can ever be wrong. My body and soul are called to yours just as you're called to my blood."

The intermixing of the sacred and the sensual was another powerful seduction technique. Brennan flashed his fangs, a familiar craze in his eyes.

"You need to leave," he bit out. "Don't worry about a thing.

Kole and I will work out every last detail. Tomorrow night, I will come for you." He stared at me like we were star-crossed lovers.

"And Rosalind," I added as a reminder.

He dismissively waved a hand. "Yes, yes. The demoness too."

"I can't wait to feel your venom inside me again," I said as I departed.

When the door clicked shut behind me, Brennan's loyal guard and I both startled at Brennan's corresponding roar leaking out into the hall.

∼

I WAS SHAKEN AWAKE VIOLENTLY. I opened my eyes to Rune's beautiful features, and this time, I was able to maintain my sense of reality. I knew that Durian was around somewhere, inducing this vision.

I thought it was going to be difficult to pretend that I was terrified, but that was actually my exact instinctual reaction. Even if I knew consciously it was Durian, all my subconscious mind saw were those hours upon hours of horrific torture.

I scrambled away, to the other side of the bed. Vision or not, the pain, confusion, and fear were entirely real.

"Please, just leave me alone!" I screamed, my bed in between us now. "Please," I said again. My body began to shake before Rune had even moved, let alone touched me.

His dark eyes were ice, his beautiful features as emotionless as a man who slaughtered for sport.

It only took one step of his heavy boot against the wood floor for me to scream until my voice was scratchy, my eyes spilling tears. Durian wasn't here to protect me. My mind was hazy with adrenaline. All I could feel was the slow sawing of a blade through my fingers.

By the time Rune made it to me, I was rocking back and

forth, my head buried into my bent knees. I refused to look at him until he forced me to, like a child hiding under the covers from the bogeyman.

"Shh, pet," Durian consoled. "Would it make you feel better if your Master slept beside you the rest of the night?"

I glanced behind Durian, but Rune was gone. I couldn't think straight. All I knew was that Durian had never once slept with me. The question had me nearly convinced I had been inside a dream all along.

If Durian was here, Rune couldn't be. I glanced down to make sure my fingers were still there.

"Yes, Master. Thank you, Master."

I crawled back into bed in a daze, and Durian slept next to me with a foot of space between our bodies. As I drifted, I felt the softest caress along my cheekbone, before it was yanked back as if by regret.

30

SCARLETT

I hadn't told Kole nor Brennan about Durian's late-night visit. I worried if I did, they'd never even attempt to steal me away. I had to trust they were intelligent enough to ensure Durian was preoccupied when they finally came for me.

I spent the evening in Durian's lap, or at his feet, or by his side, or bound to a demented altar. He didn't allow me to entertain Kole. He alternated between feeding from me, hurting and humiliating me, and offering me the strangest, barest forms of comfort. Effectively fucking with my head more than it had already been scrambled.

By the end of the night, I was exhausted and weak, and I genuinely feared what that meant for my abilities to escape. I'd hoped I would be my strongest self when Brennan came for me, but it appeared that would be far from the case.

"Silly pet," Durian said, licking closed my latest wound on my upper chest before dragging me by the collar through the hall. "Tell me who you live for."

"You, Master," I slurred.

He moved my body how he wanted it. He demanded I speak

the words he wanted to hear. He made me feel so worthless that I could hardly even sense my powers anymore.

After I'd been sufficiently traumatized, I was left on the floor in my room. The wood was cool beneath my cheek.

Someone was calling for me, but I couldn't answer. I couldn't even lift my eyelids.

"She'll wake up," a voice floated up from the darkness. Rosalind's. "Just let her nap. Then she'll be well-rested and back to her bright and perky self. She's going inside a bag, anyway. It's probably better that she's out of it."

"She needs to get in her disguise," Brennan said. "She needs—fuck, she needs blood replenishing potion."

I wanted to laugh. Of course, Brennan's chief concern was my ability to service him as his own personal blood bag.

"I'll handle the disguise part," Rosalind said. "I'll get her ready once we get there."

"The poor thing," Kole drawled. "Are we sure this is still the best idea?"

"Urgh," I might've said. I wasn't sure if I'd managed to make a sound.

"There will be witches at Black Sapphire," Rosalind said, her voice oozing calm authority. "Potions will be floating around."

"For a hefty price," Brennan muttered.

"She's worth it," Kole declared.

"Well, yes, of course, she is," Brennan said quickly, irritation in his tone.

"Gentlemen, darlings, the most handsome men in Lillian's favored palace..." Rosalind's voice was sugary, lyrical and commanding. She giggled. "We're about to go have some fun! This is the teensiest, tiniest little drawback, and it will be remedied as soon as we make it to our destination. Think about how sad our favorite human would be if she knew you were debating leaving her behind."

"We're not leaving her behind," Brennan said at the same time Kole said, "No, never."

I forced my eyes open. "Bag?"

∽

THEY LITERALLY STUFFED me inside a duffle bag. I was kept company by dildos, a flogger, lingerie, and a short blonde wig. Rosalind's perfume nearly suffocated me in this enclosed space, which may have been the point, another way to cover up my scent.

I'd heard them discussing how Rosalind was going to use her magick as a diversion. It would also be believable that my scent would linger on Kole since I'd been serving him all week. This was only if we were stopped by anyone, which was unlikely, as neither Kole nor Brennan were bound by any rules. And surprisingly, neither was Rosalind. It was apparently typical of her to leave with elites to spend a night on the town. It baffled me that she was free to go anywhere and chose to stay here.

Brennan, Kole, and Rosalind snuck through the castle using routes less likely to be monitored or used. They preferred not to be spotted, especially by anyone close to Durian. Guards weren't ones to gossip, but courtiers were snakes.

I drifted in and out of consciousness the whole time. Rosalind had been right. It was for the best, given every time I awoke, I wanted to have a very dramatic panic attack.

My mind drifted back to Crescent Haven. I missed the forest, its tall trees, and aboveground roots. I missed Jaxon. I knew that I hadn't been happy there, but it was still *home*. I missed having a home.

It was actually quite easy to imagine Rune growing up in Crescent Haven. Sitting outside somewhere, thumbing through a book, dreaming of a better life for himself and his sisters. Staring up at the stars as he envisioned faraway lands. Playing in the forest as a young boy, seeing himself as the fiercest knight, the most virtuous protector.

I tried to imagine him younger, without his shadow magick tattoos. Still broody and intense, frighteningly intelligent, harboring the ambition of becoming a writer rather than a warlord. It was a vision that made me smile in a secret, sleepy way, as I was jostled around in the sex toy bag.

"Almost there," Brennan said, maybe to me.

I made a feeble, unseen thumbs up. I needed Rune's secret forces to get Rosalind and me the hell out of this place as soon as possible. Kole and Brennan weren't thinking clearly, too lost under the careful spell I'd cast with powerful succubus magick. Even in my weakened state, I knew the truth. Durian could discover I was gone at any point. No matter how careful they'd been, it wasn't going to be impossible for Durian to connect some dots and go on a vicious rampage until someone pointed him in the right direction.

I had no intention of entertaining these men a minute longer. They'd gotten more than enough of me already. I'd done what I needed to do, and now it was time to leave them behind. As soon as someone fed me a blood replenishing potion, it was game over. Plus, I was an immortal. I was healing far faster than a human.

A shout pulled me back to full-consciousness.

"We're starving!" a woman screamed.

"Not our problem," Brennan hissed.

"It's a human whore. What else is it good for other than providing a nice meal?"

"Do you know who we are?" Kole asked, his voice raised.

I was set down on the ground.

"Of course you wouldn't know what it's like in the streets, pretty boy," the same female voice who initially shouted said. "Lillian's prophet was supposed to make blood rain from the sky, pour from faucets. A river of blood—that was what was promised. But the blood has dried up. It was *better* before him. At least we could still hunt in turned territory. Do you know how many mortals fled to their side?"

"Enough! Enough of your ignorant blasphemy," Brennan said. "This is Rune and his army of bastards' fault, not your future king's. Show some damn respect. You're speaking to *Lord* Brennan, second cousin of Ivan Ardente."

"We don't give a fuck who we're speaking to," another voice growled. "Your *ignorant peasants* are starving, *my holy lordship*."

Rosalind squealed, and I heard several whooshes, weapons meeting flesh. There was a scuffle near me, and someone's foot hit my ribs.

I gasped, involuntarily shifting.

A pause.

"Why'd your bag move?"

"What's in the bag?"

Shit.

The earth rumbled, and the sound of crashing, like a building collapse, had my hands over my ears. Were they protecting Rosalind? I didn't trust these bozos to keep her safe. A lump amassed in my throat. My body was squished and cramped.

When the bag was unzipped, a hand flew to my mouth to stifle my scream.

Brennan's features came into view, his chestnut hair tousled. "You're safe, Scar."

I wanted Rune to cut out his tongue for abbreviating my name like he meant something to me.

"Is Rosalind all right?" I poked my head out, peering around Brennan at the five dead vampires in pools of blood, a lamp post impaling two of them and the others with various combat wounds.

Kole dusted off his plum suit. He'd clearly been behind the

uprooting of the lamppost, strong earth magick settling back inside of him.

Rosalind finally came into view, giving me a small wave. She feigned nonchalance, but I saw beneath the surface at her overwhelming terror. She had trauma the same as me. The world had taught her cruelty and hatred. I wondered what her empty place felt like, which colors crowded her vision, how easily she could detach from her body and float away.

At the sound of more footsteps, Brennan pushed my head back down and zipped up the bag. I ground my teeth together, but I stayed quiet.

"Lord Brennan," an unfamiliar voice said. "And friends."

My heart hammered at the even, strong, and masculine voice. What now?

"On your way to Black Sapphire, I presume. Please, let us escort you. We heard conflict, and it would appear you encountered some nasty street pests. I offer my deepest apologies for the inconvenience."

31

SCARLETT

I needed out of this damn bag. As usual, my vision of tonight was *not* as I'd anticipated. I thought I'd be making a grand entrance, wearing some fabulous outfit and wig. I'd be spotted by Rune's men and immediately rescued. Rosalind and I would lift quadruple middle fingers as we made our grand escape.

Instead, I was trapped in a dark, stuffy space as loud music and chatter covered up my hyperventilation.

Finally, mercifully, I was set back down on solid ground.

"You look like shit," Rosalind said, unzipping the bag all the way.

I raised a hand over my squinting eyes, the light above golden and oppressive. The air smelled of soap and perfume.

"Private powder room," she explained.

I lowered my hand and dragged myself out of the bag. My joints were aching, my neck and spine screaming as if I'd knocked something out of alignment.

My hands met the white marble with gold veins in front of us. I slowly raised my gaze from the counter to the mirror, head spinning and vision going in and out.

I confirmed that Rosalind was indeed correct about my appearance. My long, dark waves were matted to my head and tangled. There was an unsavory puffiness to my eyes from all the crying. My skin was duller than I remembered, and for the first time I noticed how much weight I'd lost.

"I can fix you," Rosalind said with calm certainty, placing her hands on her hips and nodding.

I lifted a brow. "Good luck."

"Don't need luck," she said. "Open up, baby girl."

She uncorked a bottle of liquid I recognized instantly. It would appear that Brennan had agreed to shell out a drop of his vast wealth to heal me. How very noble and generous.

Or maybe Kole had. Both men thought I was here for them and not the other. Which was a charade that couldn't be kept up for long.

I chugged the potion.

"Now sit." She pointed to the stool beside me, adorned with white fur.

I let Rosalind go to work while the potion took effect. She, of course, was perfect and glamorous—so at least one of us had gotten to make a grand entrance. Her blonde curls were tighter tonight, and her lips were painted a shade of coral that reminded me of the clouds at sunset. Her dress matched her lips. Bunches of tulle covered a short, fitted gown that was silky and revealing.

She brushed out my own hair first before pinning it up and brushing through the ice blonde wig. It was a bob, much shorter than I'd ever cut my hair before. It fell an inch above my shoulders, straight and shiny.

The color made me think of Snow. Chills swept over my skin, and I smiled, imagining seeing my best friend again. The woman who taught me how to love myself the way I'd always deserved, the love that had kept me alive and fighting even when I thought Rune hated me.

I understood now that self-love was the love that had always mattered most, from which all other love rippled.

Rosalind stopped applying blush to my fair skin. "Are you thinking about Rune?" she whispered.

"No," I said, my hands trembling now—with love and fear and heartache and hope. "I'm thinking about Snow. I can't wait for you to meet her."

Rosalind's features hardened in a way that frightened me. She continued applying my makeup in silence, and soon, my strength mostly returned. My body still hurt all over from Durian's merciless assaults and being stuffed in a duffle bag, but at least I could stand without falling.

I saw a whole new person in the mirror. My blue eyes complimented my icy hair, making me appear like a goddess of winter. Rosalind had expertly disguised my tiredness and puffiness, and my succubus powers could do the rest. I consciously tapped back into my magick, coaxing it from its dormancy after Durian had beat it down. I was out of the castle. I was so close to freedom I could taste it sweet and cool on my parched tongue.

"I can't go with you," Rosalind said suddenly.

I froze. "Why not?"

I thought I'd convinced her. I didn't understand why she still clung to her life with these vampires, who only kept her around for entertainment. Or worse, for future subterfuge. I knew she thought they offered her protection, but I'd made it clear Rune and the turned would offer the same without her having to give anything in return.

"Better the devil you know than the one you don't," she said. "Cliché, but true."

I tried not to get frustrated with her, swiveling on the stool to look up at her. "I can assure you that in this case, that is far from the truth. Forget trusting the turned. Don't you trust me?"

Rosalind's eyes darted back and forth between each of mine.

She was scanning for something she might never find. Not when her judgment was eclipsed by fear.

"You said you were going to help them—the other slaves. Instead, you're only saving yourself," Rosalind snapped.

My heart sunk, and my stomach twisted with guilt. "I can't save them while Durian slowly kills me. I'm a secret succubus, not a witch or a vampire. You know as well as I do that my body is human." I glanced down at my legs, the way they'd lost their muscle tone, covered in marks and bruises. Durian was ruining my body as much as he was ruining my mind. All of me was becoming smaller. "I can't do a thing if I'm dead. If my body doesn't give out, my mind eventually will. I'm working out a way to help them, to help all slaves and all of Valentin."

"A bit grandiose, no?" Rosalind's voice had a note of meanness to it, and it made my lip wobble.

I felt betrayed. I couldn't read her true intentions right now, and worse than the betrayal was the nagging worry that she might thwart my own escape. Had I misread this whole situation?

"Maybe," I snapped, rising to stand. "But I'm a slave who gets tormented and assaulted every day, and then instead of escaping in my sleep, I'm plagued with visions and nightmares all night long. While I'm slowly losing my fucking mind, you're getting the princess treatment and doing as you please. So I think I'll politely decline your judgment on my character."

Rosalind laughed, bitterness contorting her usually beautiful face into something nearly unrecognizable. "There it is. You still think my life is a fairy tale. You don't see me as a friend. You see me for my usefulness, just like those vampires you hate so much." Her lip curled. "How's all that hate fucking going, by the way? How many enemies are you bedding? I've lost count."

"Fuck you." I shook with pain and rage, the knife twist of being so horribly misunderstood.

Then, I replayed that thought—about feeling misunderstood—and my glare melted.

"I'm sorry," I said, surprising the both of us.

Confusion flashed in Rosalind's eyes.

"You feel misunderstood. I know your life is far from perfect, which was why I was trying to save you from it. We don't have to trust each other fully, but dear gods, Rosalind. Can we at least both admit that we're each trying to do what's best with the undeniably shit hand we were dealt at birth and every day since?"

I saw reality for what it was again. Rosalind went from a spitting viper to a wounded, frightened hound. She looked at the ground, her features losing their rabidness.

"You are my friend. At least from my perspective," I said.

She made a sound that sounded like a high-pitched *hmmph*. She turned away from me, toward one of the walls with dark floral wallpaper. "I understand now the male urge to punch walls." She huffed. "I hate you, Scarlett."

"I love you too, Rosalind."

She took in a few more deep breaths and let her shoulders slowly drop back down to a relaxed position. Her fists unclenched.

She turned back to me, fighting the urge to smile. "I know you're playing games with those stupid men. I know you're good. Way better than I am. I want to hurt you because you make me feel insecure."

I shook my head with a grin. "You make me feel insecure, too, if that helps. You're so self-assured and confident, and you're perfect at wielding your powers. Even the slaves love you, and most of them hate my guts. Like other women have hated me my whole life."

I got changed into my club attire as I spoke. We were, unfortunately, still on a time crunch.

"You'll learn, honey," Rosalind said softly. "You're not dying any time soon. You have all the time in the world to hone your craft. One day, you'll be running circles around me. You already *are* in many areas. Everything that appears natural, I've spent years perfecting. Including finding ways to avoid the nasty jealousy of bitter girls and dumb boys."

I stared at myself in the mirror. I was in a full, deep blue lingerie set adorned with tiny crystals that reminded me of the stars. Overtop was a sheer, matching blue tulle dress that fell off my shoulders and came to my upper thighs. Maybe I would've felt beautiful had I not been covered in bruises and ugly knife and bite marks.

I no longer recognized my own body.

"You need someone on the inside, anyway," Rosalind said. "I want to help."

I locked eyes with her in the mirror before pulling her into a hug. She was stiff at first, just as I had once been.

"I believe you."

I slowly released her, and her face appeared beautifully vulnerable, like ice melting to a gentle stream.

She brushed a blonde strand out of my face. "Let's get your ass back to your tattooed hottie."

∽

BLACK SAPPHIRE WAS INDEED a den of sin. Even if I knew Rosalind had only been lashing out, I still felt a stab of guilt in my stomach each time I locked eyes with a drugged human. How many of these mortals were slaves? Two-thirds? More?

Even if they weren't slaves, how many of them were sober, in their right minds, and truly consenting? Very few, I imagined.

Just like the palace, the energy here was oppressive despite my ability to feed from its collective desire. This magick didn't feel as good in my veins as what I gleaned from a good, clean seduction. I was profiting off cruelty to even taste the room's sex and violence as it slid inside me.

As much as I wanted to ditch Brennan and Kole, I knew they were who Rune's mortal eyes were looking for. I was sure Rune had described me to them, too, but staying near my marks was the only way for my rescuers to know for sure I was who they were after.

In this private section for the wealthy and powerful, bodies were tangled up with each other on fur rugs, and vampires gathered in groups to talk and feed together. Loud music wove through the space, and I caught glimpses of sensual dancing in my periphery. Laughter and chatter echoed in from the adjacent room. One peek through the door alerted me that they were pitting humans against each other in sadistic competitions while vampires crowded around. At the first sign of sexual assault, I averted my eyes.

Again, guilt churned inside my stomach, and I thought of Isabella. I had so many conflicted feelings about her. It broke my heart to know she'd endured the same horrors that I had. At the same time, I'd started to see her abuse and neglect for what it was. Resentment, guilt, shame, and grief were a tangled mess in my heart.

I looked for her as we passed through the club, my hand in Rosalind's arm. Had Rune given up his search for Isabella now that the borders were closed?

A group of vampire men stopped talking, their eyes immediately drawn to us. Brash swagger and the cruelty of undeserved wealth oozed from their skin.

One of them was in front of me in a flash. "What are you two beautiful creatures doing unattended?"

"Returning to our attendant, Lord Brennan," I said firmly.

The man's jaw ticked, and he took a step back. He pointed to our right, where there was a bar and several lounge areas, vampires covering every inch of the floor.

"Thank you," Rosalind chirped, and the man snarled in response.

The boys were deep in conversation at a standing table when Rosalind and I found them. They were sharing one of the servers in a sparkly bejeweled dress, drinking from each of her wrists as they spoke. They seemed passionate, but not heated. Brennan grinned widely, and Kole appeared charmed.

My ego-boosting tactics had created a self-fulfilling prophecy. I was pleased with my work. I'd connected two powerful men who wouldn't have ordinarily gotten a chance to connect on this level of comradery. I didn't *exactly* know how I would use my ever-expanding, ever-strengthening web of influence to save the world, but I couldn't deny the potent effects of my magick even as a beaten down slave.

What was I capable of when I was my most powerful self?

Incubi and succubi have toppled entire regimes when they've gone undetected...

Again, Rune's words floated around my brain like wisps of shadow.

When Brennan noticed me, he looped his arm around my waist and pulled me closer. Kole frowned, and Rosalind was quick to make contact, pulling Kole's attention from us to her.

Brennan's fingers dug into the fresh wounds Durian had cut into my stomach, and I winced.

"He doesn't deserve you," Brennan said, elixir on his breath. His grip hadn't relaxed despite the pain he saw it was causing me. "Has he ever touched you in a way that has brought you pleasure?"

I didn't have to fake the discomfort and disgust in my features, the sadness welling in my eyes.

"No," I said.

The last time I had experienced pleasure, let alone my own desire, had been when Rune was claiming me. He'd promised me forever. And that promise had felt unbreakable, unending, destined. I missed living inside our love story.

I missed waking up in his arms and believing that no man could ever hurt me or touch me again. No man except the tortured, beautiful monster who gifted me the cruelest rapture and sweetest torment.

I locked eyes with Kole. I needed to be careful. In order to maintain my foothold inside Durian's palace from afar, these men would need to believe that I'd been taken back to Rune without my knowledge and against my will.

My features filled with easygoing delight. "I want to thank both of you gentlemen for orchestrating this night of fun." I shifted on my feet, as if I were nervous, drawing out their sympathy. "Which would you prefer? Dancing? Or… downstairs?"

Brennan and Kole exchanged a glance before both pairs of eyes drank me in, relishing my display of joy and gratitude. The promise of having me in a way I'd never given them before—a way I never would.

"You've barely seen the place," Brennan said. "Neither of you have." He nodded at Kole. "How about we—"

A nearby scream was the first note in a beautiful symphony of chaos. I pretended to react with fear, but I only relaxed.

"Fire!" someone shouted from behind us.

A group of men to our right broke out into a brawl. "Spy! Someone help!"

I looked at Brennan and Kole, and they each puffed up their chests and moved in front of me.

"Stay with her. I'm going to see what's going on," Brennan said to Kole. His ears had perked up at the mention of a spy.

But as soon as Brennan stepped away, the cacophony soared to new heights. A blast of wind slammed into the bar next to us, sending glasses flying back against the walls and floor, shards flying everywhere.

Rosalind and I ducked, shielding our heads. Luckily, most of it had flown in the other direction.

"You okay?" I asked her.

Kole turned and asked me the same, altogether ignoring Rosalind's existence.

"Yes," Rosalind whispered, and I nodded in return.

The fighting got worse as more vampires were pulled into the fray. I locked eyes with Brennan across the room, his face contorting in confusion.

"Behind you!" Brennan shouted at us—at Kole.

Too late. My vision went dark as black fabric was shoved over my head.

I flailed around. These were the good guys, right?

Right?

Rosalind screamed next to me, and I felt myself get hoisted up into the air and slung across a shoulder. Which did wonders for my aching limbs and various wounds.

This was a long day of pain, sensory deprivation, and manhandling.

And *not* in a hot way.

When cold air brushed across my bare skin, I relaxed again. It was the second time I'd been outside since I'd been kidnapped.

After a few more minutes, I was set upright, my hood removed. Rosalind was next to me, and in front of us were two buff men with wolf pack tattoos.

I thought of Jaxon.

"You're Scarlett?" one of them asked, pointing at me. He had brunette hair that brushed his shoulders and a jawline that could cut fruit.

I nodded. "Yes."

These were the good guys.

"And you're the friend?" The other pointed at Rosalind. His

black hair was cropped, his muscles bulging through his ripped white shirt.

Rosalind looked him up and down before nodding, her features turning sultry. He was having none of it. He shook his head and grunted.

"On our backs and hold tight," the first one barked, glancing back over his shoulder. Smoke rose in the distance. We were in a secluded alleyway, with no other figure in sight. With two succubi in a district of starving vampires, I knew that wouldn't be the case for long.

The men began to shift before I had time to process what had just happened. Shirts and pants ripped; bulging muscles pulsed and stretched and sprouted fur. I blinked, and my jaw dropped. I'd seen Jaxon shift countless times, and yet it never failed to fill me with awe.

We'd been found. I was *outside*. With Rune's men. Away from the palace and away from Brennan and Kole. I trembled, worried this was one of Durian's cruel visions or some naive dream.

The two giant wolves lowered themselves to the ground. When we hesitated, one of them growled.

Rosalind met my eyes and shrugged. To my surprise, she hopped on one wolf as I climbed on the other.

It happened so fast. My legs clamped around strong muscle and thick gray fur, and my arms wrapped around my wolf's upper back. In a flash, two succubi were riding giant wolves through the streets of Hatham.

I didn't need to know anything about geography to know we were riding to the border.

32

SCARLETT

"I thought you said you weren't coming!" I yelled to Rosalind, competing with the rushing wind against our eardrums and the giant wolves' impossible speed.

We hung on for dear life. Our heads tilted toward each other as the city zoomed past us in the periphery.

"I wasn't! But they were just so sexy! I had a hard time saying no!"

The wolf underneath me grunted. My laughter was covered up by the wind. I laughed so hard that I cried, my tears dropping from my cheeks into the blanket of gray fur.

Rosalind turned away, maybe to give me privacy to go into hysterics without her concerned gaze. I lifted my head up and watched as our wolves deftly moved through alleys and side streets. On occasion, we'd spot a perplexed vampire or two, but none thus far had cared enough to pick a fight.

"Scar, dim yourself!" Rosalind said. "Just in case!"

That was another thing Rosalind had taught me. Being in control of my powers meant that I could also consciously make myself less alluring, shutting off my broadcast instead of pushing it outward.

I was caught between feeling like I was soaring and falling. I couldn't feel completely free. Not until I was in Nyx. And even then, I wasn't sure I'd ever truly feel safe again.

That thought dug itself into my worn and battered heart. What if I never felt like *myself* again? Or like my body belonged to me?

I couldn't focus on any of that. I had to stay present. I could wallow when I was across the border.

That was when I heard it—the screech of a firebird. Our wolves didn't stop.

We took a sharp turn, and my brutalized thighs clamped down hard to keep myself from flying off the side of my wolf.

Hatham's biggest green space stretched out before us—a park with a garden and cemetery. From our vantage point, I could already hear the din of conflict in the distance, flares of magick shooting up into the sky between tall buildings.

It looked like the ceasefire was going well.

I scanned the skies, but it was cloudy, and I didn't hear another sound. There were likely firebird stables nearby.

We were achingly close to Talomon. We were charging past dark fountains, statues of Lillian, and barren trees. I glanced over at Rosalind, and my heart ached when I recognized the sheer terror in her warm brown eyes.

Talomon was the border district under turned control that separated Hatham from the heart of Aristelle—Lumina, Nyx, and River, the districts that were home to most mortals and turned.

At the sight of a blue flare in the distance, our wolves redirected themselves toward it.

We reached a large square where we slowed. The cobblestone was cracked, blackened, and ripped up from the streets. Rubble was everywhere. Buildings had collapsed or were significantly rundown. The street was wide enough to serve as a firebird landing strip. A desecrated Lillian stood in the center, her right arm and head missing.

I took the opportunity to pull my already half-on wig the rest of the way off, loosening my real hair from its pins and ties.

Two grand streets forked on either side of Lillian. The flare had come from the right, in between two rows of tall, white buildings whose once-beautiful exterior ornaments were half-crumbled. My wolf jumped over a lion's head and gargoyle that had fallen.

A horde of vampires were currently brawling far in the distance. A hazy magickal ward flickered behind them with translucent red energy.

My heart slammed against my ribs. How many were turned and how many were born? Was this planned, or were we in trouble?

I didn't have time to dwell on these valid concerns, because a firebird suddenly appeared from behind the buildings to our left. Its talons were sharp, its fiery eyes warlike.

All the air left my lungs at once.

Rosalind met my eyes, her face ten shades paler than her usual pallor.

Durian and Brennan. They were the riders heading straight for us.

A violent wind slammed into us, and our wolves growled in response as they forged ahead. I looked forward, my heart stuttering when I saw a dark cyclone churning, far lower than any naturally occurring clouds.

My neck seared heat, like an invisible collar.

As the shadows circled, the earth rumbled, and power was thick as blood in the air.

An ear-splitting explosion sent the brawling vampires scattering, some of them thrown an unforgiving distance by the growing cyclone. The field of darkness enveloped all movement, obscuring Talomon from sight.

A man stepped out from the shadows, completely unaffected by the unearthly winds.

His hands rested casually in his pockets. His eyes were nearly as dark as his hair, and when I met them, their intensity pierced straight through me. He wore coal-colored, elegant attire. But nothing was as pitch black as his tattoos, his cloud of deadly onyx.

He was a dark god, a being that didn't belong in this realm.

My body trembled with fear—recognizing the brutal coldness in his features. But my soul reached for his, drawn to that confident, devastating smirk.

I peeled my eyes from Rune just in time to see the firebird sharply descending, talons outstretched. Durian's eyes had never appeared more wrathful.

Fucking *think*, Scarlett.

Nope. No time for thoughts, only instincts.

I reached a hand toward the firebird. I had to keep up my charade. It was the only way I guaranteed my survival either outcome. I needed to stay on the board, to ensure my succubus games remained viable no matter what happened.

It only took three seconds, barely enough time for my eyes to flit from Durian's to Brennan's, before shadow vines had wrapped around the poor firebird and jerked it back. It took that same amount of time for Brennan and Durian to deftly jump ship, allowing the bird to crash into a building behind them. A small object flew toward us at an inhuman speed, light reflecting off metal. More firebirds called in the distance.

Beside me, Rosalind let out a sound that twisted my guts into knots. It was a cross between a scream and a gasp, like all the air had been knocked from her lungs. My wolf screeched to a halt, whimpering.

Rosalind had fallen to the ground, a dagger lodged in her stomach. She was panting, confusion drawing her beautiful features tight. Her wolf nudged her hand and then looked to me.

I clumsily jumped to the ground. "You can't leave her," I whispered. "We can't leave her." I stepped forward, but my wolf growled, startling me. Someone—I thought Rune—yelled an order in the distance, but I couldn't make it out.

In a flash of vampire speed, Durian and Brennan stood twelve feet in front of me, and Rune was just as far from my back. The wolves took off.

I knelt by Rosalind's side. She stared up at me, rapidly blinking. She mouthed just one word.

Go.

"Do not take another step!" Brennan roared at Rune, and I felt wind at my back.

"Pet clearly wishes to stay with her Master," Durian spat. "I have men waiting to—"

"I tire of your sniveling, meaningless words. They will no longer be tolerated," Rune said, his tone ice.

My neck grew hotter. A tear slid down my cheek.

I glared at Brennan and Durian, my vision blurry. "Why? Why would you hurt her? She didn't do anything wrong—we were both kidnapped." Even in my terror, I continued to lie and manipulate. I continued to use the only weapon I had.

"I missed," Durian said with a dismissive wave of his hand. His lip curled. "You will be punished severely for speaking to your Master that way, you useless whore."

"What did I fucking say?" Rune roared. Foundations crumbled, the air grew dark, and a flood of screaming shadows moved past me and slammed into Durian and Brennan. "*About. Hearing. More. Of. Your. Nasty. Words.*"

Rune's voice boomed, as if he were speaking to every born in Hatham, or perhaps every being in the realm.

The ground beneath Durian and Brennan rotted. I couldn't see them through Rune's onslaught of shadows, as if they'd been swallowed by death and void. Glass and rubble fell from nearby buildings. A creature dipped from the sky. The light in Rosalind's eyes went out. She mouthed *go* one last time before a line of blood spilled from her mouth and the muscles in her face fell slack.

It wasn't blood that rained from the sky and flooded the streets. It was wrath. Mine and Rune's both, twisted up together the same as our souls, the same as those giant roots in our home village.

I screamed when strong hands grabbed me, dragging me away from Rosalind's unmoving form. My body was once again a doll to be moved at will. My stomach dropped, and my legs planted on something that felt like rough, reptilian skin. I saw nothing but darkness. I flailed around, and too many limbs held me still, their grip firm yet gentle.

"Shh, baby," a voice whispered in my ear, breath cool and tickling.

Baby. Not pet, not whore, not worthless cunt.

"You're safe," Rune said.

I shook, blinking away visions of Rune torturing me in sociopathic silence for hours on end.

"Why can't I see anything? How do I know you're real?" My voice was shaking as violently as my body, and Rune's form went rigid, his fingers soothingly trailing through my hair.

"My shadows. I'm shielding us from Durian's visions with my shadows until we're far enough away. There's a distance limit on his powers."

Soon, the darkness cleared, and I peered down below at two men kneeling with raised arms in a rotted, crumbled wasteland that spanned an entire street. Brennan had shielded himself and Durian with his defensive magick.

They'd killed Rosalind like she was nothing. Durian had been aiming for a wolf.

I sobbed.

"You're okay. You're safe. I'm trying considerably hard not to accidentally squeeze you to death," Rune said, his voice strained with uncharacteristic raw emotion.

Other shadowbirds appeared around us, and I caught a glimpse of both Mason and Uriah on their own creatures. A wave of that same translucent red magick extended from another turned's palm, as if patching up a protective border.

We were in Talomon.

I was in Rune's arms.

I'd led Rosalind to slaughter.

"Can you tell me if you're injured, please, Little Flame? I don't want to push you. You don't have to talk to me. Just tell me if you need emergency healing."

I relaxed, just an inch, at his use of my pet name.

"I'm fine," I whispered. I wasn't sure if he could hear me. "Rune," I whispered, sobbing again, reaching to feel the strange, silky skin of his shadows around my torso, his chiseled arms holding me against his chest.

At my touch, Rune trembled. "Hi, baby." His inhales were uneven, his body vibrating with the exertion of his power. "I'm here. I'm here, and I love you. I'm here, and you're safe. You will never be unsafe again."

33

RUNE

Scarlett had somehow lost even more weight since I'd last seen her. When she'd faced down Brennan and Durian, she'd been impossibly tiny. Any more time with Durian, and I knew without a doubt she would've withered away, no matter how strong she was.

That was half the reason I exploded. Seeing what they'd done to her. The disgusting fucking bruises and fresh wounds all over her skin. Her barely covered body, despite it being the dead of winter. It seemed like she couldn't even feel the cold, utterly detached from her physical existence more than she'd ever been before.

The other half of my reason for unleashing every last drop of my rage was the way Scarlett had reached for Durian. She'd been guaranteeing her survival if she were to be recaptured by playing into Durian's delusion that she would rather be with him. Brennan's delusion, too, clearly.

My Little Flame no longer trusted me to save her—to protect her from all monsters but the one who owned her perfect, beautiful heart.

She had every right to no longer believe in me.

But I would've sooner died than allowed Durian to say one more disgusting word to her. When he'd called her a useless whore, right after killing her friend before her eyes—I just fucking lost it. I saw nothing but oblivion and the deepest, hungriest fury. I wouldn't have cared if I'd created a martyr out of Durian and killed him on the spot. I would've exhausted my power to break Brennan's shield and obliterate them both, if I hadn't known that he had backup on the way. I wasn't about to risk Scarlett's life by provoking the war's first battle with her in the middle of it all. Scarlett's rescue was always meant to be an extraction. A bloody one, but still. In and out, as quickly and efficiently as possible. Though I did enjoy killing as many born as I could on my way. If the kingdom inquired, I'd use the borns' tried-and-true *self-defense* justification.

Fuck a ceasefire. I didn't give a single shit when I knew that the most I'd get was a half-assed slap on the wrist from a spineless courtier. Valentin was on her own. She always had been. I wasn't about to act with reckless abandon, but destroying an entire born camp on the border and effectively castrating Brennan and Kole in front of their men? Priceless. More than fair in this game of retribution and justice.

Scarlett had gone quiet shortly into the flight to Nyx, occasionally sobbing, but mostly just melting into me as I held her tight. Her small body was weaker and thinner in my hold, and it made me grind my teeth together with fury.

But my anger would be selfish from this moment forward, and I would keep as much of it to myself as possible. Scarlett needed the safety of the man who loved her. Not the wrath of her jealous God.

When we landed, I carefully helped Scarlett off Millie's back. When she met my gaze, she flinched.

"Sorry," she said.

"It's okay, sweet girl. You're okay."

I steadied her and then stepped away, giving her space as she took note of the other turned hopping off their shadowbirds. She looked up at the Gothic castle before us.

I fought the urge to touch her, to pull her back into my arms. She met my eyes again, and I grew predictably lost in those mesmerizing pools of blue. They sparkled, reflecting the witch lights illuminating the path to the castle's rear entrance.

My clan had the good instincts to leave us alone. Mason and Uriah merely nodded as they walked past.

Silent tears streamed down Scarlett's cheeks. She appeared terrified of me, and I was half-afraid she was about to bolt.

Instead, she quickly launched herself into my chest. And the move broke something inside of me. Or maybe it had knocked something loose.

I wouldn't have been able to stop my shadows from crawling all over her if I'd tried. One of my hands rested on the back of her head, the other on her upper back. We were locked like this for what could've been years or the briefest of seconds. We were two halves of a whole, two souls who were always meant to find each other, in any lifetime and any world.

She would never leave me again. There was no place in this world my Scarlett could go where I wouldn't be able to hunt her down and drag her back where she belonged.

It felt like I could finally breathe again after weeks without oxygen. Knowing she was safe, that she was away from those who'd been hurting her, meant more to me than any other truth ever had.

I pulled back, my hands now cupping her face in my broad palms. That first failed rescue had affected me more than I'd thought. It was hard not to fear she might fade away again.

This woman was the only thing in this world that could make me think and behave so irrationally, like a man possessed. I was thoroughly convinced I'd set myself on fire just to see Scarlett give me one of her beautiful, dangerous smiles.

I fell to my knees before her.

She stared at me in shock, glancing around before she refocused on me.

I didn't want to make this about me, but I needed to show her where she stood before I said it aloud. I needed her to see that I was at *her* service. I would apologize in whatever way she desired, for as long as she desired, until she felt safe with me again.

Until she believed in me again. Believed in us. In our soulmate love—dark, powerful, and all-consuming.

A shudder rolled through her, and she swallowed. "What are you doing?" Her voice was scratchy and raw. Her small hand reached for my face, and I leaned into her touch.

"Showing you how much you mean to me. How much you will mean to me forever. Now is not the time to tell you everything I need to say. But I will start with this: Scarlett Hale, my soul has been in love with yours since we were nothing but flecks of stardust. I would sooner die than let you believe otherwise ever again."

Her features crumpled. I saw evidence of the heartbreak I'd caused her pour from her eyes and twist my own heart in a tight fist. I'd broken her, just as I'd been broken when she was taken. She'd not only been tortured and harmed, but she'd endured it all believing I'd abandoned her.

"Please stand up," she said, dropping her hand. She looked around nervously, even though we were alone now. The only potential onlookers were stable hands guiding shadowbirds back to their stables.

I smiled at her. "Does it make you uncomfortable to see your God on his knees before you, Little Flame?"

Her eyes flashed, her lips quirking up. "It would've been more dramatic of a move if you weren't so freakishly tall."

A joke. She'd given me a half smile and poked me with that jagged wit, and it was as though she'd given me the whole world.

I stood, giving her back the comfort of eclipsing her with my size. "You have complete control over anything that happens to you from this moment forward, baby. My only humble request is that you allow me to take care of you, provide you with food and let a witch heal your wounds."

I lightly stroked her cheek as she parsed carefully through my words.

"If ever you want me to leave you alone, or to stop touching you, tell me. I will never be offended. It will only harm me if I cross your boundaries because you were too scared to make them known."

I tried not to look at the fang marks on her neck, on her breasts. The blue and purple bruises on her arms, the jagged red lines on her thighs. Worst of all, Durian's name once again carved into her stomach.

Fuck, had I been hurting her when I'd held her or picked her up? How much pain was she in?

"Okay," she said softly. Her eyes were dimming fast, and her cheeks turned slightly pink.

It fucking broke me that they'd done this to her, and it was *she* who felt ashamed. I fought the urge to clench my fists. A muscle in my jaw twitched. In the distance, heavy doors creaked shut.

"Stay here, sweet girl. Focus on your senses—what you can smell, hear, feel, and see. I'm unbelievably sorry you lost your friend today." Behind Scarlett, Snow was making a quick approach, a white fur jacket slung over her arms. "I don't want to overwhelm you, but there's someone who really wants to see you," I said gently, nodding behind her.

"Oh, honey. You must be freezing," Snow said, covering her mouth as a sob escaped her lips. She draped the coat over Scarlett's form. "May I hug you? It's okay if not."

Scarlett slipped her arms inside the coat as she faced her friend. She stared at Snow for only two seconds before launching at her too. It melted my damn heart until I wasn't sure it was in my chest any longer.

Snow was in her lavender jacket, her face stricken with emotion as Scarlett folded into her embrace.

"Anything you need, Scar. Just tell me. Rune and I bought seventeen different flavors of ice cream."

"That many flavors exist?"

"Baby, there are hundreds of flavors of ice cream," I drawled. "You don't like any of those and I'll get you a dozen more."

Scarlett slowly left Snow's hold and raised a brow at me. "Always so intense," she said, wiping away her tears. "But for ice cream, I'll allow it."

I watched Scarlett's face carefully, saw the exact moment when she grew uncomfortable. Her lips turned down, her eyes glassed over. A flip switched, and instead of focusing on us, she receded deep inside herself.

Snow and I exchanged a glance.

"Let's get you inside," I said softly.

Scarlett walked with us without another word, sniffling and teeth chattering.

In the back foyer, a few of my men stood guard. I didn't miss the way Scarlett startled when she saw them. They quickly averted their eyes as we passed.

"Do you want to eat in my private dining room, Little Flame? Where we ate breakfast…" I trailed off, and Scarlett looked up at me, eyes rounded.

Where I'd fed her breakfast from my lap, was a more apt description.

"You could eat there alone, or with us," I continued. "Or you could go straight to somewhere private. Whatever you want."

Healer witches were quick to find us in the hall, and Scarlett flinched when she saw them, too. She came to a sudden halt, leaning closer to me as she stared at the female witch wearing all black. I wondered if this healer reminded her of one of the *aunts* we'd learned about from Isabella. It was likely they wore all black in reverence for Lillian, just as their predecessors did.

The witches kept their features neutral but warm-leaning.

The woman in black spoke up. "We're ready whenever you are," she said to me.

"Whenever *she is*," I corrected. I drew Scarlett's eyes to mine. "Would you rather be healed before or after you—"

I stopped myself. Scarlett looked up at me in utter overwhelm, in and out of dissociation. I wanted her to know she had agency, that everything was her choice. But I could see that she was in no state of mind to decide what was best for herself.

"Snow, could you have attendants bring food to my chambers?" When Snow nodded, I focused on the witches. "Tarwin, you're dismissed for the night. Belise, you can come with us."

Belise, being thin, male, and in bright magenta and several golden bracelets, was far less likely to subconsciously trigger Scarlett's memories of the wretched slave handlers.

"Is this okay, Scarlett?" I asked.

She nodded, noticeably more at ease when Tarwin left. And when she realized she didn't have to make any decisions right now.

In the entrance hall, Scarlett scanned each piece of art, each sculpture. I moved at her pace, gently guiding her toward the stairs.

After a few steps, she said quietly, "There wasn't a lot of art in that place." She sighed. "And the art that was there was… garish. Repetitive. Soulless. I think that says something."

Fuck, I'd missed her.

"I think that says something, too, Little Flame."

34

SCARLETT

"Can you please leave?" I asked Rune.

He paused as he handed me a glass of water, his fingers brushing mine. He showed no disappointment, no anger or hurt, even as I scanned his features for any negative reaction.

Belise, the healer witch, was setting out his tonics and salves as I lay on the carpet in Rune's living room in his private chambers. He radiated a soft, comforting green witch energy, ruled by steadiness of the earth and her natural remedies. I was glad Rune sent the other witch away. Even though I knew she wasn't an aunt, she reminded me of a younger Aunt Carol. I couldn't help but recoil, remembering all the times I'd been healed only to be cut into again hours later.

"Of course, baby," Rune said.

I kept my coat closed tight over my body. I refused to let Rune catch any more glimpses of how ugly my skin looked, how withered I'd become, the evidence of where other men's hands had been. I felt gross and ruined. I wondered if he was disgusted —if it was hard to look at me. I wanted to go back to how I was before as soon as possible.

Rune noticed me compulsively tugging at my coat.

"You can come back when it's time to eat," I said quickly.

Rune's gaze had always been intense, prying. Before, I'd secretly wanted him to stare straight through me—to see what no one else had, what no one else had bothered to try. But now, I wanted to hide.

Rune nodded and left without another word. I didn't miss the brief flicker of pain. The *pity*. It made my skin crawl.

Luckily, it was easy to slip out of my skin entirely when Belise tended to my wounds. I stared into nothing, mumbling affirmatives whenever they were necessary. In my chest, a weight had amassed, an unshakable lump of grief and guilt that made it hard to swallow.

I wasn't allowed to see nothingness inside my dissociated mindscape. I forced myself to see her—Rosalind—picking apart our every conversation, ending with her pink lips forming the word *go*.

She'd chosen to stay with the born because she was scared, because this world had been as cruel to her as it had been to me. And she'd changed her mind because she'd decided to trust me, to dream in my better tomorrow. I'd saved myself at her expense. Just like she'd originally feared.

"Hey," Belise said, sitting cross-legged in front of me. His tanned face was as gentle as his touch, his dark eyes watching quiet tears fall down my cheeks. "Everything should be on the mend. I noticed some deeper bruising around your ribs. Are you in any pain?"

My vision refocused. "I don't know."

He nodded. "You can send for me if you start feeling any discomfort. I'm also trained in trauma integration and processing."

I frowned and sat up an inch straighter. My muscles tightened.

"Just something to think about in the future," he said,

gracefully rising to his feet. His golden bracelets softly chimed against each other.

After a tentative knock, I hurried to pull the fur coat back over my body and fasten it tight. Snow and Rune entered, attendants behind them with platters of food.

When I stood, blood rushed to my head and inky splotches overwhelmed my vision. I faltered, and Rune was in front of me in a flash. He steadied me, and I felt dramatic and annoying. My brows furrowed and cheeks heated as I stared up at him.

"Don't look at me like that, Little Flame," Rune murmured. His lips curved. "You're the one who can't stand upright."

Our little dance was familiar, comforting—my irritation, Rune's cocky dominance. He removed his touch, and his smile grew as my glare deepened. I was angry for reasons I couldn't consciously understand. But perhaps top of the list was his uncanny ability to understand exactly what I needed from him and when.

I'd missed him. In a way that couldn't be expressed through language.

"Can I sleep soon?" I mumbled.

"After food," Rune said.

He gently guided me to his personal dining table, where Snow was unboxing pastries and sandwiches from Marigold's. I looked to the arched windows where the curtains were tied back. Lights twinkled outside, showing off the beauty of Aristelle.

"This is too much," I said to them, eyeing the insane amount of food. "You know I'm only one person, right?"

I tried to smile, to show my gratitude, but I was waning fast. Belise's healing magick had infected my tired muscles with soothing energy.

"You'll need to eat tomorrow too," Snow said. "Plus, Uriah makes sure no food goes to waste in this castle." She made a face of disgust, but her lips soon quirked up.

Weird. I'd clearly missed some things. My heart squeezed, and I sat down at the table. I wasn't hungry, but I also didn't want to hurt Rune and Snow. And eating was the only way to sleep as soon as possible.

Snow sat across from me, and Rune sat next to me. Both of them pretended to eat, to avoid staring at me instead. Which was kind of them.

I forced down bites of everything, feeling guilty that I couldn't taste or enjoy any of it. I'd stopped finding pleasure in food weeks ago. Durian had controlled everything I consumed. Every drop of water, every morsel of sustenance.

I still had his depraved scripts imprinted into my brain. My purpose had been to please him. I had no free will except the magick I'd used against him and his men. On my next bite of food, I looked to Rune, seeking that same approval and scanning for the threat of punishment.

And when his dark eyes locked on mine, I startled.

Rune's face fell, and I stared down at my plate.

"I'm sorry. I want to sleep now," I said. "Thank you for the food, and tell Penn I said thank you too."

Had I eaten enough? Were they going to be angry with me for being ungrateful? Exhausted tears welled in my eyes, and I hated those too. Because I was sick of all the pathetic crying. It didn't help me, and it sure wouldn't bring Rosalind back.

"You don't have to apologize, Scar," Snow said. "I'll be here tomorrow. Everyone who loves you will be here tomorrow. And we don't need anything from you. You can move at your own pace. No one has any expectations."

Gods, I wanted them both to stop looking at me. "Okay, see you tomorrow." I fled the room, and I realized quickly that I didn't really know where to go except to Rune's bedroom.

The room was dark, a lone lamp dimly lit on the bedside table. I collapsed atop the dark bedding, impossibly plush beneath my weary form. I didn't bother getting under the covers. Every time I began to drift, I was jolted by the terror of being unsafe, of being somewhere unfamiliar. I saw the faces of the born, felt their hands on my body.

"Little Flame," Rune's voice came from my left.

I jerked awake and opened my eyes, my heart hammering in my chest as he came into focus.

"I'm going to sleep in my guest room. It's on the other side of the dining room. I'm around if you need me, but I won't disturb you. There are clothes for you on top of the dresser."

I stared at him. His weaponized body, his shadow tattoos that still lightly thrummed with power. My body was fearful, but the rest of me had never been more conflicted.

He headed for the door.

"No, wait," I said, the words coming from somewhere broken and frightened. The part of me that yearned for my mother, the part of me that forgave my abusive sister because I hoped I could inspire her to love me again. "Can you please hold me?"

Rune returned to my side, his own features conflicted as his face crumpled. "Are you sure? I don't know if that's—"

"Please."

He didn't fight me. He lay on the bed next to me, and his shadows instantly reached for me—thorns tucked as they skated over my body. I rolled onto my side to face him.

"You're terrified of me," Rune whispered.

"I'm sorry," I said.

"Please stop apologizing."

"It's because of the hallucinations," I said quickly. "Durian plagued me with visions of you torturing me for weeks. I know they weren't really you, but my body hasn't figured that out yet. They felt real. I'm not crazy."

"Of course you're not crazy, Scarlett," Rune said, his jaw tensing.

I knew he was hiding his wrath from me. Still, I scanned for evidence of it—the way his shadows coiled around my limbs, the heightened power in the air despite his magickal depletion.

"Do you want to bathe and change into something more comfortable?" he asked. He noted the look of panic and exhaustion on my face. "Or at least get out of your coat and under the covers, maybe?"

I shook my head.

"Is there a reason for that as well?"

I stiffened. "Fine, close your eyes."

Rune's lips turned down, but he obeyed without question. I sat up and yanked the coat off, refusing to look down at my ruined body as I receded under the covers. All the while, Rune was still, his eyes glued shut.

"Okay," I said softly. "Come on in."

Rune smiled, looking at me like I was the most precious thing he'd ever seen. It made me feel like I was falling—how it felt to swing by the forest and stare up at the stars.

"Thank you, baby," he said. He watched the way I kept the sheets pulled tight around me as he joined me underneath the covers. But he didn't comment on it, just kept his eyes on mine.

He was the same, yet irreversibly different. We both were.

"You really need to sleep," Rune said. "This castle is the safest place you could be."

"I want to know what happened," I whispered, my voice scratchy and raw. "When did you decide you loved me again?"

Like parting clouds, Rune's shadows loosened, and his eyes filled with heavier emotion than I'd ever seen in them. That vulnerable, deep pain that he could reveal only to me—the humanity that terrified him and cracked him wide open.

"I never stopped, Scarlett," he said. "And I tried, believe me." He slowly traced the side of my face, his lip twitching. "I was hurt. I thought that you were an enemy plant who didn't truly love me. I was angry with you, but with myself most of all.

Because even if I knew you were a beautiful delusion, I still couldn't cut you out of me no matter how deeply I dug."

"You didn't even give me a chance," I whispered. "You believed a false version of reality so easily, after everything we both felt, after I gave all of myself to you. After you promised me forever."

"You didn't feel real," Rune said. "You never have. None of it's an excuse. I fucking hate myself for what I did to you and what happened because of it."

Rune had never felt real to me either. It had been just as easy for me to believe that he hated me, that I was a parasite and our love had been fabricated all along. We'd each succumbed to our own worst fears about ourselves and what we deserved from this world.

"I failed to protect the woman that I love, and I will never be able to forgive myself for that. I certainly don't expect you to forgive me."

I slowly reached my own hand out to trace his sharp jaw. Rune closed his hand over mine as it rested on the side of his face.

My lips wobbled as I smiled. "Always with the melodrama."

Rune stared at me blankly for two long seconds. He rolled his eyes, though his lips curved. He gently thumbed away one of my stray tears. "We don't have to hash it all out tonight. You should sleep."

I opened my mouth to say more, but Rune twirled his finger for me to turn over. I was too tired to fight him. I wasn't sure I even had the ability to put together another coherent sentence. I shifted so that my back was to his chest, his arms and shadow limbs locking around me. I deeply exhaled. I forgot about my body. I forgot about my broken heart.

I remembered how it felt to be safe.

I remembered how it felt to be Rune's.

35

SCARLETT

I slept dreamlessly, bathed in darkness. When I awoke, my body was tight and sunken into the mattress, and I was held in a snug embrace. When I caught sight of Rune's shadow tattoos, I screamed.

"It's okay, it's okay," Rune said, stroking my hair. "You're safe. I would never hurt you."

I cursed, cringing as my heart hammered violently. "Instinct. I'm s—" I stopped myself before I apologized again.

"Good girl," Rune praised. "You could stab me a few times, and you still wouldn't need to apologize."

"How many times are permitted, exactly?" I turned over, silently yelling at my body to stop trembling. Sunlight managed to leak through a gap in the dark curtains, and I wondered how late in the day it was.

"Let's start with one and see how we feel after."

"That seems fair."

Rune pulled me into his chest and kissed the top of my head. "It's humiliating how much I missed you."

"Good."

Rune chuckled, the sound of it rumbling through both of us.

My cheek was smooshed against his chest. He was in a black short-sleeved shirt; he must've shed a layer while I slept. When I realized I'd stopped shaking and had relaxed against him, something inside me melted.

And when he pulled back to study my face, I knew he felt the same relief. "Do you still want me here?"

I nodded. "But I need to shower. You're kind not to mention my current... scent."

Rune lifted a brow. "Fucking intoxicating and divine?"

I squirmed. "You don't have to lie or treat me differently because of what happened. I'd prefer you didn't."

"I wasn't lying, Scarlett," Rune said. He stared at me in that way he did—like he wanted to pry open my ribs and pull out my heart to examine it from all angles. "But I wouldn't be a good man if I didn't take what has happened into consideration. That doesn't mean I'm dishonest or pitying. It means I care about your well-being and refuse to let your trauma get shoved under the rug, nor will I ever consciously perpetuate your suffering."

I shrugged out of his hold and sat up.

"Baby, don't do that..." Rune sighed, sitting up to rest against the headboard. "You don't have to face it today. Or even tomorrow. Focus on letting yourself heal and feel safe. Let's get you showered and in your own clothes."

His gaze dropped to my chest, and I panicked, quickly pulling the sheets back up to my neck. I'd forgotten I was still in lingerie and a sheer dress.

"I can handle it, Scarlett," Rune said. "I will employ methods of torture unseen in even the deepest pits of the underworld for every bruise. For so much as an unwanted stare."

After the healer, most of my marks were likely gone or substantially faded. But I still wanted to hide the weight I'd lost, the way my body had changed.

"I know you will," I whispered, looking away. "I don't want you to see me right now."

"That's okay. You don't owe me anything." He rubbed his thumb over my hand. He dragged his eyes back up to mine, pondering something. "You're not hiding yourself to spare my feelings, are you?"

I shook my head. I took a deep breath.

"He ruined my body," I whispered, and I regretted the words instantly, the way they scraped up my throat and hung in the air for far too long between us.

Rune leaned forward, his gaze fierce, certain, inarguable. I couldn't help but fall prey to his gravitational field of authority, his power thick in the air.

"No. He. Didn't." Though his voice was steady and quiet, I could tell he was vibrating with rage. "Scarlett, you are as beautiful as that day I found you in Noel's Tavern. And I will not rest until you see yourself exactly as I see you, just as I promised when fate intertwined our lives and brought you to my city. You are perfect. You always have been. You always will be."

Noel's? I'd nearly forgotten the fact that Rune had been stalking me for longer than I'd ever realized.

I tasted bitterness on my tongue, driving the urge to cower and lash out. "I don't feel *perfect*," I said. "I feel ruined."

"That's okay." Rune kissed my forehead, deeply inhaling. "Feel what you feel. But feelings and thoughts are not always reality. Especially when they've been planted inside us by those who wish to make us small."

I shuddered when Rune's lips brushed my skin, and I still felt them there after he pulled away. It was hard to believe I was free. This all felt like a strange dream. And Rune's love was far less understandable than my escape. Flashes of yesterday arose from the abyss, and I struggled to remember every detail.

"It was Snow, wasn't it? She told you the truth about who I was," I said, putting two and two together now that I'd had more time to think. Snow had seemed friendly with Rune. More than that—it was like they were actually close.

"Yes," Rune said. "She barged inside my castle, and she fought for you exactly how you deserve to be fought for. I deeply respect her, and I'm grateful you have her in your life."

"But, Rune..." It was excruciatingly hard to say, and I was terrified it would lead to me losing him all over again. But I had to say it. I couldn't live a lie. "Are you sure you truly love me? I know succubi can't induce love. But what if it's not love you feel? What if it's all still a grand manipulation, even if I didn't do it on purpose?"

Rune smiled, brushing a thumb against my cheek. "Sadie, my mentor, showed me that I'm immune to succubi magick the same as I'm immune to bloodlust. It may damn well feel like you've hexed me, but you played fairly. I really, truly love you, Scarlett. More than any man could ever dream of loving you." He leaned in, glancing at my lips, tracing every angle of my face before landing back on my eyes. "Now go get in the shower. You reek."

I snapped out of my stunned stupor to glare at him. I huffed and turned my back on him, slipping out of bed and making my way to his bathroom while he laughed. It was only when the door was shut behind me that I realized I'd revealed my body.

I still burned with shame. But not nearly as much as before.

I raised my fingers to my lips as I leaned back against the door facing Rune's lavish bathroom. I traced the way they'd curved into a small smile.

Everything that had happened, everything that had gone horribly, heartbreakingly wrong—and still Rune's declarations made me feel like a woman who was hopelessly addicted, endlessly obsessed with him. Everything in this whole fucked up world paled in comparison to his sneaky roots wrapped around my heart.

He was immune to my magick. All this time, I thought

everything about us had been a fabrication. I still had many unanswered questions. There was still so much hurt. Yet, our love, our destiny—if he had never been manipulated, then Rune might've been the most real, untainted connection of my entire life.

I struggled not to fall to my knees. My reality had shifted back another one-hundred-eighty degrees.

I ripped off the sheer dress and lingerie with little care and tossed them aside. I walked to the grand shower and turned the knobs, letting the cascading water heat as I stood back and watched the steam.

Sadie... who was this woman, and why did her name sound familiar? I remembered now that Rune had mentioned her before, when he was explaining to me why he no longer entered bloodlust. How powerful did she have to be for her to be a mentor to *Rune?*

Belise's healing salves washed down the drain, leaving mostly unblemished skin in their wake. I wished the wounds behind my eyes were so easy to erase.

∼

MY NECK FELT naked without Durian's ugly collar. I found myself reaching for my throat every once in a while, thumbing where that O-ring used to rest.

I barely remembered being in the shower, as if I'd skipped forward in time. Now I stared at the clothes laid out on Rune's bed—an oversized white sweater, black cotton leggings, and cozy-looking socks.

Damn him, I couldn't be mad he'd dictated my wardrobe. This outfit was exactly what I wanted to wear, and he knew it. It covered my body, it was comfortable, and it was cute without being remotely showy.

I could, however, be mad at him for the breakfast—or maybe

lunch, who even knew what time it was—spread on his dining room table.

My anger at the exorbitance had nowhere to go, as I stood in his beautiful dining room alone, no sound of life coming from anywhere in his chambers. Plates of fruit, more sugary pastries, meat and cheese, fizzy water that was no doubt spiked with vitamins and minerals, knowing Rune...

"Hello?" I called. This was absurd. But I was thirsty, and surprisingly, I was hungry too. I thought I'd lost that sensation a while ago. I poured myself a glass of the sparkling drink, and when I sipped it, it reminded me of that first night I met Rune. He'd forced me to drink water with electrolytes, citing that I looked pale. From the very beginning, Rune had taken care of me, in a way that was equal parts sweet and deranged.

Wait. Was that when he'd dosed me with his blood?

"Hello?" I called again, this time a tad more irritated.

I grabbed a stupid square of cheese and a stupid slice of meat, tentatively placing them on my tongue. I chewed and swallowed.

Food still wasn't the same, but it was better.

I found myself standing at the head of the table, grabbing pieces of food here and there, eating angrily until I forgot why I was even angry.

I walked around as I replenished myself, admiring Rune's art. Stars and mountains, roses and whorls of gold, vines and thorns. I spun, taking in the marble sculptures and intricate fixtures on the walls, the little touches that gave this room both warmth and familiarity paired with brushstrokes of the indescribable divine.

Then I looked up at the ceiling. I quickly swallowed my bite of a cinnamon pastry. My eyes widened, and my mouth fell open. It was a captivating cross between a deep, dark ocean and a night sky—a golden sliver of moon, nebulas and auroras, waves of deep blue and crackles of onyx. It was fire and water, darkness and light, like mine and Rune's souls had exploded into the cosmos. All I could do was follow the art, my feet moving with a mind of their own as I stared upward. I stumbled over a step, and I found myself inside the main living area, where the ceiling was even taller and grander.

My lip trembled, and I didn't know whether to laugh or smile or cry or yell for Rune again. Because the stars and oceans and deep darkness faded into brightness—a painting of me, in Helia's golden dress, grinning and blue eyes bright. I understood my nickname now, the way Rune saw me as this flame of hope that refused to die. I was on fire from within, the shimmering fabric clinging to my curves as I stood mesmerized, gazing at the world.

I looked like I was in love.

With Rune, with Aristelle, with this messy, painful, unfair existence.

And only a man hopelessly in love with me could've commissioned such a piece. Only a man insatiably obsessed could've captured me for who I was, half Helia's sun-kissed dreamer and half daughter of the goddess of lust, darkness, and chaos. A beautiful, sinful contradiction, just like the vampire afraid of his own humanity.

"I was wrong, Scarlett."

The voice nearly made me jump out of my skin. I twirled around to see Snow drawing her eyes away from the ceiling and down to me.

36

SCARLETT

Snow smiled, her icy blonde hair a few inches past her shoulders now, her bangs slightly longer too. She wore a black sweaterdress and clunky platform boots. A silver pentacle necklace hung low on her chest.

"Rune is unhinged, yes," she said, lifting her brows and shaking her head. "There are many actions of his I do not condone and never will. But my primary concern is you. Your happiness, your safety. He loves you deeply, and the pain he suffered when you were taken was difficult to watch. Yet he somehow managed to rule Aristelle and rescue you without making a single rash decision that endangered masses of mortals. I was wrong about him."

She took a breath, her features turning more serious. "If you decide he isn't what you want—tomorrow or years from now—I will always be your getaway rider. I'm team Scarlett, not team broody, arrogant vampire." Her mischievous grin dissolved as she stepped toward me. "Against all my initial judgments, however, Rune seems to care about your happiness above all else. Doesn't mean I won't be watching him *very* closely." She made a serious face and crossed her arms, and I laughed.

Snow relaxed at the sound of my laugh. Her eyes welled with emotion. Before she could politely ask, I hugged her.

"He didn't leave you alone, you know," she said over my shoulder. "I was here the whole time—in his private library, reading a filthy book." She pulled back and waggled a brow, and I couldn't help but giggle again. "We thought it might help your appetite if we gave you space."

Snow took both my hands and squeezed. My heart was a puddle of goo, and I tried to push past the discomfort so I could fully bask in Snow's warmth. How could I not? When yesterday, I was a slave, and my future was no longer guaranteed. When I'd watched my friend die before my eyes.

How could I not lean into love when there was a time that I thought love was for other people, and not for me?

I'd been wrong too.

"It did help my appetite," I affirmed. "I love you so much. I thought about you all the time." The clouds over my heart cleared, and I wondered if Snow saw it too—the space opening inside my aura that had once been opaque and impenetrable. "Isabella's voice used to be the loudest inside my mind. She'd been clipping my wings, just like you said. But when I was at my lowest, when I thought Rune had abandoned me and I was better off dead—your voice was the one that kept me alive when I no longer had my own inner strength. You were the one who showed me that romantic love was not the foundation. Rune isn't a missing puzzle piece to make me whole, to fill all of my voids."

Snow rubbed her thumbs against my hands, and I thought of Rosalind. Snow nodded at me, pride in her eyes.

"I might feel broken right now, damaged beyond repair. But it's your voice I hear when I dream of a possibility that one day, I might claim that wholeness all on my own. His love, your love, Penn's and everyone else's—it's all going to help. But I see now that the more love I give myself, the more love I can accept from all of you."

Snow's grin wobbled. A mirrored tear fell down her cheek. "You don't sound like an evil succubus to me."

I let out surprised laughter at her dark joke, and she joined me, letting go of my hands.

"Or I've gotten better at it."

Snow shrugged. She leaned in, the dark mischief in her eyes blooming. "Good. All jokes aside, you deserve to embrace who you are, Scarlett. You deserve to own your magick after feeling powerless for so long."

I deflated, this conversation suddenly making me feel exposed. I was still caught halfway between shame and acceptance. My powers had helped me escape, and they'd hurt those who had brutalized me. But they'd also sowed uncontrollable chaos. I was still responsible for the deaths of two innocent humans. And for Rosalind's death, too.

"I couldn't agree more," a new voice said from behind me.

My cheeks burned. I wondered how much he'd heard.

Rune was a shadow, by my side quicker than I could track. Guilt lodged in my stomach, reminding me that while I was safe, thousands of slaves weren't.

I'd started something in that palace. Something that could be *useful.*

Rune watched my face, his smile falling the exact moment I went somewhere cold, dark, and empty.

"I heard you laugh," he murmured, distracting me. He looked up at the ceiling, a dangerous smirk on his lips. "If I could've captured that sound in the painting, I would've." He bent to kiss my temple.

"Oh, gods," Snow said, wrinkling her nose as she watched us. "Go back to being a tortured warlord. I can't handle this version of you."

Rune snaked his arm around my waist and peeled his eyes

off me to level his gaze on Snow. "Don't you have naked forest frolicking to do with your coven, *witch?*"

Snow rolled her eyes, clearly fighting off a smile. When I giggled, both pairs of eyes flew to me.

"What do you want to do today, my love?" Rune asked.

The question was simple, a gentle declaration of my freedom and agency. But, to me, it was a field that extended forever. It was too big to grasp, reminding me of all the ways I'd been constrained and controlled before.

I knew everyone expected me to crawl into bed and refuse to leave again. But the thought of wallowing to that degree was not only humiliating, it was also shameful. I couldn't do that to Rosalind. I couldn't do that to Lana, Mairin, and the slaves I left behind. To the mortals who had already been sacrificed for Durian's bullshit holy war.

None of them got the luxury of becoming a hollow shell of a person, so neither should I.

"I want to go out," I said.

The briefest flicker of surprise shone in Rune's molten brown eyes. "Done."

"I promise I'll see Penn, Eli, and the others soon," I said to Snow. "But for now, I was hoping I could interact with people who aren't going to treat me like…"

I struggled to find the words. Snow understood anyway, nodding and filling her features with warm understanding.

"No expectations, remember? You guys should go do something, just the two of you," she said. "I'm volunteering at one of the care centers today before my shift at Odessa. Not the one—"

Snow and Rune both froze, Rune's hand halfway down the length of my hair.

"What?" I asked, looking between them. Rune's face was infuriatingly blank, and Snow appeared uncomfortable.

Snow cursed. "I'm sorry. I've barely slept. I wasn't thinking."

Care centers? Like for traumatized trafficking victims?

I took a sidestep away from Rune, my heart panging. "You're not sticking me in one of those places, are you?"

Rune tilted his head. "Fuck no. As if I'd let you stay anywhere but this castle."

Snow shot him a glare, but Rune didn't back down. I didn't give a shit about Rune's domineering protectiveness, currently. I wanted to know what they were hiding from me.

"I don't need anyone walking on eggshells around me," I said, frustration leaking into my tone. "I'm not a victim. I'm a person. Do not treat me like I didn't *fight* to be standing with you both right now. Neither of you have any idea…" I shut my mouth, a fury of buried emotion battering against my mental walls.

Rune's shadows vibrated with power. He seemed to be calming himself down, his features slowly relaxing. He reached for my hand and brought it to his lips.

"I made good on my promise, baby," he said. "Just before you were taken, I found Isabella. We rescued her cell of slaves before they could be relocated to the palace."

～

Rune was taking me to a café in River. Other than stares from everyone we saw and brief exchanges between Rune and passing turned, our walk was uneventful. Rune didn't miss the way I startled at every noise.

"Stay close, Little Flame," he whispered, kissing the side of my head as I held onto his arm.

My stomach fluttered as I looked up at him. This tall vampire built of lean muscle and dark magick, who simultaneously ruled an island and cared for me like I was the only thing that had ever mattered to him.

I shed a lone tear as I observed the city. The frigid air was a bit quieter, more solemn than before I'd left. But crystalline domed temples still shimmered under the sunlight. Buildings were architecturally breathtaking—various shades of cream, white, black, and dark jewel tones. Some were decorated with blooming flowers and creeping vines, despite being the dead of winter. Vampires and mortals, alike, poured out of restaurants and shops to gather on the cobblestone streets.

Had Isabella bothered to leave the care center to see how wrong she'd been about Aristelle? No. That seemed unlikely. Even if she did have the gall to explore the city of vampires, I'd bet she'd find a plethora of reasons to hate everyone and everything she encountered.

We'd traded places, she and I. She'd been saved the same night I had been kidnapped. And I didn't know how I felt about that truth, or even about her, anymore. I was glad she was safe, along with all the other rescued slaves. I was grateful to Rune for rescuing her even after he'd unclaimed me, for fulfilling such a lofty promise.

But I didn't want to see her. Not yet.

"This is it," Rune said.

I barely glanced at the tiny café, its patio lit up by string lights. I was looking at the view of the city from this high vantage point. The sun was starting its descent, bathing the world in warm, summery shades of pink and orange. The clouds were wispy and sparse. I could delude myself into thinking, for the briefest of moments, that nothing had changed —that the city was peaceful because the born were merely a nuisance, and not because we were in a tenuous ceasefire while the kingdom decided our fate.

Rune grabbed my waist, letting me gaze in silence at the city I adored. I backed up into his chest.

I jolted at a nearby burst of laughter, and Rune gripped me tighter. A few turned were nearby, watching the sunset over the city. When someone played a fiddle tune, shivers brushed across every inch of my skin, strongest down the length of my spine.

A woman sang, and I recognized the song immediately.

I spun. A woman and man had set up on the patio of the quaint café in a nook where a table had been pushed aside. The man was vigorously playing the fiddle, and a woman's voice poured across the street, tickling my ears as it rose and fell like lulling ocean waves.

"Is that—is that *Frida?*" I squeaked, grabbing Rune's arm in disbelief and excitement.

Rune chuckled, and his eyes lit up as he studied my face. "No, she's long passed. But I found musicians from that region who were familiar with her work."

"How... Rune!" I was so flustered I couldn't string my thoughts together.

He gently pulled me forward, and we sat down at a table under the warm-toned faerie lights. On our table, a pair of thorny burgundy roses were displayed in a black vase.

When Rune had been off on official clan business, and we'd fallen deeper in love through notes short and sprawling—he'd often sent me to his favorite spots in the city. To taste foods he thought I'd love, listen to music, read poetry, observe beautiful holy sites. And everywhere I'd gone, I'd imagined a future where we could go places together, where we'd no longer have to hide.

I'd imagined this moment, right now, countless times.

Rune had made sure I was sitting in clear view of the musicians, and I was caught between staring at them and staring at him. Either way, I was endlessly mesmerized, caught under a spell not of my own making.

"This is only a drop in the ocean, baby," Rune said. "You have no idea the lengths I have gone to keep myself sane. Since you were taken, I've spent every free moment making sure you came home to everything you've ever loved, in their most beautiful forms."

"You are so... *you,*" was all I could utter, nervously reaching for my throat. When I felt my own skin, it shocked me. It was hard to rid myself of the paralyzing fear that I'd forgotten my collar, and Durian was going to hurt me until I left my body.

I blinked and reset, dropping my hand back down.

The music cascaded over me like the most refreshing bath, and damn this man, I didn't jump out of my skin when someone dropped silverware. I barely processed the fact that we were the only ones on the patio besides the wait staff and the musicians, or the inner circle vampires standing guard a reasonable distance away.

All I could think about was Rune. It was that easy. I'd fallen right back into his web of words and shadows.

Rune grinned, leaning back in his chair as his broad hand closed over mine on the table. "I know why you asked me if I was sure I truly loved you, but gods above and below, Scarlett, what a ridiculous question."

My lips curved and my eyes welled with awe. But I couldn't find words. His love slammed into me just as hard as it had when I'd sat in Durian's lap across from him. This wave of desire that was entirely selfless. Desire for my contentment, my well-being, my joy, my every taste of beauty. My *freedom*.

How wrong I'd been about it all.

How terribly, heartbreakingly wrong I'd been about the jailer of my heart and the owner of my body and soul.

He held my gaze by force. "I love every single part of you, from the wicked to the sublime. That powerful mind of yours, equally infuriating and captivating. The delicious chaos of your soul—the way it yearns for adventure and novelty, sex and power, comfort, love, and belonging. You became my entire world without even a drop of magick. We are inevitable. We always have been. And I will never stop showing you how hopelessly entangled my soul has become with yours. It is my deepest regret I ever showed you anything less."

I looked at our intertwined fingers. The song Rune had once overheard me sing faded into the next one.

"I can't do anything *but* love you," I said. "That doesn't mean I'm not still hurt at the ease you cast me aside, believed the worst about me without even giving me a chance."

"As you're allowed to be," Rune said. "Just know that it was far from easy. It was all a bluff. I hadn't ever truly let you go. I could never. Tell me to get on my knees again and grovel, to do anything at all to prove to you that I'm yours—and I'll do it, Scarlett. Every day for the rest of our lives, if that's what you desire."

The waiter—a turned vampire—barely glanced at us as he brought a carafe of water. I waited for him to leave before I spoke.

"Aren't you worried about how that will look to your clan?" I asked softly.

Rune leaned forward. He glanced at my lips, his intense gaze trailing back up to my eyes in a way that had my heart skipping a few beats.

"Scarlett, my love, I would kneel before you in front of the entire damn world."

His shadows curled around my arm, and I gasped when the tip of one crept up my neck and gently brushed my chin.

"I was a fool to ever fear you'd make me weaker. You have brought all parts of me into balance. You've made me softer when it matters, led me to ask different questions, to fight the complacency of immortality. You've made me stronger."

I homed in on the tips of his fangs, and my stomach dropped.

"The born worship a woman and yet treat the rest as inferiors. And that makes them stupid and weak. I would be more powerful than their best man on my hands and knees in prayer before you."

37

RUNE

I'd moved my chair to sit next to Scarlett instead of across from her. I couldn't get close enough, not even when my fingers brushed her lips as I fed her a piece of bread with a spread of olive oil and herbs. I'd ordered her a taste of nearly the entire menu, much to her disapproval and my corresponding amusement.

"I should've seduced the vampire lord of Aristelle years ago," she said with a sigh, sipping her water as she stared into my soul.

It was reassuring to see that she was still a raging brat.

Her eyes narrowed. "We still haven't addressed the fact that you'd stalked me before I came to Aristelle."

I twirled a strand of her hair around my finger. "We haven't addressed many things."

She leveled a pointed stare.

I told her all of it, our voices low as the music filled the air. I surrounded us with a barrier of shadows, extra protection against prying ears.

I told her about my sisters, how I visited their graves and my mother's every year or two in early autumn, the time of year my sisters were slaughtered by the born. I explained how I'd gone to the forest, where I'd found their bodies, and I'd heard a girl sing with the voice of an angel.

"I kept going back to Crescent Haven, all those years, to remember my *why*—why I'd claimed this city for the turned, why the born were undeserving of any semblance of power in Valentin, and why I'd sought out my mentor and asked her to rebirth me into an immortal capable of protecting the powerless and the vulnerable."

Scarlett stared at me with her big blue eyes, absorbing my every word. Her brow furrowed occasionally. Sometimes, she hid her reactions, and other times, her emotions leaked out beyond her conscious awareness. When I talked about my sisters, she'd found my hand and held it tight.

"Or at least, that was my surface level rationalization," I said. "In truth, what I wanted most was to remember what it felt like to be human. To fear death. To yearn for dreams forever on the horizon. To live and love viscerally, subconsciously understanding that nothing is guaranteed, and it could all end in an instant."

"I reminded you of your human self," she said, the strikingly clever, intuitive girl. "I made you feel vulnerable, just as you secretly desired. And it was everything that Rune, the vampire lord of Aristelle, could never allow."

"It wasn't right," I said, shaking my head as I fought to maintain eye contact. "To watch a child in secret, even if it was for the briefest moments. I just wanted to see that you were okay, that your flame still burned bright. You were the lifeblood of that village, the only thing of interest for miles. I wanted you to have the life that I couldn't—the life I gave up when I chose to become a monster instead."

"You're not a monster," she whispered, the sole source of light and warmth in this enclave of shadow. "Like I told you before, your rise to power had always been an act of love. You chose to preserve your humanity when it would've been far easier, and far less painful, to succumb to the apathetic cruelty of vampirism instead."

She was far too generous with me. It was hard not to think of her as human. Who knew demons could be this damn sweet?

"When you were on the cusp of adulthood, I knew I could never see you again," I continued. "It had never been right, but it was even less morally sound to watch an adult woman. I couldn't risk you seeing me, or ever interfering with your life. So I stopped. But then, six years later, I had an excuse to return. Known trafficking scouts were in the area, looking for high-value marks for Durian. I followed them to Crescent Haven and eliminated them, but I'd been distracted for long enough during the night for them to send word of you back to their vampire contacts."

Scarlett mulled this over. "Distracted by what? Also, how in the hell would it be less creepy to watch an adult rather than a child?"

"I suppose I have the same answer for both questions," I said, shifting slightly. It wasn't often I felt the heat of guilt crawl up my spine. "When you were a child, I checked in on you because you fascinated me, because you reminded me of the man I'd killed to become what I am now. It was innocent, or as innocent as such an act could be. But when I saw you in Noel's, as a twenty-three-year-old woman... my obsession twisted, no longer anything close to pure and decent. I'd grown distracted because I saw just how easily you drew the obsession of other men, too."

Scarlett stared at me, her eyes flitting through every emotion imaginable. Most surprising of all was the unmistakable scent of her arousal that had my fangs aching in my gums. The wicked little thing settled on anger even as she shifted her thighs closer together. But when a spark of confusion and shame eclipsed her features, I was quick to distract her again.

"I was distracted by *you*, as I have been every day since. I saw you being followed, and I wanted to make sure you were safe before I left you for good." I glazed over the details of that night. She could connect the dots on her own. "I hadn't realized your sister had been taken until you told me. Until then, I was utterly perplexed by how you'd ended up in Aristelle after you'd been set on traveling with your friend."

Scarlett went heartbreakingly silent for a moment, and I knew her well enough to tell the exact moment she thought about those disgusting drunks groping her. Then, as she always did, she pulled herself back to me. She continued to choose life, no matter how fiercely it had shoved her down.

Even if I didn't deserve her, I prayed she still wanted to be mine after everything I'd done.

I awaited her verdict patiently. As if her decision to leave me of her own volition wouldn't shatter this immortal heart she'd made irreversibly exposed.

"I should be disturbed," she said. "I should be running."

I stroked her cheek. "Go ahead. You know I love a good chase and capture."

Her breathing grew shallower.

"You should hate me, but you don't." My voice was low, a gentle caress of her buried truths. "You still can't do anything but love me."

She glared at me in confirmation, adorably frustrated. "You dosed me with your blood my first night in Odessa."

"Yes."

"You're insane!"

I smiled. "Yes."

"You saw me as yours the very first time we met."

"Yes, baby," I drawled. I moved closer to her, staring at that spiteful mouth. When she bit her bottom lip, I wanted to run my tongue where her teeth had been. "I told you that you've always been mine. My soul has always known. I fed you my blood so I could track you in a city full of vampires who wanted a taste of you and men who wished to hurt you. I fed you my blood so I could protect you, my soul. And I fed you my blood because it made my cock throb to see you marked by your God."

Scarlett gasped. Her eyes were ferocious, and it made me grin.

"Run from me, Little Flame. I dare you."

Her heightened arousal was driving me into an insatiable craze, reminding me that I'd broken my promise to Uriah. I'd let myself become far too hungry and depleted. I hadn't fed since I unleashed my shadows upon Hatham and saved Scarlett.

I couldn't drink another's blood. Not with Scarlett sleeping in my bed, traumatized and clinging to me for safety. Not with her intoxicating scent all over the castle. It would feel like yet another betrayal. The thought of drinking someone else's blood, even from a chalice, made me sick.

"Why are you so hungry?" Scarlett suddenly asked, cocking her head.

She might not be able to manipulate me, but she had clearly gotten better at reading desire.

"I'm not," I lied.

"Why are you lying about it?"

I let out a long, exasperated exhale. Damn this woman. "Because it wouldn't be right to tell you the truth."

"Do it anyway," she demanded, leaning back in her chair.

"Because all other blood tastes like shit compared to yours," I said, gritting my teeth. "Because drinking from another goes against my every instinct, my every desire. It feels like I'm being unfaithful to you, after I've already betrayed your trust and failed to protect you in the most basic of ways." I glanced at her collarbone, how it protruded more than it had before. "Feeding from you, of course, is out of the question. I know it's best for everyone if I just close my eyes and replenish myself from a willing donor. It's what's best for you, most of all."

Scarlett didn't speak, and for a moment, I was terrified that I'd frightened her. I watched her eyes for signs of dissociation, but they remained sharp and focused.

"I'm not going to run from you," she said. "Unless it's because I *want* you to chase me."

Her voice was soft, but her lips flashed that dangerous smile I thought I'd have to wait weeks to see.

"You can feed from me," she said. "I don't want you to suffer."

"Fuck no. Absolutely not."

My body was screaming for her, but luckily that wasn't the part of me steering the ship. This had been a wake-up call. I needed to choke down someone else's putrid blood as soon as we arrived back at the castle.

My shadows receded so she could listen to the live music again. It was extremely unlikely that anyone could hear us anyway, but I wanted to ensure it when it came to discussions of Crescent Haven.

Scarlett watched the musicians, her frown easing. "Rune, it's okay—"

"No." I watched her fight the urge to brat off. "It's only been a day. I don't even want you to *think* about doing anything for anyone but yourself."

She suddenly looked around, her eyes snagging on a human man on a vampire's arm.

"Do you think Durian has mortal spies?"

I opened and then closed my mouth, staring at her in confusion. "What?"

This was likely another reverberation of her trauma, her inability to stay focused on the topic at hand. Or maybe she just didn't want to think about feeding, which was understandable.

I, myself, couldn't think about how she'd been used and brutalized without my shadows leaping from my body ready to peel born skin from bone.

It was more difficult to read her than it had been before she was taken. Not that it would stop me from adjusting, making sure that I understood this new version of her just as well as I did the last. I'd never stop trying to peer inside every dark corner of her entrancing mind.

She repeated her question, her eyes narrowing.

"It's possible, but not in any meaningful way. His fanaticism tends to produce more religious agents of chaos than organized infrastructure. There are mortals who have been duped by him, sure, but they're mostly impoverished, uneducated, and relegated to the born districts."

I watched the way Scarlett had pulled back from me, her gaze still flitting around at the lookout behind me.

"They're not going to try anything, Scarlett, I assure you," he said. "Especially not through mortals they see as inferior and undeserving of rank."

"What if word gets back to him that you and I are going out on dates in the city?"

I had to stop myself from asking a second, incredulous *what?* Because her line of thinking was not at all what I'd first imagined. I tensed, my shadows trembling and hunger multiplying the more power I restrained.

I searched her eyes furiously. "What the fuck does that matter?"

She flinched, and I instantly regretted cursing and using such a harsh tone.

"I'm sorry," I said.

That nagging vision from when I'd rescued Scarlett reached up from my mental caverns—when Durian and Brennan had flown closer to her on their firebird, and she'd reached for them.

"You weren't just ensuring your safety. It wasn't merely because you didn't trust me to save you," I said quietly. "When you pretended you were glad your kidnappers had found you."

She was quiet. Rage was hot and thick under my skin. The

ground trembled, and my nearby men and women glanced back at me briefly to assess.

Scarlett's eyes rounded. As soon as her hands began to shake, I closed my eyes. I whispered to my shadows, begging them to calm the hell down, no matter how badly I wanted to pull Scarlett close and never let her take more than three steps away from my side.

"I told you I fought my way back to you," she said. "You might've gotten me over the border. But I got *myself* out of that damn palace. I was the only slave with power. And I still owe it to everyone I left behind to make it all *mean something*." She paused. "I created something in there, something that started small and became so much bigger. A web of influence, a network of division. I don't know how yet, but I'm going to figure it all out. There's a way to stop this war before it destroys this island I love, this island I've barely gotten a chance to see."

I was reminded of Sadie's words I'd tried desperately to forget. She claimed Scarlett was more than a survivor, and that there was a way to rescue her while maintaining her position as an *asset*. A weapon. An object, just as she'd been traumatized to believe she was her entire life.

My eyes flew open. "I will not allow you to throw your life away," I hissed. "You deserve to live for yourself, after everything you've endured."

She crossed her arms and opened her mouth, but I cut her off.

"It has been *one day*, my love." I dragged a hand over my face as I struggled to hide the frustration from my voice. "You have to stop running. When you don't face the past—when you shove it inside a back room and slam the door on it—it will *always* escape to ruin your present and future when you aren't looking."

"Is that what you did?" she asked. "Threw your life away? Used your trauma as fuel to fight a war instead of truly confronting it?" Her eyes darkened. "Stop projecting yourself onto me."

I shook my head. "No, baby. You have it all wrong." I reached for her clenched fist. "It was only because I made peace with the past that I was able to forge Valentin's future."

I watched as Scarlett's anger reached its peak and then washed away. Her hand relaxed under mine. There was still a spark of defiance, an unwillingness to hear what I was saying. I intuitively knew she'd only decided to hide her thoughts away rather than change them. And I couldn't let it provoke my anger or my fear of losing her again. I couldn't drive her away and out of my reach.

She glanced at the musicians. "It doesn't sound the same as it did before." Her gaze fell to her food, grief in her blue depths.

I wanted to pull her into my lap. I wanted to hold her tight enough to erase what had happened to her. But that was the same poison I needed to help her remove from her mind—the inability to accept reality and live life on life's terms. We both needed to make peace with the unspeakable in order to feel safe again.

I read her body language, the way she was closed off. She'd reached a limit, exhaustion weighing her shoulders down. When she began to make herself smaller in her chair, hide her mind away from my prying gaze, I knew it was time to leave.

"And it never will," I said, and her heartbroken eyes snapped to mine. "Nothing will ever taste, sound, feel, or look the same. It's not supposed to."

Her sorrow at my words broke me. She stared at me, waiting, nearly begging with her eyes for me to give her the answer she wanted to hear. But I couldn't.

"You'll adjust, Little Flame. And one day, you'll wake up and realize that after you've given yourself ample time, healing, and grace, it will all taste, sound, feel, and look better than it ever did before."

38

SCARLETT

In the middle of the night, I woke up to the sound of my own screaming. Rune's face was inches from mine, and I scrambled away, off the side of the bed and to the corner of the room. I pulled my knees to my chest and buried my head.

"Please, please, please," I sobbed, snot dripping down my nose. "Don't." I imagined a blade sawing through my ligaments, and I prayed for Durian to come, to make Rune disappear.

My eyes were shut tight, but I felt the gentle stroke of a hand through my hair.

"Thank you, Master," I choked, relieved as I sucked in air.

The touch halted, and I slowly opened my eyes and looked up.

Rune stared back.

I shrieked, backing up so quickly that I slammed my head against some sharp corner. A stab of pain erupted at the back of my head. My vision blurred, my body unable to sustain this level of terror as it slowly lost all sensation.

Rune cursed, and it didn't make sense—because the Rune who hurt me didn't speak, other than that time he told me I was dead to him. He didn't react this way. He was cold and uncaring.

"You're safe, Little Flame," Rune said, his voice trembling, his face racked with horror. He hesitated, holding himself back and away from me as my confusion slowly morphed into understanding.

My eyes darted around. I wasn't in my slave chambers. I was in Rune's bedroom. The Rune who tortured me didn't call me Little Flame.

I met his gaze and rubbed the back of my head. "I'm sorry."

His face was utterly tortured for another second before he erased it all, replacing his crumpled features with calm and warmth.

He crouched down in front of me, and I nodded at him, giving him the unspoken permission he needed. Rune scooped me into his arms and brought me back to bed, holding me sideways in his lap as he leaned against the headboard. He gently stroked the back of my head, and his shadows crawled over me in smoke form.

"You're safe," he whispered. "You're okay."

I cried softly, my poor body confused by the conflict between my memories and my reality. The trembling was slow to ease.

"I don't think it's best for me to be sleeping with you, baby," Rune said.

I tensed, grabbing his arm. "No, please don't make me sleep alone." The nightmares would still be there, and if I was alone, it would remind me even more of my living arrangement in the palace. I needed Rune.

"I'm hurting you, Scarlett." He felt the back of my skull to assess the severity of the bump.

I tried not to wince. I didn't want to see the healer right now.

"No, you're not," I said, my voice wavering. "It's not you. I'm sorry. I just get confused. It won't happen again. Please don't leave."

"Shhh," Rune soothed, pulling me tighter against him.

"You're not in trouble. You didn't do anything wrong. I will never leave you."

I slowly relaxed, letting Rune guide me back to my body. I told him what I heard, what I smelled, what I saw and felt.

"I used that technique while I was in the palace," I said.

Rune made no reaction, only kissed my forehead.

"Who taught it to you?"

"Sadie." He gently moved us under the covers, my head resting on his chest as we lay in the dark. "She can't wait to meet you. But wait she must," he said dryly.

"Wait... was she the witch who was at the meeting with Kole?"

A pause.

"Yes."

Several loose ends suddenly tied themselves off all at once.

"She was the mean domme who calls Kole a disgusting little rat!" I said, rising from Rune's chest to stare at him with wide eyes.

I smiled in spite of myself, catching an utterly bewildered Rune off guard.

"That sounds about right," he said, his eyes narrowed.

I lay back down, my smile fading as I thought about it more deeply. "And a witch is your mentor, because she's the one who made you a vampire. She's behind all of it."

Rune was silent.

"*All of it,* is a stretch, but she'd enjoy that interpretation."

"Oh," I whispered. "No one knows, obviously, except the turned. But how? How have none of you ever let it slip?"

"Part of the initiation process, and no, I will not be elaborating. You already have more than enough information in that conniving, vicious little mind to get yourself killed fifty times over."

Some kind of magickal binding, I assumed. Sadie was ancient in witch years. Yet she still appeared young. A testament to a very large, dark amount of power at her disposal.

"You think I'm vicious and conniving?"

"Terribly so," he said.

I scoffed, and a chuckle rumbled through his chest.

"I adore you for it. I adore you for it all."

Rune cleverly steered me away from my scheming and back into his arms. I wanted to connect more dots. Inside my mind, a game of chess was in motion. Lines were drawn between actors, connections fused between great powers and divisions carved between others. I used to gamify seduction to distract from the trauma of existing as a sex object. Now, I was playing war games.

Did it count for anything that I was self-aware of my own denial?

Against all odds, Rune was able to soothe me back to sleep.

∽

THE NEXT DAY, I woke up depleted. I was exhausted in a way that weighed down my soul as much as my body.

"Your body is recovering," Snow told me over breakfast. "Give yourself grace, Scar. You're only hu—" She paused, her eyes flashing. "Demon."

I snorted, and we both entered a fit of much needed laughter.

Rune was off doing clan leader things, and we were in his private dining room, faced with another insane array of food.

"Are you sleeping here in the castle?" I asked, swallowing a bite of smoked salmon and cheese on toast.

"Yep," she said.

"With Uriah?"

She sprayed orange juice out of her mouth and maybe her nose before coughing like she was on the verge of death.

"Sorry, sorry," I said. She glared at me as I laughed even harder than before.

She chugged water and cleared her throat. "No. Though he is, unfortunately, sleeping next door to *keep an eye on me*. I've been here for a couple weeks now, actually. It was just easier."

Snow had been staying in the castle, with vampires she at one point had despised, since I'd been taken. I fiddled with the tablecloth, imagining her, Rune, and his favorites gathered around the fire together because of *me*.

I brushed the strange image away.

"I haven't missed anything of note between you two?"

"No!"

"Are there… feelings? Yearnings?"

"Yearnings," she said with an eye roll. She violently bit into a scone. "He's obnoxious. And brutish."

That was so not a direct answer. And then she abruptly changed the subject.

"Rune wanted to see if you had any desire to hang out in the library?" Snow asked casually, doing that thing they were both doing where they pretended not to scan me for clues about my current mental state. When they *absolutely* were.

"Not yet," I said.

Rune wanted me to visit my favorite room in the castle, the room of music and stars, with an endless collection of recorded music from all over Ravenia.

But what Snow and Rune didn't understand was that it would only hurt me. I didn't want to be reminded of how little pleasure I experienced doing things I used to enjoy. How prone to exhaustion and mood swings I'd become. How hard it was to focus, how far I jumped out of my skin at the faintest noises.

I wanted to go back to how I was before. My body, my mind, my interests and hopes. Rune had broken my heart when he'd told me that was never going to happen.

"Want to read? We can stay in, or bundle up and go outside?

It's cold, but it's sunny," Snow said, reading my features for hints of my desires.

"Sure, let's sit outside." I lifted a brow. "Are you hoping hunky vampires are out there sparring while you read smut?"

"I hate you so much right now."

Snow glowered, and for a moment, I saw Rosalind instead. I was back in Black Sapphire, when Rosalind told me she hated me, but what she really meant was that she hated that she loved me.

"I love you too, Snow."

39

SCARLETT

Snow and I were in big coats, hats, and gloves, lounging together in the gardens. Attendants set us up with chairs, pillows, blankets and a table of snacks. Several guards were posted around us, reasonable distances away.

In the training field, vampires were sparring. And Snow may or may not have peeked out at them over her book on multiple occasions. Desire was ripe in the air, and it made me laugh to myself.

Snow shot me a frustrated glance. "Stop that."

I raised up my hands. "I'm only reading." A true double entendre. Soaking up desire had me relaxing back in my chair, my spirits lifted. I wasn't going to manipulate anyone. But I couldn't deny that the act of feeding did wonders for my exhaustion.

I looked back down at my book, *The Taming of Marianne*. I hadn't made it far, yet I was fairly certain the main characters were a few pages away from jumping each other's bones. And not in a normal way. In a very kinky, Rune-and-me kind of way.

I couldn't wait to tease him about his personal library of indecent literature.

"Scar—um, do you know what that one's about?" Snow asked, jolting me from my current page. She glanced at the book in my hands with a frown.

I met her concerned gaze. "Kinky sex between a human and a vampire?"

She hesitated. "Well, I suppose. But it's pretty old, and I just—it's not very consensual at times, and extremely dark. It's more like she's his... slave."

Snow's features twisted with discomfort, watching my face closely.

I blinked at her. "It's fiction. I don't mind." I furrowed my brows. Her description of the plot only turned me on, but I knew she was trying to say that I shouldn't be reading something that mirrored my trauma. My cheeks burned. "I appreciate your concern, but it feels different to me. It's fantasy. An escape. And I—I still want to be able to enjoy sex."

The dark and depraved kind, but I kept that qualifier to myself. Snow appeared pensive, and I could tell she didn't quite understand. And maybe that was okay. I wasn't sure Snow was into the same things that I was in bed, but I did know that she'd taught me not to be ashamed of my sexuality after years of being scorned by Isabella.

"If I feel triggered, I'll stop reading," I promised. "But between these pages, I'm safe. It's not even remotely the same. Here, I have power. When men have hurt me in the real world, I've had none. Does that make sense?"

"Yeah, it does," Snow said. She offered me a small smile. "Controversial or not, that's the book that started it all for modern kink. It's what gave us the word *sadism*."

"You're a walking encyclopedia sometimes, you know that?" I teased.

"It should come as no surprise that I was bullied relentlessly in school."

I shook my head. "Give me a list of names." I pinned her with a serious face, setting my book down in my lap. "I'll succubus the shit out of them."

Snow laughed. A couple of vampires looked over at us from the sparring matches, and they were promptly yelled at by Mason.

I wondered where Rune was. That thought became more pronounced the longer I read, lost in this faraway world that was somehow both achingly familiar and exhilaratingly foreign. To say the romance between Edgar and Marianne was dark was an understatement. And yet, just like Snow, I found myself sitting perfectly still, my bottom lip sore from how hard I was chewing on it.

Snow suddenly squealed, launching her book into the dead grass. "Ugh! I hate this stupid book and I'm never reading again!" She was breathing rapidly, her face moving from anger to regret. "Oh, hell. I shouldn't have thrown that."

She bent down and picked up the book from the grass and dusted it off, mumbling an apology to the inanimate object.

When she rose back up, she was nose to nose with an amused Uriah.

I bookmarked my place and closed my own book. I now had different, but equally entertaining, content to consume.

Snow reared back, wrinkling her nose. "First, ever heard of a thing called personal space? Second, you're all—smelly and sweaty."

Uriah stuck his hands in his pockets. His honey blond hair was tucked behind his ears, his rugged features radiating confidence and delight. Like the others, he wore all black. The tips of his razor-sharp tattoos brushed the base of his neck and hands.

He grinned, and in a flash of movement he'd ripped the book from Snow's palms and held it up.

She squealed and leaped for it, but he was tall enough to keep it out of her reach and block her as he scanned the pages.

"Just as I suspected," Uriah said, shaking his head and making a low whistle. He returned the book right as Snow conjured glowing lunar magick in her palms.

She snatched it away. "You still don't know how to read?"

He chuckled, pouting his lower lip. "Big strong man only know how to kill. No good with words."

Snow smirked. "I love hearing your inner monologue spoken aloud."

I crunched too loudly on my palm full of almonds, and Uriah slowly dragged his eyes to me.

"Hello again, Trouble," he said with a wink. Then, his eyes widened. "That was a wink of friendship," he said quickly. "Don't tell Rune."

I laughed. "I didn't interpret it any other way. Hello again, Uriah."

We'd always had the best banter out of all the inner circle members Rune had forced to follow me when he couldn't. Unlike Mason, I'd always read that Uriah was kind of rooting for me. Though Mason had clearly changed her tune after everything that had happened.

"Bold of you two to be reading such naughty literature in broad daylight, in front of a legion of bloodthirsty monsters." He flashed his fangs, his eyes back on Snow.

Snow placed a hand on her hip. "Leave shame and secrecy out of it. It's just sex. We all have it." Snow raised a hand to her mouth. "Oh, sorry, Uriah. *Some of us* have it."

He clutched his chest and stumbled backward. "Ouch, Blondie." His rakish grin was soon to return. "Ready for another session?"

I raised a brow at Snow.

"He means hand-to-hand combat. Self-defense," she said as she shook her head. She focused back on Uriah. "I'm hanging with Scar, as you can clearly see." Then, she lowered the sass, shifting on her feet. "Later tonight?"

Uriah's smile remained unchanged. "Can't wait. Need at least one form of release, right? Call it my version of sexy novels."

Snow chuckled dryly. "As if you all don't already get plenty of barbaric *release* these days..."

I interjected. "Can I join?" Then, I realized maybe they'd want to be alone. The mutual desire between them was so ripe that one nudge from me might induce public sex. Not that I'd ever interfere. "Or, actually, could I just snag a session of my own sometime?"

Snow and Uriah both slowly turned toward me. I stood to join them.

"I think it would be easier to focus on learning with you than with Rune," I explained. "And I need to understand the basics."

"Right, well, that's some sound logic, Trouble," Uriah said. "But you know I'm going to need Rune's stamp of approval on such endeavors."

Snow huffed. "Scarlett is her own person. You vampires and your—"

"Blondie," Uriah said. "We've been over it."

Snow, surprisingly, relented. Something unspoken traveled between the two of them, and it seemed—intimate, in a way that had nothing to do with sex.

She nodded, staring into Uriah's eyes with considerably less fire than before. We all three startled when a fourth person approached from behind nearby shrubs, following along the stone path until she reached our enclave. Our guards eyed her, but they weren't concerned.

The woman was short and curvy, with long black hair that was messy and littered with pieces of dead leaves and small twigs. She ran her fingers through her hair as if that would solve the problem, scrunching her button nose and shrugging when she realized it was futile.

"Imogene," Snow said with small wave.

I could sense shifter magick radiating from her. She looked between the three of us, but her eyes decisively landed on me.

My first instinct was to tense, to wonder what I'd done to earn this woman's derision. But Imogene was quick to break out into a cheerful smile, nearly skipping the rest of the way to join our little huddle.

"Hi, Scarlett," she said, perky and warm. "Pleasure to meet you."

Sexual energy radiated from her aura in waves. I had the succubus intuition that she must've been rolling around in the grass with someone back in the woods that separated the castle from the rest of Nyx.

She glanced back at the chair I'd been sitting in, pointing to the book I'd left behind. "A classic." She giggled. "Mistress says she knew the human woman who wrote it."

Mistress. The word triggered unconscious visions of my time in the palace, forced to entertain Kole, to let Brennan feed from me—to let them all touch me, humiliate me.

I shuddered. Everyone's eyes moved to me. I flushed with embarrassment. "I'm sorry," I mumbled, quickly changing the subject and rooting myself back in my present reality. "It's nice to meet you too, Imogene." I opened my mouth to talk to her more about the book, but I was interrupted by another form approaching from the direction of the castle.

Uriah glanced over his shoulder and nervously chuckled.

"Kitten," Rune's mentor said, lifting a single, perfect dark brow as her green eyes homed in on Imogene.

Imogene smiled sheepishly. She fell to her knees as the infamous witch approached. She bowed her head.

Something sick and slimy crawled around my stomach when Sadie greeted her sub with a delicate stroke of her hair. I had to make a conscious effort to fight my traumatized, subconscious brain—to remind it that this was consensual, and the shifter was not actually a slave.

Sadie's gaze slowly met mine. She was gorgeous. Her brunette hair was shiny and meticulously styled, her lips painted red, the same color as her stylish leather jacket that brushed her calves.

"My apologies for the intrusion," she said. "Kitten is always looking for new friends. She just can't help herself, can she?"

Her eyes fell back to Imogene, gesturing for her to rise. Sadie placed a long red nail under her chin and shook her head in gentle chastisement as Imogene giggled.

"Very bad girl," she said, though her tone was lighthearted.

It made me relax—to see that underneath Sadie's scary domme façade, she had nothing but love and care for the bubbly shifter woman. I could see it reflected in Imogene's desires and body language.

"Hello, Scarlett," Sadie said. She extended a hand, and I shook it. Her grip was firm, and she was quick to release me. "I didn't intend to introduce myself today. I'm sure I'll receive an earful about it later."

Was she being truthful? It wasn't like Imogene was really causing us trouble. I couldn't discern, because Sadie's desires were hidden just as they'd been at the meeting.

"I'd prefer not to be treated like a glass object on a shelf," I said.

Uriah cleared his throat. "I'm going to head back. See you ladies later."

Sadie grinned at him. "Off to send Rune a warning flare?"

Uriah didn't say anything, only laughed nervously and jogged back toward the training field.

Snow stepped closer to me, and I could read trepidation in her features. Sadie glanced at her, offering a polite smile that didn't quite reach her eyes.

"Would you like to take a walk, Scarlett?" Sadie asked. "*No* is a perfectly acceptable answer."

Rune, Snow, and Uriah clearly thought a walk with Sadie

was a bad idea. But if I were being honest, that only made me want to do it more. If not for sheer curiosity's sake, then certainly out of irritation with everyone treating me like I was fragile no matter how many times I told them to treat me the same as before.

I nodded. "Okay. Let's walk."

40

SCARLETT

"I'll be back soon," I said to Snow as Sadie murmured something to Imogene. Snow sighed, but she didn't fight me.

Sadie and I traveled down the garden path, heading toward the thin patch of woods and away from the castle. I knew it was cold out, but it was hard to feel the biting air on my skin. My body and I were no longer fully connected. Our lines had been compromised.

"What's up with the weird energy between you and Snow?" I asked bluntly, because what did I have to lose?

Sadie laughed. "My fellow witches have always been wary of me, worrying that I'm dabbling with forces beyond my control. They think that I perhaps have too much of the wrong kind of power at my disposal."

"Do you?"

"Matter of opinion."

Snow didn't even know that Sadie had created the entire race of turned vampires. I couldn't imagine that would help her wariness.

I glanced at Sadie. "You showed Rune that our love was real,"

I said. "Why? Aren't you worried about how that will affect your own interests? Wouldn't it have been easier to let him believe otherwise, to be fueled by hatred instead?"

Sadie peered over at me, an amused smile on her red lips. A harsh wind whipped her dark hair back. "I value the truth, Scarlett. And I also value my relationship with Rune." She sighed. "Being fueled by hatred is not as effective as you'd imagine. Far better to be fueled by love."

This answer took me by surprise, and yet, I wasn't sure what else I expected from a darkly powerful witch whom Rune admired.

"Don't misunderstand. Love for justice can necessitate brutality. Love for a better future can necessitate war. Love for mortal life can require the harshest acts of vengeance and retribution. The dichotomy between love and violence can send the weak minded into a state of panic. But this is the fundamental difference between the turned and the born. Our side values power gleaned from love, and their side values power for power's sake. A nasty business indeed."

I remembered Rune explaining why he'd gone back to Crescent Haven all those years. To remember his *why*. He was a protector of mortals, forced to posture as a ruthless clan leader in order to remain effective.

It was not dissimilar to the way dominants played their strict, sadistic roles with their submissives, both parties understanding innately that underneath the game lay only respect and care.

"Also, I knew that if Rune fell for a woman after centuries of keeping everyone at arm's length, I would come to value my relationship with her as well," she said. "I do not wish to treat you like a glass object on a shelf, my dear."

Her smile was hovering dangerously close to flirtatious.

"Good," I said. "I get it. I was only just rescued. Everyone expects me to be crying in bed all day or something. But I don't *want* to be that weak, useless version of myself. I refuse to be. I want to be of service to something bigger than myself."

The playful flirtation melted, and Sadie stopped walking, turning to face me. The approval in the planes of her face eased something tight inside of me, unraveling the ball of tension in my chest until I could inhale deeply again.

"I have a feeling you've received your own fair share of derision for your dark and powerful forces, no?"

My skin was suddenly too warm under my layers. I frowned, thinking of Isabella and the women in my village who'd bullied me relentlessly. One of my worst bullies, Emeline, had spent years mimicking how I spoke and how I dressed, copying my every move, all the while launching cruel campaigns against me in the name of Helia. At one point, her behavior had become so delusional and psychotic that I feared she was going to try to wear my skin as a suit.

Women's obsession was sometimes worse than the men's—more vicious and long-lasting. No matter how much I tried to keep my head down to give them less to work with, they couldn't let it go so long as I still breathed. Jaxon had been my only protection, my only relief. It was heartbreaking how long I'd been dimming myself as a form of protection.

"You could say that." I laughed in a dark sort of way.

"Jealousy is the most destructive force in the world," Sadie said. "It's a poison that erases our ability to discern reality, to understand truth. It allows others to control our moods, dictate our actions and our desires. True power is gleaned from within. And that is why Durian and his men make stupid moves. Their envy and spite will spell their downfall."

I considered her a moment. I wanted to confirm her suspicions with my own intel about Durian, Brennan, and Kole. I yearned to hear her perspective, to measure her wisdom and knowledge against my own. But I also hesitated. I knew Sadie was too ancient and powerful to trust on intuition alone.

I remained silent for now.

"You're so young, Scarlett. To be as mature and strong as you are, after enduring ordeals that would've ruined most beings, is a testament to your endless potential. Not as a weapon. But as a powerful, dangerous woman."

The wind picked up. Crows squawked in the distance. Sadie took one step toward me in her shiny black heels. A twig snapped underneath her right foot.

Her words reached somewhere deep, to a part of me that had been yearning desperately for attention and validation. It was the part of me that wanted to make my life—this magick, this anger, this injustice and trauma—to *make it all mean something.*

"I can help you release what has been holding you back," she said. "The nasty jealousy of weaker women, the bitterness of mediocre men, the fear of taking up space and calling attention to yourself. These things no longer serve you, and it is time to let them go."

I thought of those dead humans. I thought of Rosalind.

Then I lifted my chin and stared into Sadie's sharp green eyes. I imagined the freedom her words promised.

"I can help you come to terms with who you are and the path that has brought you here. I can make you stronger. I can prepare you for battle, in whatever form it takes." She took a small step back. "But *only* by your will and direction. This is your destiny. No one else's. Not even darling Rune's."

"What if Rune forbids it?" I asked.

Sadie smiled, all calm certainty and authority. "He won't."

∼

RUNE FOUND me in a nook in his private library, adjacent to his locked study. It was filled top to bottom with books, a sliding wooden ladder to reach the higher shelves. The ceiling was a depiction of the gods who resided in the heavens, Helia and Selena included.

I'd scooted a cushioned, circular white chair over to the farthest corner, next to a window with the curtains drawn. I felt safest protected by bookshelves and walls in a position to see the entire room. Escaping into a book had helped more than I'd ever thought it would. It was like leaving my body in a healthy way, allowing my mind to wander somewhere else without the stress of dissociation. I understood now why Rune had fled into books his entire childhood.

I wondered at what age he'd read the kinky classic I now held?

When he entered, I jumped, my heart hammering.

Even if it didn't make any sense—given I'd found it in his own library, and Rune and I had done far more than see each other naked—I quickly closed the book and wedged it in between the blanket and pillow beside me.

Rune's dark eyes landed on me, and when he came into full view, my heart stuttered for an entirely different reason than a trauma response.

It appeared as though he'd tried to clean up his appearance, but he had missed a few flecks of blood on his neck and face. Those thorny vines were thrumming with power, the faintest tinge of darkness leaking from his skin underneath his black clothes.

He'd clearly just arrived back from killing or torturing enemies. And that knowledge only compounded the heat in my core.

I stood up, glancing behind me to make sure the book was out of view.

Rune lifted a brow. "Did you seriously just hide *The Taming of Marianne?*"

My face heated. "Um, no…" I lied.

There'd been a hint of anger in his eyes when he'd first

found me, but it melted into amusement the longer I consumed him with my gaze.

"Sorry, I should've showered and changed before I checked in on you."

"No," I blurted, and his eyes flashed. "The blood is hot."

Rune smirked and shook his head. He opened his mouth to speak, then stiffened when I approached him. I stared up at him. Lifting my hand, I traced the brutally beautiful planes of his face. My gaze devoured the evidence of violence splattered on his dark clothes, his flawless skin marked by shadow. His sleeves were rolled up, revealing his toned arms.

"Enjoying your read?" His voice was strained all of a sudden.

I nodded. "Uh-huh." His scent was intoxicating—masculine and woodsy, undercut with the smell of winter and pine, fire, and musk. I inhaled deeply, remembering what he looked like underneath his clothes.

"Gods, Scarlett," he hissed. "Please tone it down."

"Tone what down?" I asked while running a finger along the pulsing vein of his forearm.

He glared at me. "Your arousal that is growing stronger by the second."

I watched him try and fail to hold his breath. I hadn't been this aroused since... Rune had claimed me. I might've felt the slick familiarity of shame if I wasn't so consumed by my own lust, dormant for too long. I welcomed the sensation. It was a win—to know I could still experience real desire that belonged only to me.

"Why should I?" I asked softly, reaching to touch his face again.

He grabbed my wrist, lightning fast. His shadows slithered toward me, moving from smoke to solid limbs as they tucked in their thorns and wrapped around my ankles, rooting me to the ground.

"Because you're driving me fucking insane," he growled. "I

can't feed enough to rid myself of the desire for your blood. The least you can do is read some nice, wholesome literature and stop undressing me with your eyes."

The humor he'd tried to lace into his words was rendered less effective with the obvious swell of his cock in his black pants. His shadows only continued to crawl up my body and tighten. His eyes darkened, his body rigid as stone as the room flooded with power.

"You fed from someone else?"

"I had to," he said. "I don't even know whose blood it was, only that it was a male volunteer. It was in a chalice and unceremoniously choked down for fuel."

"I want you," I said.

Rune groaned, his eyes closing as he massaged the bridge of his nose.

I reached for him with my free hand. I traced his jaw before moving my fingers to the back of his head, running them through his soft strands of dark hair. I couldn't move my legs to stand on my toes, so I gently pulled him to meet me instead.

Rune's eyes flew open, understanding what I wanted. He stared into my eyes first, assessing. "Are you sure?"

I nodded.

He studied my lips, then cursed.

He bent, and the moment his lips met mine, the entire world melted into the sweetest darkness.

41

SCARLETT

At first Rune was gentle, teasing, as if getting reacquainted with my lips. Then he sighed into my mouth, holding my face in his palms as he consumed me. His tongue brushed along my lower lip, where I'd been chewing as I read about Edgar dominating Marianne.

My body was flushed with pleasurable tingles, and I was frustrated with my inability to move, to tangle my limbs with Rune's or tackle him to the floor.

For a frightening moment, I was back on Durian's demented altar—screaming and fighting against the magick that held me down as he carved into my flesh with a sharp blade.

Stop. *Stop.*

Rune pulled back immediately. He scanned my eyes. His shadows began to recede.

"Why?" I rasped, trying to catch my breath.

"Little Flame," he said softly. "You stopped kissing me back. I felt the change in your body."

"It was only for a second," I said, frustration in my voice. "I'm fine. It was just a memory, but I pushed it down. I'm still in my body, and I still want you."

Rune moved closer to me, his shadows gone, but his hands still holding my face. "Baby, I will not hurt you. Not like that."

I took a step away, out of his grasp, as his hands fell slowly back down to his sides. "So because evil people did evil things to me, I can never again have sex or experience pleasure and desire? How is that fair? Am I to become a Helianic nun so I never get hurt again?"

That would be a pretty funny life choice for a succubus, but I didn't currently have the capacity to appreciate its comedic value. Angry tears burned my eyes.

"Of course not," Rune said, pain in his dark irises. "It's only been a couple days. It's all still fresh and unprocessed. I'm not here to cater to your every fleeting desire, Scarlett. I'm here to take care of you and put your well-being above all else, even and *especially* when you can't do that for yourself."

"Kind of patronizing to think you know what I need better than I do," I snapped.

Rune shrugged, an infuriating immovability in his features. "Call it whatever you want. But I know when you're no longer present and capable of giving consent, and I think it's fairly bloody reasonable to exercise the most extreme level of caution right now. And it's more than that. I need you to understand that *pushing it down* is an unsustainable way to cope with trauma."

The anger was back in his eyes, and he raked a hand through his hair. "I spoke to Uriah and Sadie."

I glared at the floor. That was why he'd been irritated when he'd first found me.

"Talk to me, Little Flame. Tell me what you're thinking," he said.

I looked back up. "Why should I? You're only going to shut me down."

Rune sighed, his face softening. He reached for my hand, kissing my knuckles before guiding me to sit with him on the nearby loveseat. He was comically large on the dainty piece of furniture. I nervously picked at a nail, pulling my thoughts together through the haze of anger, lust, and confusion.

"I wasn't merely a passive, broken victim in that place," I started. "Sometimes I was. Sometimes I was even worse—sometimes I tried to help the other slaves, and I failed." I took a deep inhale, refusing to look at him. "I got two humans killed."

"How?" Rune pulled my legs into his lap, taking my hand and rubbing his thumb soothingly over the top.

It didn't feel like I deserved this tenderness, but I let it soothe me, anyway. I forced myself to meet Rune's soft eyes, teeming with understanding and care.

"I pulled as much attention as I could off them and onto me. They had no defenses, no magick. And I—well, Durian had forbidden anyone from touching me sexually or killing me. I had protections that no one else had, and they hated me for it, and I hated myself. I wanted to take as much of the abuse as possible, to give them a reprieve."

Rune stared at me. His jaw flexed, his body tightly wound. I could tell he was trying extremely hard not to show his wrath that threatened to explode from his every pore.

"They put me on a cross and made the other slaves hurt me," I said, my voice breaking. "I only created a frenzy. Guards threw humans at vampires in bloodlust to distract them from me and my addictive blood," I spat out the words, disgusted with my selfishness and callousness. "Then you showed up, and you told me what I thought I deserved to hear—that I was dead to you, that I belonged with the born. You said I was ruined."

Rune's thumb stopped his gentle caress, his grip on my hand tightening. His tattoos shifted on his skin.

"Sometimes, even though I know it wasn't really you who said those words—I still worry that it's the truth. I worry that you look at my body and see all the places other men have touched. You see the weight I've lost and the way my time as a slave has changed me physically, and you're disgusted. And maybe that's partly why you won't touch me sexually."

As the words poured from me, it felt like a space had opened up that had once been closed and locked tight. I was uncomfortable and raw. I wanted to be back in a secluded corner, lost in a fantasy realm instead of facing this god of wrath who saw straight through me and into my soul.

"Scarlett, my soul," Rune said, his voice bleeding rocky emotion. "When I look at you, all I see are stars. I see the woman I was born to love. The fact that other men have touched you does not affect how I see you. It affects how I see *them*, and all the ways I plan on killing them slowly, painfully, and damn artistically."

He placed his hands on my legs, giving his head a little shake as he exhaled roughly. "My refusal to hurt you is because I love you. My attraction to you is as fucking insatiable and concerningly obsessed as it's always been."

When his eyes burned into mine, I couldn't do anything but believe him.

"Trauma has a nasty way of breeding shame. When we feel powerless against our abusers, it is easier to turn that loathing inward instead," he said. "I told you about my upbringing. Though I tried my hardest to distract my father from my sisters and mother by provoking him to attack me instead, sometimes I failed. Sometimes I wasn't there. I used to feel responsible for every time I couldn't stop him, or every time I made things worse. It took a very long time to forgive myself, to understand that I was a child too, and my father was the one who had failed as a man and a human being. That wound followed me into war. I experienced the same guilt for every vampire and mortal lost, each time I was unable to prevent a tragedy. If I didn't feel responsible, then who would? That was the question that weighed heavily on my heart."

I stared at his broad hands on my lower thighs, warm and

comforting, like he was holding space for me that I didn't know how to hold for myself. In showing me this parallel with his own life, he was making me feel less achingly alone for the first time since I'd been taken.

"And it still does. These patterns of thinking and feeling don't ever leave us. We carry them always," he said, drawing my eyes back to his. "But their weight doesn't have to be so heavy. They can go from overwhelming to fleeting, rigid to soft. I didn't push down my trauma to become the man I am today. I integrated it into my whole being. I talked about it with someone I trusted, and I allowed her to help me break free from the tyranny of the past. Punishing myself for what happened to my mother and sisters was a waste of energy. It didn't help them, and it didn't help me. I honored them by focusing on how I could aid others, and that started with first getting right with myself."

I slowly unwound my tightened muscles, and I did something much more difficult than fighting. I *stopped* fighting.

"I hear you," I said, and for the first time, I truly did. "But I still want to do more than just heal. Our time under this ceasefire isn't endless, and judging by the sexy blood splatters on your skin and clothes… *ceasefire* is also a misnomer. I want to help, and I believe that I have more of an ability to do so than anyone is giving me credit for."

Rune slowly nodded. "I hear you, too, Scarlett. And I want to gently push you to consider the idea that the deaths of those slaves are stains on born demons' souls, not yours. Their fates were tenuous no matter your involvement," Rune said. "You gave me an example of a time you failed. I also want to hear about the times you *won*. Because you're wrong. I do believe in your power to help. It's because I believe in you so vehemently that the prospect of sending you back into the line of fire terrifies me so damn much."

I felt a light return to my eyes, and as soon as Rune saw it, that light reflected back to me in his. Sadie had been right. Rune had never tried to clip my wings, no matter how much I anticipated it, prepared myself for it. Damn this man, but he really was as perfect as he carried himself to be.

He was downright terrified of losing me, but he was still willing to risk it. Because, to him, I was a woman, not a slave. I was not an object, no matter how aroused I became at the thought of him treating me like one.

"Uriah and I can train you. Sadie can mentor you. We will listen to your ideas and help you formulate a plan of action." He paused, pulling both my hands into his. "My only condition is that you see a healer, someone who isn't me or Sadie, whose only aim is to help you process the horrors you've endured. I cannot force you to feel better, Scarlett. It's something you have to choose for yourself. You don't have to be fully healed in order to fight. Nor do you have to be completely healed in order for me to touch you. But for your safety and the safety of my clan and all of Valentin, you cannot work with us until you are willing to begin the healing process."

I'd had it all wrong. I stared at Rune, searching his words for evidence that he was holding me back. But he wasn't. Not at all.

"If I had it my ego's way, I'd refuse to ever let you even consider making yourself vulnerable again." He grabbed my chin. "I'd chain you to my bed and never let you out of my fucking sight, and any man who breathed near you in a way I didn't like I would kill on the spot."

I giggled, and Rune's lips quirked up. His eyes softened at the sound.

"I will still do those last two things, on occasion," he said.

"Big of you to admit." I rolled my eyes, still toying with a smile.

"But I will not stand in the way of you forging your own destiny. I will not allow you to live with any regret."

I crawled into his lap, straddling him as I looped my arms

around his neck. "And that is why you're the only man who has ever held my heart in his palms, capable of crushing it with just one squeeze. That's why I love you so deeply it terrifies me. Our love is vast enough to get lost in. The oceans and the cosmos can't even compare."

"Mm," Rune uttered, long and drawn out. "Look at you and your beautiful sentences, baby. I must truly be a god to have captured a powerful succubus under my spell. To have turned her into such a soft, docile little creature just begging for my love."

I pulled back, but he held me in place with his hands gripping my hips.

"I'm the one who has ruined you, Little Flame. It's a good thing you're mine, in this life and all the next."

My eyes narrowed, and Rune's self-satisfied smirk only widened under my glower. I melted, laughing at his ability to burrow this deeply under my skin. It was only fair, as I'd clearly carved a place for myself under his.

"Okay. I'll tell you about the times that I won," I said, harkening back to earlier in the conversation. "*When* we're ready to talk about a game plan." I slowly trailed a circle on his chest, finding the strength I needed for my next words in Rune's rigid muscles. "Is Belise on staff today?"

Rune melted, pulling me down to kiss my forehead. He exhaled slowly, as if in unspeakable relief.

"Yes, baby. He's ready for you whenever you are."

42

RUNE

I sat on my personal patio, overlooking the city in solitude as I reflected on the past week.

Over the past six days, Scarlett had slept long hours, had slowly begun to eat normal quantities again, and had seen Belise for two sessions a day, morning and night. I never pried, but from what Scarlett had freely revealed, I knew that he was offering her a blend of talk therapy and somatic healing witchery. His methods aimed to allow Scarlett the opportunity to reconnect with her body and release the trauma stored within it. Sometimes, she seemed better after a session, more herself. Other times, she was quiet and tired, or emotionally volatile. Sometimes she wanted to be alone, and other times I held her as she cried in my arms.

While Scarlett worked with Belise, I worked with Sadie. It had been a long time coming, but I knew that in order to be the man Scarlett needed me to be, I had to heed my own wisdom.

Because while I was careful to hide my horror from Scarlett when she revealed more about her time with Durian, the truth was that each reveal was killing me inside. Even the things she let slip in passing, like they were no big deal, made me want to grind my teeth so hard they fissured.

I hated myself for all of it. I *blamed* myself for all of it. It was that core wound all over again, the one that led all the way back to the day I found my sisters' dead bodies in Crescent Haven's forest in early autumn. And even further back, when I first remembered my father striking my mother.

I'd seen what Evangeline had in her basement—those sacrificial altars for ritualistically feeding from slaves. I'd also seen what Durian had done to Scarlett's body with a blade. His name had been carved on her stomach not only at the meeting but also when she'd been rescued, and it had been fresh. I had the sick intuition that he healed the wounds of his brutalization only to perform the acts all over again, like the demented, sociopathic freak that he was.

I wanted to rage, to unleash the feral noise building in the back of my throat. I wanted to shake the castle's foundation with my wrath. But I couldn't do that to Scarlett. I couldn't frighten her like Durian's nightmare vision of me had already terrorized her for an entire month.

It was all so vile, and yet Scarlett couldn't always see it. She kept repeating how much worse it had been for others, and how it could've been far worse for her. She was champing at the bit to step into her power, to fight for Valentin in whatever way she could.

And I equally adored her for it and was selfishly infuriated with her because of it. The mere thought of her being harmed again, by anyone or anything, tested every ounce of my self-control.

Sadie was helping me work through these weaknesses, and I tried not to be furious with her, too, knowing full well she'd encouraged Scarlett to forge ahead on this path. None of us could afford to let our emotional baggage rule our minds and our actions. Not with Durian only continuing to try to manipulate King Earle and his council while they deliberated, or with Kole still fucking around inside the palace doing Lillian knew what. Or with the born continuing to gather at the border, building defenses and carrying out supposedly rogue suicide missions in border districts.

Every move needed to count.

I forced myself to practice gratitude, one of Sadie's suggestions that I followed despite my reluctance. Because for whatever reason, I respected the ancient witch and her occasional bout of nonsense woo-woo therapy.

I thought about the way color had returned to Scarlett's cheeks, the darkness under her eyes receding. I thought about how she was eating more, and she'd had two nights in a row without nightmares. I thanked the gods for her willingness to feel better, to listen to her healer and accept help.

Above all, I expressed my endless gratitude that she was back with me for as long as fate allowed. My Scarlett was safe. She slept beside me, just as I'd always dreamed and hoped, even more desperately after she'd been stolen. And that was enough. It was more than enough.

"Rune."

I turned to see Uriah step onto the patio. "Sorry to disturb you while you indulge in your nightly ponderings," he said. His humor fell flat, his features tight. "Durian has sent another letter."

"About the impending war? Negotiations? Lillian's divine will? To ask me about my day? Literally *anything* other than what I think you're about to say?" I asked bitterly, already shaking with fury.

"Sorry to disappoint," Uriah said, scratching his head. "He's still rattling on and on about Scarlett. Paragraphs upon paragraphs. Very wordy, lots of purple prose. He'd benefit greatly from a good editor."

I laughed dryly, rubbing my mouth and rising to my feet to

face him. "I can't say I blame him. I might've done the same if I lacked self-control, half a brain, and a modicum of sanity."

"Your writing would've been far easier on the eyes," Uriah added, crossing his arms. His smile faded. "He says he's going to commit an atrocity for every day that she's gone. Sacrifices for Lillian, other fucked-in-the-head language that doesn't need repeating."

"He wants her to know," I said. "He wants to hurt her. To give her even more incentive to fight me and find her way back to him."

"Are you going to tell her?"

I listened to the sound of late-night comradery out in the training field. I picked up on the sound of a woman's laughter carried in the frigid breeze.

"No. It wouldn't help her to know. It would only harm her."

Uriah nodded. "I think you're right about that." He gazed out over the city, familiar anger crossing his features that let me know he was thinking deeply. "Rune, he... he might want to punish her for being here, but he still legitimately believes she was taken against her will and wants to be with him. He believes she was given to him by Lillian. He's fetishized her blood. And her, um, pain. He sees them as these sources of holy power."

I ground my teeth, my every muscle straining and flexing.

"And I don't say this to hurt you, as I don't think a lot of it is worth reading for your own sake. I say it to point out that, yes, we may have underestimated Durian's powers of persuasion and intelligence, but I don't think we were wrong that there's a fundamental screw loose. And I think Scarlett was working on that screw, deepening that vulnerability. He doesn't sound sane. He doesn't sound like someone who knows for certain his holy book is fabricated and his religion is a mere political ploy. My read is that he believes his own delusions, or at least some of them."

I used Sadie's techniques to ground myself, to steady my

breathing. I thought about what Uriah was actually saying instead of getting lost in the swell of my emotions.

"Kole isn't stupid," I said. "He doesn't despise us for idealistic reasons. He's not truly buying into the religious nonsense, and if it's interfering with Durian's ability to lead, that will become intolerable to someone like Kole. Entertaining psychotic children isn't like him. There's something there that we're missing."

Uriah looked down at his feet, squinting before slowly raising his gaze. He shifted nervously. "Scarlett was close to him, no? You think she might understand Kole's current state of mind? Or… could find out?"

I wanted to cut off Kole's pathetic excuse for a cock for merely thinking about Scarlett, but I feared he might enjoy that too much.

"No one can get to her through a letter," Uriah said.

A half-truth. "She's getting better. But it's only been a week."

Fuck, I just wanted to protect her from it all. I always had. My only solace now was that her succubus nature made her immortal like me. It was a truth we hadn't even begun to unpack, and I wondered how much Scarlett had gotten a chance to consider her new reality. At least now I knew that war would not ruin her life. She would still be here, by my side, when this unchanging world moved into its next season of stability.

"I want her to have more time to grow stronger. Nothing has changed. We'll loop her in soon."

Uriah tilted his head. "Reasonable and understandable. I'm glad she's back." He grinned. "Because that means we have you back, too."

43

SCARLETT

It had been two weeks since I'd started healing.

When Belise massaged my hips, I started to cry. "Checking in—still okay? Need to stop or break?"

I shook my head. We were in his private healing room, the air smelling of lavender and mint, the energy calming and safe. Warm morning light trickled through the rainbow-colored curtains. I lay on his massage table, where we did a mix of energy work and massage therapy.

His touch was caring, non-threatening. His desire was to heal and nothing more. I used to compulsively check his desires every few minutes, preparing myself to flee each time. But now, the impulse was curbed by my trust in him and his intentions. He'd been incredibly patient, moving at my pace and letting me enforce my own boundaries.

When he pressed into my hip muscles, I winced with discomfort. "What guilt are you holding on to here?" he asked.

My tight bundle of nerves and muscle fibers strained against Belise's call to loosen, to let go.

"I still haven't seen Isabella," I said, the first thing to come to mind.

I was learning how to let my unfiltered thoughts pour out. It was the only way to access the parts of myself and my past I'd shoved down for so long. In this room, I allowed those dark corners to see the light, inch by inch.

"She was my entire purpose for coming to Aristelle," I continued. "No matter what she did to me, what she allowed men to do to me... I was still the reason she was kidnapped and harmed. And now, she's free, just like I'd vowed. She's staying nearby and I don't even want to see her, and I feel crushingly guilty about it."

Belise nodded. He was in a loose and flowy purple gown embroidered with golden flowers.

"It's not selfish to take care of yourself, Scarlett. Do you think Isabella would receive you with love?"

"No," I choked out, a tear sliding down my cheek.

"Do you think she would express gratitude for your sacrifices on her behalf? Before *and* after she was taken?"

I shook my head and closed my eyes, releasing my old beliefs and opening myself up to the truth. It was getting easier and easier every day.

This time when he worked my muscles, they untightened.

I hadn't even realized how restricted and stiff I'd been before our sessions. I knew my mind had been damaged, but I hadn't fully understood how it had been impacting my body until now.

And I cursed Rune. Because he was right. I *did* feel better. I got better every day. Even if some days, it didn't seem like it. Belise taught me that releasing trauma wasn't always pretty. Sometimes it came out as violently as it went in.

I kept going. I kept doing the hardest work of my life for many reasons. Rune's praise, Snow's pride, the promise of doing something to help other trauma survivors.

But also, for *myself*. It turned out that no matter how much shame I carried—all the beliefs I'd been taught about taking up too much space, being selfish, unworthy of love, and an evil succubus who had to earn everyone's approval at all times... I'd never lived solely for *me*. I'd been conditioned to live for Isabella for so long that when Rune showed me how to act on my own behalf, it terrified me. I thought it made me a bad person to choose myself over anyone else.

Now, I was beginning to understand that I was of no use to anyone if I behaved out of guilt rather than love.

Belise moved into energy work, letting me stand as he burned a bundle of herbs and made circular motions around my energy centers.

When he got to my heart, I spoke, and it came from a deep place in my mind—untethered and unfiltered. "Do you think it affects someone, forever? To have their first introduction into this world be their parents disposing of them?"

I wondered what my birth parents were like. Was it my mother who was human? Something told me it was. Or at least that whichever parent was human was the one who left me in Crescent Haven. Were they running from something? From my born vampire side? Nothing in Isabella's diary had indicated anyone knew anything about who'd left me and why.

Belise stopped, his eyes warm. He shook his head lightly. "Sometimes we're given family, and other times we choose it. Neither is better nor worse than the other if both meet us with love and nourishment." He guided me to take a deep breath with him. "Has your upbringing affected you? Of course. We're affected by our early lives forever. But we can change the story, change ourselves. Nothing is ever stuck. We need only acknowledge each root before altering the trees in our mental forest. We have the power to break patterns and start new growth. For ourselves, and for everyone around us."

He moved to my throat, changing his movements now as he concentrated. Something shifted inside of me, and I allowed it. I heard music float up from my memories, and instead of grief, I felt hope.

When we finished, I was light and unencumbered. I saw movement where there had once been stagnation. I heard melody where there had once been silence.

I'd been worried that in letting go of the past, I'd be letting go of who I was.

But that wasn't true. I was more myself than I'd ever been before, and shockingly, I actually *liked* the woman I was becoming. I was rooting for her.

∼

I'D SPENT the afternoon with Snow, Penn, Eli, Winnifred, and Tera. Out of fear, I'd been avoiding them since I'd been rescued. But I knew it was time to let go and trust instead. It turned out, everyone else liked who I was becoming too. I'd only cried a little when I'd melted in Penn's arms and felt her motherly warmth wash over me.

The rest of the day, I was able to acknowledge what had happened without sharing too many details or hiding from my friends' empathy. Then I got to enjoy their company like I used to, pretending we didn't have a dozen guards watching us from a distance at all times.

On the way back, Snow looked over at me and grinned. "When we were in the coffee shop, Eli turned to me and whispered that you'd changed. He said you were bolder, brighter. Succubus or not, he said you were powerful and compelling on your own merit. You were more *alive*."

"Was I still as funny as before? That's what I care about most."

"Your wit was sharper than ever," Snow said with a roll of her eyes.

I smiled at her. "Thanks, Snow. I'm glad I saw them, and that everyone's staying safe."

Snow frowned, and I sensed the unmistakable flare of desire

to say something important. But she didn't act on it, and I didn't force her to.

Back at the castle, I made my way up the grand staircase. When a voice stopped me, just before I entered Rune's chambers, I nearly jumped out of skin.

"Scarlett," Mason said, then mumbled, "Sorry."

I turned to face her. She cleared her throat, glancing around the empty hall.

"I wanted to give you space at first," she said. "But I believe it's time I make my amends."

Her deep brown skin was warm under the dim witch lights, her broad, muscular body as deadly and intimidating as ever. Nothing about her face indicated anything but ruthlessness and detachment save for the briefest flicker of discomfort in her dark irises.

"My highest priority, at any given moment, is to protect Rune and our clan," she said, her voice dry and devoid of emotion. "I do not deviate from my duty to Valentin and my loyalty to the turned, but I am not infallible. On the surface, it looked bad. Your proximity, your nature, your origins."

"I know," I offered with a small smile. "It looked like a disaster."

Mason's lips quirked up, relief in her features. "You were important to Rune, the man I respect above all others and always will. I should've done my due diligence. I should've given you a chance, an opportunity to tell your own story. If there's something I can do to make up for my part in your suffering, I hope you will let me know. I am at your service."

I exhaled. "Mason, I have no room in my heart for useless resentments. I forgive you. You can make it up to me by continuing to protect Rune. I don't blame you for being wary of me during times like these. But I do blame you for never giving me the opportunity to prove you wrong. Believe me when I say that I, too, respect Rune more than I've ever respected any man before him." I lowered my voice. "But don't tell him that. His god complex hasn't been nearly humbled enough by all of this."

Mason snorted, offering as close to a smile as I was ever going to get from her. Then, she stiffened.

The voice at my back sent a shiver down my spine.

"What was that, Little Flame?"

I slowly turned to face Rune. His smile was downright sinister as he leaned against the wall, watching me closely.

"Do repeat yourself."

The tone of his voice had the hairs on the back of my neck standing in high alert. Muscles low in my stomach tightened, and my cheeks flushed.

Mason couldn't have made a faster exit. I blinked, and she was gone.

Rune grabbed me like I weighed nothing, swinging open the door to his chambers, shutting it, and shoving me up against the other side in a quick burst of movement. He gently caressed my cheek as I panted, lust burning beneath my skin.

We'd been toeing closer and closer to an explosion the last couple days, but we'd both been too busy to find much time to be alone. And Rune refused to let me skip sleep right now.

His desire tasted better than any I'd ever consumed before. Now that I understood I was a succubus, it was easier to feel these beautiful threads connecting his soul to mine—the way he bled for me just as I did for him. His desire was rich and golden, starlight against the deepest darkness of space. I pulled it into my veins, dipped into it like steamy hot springs.

He pinned my arms up above my head with his shadows, searching my eyes until I gave him a small nod of approval. I no longer grew irritated by his consent check-ins. I let them melt into our play effortlessly, an extension of Rune's protective dominance that made me desperate for him as much as his wickedness.

"You think your God needs humbling, Scarlett darling?"

I stared up at him innocently, batting my eyelashes as my lips curved. He inhaled roughly, his lips skating over my earlobe as I shuddered. He kissed my jaw, then next to my mouth, finally landing on my lips where he tugged at the bottom one with his teeth. At the brush of his fangs, my core grew molten, screaming for his touch.

"I feel as though today's daily groveling should be performed by tongue," he whispered, his breath tickling my ear. "How's that sound, baby?"

"We'll see if it's to my satisfaction," I said. A bluff, seeing as I was fairly certain I might come undone on Rune's tongue the moment it slipped between my thighs. He might've been able to make me come right now with that dangerous, penetrating gaze alone.

"Oh, is that so?" He chuckled darkly. "How much longer do you think is fair that I allow you to brat off without consequence?"

"Forever," I giggled.

Rune drank the sound, his lips capturing mine as he made a low, guttural noise that had me surging heat in response.

"I think not, little demon."

At first, the pet name jolted me, and then I found myself smiling at its meaning. Rune knew exactly what I was and loved me for every dark piece.

His shadows released my wrists, and he effortlessly pulled off my oversized red sweaterdress and underwear. I had a momentary surge of panic as I stood nude before him. But the look in his eyes—unwavering devotion—paired with the lust hemorrhaging from his every pore, kept me grounded in reality.

He leaned in close, his gaze holding mine in an iron grip. "You. Are. Fucking. Perfect."

He scooped me into his arms. Our lips locked again as he carried me, and I couldn't get enough of him. I explored his mouth with the tentative stroke of my tongue, and Rune growled, his grip on me tightening.

When he lay me on a fur carpet, my eyes fluttered. This living room's ceiling took me surprise as it always did.

I stared at myself in that golden dress I wore to the opera, surrounded by the glimmering lights of Aristelle from above, bleeding into shadows, stars, and oceans. Everything I loved, and perhaps everything Rune loved, too, carefully painted on the ceiling in rich color.

I smiled, and Rune looked up to see what I saw.

He dragged his gaze back down. "Good girl, baby, keep those pretty blue eyes on the ceiling. I want you to see yourself through the eyes of a man eternally obsessed with you. I want you to ponder the depths of my captivation as I show it to you with my lips, my tongue, my teeth..." He kissed my neck, and I struggled to keep my eyes open as my nerves erupted with waves of tingling pleasure. "Only a man lost in devotion to you could've commissioned such a painting. Only a man who dreamed of you every night, thought of you every minute of every day, who checked the blood bond compulsively to know exactly where you were and how fast your vulnerable heart was beating—only he could've captured your beautiful soul in art."

I choked on emotion, seeing the way Rune's thorny shadows reached for me in the painting, just as they coiled around me now.

There was a time I feared Rune hated me. But worse were the moments I wondered if he still thought of me at all.

Meanwhile, he was protecting my friends. Finding me the best healers in Aristelle. He was commissioning art, redecorating the castle—I found new little touches every day—gathering my favorite foods, new clothes, books and music... and who knew what else I'd yet to uncover? He hadn't stopped loving me, and it wasn't merely a passive feeling. No, Rune was consumed by his love for me, and he showed it to me with a thousand different actions even more beautiful than a thousand of his beautiful words.

"I thought of you just as much," I whispered, his lips on my collarbone now. "I thought of you even when it only brought me pain. I couldn't stop. No one could carve out that love from my skin, not even you."

44

SCARLETT

Rune checked my eyes, and I smiled at him as my core ached. My lips quivered. When he licked away a stray tear, I squealed and laughed in surprise as I reached to shove him away. His shadows were quick to pin down my arms.

"I promise I have the utmost empathy for your pain, but gods above, you're beautiful when you cry," Rune said slyly, tonguing his fangs.

"You're demented," I said, repeating my exact words the first time he'd licked one of my tears in the music room.

He repeated back his original response. "Thank you, baby." He lifted a brow. "I wonder, Little Flame, is this your sneaky way of begging me to once again use my shadows for nefarious purposes?"

I wondered what shade of red my cheeks were right now. "No!" I bit my bottom lip. The nerves between my thighs pulsed.

"So bashful for a succubus. Are you playing games with me, baby?"

I shook my head, and suddenly two of his long fingers were pressed against my lips.

"Suck."

He pushed them past my lips, and I did as I was told. As they went deeper, I locked eyes with myself—the version of me painted on the ceiling. The version of me that Rune saw in his dreams.

I swirled my tongue against Rune's digits. He pushed too far, and I gagged. He made a low sound of approval.

"That's my perfect, good girl," he praised.

I fell into his praise the same way I fell into his desire. I kept waiting for my trauma responses to start firing, ruining everything before it began. But just as I'd always known, what had happened to me in the palace was *nothing* like what Rune and I did. Not even Rune at his most sadistic was anything like Durian. Not even close.

In fact, it was an act of delicious vengeance that I could enjoy Rune's lips brushing over the peak of my breast. The sweetest, purest spite warmed my stomach, knowing that none of the men who hurt me would ever have me like this.

Rune's slick fingers found their mark between my legs, and I writhed as his mouth closed over my nipple at the same time. He lightly sucked, and my eyes rolled back.

I felt a jolt of panic. "Sorry," I quickly said.

Rune paused. "Sorry for what, baby?"

"I looked away from the ceiling. I'm sorry."

My heart hammered, and Rune's palm skated across my chest, stopping over my racing pulse.

"Sweet girl, look wherever you wish," he said. "Let go. I'm here to catch you, not punish you."

Underneath his palm, my heart slowed. I remembered that Rune and I were playing a game. He was only pretending to be scary because I liked it. I glanced at the oceans and stars, the shadows that desperately reached, and I did as I was told.

I let go.

He resumed his worship of my body, pulling the other nipple

into his mouth. At the scrape of fangs, I made a throaty moan. His shadows held me down while his free hand skated over my skin soothingly. He pushed lower, his lips meeting my navel. His slick fingers worked my clit again, slowly ramping up their intensity as I bucked.

I allowed my eyes to shut, lost to sensation I hadn't felt in too long. All of me had been brought back to life, and I drowned in the high of our shared pleasure intertwining in threads of darkness and light.

A limb I couldn't account for brushed my lips. How many hands did Rune have?

"Oh."

Rune chuckled as a tip of shadow solidified and entered my mouth. It was slick and cool on my tongue. It tasted like... how Rune smelled. Fresh, woodsy, and crisp. It was divine.

The shadow slipped out and down my body, slick with my saliva. At the same time as the shadow teased my nipple, another one was at my lips again.

Rune's mouth closed over my clit, his fingers teasing my entrance. When they slipped inside me, and his tongue began to pulse, I melted into the fur beneath me. Boneless, thoughtless, my skin engulfed by fire.

Both of his damn shadows were teasing my nipples, and the act was beautifully degrading. I was flooded with so much rapture that I couldn't feel anything else. My every sensation was devoted to pleasure and desire, and I had the distinct thought that *this* was what I was made for.

I was made to be Rune's. My body was forged for him the same as my soul.

"Please," I somehow rasped. "Please may I come?"

One of the shadows teasing my nipples suddenly developed sharpness, as if the thorns had untucked. Their gentle scrape against my sensitive peak had a scream building.

The other shadow, still smooth and slick, crawled down my

body. Rune hadn't answered me, still feasting on me like a man starved. He slid his fingers out of me. I knew what was coming.

The words that left my mouth were entirely indecipherable as his shadow impaled me. Rune chuckled, the vibration of it sending shockwaves from between my legs outward. The limb curved and expanded inside of me, hitting a spot that finally knocked my scream loose. I was impossibly full, overloaded with a beautiful blend of discomfort and euphoria.

Rune lifted up an inch, and I opened an eye to meet his hooded gaze. My stomach tightened, my legs shaking.

His fingers circled lower at my second opening, and he grinned when my eyes widened in terror. I shook my head.

"One day, I'm going to claim this hole too, baby. I'm going to fill all of you. You will be nothing but *mine*. You will have no purpose but to take it all like a good girl and thank me for every inch."

To drive the point home, another shadow was skating up my neck, brushing over my lips before dissipating back into smoke. Rune's filthy words had me unraveling past the point of return. The waves of pleasure crested.

"*Come.*"

His tongue returned to its groveling, and I looked at the ceiling one last time before I exploded just like the brushstrokes of those luminescent nebulas. I wasn't sure if I was screaming again or pleading. I'd left my body in an entirely different way than ever before, and I wasn't sure how much time had passed by the time I returned.

Rune's pulsing ceased, and he kissed my sensitive bud. His shadow slowly withdrew from me, wrapping around my stomach possessively now instead.

"Was that satisfactory, Little Flame?"

I couldn't speak. Rune trailed a finger down the center of my chest. He grinned when he touched the nipple he'd tortured, and I squirmed.

"Oh, do you think I'm finished with you?" he asked, his voice deceptively sweet. "That's so cute."

He kissed my forehead. When I still had no words to give, he laughed and gracefully rose to his feet.

Head swimming and body weak, I pushed up to rest on my forearms and watch Rune pull off his clothes.

How was this man real? His body was sculpted into a weapon: tall, lean and with too many muscles to count. Whorls of shadow marked his fair skin, paired with those beautiful, deadly thorns.

"Don't bite that lip, baby. Or I'll be forced to bite it harder."

I released my bottom lip, still staring at his looming, intimidating form. When his cock sprung free, my eyes dropped to a new focal point. It was a truly terrifying appendage.

"Fuck, Scarlett," Rune groaned. He stared right back, his eyes scorching. "Do you even know what that does to me? To smell your blood surging with *fear* when you stare at my cock?"

"Um," I croaked. I cleared my throat. His cock pulsed, and I swallowed. "I suppose I can see what it does to you."

Rune stroked himself as he looked at me, and it made my core burn with heat all over again. It made me feel powerful, mentally and magickally—to see him just as insatiable as I was, unable to stop himself from acting on his lust as he stared at my body.

He pointed to the ground in front of him with his free hand. "Now, little demon."

When I smiled, his eyes narrowed. I made a show of crawling to him, arching my back, delighting in the way he groaned and gripped himself tighter. My mind flitted to crawling to Durian, but with my focus on Rune—with my focus on how fucking *good* this felt—the flashback melted away before it could take shape.

I knelt in front of Rune, staring up at him as I arranged my features into faux innocence.

"Does my obsession taste good, my wicked succubus?" he asked.

Just that one word—*my*—made all the difference.

I nodded. "More please."

Rune unleashed a low growl from deep in his throat. "If you get to feed from me, I think it's only fair that you return the favor."

I locked on his eyes, my body surging with a euphoric mix of terror, power, and desire.

Rune paused and pulled me to my feet. His grip on my chin was soft. "Check-in time. You do not actually owe me your blood. Do you still feel okay, and do you wish to proceed? We can go straight into aftercare, and I would still be the luckiest monster in the realm."

His dominant mask dropped, revealing the man who merely loved me. I tiptoed to briefly brush my lips against his. I checked in with my body and assessed my own needs, something Belise and I had worked on.

"I'm only scared in a good way," I whispered. "I want to keep going. Just—still no impact or blades for now."

He nodded. "Baby, I would never forget your limits," Rune said. "You're safe with me, always."

I wasn't sure I even understood what consent was before I'd met Rune. Even sexual experiences that weren't full-on assault no longer met the standards Rune and Belise had taught me. There had been far too many times I'd been pressured or coerced, where safety and limits hadn't even made it onto the checklist of prerequisites. Deeper than men's callousness, thoughtlessness, or straight-up negligence was my own ignorance about my desires and needs. I owed *myself* amends for all the ways I'd let myself down over the years. Yes, poor behavior was always the fault of the perpetrator. But never again would I willingly stay in situations that harmed me, sacrifice myself for another's pleasure, or ignore warning signs.

Because of Rune, Snow, and my healer, I understood more each day what I truly deserved—and the kind of treatment I would *never* tolerate again. Not that I would ever have to. Because I belonged to Rune, and he belonged to me, and there was no safer place for my body and soul.

"Feed from me," I said throatily, but underneath my words I said *I love you, and I trust you.*

Rune gripped my throat. "As if you have a fucking choice," he said, and I knew that he was also saying, *you always have a choice. You're safe with me, and I love you, too.*

I gasped as I struggled to breathe, and Rune's shadows bound my wrists together in the front. He let go of my neck and lifted me into his arms bridal style, his shadows binding my legs now too.

When he carried me to his bed, it was as though we were overriding the first time he had claimed me.

"You were never unclaimed," Rune whispered, reading my thoughts as he straddled me and shoved my bound wrists over my head.

He freed my legs, giving me plenty of wiggle room now that he'd heard how Durian had fed from me on the demented altar. One day, I wanted to be able to do everything with Rune, but I knew I had to be gentle with myself and accept that some things were off the table for now.

"You have always been mine, and you always will be." Rune kissed on either side of my mouth, and his hard cock pressed against my stomach. "And in return for an eternity of filling your tight little holes with shadow and cock, you're going to fill my veins with your blood—the blood I haven't gone a minute without thinking about since it first met my tongue." He glared down at me. "Isn't that right, baby?"

"Yes, Rune."

"Tell me, how have your first sessions with Uriah gone?"

I stammered, confused by this sudden shift in topic as my

thighs shifted closer together. A drip of moisture from Rune's tip met my stomach, and I licked my bottom lip.

"I—I'm getting stronger every day. On my way to becoming a vampire-killing machine."

Rune chuckled at this, glancing up at my bound wrists and then back down to my lips. "Don't think that after I ruin your pretty pink pussy, you're going to be allowed to skip tonight's session."

I swallowed, and Rune watched my throat bob.

"The new recruits haven't quite learned that their eyes are at risk the longer they stare at you," Rune murmured. "I think I'll send you to the sparring field with cum dripping out of your perfect cunt and my scent and fang marks covering every inch of your skin."

"Rune," I gasped, and his lips captured mine before I could utter another syllable. His tongue claimed my mouth, and his cock throbbed.

He teased my entrance with the tip now, and gods, if I thought I'd been filled before…

There was no way in Lillian's vast underworld that *thing* was fitting in my ass. Rune had better have been posturing earlier. Knowing him, I feared that was not the case.

I only had time to worry about the hole at hand as he began to stretch me. He raised up and covered my mouth.

"Scream into my hand, baby, you know how hard I get listening to your cries."

I didn't have much of a choice when Rune thrust violently, his groan swallowed up by my muffled scream.

"Good girl. I knew you still remembered how to follow directions," he said condescendingly, sadistically laughing as my eyes rolled back and I cried out against his palm.

I was impossibly full, and Rune was unrelenting, barely giving me a chance to acclimate. His desire was suffocating, as if a dam had broken irreversibly, and I lay victim to wave after wave of his pent-up aggression and lust.

He squeezed the sides of my throat, and I well and truly saw stars. The moment I thought I was reaching a limit, Rune let go and sunk his teeth into my sensitive neck.

I came. *Hard.*

Orgasming apparently made my addictive blood only that much more delicious. And that fact compounded my instinctive terror, which *also* made my blood tastier.

The way Rune's cock swelled as he violently drove into me, impossibly deep, gave further credence to these truths.

As soon as I wondered if I was in danger, Rune's venom entered my bloodstream. I sighed, my eyes fluttering.

And yet again, it was nothing like when Durian or Brennan had fed from me. Because I fucking *wanted* this. Waves of pleasure swept over me and grabbed ahold of my fading orgasm, bringing it back and extending it for what could've been hours.

Rune's fingers entered my mouth as if to pacify me, and I sucked on them to keep from screaming again. My voice was going to be gone tomorrow, guaranteed.

I was delirious by the time he'd clotted that bite and moved onto the next, leaving a trail across my neck and down to my breasts. His tongue flicked over a hardened nipple, sucking soothingly at first, letting me ride these melting, everlasting waves and giving me a brief reprieve from his cock.

Then he bit down, his fangs piercing the sensitive skin above my nipple. His fingers were back in my mouth, giving us both something to suck on.

I moaned against his fingers. I didn't know where I began and Rune ended, feeding off each other as my threads of magick wrapped around him and his shadows twisted around me. We were forever bound. I knew in my bones that not even the gods could rid us of each other.

45

RUNE

With Scarlett's blood coursing inside of me, and my desire fueling her frightening, dangerous succubus magick, we were bound together more inseparably than ever. We were making each other even more powerful, unstoppable.

Not even the gods could rip us apart. I would like to see them fucking try.

In any realm, in any world, I would track my Scarlett down by her scent and drag her back to me. Kicking and screaming if necessary, as that would only make my cock throb even more painfully than usual.

I was ravenous, no matter how much blood I stole from her flawless, milky skin. Seeing my fang imprints all over her was driving me even more wild. I couldn't get enough. Not of her essence, not of her cunt, not of her beautiful soul and her every last cry of pleasure and pain.

I was back between her legs, devouring her as she came a third time, her juices as sweet as her blood. As soon as her waves of pleasure began to ease, I sunk my teeth into her inner thigh, extending her orgasm as I satisfied my thirst.

If I'd been anyone else, I would've already killed her. That was how out of control she made me feel, how she made *everyone* feel. It was almost implausible that she'd survived being fed from by Durian and Brennan, though she'd told me she used her succubus magick on multiple occasions to make them both stop. Also, Durian seemed demented enough to not respond to desire as most men did, given his nauseating predilections.

A primal rage took over me, to know that other men knew how my Little Flame tasted and they still roamed the earth. It didn't matter that Brennan had only had her once. His head was going to roll. I didn't break promises when it came to my Scarlett.

I closed this fresh bite and moved eye-to-eye with my precious, devious, breathtakingly beautiful girl. I used that primal rage when I slipped inside her forcefully, feeling that pretty pussy clench around me. I groaned, overloaded with pleasure. I couldn't compare it to anything else in all my centuries. Scarlett still hardly felt real.

"Look at me while I mark you with my cum, baby," I said, my voice sweet even as I brutally used her.

Those heart-stopping blue eyes locked on mine. Her lips parted, and her features relaxed with rapture.

I'd stopped well before she'd lost a dangerous amount of blood, but I'd be sure to feed her half a replenishing potion to be safe.

"What do we say, Little Flame?"

It was ridiculous how adorable she looked right now, brows drawn tight as she scrambled to string a coherent thought together.

"Manners," I said softly, glowing with amusement and endless love.

She smiled dreamily. "Thank you, Rune."

I grabbed the headboard, impaling her as my balls tightened

and she moaned. I finished as I stared into my own soul through her eyes.

"Good girl," I praised, softly stroking her hair as I quickly assessed her body for any open wounds or other points of concern.

I'd been notably gentle with her despite the intensity, careful not to get into much pain play after she'd revealed more details about her traumatic experiences in the palace.

After receiving the most endearing affirmative noises in response to my check-in questions, I gave up on trying to get a full word out of her and pulled her against my chest. She wrapped around me like a vine, contentedly sighing and listening to the steady thrum of my heart—the heart that beat only for her.

I laughed softly as she clung to me and made another incomprehensible noise of pleasure.

"I'm going to assume that today's groveling was *more* than satisfactory," I murmured.

"Mm."

∼

I DIDN'T WANT to intimidate Scarlett, so I arranged for our first deliberation meeting to occur only with Sadie, Uriah, Mason, and me in attendance. I'd be able to delegate and inquire further with others in my inner circle after we discussed the basics.

We sat at one end of the deliberation table, and I enjoyed forcing Scarlett to sit at the head. Sadie and I flanked her. Uriah sat next to Sadie, and Mason sat with me.

I'd heard a lot over the past few weeks from her about her succubus web of influence. But I'd been steering her into treating her healing as her first priority. A full picture of Scarlett's master plan was taking shape just as she was starting to feel better in her own skin.

It was terrifying.

I was on the precipice of losing her all over again, and I couldn't do a thing about it without being like every man who'd ever hurt her.

I wanted Scarlett to soar. I wanted her to have it all. But I simultaneously wanted to tie her little wrists behind her back and keep her by my side or in my lap at all times. Where she couldn't be harmed.

As Scarlett spoke, I took comfort in my fang marks on her neck, briefly deluding myself into believing that they would protect her from what was to come.

"As I've already mentioned to each of you before, I believe that a civil war can be stopped before it begins," Scarlett said. "It's what's in the best interest of the born, the mortals, and us, and it's certainly in King Earle's too."

I enjoyed that Scarlett placed herself with the turned in her use of the word *us*. Another tiny comfort as my shadows threatened to reach for her and my every muscle clenched in anticipation.

"We have to show each party this reality and shake them out of Durian's illusions," Scarlett said.

She slowly grew more and more comfortable from her seat at the table head, her eyes lighting up with passion. She exuded power and conviction, and it was fucking sexy as much as it was frightening.

"Durian is punching above his own strength, and if his second in command knows it, then others surely do too. I'm going to tell you everything I know, and I'd appreciate if you filled in all the blanks just as I will try to fill in yours."

Those vicious, big blue eyes landed on each of us, and I could only grin and nod in response.

"Go on, baby," I drawled, if only to earn that ruthless glare. It went straight to my cock. Visions of bending her over this table after the meeting were becoming more likely by the minute.

"There are many places we could begin, but I'll start with our biggest threat, the kingdom. I think Kole is concerned about Durian's connection with King Earle," she said. "At first, I thought Kole wasn't giving you all a chance at the meeting because he was born and had no interest in siding with the turned. I can read desire."

She paused, hesitating despite that fact not being news to any of us. She'd been conditioned to hate what she was since before she had a name for it.

"So I could tell at the meeting that Kole wasn't interested in anything you all had to say. He didn't want to punish the born, and he was only triggered when Durian seemed to be disrespecting Earle and the kingdom. I'd made the wrong assumption. I may be able to read what people want, but I don't always know *why* people want things. Kole is looking out for himself most of all. But he's also looking out for King Earle. He's *concerned*. I don't know a lot about Ravenia other than that the kingdom is now at war with rebel forces…"

Scarlett looked around at all of us.

I stepped in. "King Earle has been alive for nearly one thousand years. He is obsessed with preserving his legacy, now more than ever. Not only have turned forces risen up against the nobility and King Earle's rule broadly, but several members of his own council had been plotting against him. Those dissenters are now in hiding, but their impact remains. He feels attacked from all angles and whispers from Ravenia say that those closest to him are concerned about his state of mind."

The wheels of that adorable little mind spun and spun.

"Just like what happened in Valentin, a long reign of immortals can breed a level of arrogance and apathy that must be checked," Uriah said, ever the bleeding heart. "The born in Ravenia saw what happened here and thought that it couldn't possibly happen to them, but they were wrong. They've royally pissed off the mortals who sustain them, and now they're paying the consequences."

"Kole is a true loyalist, no?" Scarlett asked. "He wouldn't have been a dissenter?"

Sadie nodded. "Correct. He's always sought to protect Earle and the monarchy. He's in love with customs and traditions, and he believes that there's no greater honor than to *serve*." Sadie smiled slyly.

Scarlett shifted uncomfortably, glancing at me. She was waiting for my anger, for my hurt, directed toward her for doing what she needed to survive. She'd never receive it.

"He called it island madness. That's what the born in Ravenia think of the born here. He even said that slavery was low-class behavior," Scarlett said. "It confused me, because I always thought that the born were the same everywhere."

"I think we've all learned valuable lessons recently about assumptions and treating entire groups of people as monoliths," Sadie said with a nod.

Mason and I tensed, exchanging a glance.

"Consider me sufficiently humbled," Mason offered, still throwing olive branches at mine and Scarlett's feet.

I would eventually tell her to knock it off, but for now, it was satisfying to watch her squirm and work double to earn back approval.

"It's true that the slave trade in Ravenia has been growing, but yes, it's not kingdom-condoned," I said. "Whether the nobility in each region partakes is another question, but slaves certainly aren't paraded out in the open in King Earle's court." When Scarlett's eyes flashed with pain, I quickly forged ahead. "It goes against traditional customs of seduction and mortal-vampire relations that have maintained relative peace for thousands of years. It's when those protections are eroded for the general populace that we end up with clans of turned vampires and rebelling mortals. The slave trade has been a means for born vampires on the bottom of the power and wealth hierarchy to climb higher. What was once a rarity has become widespread, and we fear that Durian's religion is spreading in tandem with trafficking, one reinforcing the other and vice versa."

Scarlett nodded. "That's what Durian wants. He doesn't only think of himself as destined to rule Valentin. That's just phase one. He believes he was destined to rule Ravenia, too. He admits it freely, around safe company. Now I'm seeing how poorly such an admission would reflect on the born to someone like Kole, and especially to King Earle..."

"Yes," I affirmed. "It would be devastating."

I memorized the way Scarlett looked right now, her blue eyes bright, her cheeks faintly pink, her shoulders straight and confident. She'd been dressing more and more in her preferred style, no longer hiding her body away completely. Today, her dress was black, perhaps to match my clan's attire. It was still conservative, with lightweight fabric that came to her wrists and low on her legs, a dainty bow at her collarbone. But it clung to her curves rather than hiding them away, and that was progress.

"I can work on Kole, especially with Sadie's help," Scarlett declared, and I fought the urge to clench my fists where they rested on the table. "Exposing Durian to him and Earle is a crucial component to the plan, not only as traitorous but also as unfit to rule even Valentin." Her brows furrowed when she looked at me. "What's Kole's vendetta against you?"

Her insight startled me, even though it shouldn't have at this point. "He was in the running to rule Valentin on behalf of Earle."

Scarlett's eyes widened. "Well, that's surprising."

Sadie snorted. "Couldn't agree more. Rat certainly wasn't born to rule."

Scarlett giggled, as she did every time Sadie called Kole *rat*. I grinned as I watched her, my smile fading the moment hers did.

"He blames you all for his lost opportunity to rule," she said, "because King Earle decided ordaining Rune and the turned as custodians of Valentin was the smarter move, rather than taking back the island under complete kingdom dominion."

Sadie nodded. "I was able to *convince* Kole to vouch for us at key moments, spinning the illusion that he was fighting for his own power by opposing Ivan and Haemon. He thought I supported his play for Valentin's lord. In reality, I was using him and other powerful born to inadvertently cement the victory of the turned. He was merely a casualty in our grand scheme to win the war *and* secure Earle's begrudgingly awarded blessing."

"Are you sure you aren't a succubus?" Scarlett asked with a small smile.

Sadie eyed Scarlett in a way that irritated me, which I knew was half the reason she was doing it.

"In a past life, darling," Sadie said with a wink.

"Focus," I snapped, and Sadie shot me a smirk that was nothing short of victorious.

"Okay, then we also need a way to mend that bridge," Scarlett said. "He has very little desire to help the turned. We can convince Kole that Durian is unfit and dangerous far easier than we can convince him to defend us against the kingdom. He needs incentive, and it needs to be ego-boosting, because most of his resentment is about his lack of promotion and perceived mistreatment by superiors. He needs to feel recognized and respected." She looked at Sadie, hesitating a moment before adding, "He may be a disgusting little rat, but I think—no, I *know*—he's tired of being treated like one. We need a new approach."

Sadie lifted her brows, and the room went quiet. All eyes moved to Sadie.

When Sadie's lips slowly curved, Uriah released a breath. I

stared at Scarlett, and I couldn't possibly be in love with her more than I already was.

Sadie nodded. "Noted."

"The next faction are the mortals," Scarlett said. "Clearly, most mortals already have reason to back us and oppose Durian, and I know you've already been working with mortals in dry lands on this front. Just like I know that those mortals' exports are crucial to Earle, especially the poisons and other weapons. Not being spread too thin during wartimes *and* the threat to exports need to be highlighted with both Kole and future relations with the kingdom. It would be stupid for the kingdom to back Durian now, even if Durian is too blind to see that."

I nodded. "Agreed on all fronts. We've received recent word that the turned in Ravenia are putting up one hell of a fight. If Earle divests resources and men to meddle in Valentin's affairs now, then he really has gone mad. He will have proved the dissenters right."

Scarlett tapped her fingers on the wood, nodding as a crease formed between her brows. "The only mortals that support the born are those brainwashed and subjugated in the born districts. I have reason to believe those mortals and the lower class born have a lot more in common with each other than with Durian and the born elites." She paused. "The night I escaped, we were attacked by a group of born who had lost respect for Durian. The way one of the women spoke of failed religious prophecies made me believe she had once believed in Durian's holy book, and perhaps had even been duped by his visions, but she'd become disillusioned. They said that the born were starving. There's a blood shortage problem in born districts, isn't there?"

Everyone glanced at me nervously, knowing I was shielding Scarlett from the current state of Aristelle. She hadn't been ready to shoulder such a weight.

"That's what happens when you erect a border and force mortals to choose a side," Uriah said. "Not to mention the attacks on blood cafés. They wanted anarchy, and they certainly received it." He massaged the bridge of his nose. "I promised Blondie that I'd say it plainly."

Scarlett peered at him, puzzled, while I stared at Uriah in utter warning. I feared his next words and what they might reveal. Scarlett still didn't know about Durian's direction of massacres and destruction in her name.

"Mortals are suffering all over Aristelle, and it's only getting worse," he said. "It's getting dark. Really dark." He met my eyes and didn't say anything more.

Heartbreak crossed Scarlett's features, and it reflected in the squeeze inside my own chest.

"Durian was clearly using blood shortages and widespread poverty as evidence against Rune and the turned, but now it's starting to backfire," she murmured, refocusing. "I think this needs to be exacerbated. We need to counter his propaganda with our own, highlighting Durian's failures."

"Already in motion," I said gently.

Scarlett's eyes rounded. "Oh. Good."

"We're also spreading the information that Durian is an illusionist. There's a reason he kept his gift a secret for this long. Mental magick breeds distrust. No one likes feeling manipulated." I smirked at her, and Scarlett shrugged in response, the corners of her lips quirking. "You're right about it all, Little Flame. Keep going."

My use of her pet name brought a satisfying blush to her fair cheeks. She tucked a stray strand of dark hair behind her ear.

"I think there's a reason Durian and Earle feel so much inexplicable comradery, and it has everything to do with their questionable mental states. Durian is blinded by his own delusions," she said. She took a deep breath, frowning before regaining her composure. "And Brennan, his own second in command, is beginning to see through it."

"Say it plainly, dear," Sadie cut in, her tone sharp as she looked at Scarlett pointedly.

My jaw clenched. I didn't enjoy seeing another dominant correct Scarlett, especially not Sadie. I shot her a glare, my lips turned down. Sadie lowered her authoritative energy as Scarlett spoke.

"*I* encouraged Brennan to see through Durian, carefully and meticulously, the entirety of my stay in the palace," Scarlett said. Mason appeared shocked, looking at Scarlett with new eyes. "I can't create new desires, but I can tease out desires already present—even if they're deeply buried—and slowly make them stronger. In this case, I searched Brennan's mind for weaknesses."

My closest comrades leaned forward in their seats now. I beamed with pride. No matter how much anger and fear simmered below the surface, knowing what Scarlett had sacrificed and what she may still give of herself in the future, I was mesmerized.

I stood in awe of Scarlett's radiance always, especially when she showed just how powerful she was, even in her darkest moments.

"Like Kole, Brennan is starving for validation. He's well-respected among the elites and what remains of Durian's devotees. He's charming—"

My jaw ticked, imagining Brennan's charming little head decorating my gardens.

"—and he's intelligent, resourceful. He bought into Durian's religion when it suited him and his interests. But now that I've grown those seeds of resentment toward Durian, along with Brennan's own self-belief, Durian's influence over him is waning. In fact, I'd bet anything he now blames Durian for my absence." Scarlett winced, now avoiding my eyes. "Brennan thinks he's in love with me, and he believes that Durian was ruining me just like he is ruining Valentin."

The room darkened for a moment, the lights flickering. My shadows begged to reach for Scarlett, to wrap around her dainty neck and show the whole world who owns her.

"Kole feels similarly, in his own kind of way. In fact," she said, swallowing, "all three men think I'm meant to be with them. And if I know anything about seduction, I'm certain that my escape has only deepened the divides I'd been digging. Their obsessions have only grown. I've weakened them, and if I make contact now, with discord in the born districts multiplying, after I've been silent for weeks… I can finish what I started."

Dark magick coursed through the room. And it wasn't mine, Mason's, or Uriah's. It wasn't even Sadie's.

It was darkly sweet, the divine unholy feminine. It was the deafening strike of lightning from a powerful storm, the unmistakable scent of violent sex, and the luxurious feel of soft, supple skin. It was the destruction and sensuality of the Dark Goddess and her beautifully deadly daughters.

We were held in suspended captivation as Scarlett told us more about what she'd heard during her time as Durian's slave. She told us about those divisions, the weaknesses she'd used to her advantage. When she told us about her friend Rosalind, she remained strong even as a single tear fell from her piercing blue eyes. She spoke of this fellow succubus with the utmost respect. And I hated myself even more for my initial prejudices against sex demons, understanding now that Rosalind was one of the reasons Scarlett had survived that place and found her power.

"I can make each man bend. Brennan will turn against Durian and *act on it*," she said fiercely, with all the wrathful conviction of Lillian herself. "This will divide the court and the elites, among whom I've already detected and nurtured a vast array of jealousies, vendettas, and dissatisfactions. Kole will be turned off by this level of discord, and he will see that the

Valentin born are a danger to Earle's legacy. He will also see that the born districts have succumbed to their own in-fighting between mortals and born alike, which will inevitably lead to a confused and divided army. We will expose Durian's contempt for his own people and reveal his religion and visions for the manipulation that they are. We will show his treason to Earle, and we will find a way to ensure Kole's recognition for a portion of our work. We can keep Kole in our back pocket, and each faction will have no other option but to submit to the rule of the turned if they hope to survive."

She stood, placing her hands on the table. "After I work on these men from afar, I will be returning to Durian's palace to ensure the final pieces fall as they should. One of those pieces being Durian's head."

46

SCARLETT

Rune's eyes were infernos as I spoke my last words.

"Will you now?" he hissed.

Sadie watched me as she worked through her own mental puzzle, those long red nails softly tapping on her crossed arms.

"By yourself, with no protection, I presume?" Rune asked.

He knew it was coming. Everyone at this table knew it was coming. I'd watched him fight to stay calm on numerous occasions, but it would seem his restraint had finally worn thin.

"You've found yourself quite the force, Rune," Sadie said. "Her intuition matches mine, and it matches yours, too. We can't rid this island of the born. There are still civilians and born children on their side. This is our path forward. We must look to the future of how to prevent another born uprising. We will ensure an end to the slave trade, and we will need to make concessions in other areas to mend the borns' ire. We are the lesser of two evils, and we must let each group come to that conclusion on their own, with our careful, guiding hand."

"We'll have the born burning down Durian's palace

themselves if we don't get to it first," Uriah said with a grin. "It's the best-case scenario."

"And what happens if the angry mob descends while you're still trapped there, Scarlett?" Rune asked me. "Need I remind you how breakable—and flammable—your human shell is?"

I shrank at his tone, and Rune's anger melted an inch. He shook his head and raked a hand through his dark hair.

"Rune," I said softly. "I know you're all hiding the full extent of the borns' atrocities against mortals, to protect me and stop me from making rash moves. That's what Snow wants me to know, right?"

Rune's eyes flashed in confirmation. He was leaking shadow now, and Sadie was shooting daggers at him in response. Uriah was silent, but I could sense unsaid truths on his tongue. His loyalty to Rune was still his strongest desire.

"I know that we can keep Valentin safe. We have more than enough to work with," I said, willing Rune to believe in me, to continue to allow me to make my life mean something. On my own terms. "If Durian's psychopathic cruelty is only getting worse, then we have no time to waste. I'll need access to the other half of Kole's linked journal. I will also need access to Brennan. Any ideas?"

Rune steepled his fingers at his lips. He was suddenly eerily calm, eyes passing over his closest confidants. "We're breaking. Leave us."

"Rune," Sadie said, irritated.

Uriah and Mason stood.

"We'll finish this later." Rune spoke to them, but he only stared at me. "As Scarlett said, we have plenty to work with, and we will begin any new directives right away. I want to speak with the other half of my soul alone."

As I always did when Rune declared his love in front of others, I blushed. I wasn't used to our connection being on full display. I once thought Rune would never broadcast his devotion to me, as if it made him weaker in the eyes of his clan. I couldn't have been more wrong about him.

That was what gave me hope that Rune would come around about this, too. He had to see that just like it was my fate to be his, it was also my fate to be in service to Valentin. To protect this island and avenge myself and all other slaves.

Rune's closest confidants headed toward the exit at the far end of the spacious room.

Sadie turned when she reached the doors. "Since no one bothered to say it aloud, let me be the first." She pinned her eyes on mine. "What you accomplished during the worst moments of your life, with barely any knowledge about your own nature, is nothing short of incredible. It is an honor to be fighting with you, Scarlett Hale."

Mason nodded, looking at me with respect.

"Agreed," Uriah said. "You've kicked ass."

"Thank you," I said softly, the tension in my shoulders melting as they each filed out and shut the door behind them.

Rune stood, and my muscles tightened right back up as I faced his looming form.

"I didn't need a break, Rune," I said. "It felt good to be useful. I know you think I'm pushing myself, and that I'm rushing into things for the sake of others, but—"

"I was the one who needed a break," he said, cutting me off.

I closed my mouth, searching his dark eyes. He moved close enough to brush his knuckle across my cheekbone, and his mask of anger was soon to melt into something sorrowful. It was the vulnerability he wore only for me.

And it shattered my heart to see Rune look at me as if he were grieving.

Grieving *me*.

I melted into his chest.

"You may write to them, Little Flame," he whispered into my hair. "These men who had no choice but to grow hopelessly infatuated with you. But you may not go to them, not until we see how our plan plays out. And I'd sooner lock you in a fucking cage before I'd let you go without any protection and a meticulous escape plan."

I peeled away from him with a glare.

"How?" he asked, his voice hoarse. The heartbreak in his features softened me. "How could you even consider returning to the place that nearly broke you? After you've spent hours crying and shaking in my arms? After you nearly withered away, and you did everything in your power to fight your way back to me?"

I clenched my fists, my heart beating erratically. I remembered how I felt standing in that angry crowd of mortals at the human trafficking rally, when they'd demanded the turned crack down on the slave trade. I'd grown so angry that I'd inadvertently encouraged the entire crowd to turn violent, to act on their most base desires.

When I'd leaked my wrathful influence, I'd been thinking about the injustice of it all. How I'd been shown, over and over again, that my body had never belonged to me. That was the message delivered by Isabella and too many men to count.

There was this vengeful, spitting snake inside me that was growing hungrier the stronger I became.

"Because I owe it to myself, and all people like me," I said. "I owe it to everyone who has ever been made to feel as though they exist only as an object to use and discard. People like Rosalind, who was slaughtered without a second thought." That angry, venomous serpent coiled around my spine. "I've been forced to cater to men my entire life. To pretend to lap up their disgusting words, to absorb their pitiful attempts to make themselves strong and to make me small. I'm willing to go back to that tasteless shithole so I can see the look on Durian's disgusting face when he realizes that the woman he tortured, brutalized, and assaulted—the woman he wrote off as nothing more than a stupid human pet—was the one who destroyed him and everything he has built." I radiated power, now molten, in my stomach. "If only to make myself fucking *feel good.*"

I gasped, nearly panting now, as my veins flooded with heat. Rune's eyes darted to my thighs, squeezing together beyond my conscious awareness.

My eyes hungrily consumed Rune's form, his beautiful tattoos and forceful presence. I no longer cared why or whether it was appropriate. All I cared about was satisfying this sudden ache between my legs.

I nearly tackled Rune. He met me halfway, lifting me into his arms as I crushed my lips to his. He cleared gods knew what off the deliberation table, objects clattering to the floor as he placed me forcefully down and shoved his way between my legs. One hand was on the back of my head, the other roaming my body.

Just before he met my lips, he stopped. "I will not lose you," he growled.

"No, you won't," I said. "I know that I can do this. This is the destiny I've always felt charging through my veins, the one that brought me to Aristelle. My destiny is *you*. And an eternity with you means slaughtering our enemies and building a better world for us all."

This was my story. Not Durian's. Not Brennan's or Kole's. It was fucking mine. My power flared, and I thought of Rosalind. Without her, I wouldn't be standing here today. Just as she'd taught me, I would stand so firmly in my power that failure was an impossibility.

When Durian choked on his own blood as his palace crumbled, I'd think of her then, too.

I went in for Rune's lips, drinking his desire as the room filled with Lillian's decadent darkness. I locked my legs around Rune as the nerves between my thighs pulsed.

"Gods, Scarlett," he said, pulling back to stare at me. "Now that I can see underneath your glamour... I can feel your power.

It's as potent as even that of my strongest clan member. Your body might be fragile, and your magick might not manifest as a physical weapon. But there's a reason that mental magick is prized above all others, *feared* and *hated* above all others."

He pulled at my bottom lip with his fangs, and I moaned into his mouth. "You're a viper hidden in tall grass, baby."

He fisted my hair at the base of my scalp and forced me to stare into his wrathful eyes. His shadows leaked from his imposing form.

"I fucking hate how much I believe in you," he hissed, yanking me off the table to remove my dress.

I eyed the tall windows behind him. His shadows were quick to close the dark curtains.

"Part of me wants to claim you in front of my entire clan—better yet, the entire city—but I know I'd end up obliterating anyone who dared witness the face you make when you're filled with my cock," he said as my dress fell to the floor and I stood bare before him. His anger only multiplied as he glared possessively at my body.

He didn't bother removing his pants, merely unzipping and letting himself spring free.

I wet my lips, and Rune was violent as he spun me around and bent me over the table. My hands pressed against the sleek wood. I heard Rune spit. I barely felt him brush against my entrance before he was driving inside me.

I arched my back. I couldn't get enough of him, enough of the pain or enough of the pleasure. I wanted it all. I wanted this unfair, cruel world to bleed for me, to fill my veins with every last drop of the pleasure I was owed.

My body surged heat, my legs shaking as I took Rune's brutality with throaty moans.

"Good. Fucking. Demon," he purred, gripping my hair again.

I cried out, and just when I thought I was reaching a limit, Rune manhandled me back into his arms. My forehead brushed his. He entered me as he held me, my legs wrapped around him. He bounced me on his cock as his tongue invaded my mouth. I groaned his name, knowing it would only make his desire sweeter.

Rune shoved me up against the window, my back on the velvet curtain as he continued to impale me.

"Tell me, Little Flame. Was it my power you used to pull these men under your spell? To make Brennan fall so pathetically in love with you?"

I didn't back down from his unflinching stare as his hips rocked. My grip around him tightened as I smiled. I felt powerful, unstoppable.

For far too long, I'd hated what I was. Leaning in was infinitely more delicious.

"Was it my blood that fueled you when you saved those slaves from Evangeline, killed any born in your way, and burned her mansion to the ground?"

Rune laughed darkly, carrying me away from the window while still inside me.

"Yes, wicked little seductress. Your blood will fuel unspeakable violence over the next centuries."

He slipped out and placed me on the carpet by the fireplace, lording over me as I knelt.

"What was it that made you so needy for me, so desperate for my touch? The prospect of violence and retribution, or talking about all those men you've trapped in your succubus web?"

"All of it," I whispered, letting the darkest parts of me rise from the abyss as I stared up at him. "The violence, the manipulation, the power. It all made me soaking wet, *my God.*"

I confessed to him on my knees—in reverence of this deity who'd promised he wanted to bathe in my darkness just as deeply as my light.

Rune's eyes went wild. His lips slowly spread into a grin,

bathing me in depraved approval. "Open that spiteful, devious little mouth for me."

I obeyed, and Rune filled my mouth with his impossible size. He slid over my tongue, and I tasted myself on his shaft. It only turned me on more, to taste my own addictiveness—the allure that made men *lose their godsdamn minds*.

"Relax. Breathe," he instructed, pushing deeper as he smoothed my hair. "What a diverse array of uses this mouth has. Lying, scheming, seducing... taking its owner's cock with gratitude."

The apex of my thighs was screaming for him. I moaned, the sound muffled as Rune stretched and gagged me. Tears pricked my eyes.

"You can rule this whole world, baby," Rune said. "But don't you ever fucking forget who rules *you*."

He used my throat mercilessly, every once in a while giving me a break or softly guiding me to relax.

When he finally pulled out, my face half coated with saliva, I was desperate for a reprieve from my scorching lust. My power was rich in the air, ever-strengthened by the obsession of Valentin's powerful vampire ruler. I was panting, my clit throbbing as I ached with need.

It was exhilarating to be humbled by Rune, the only man capable of truly bringing me to my knees, of earning my submission and service.

The only man who'd ever beaten me at my own game—who'd ripped me off the board completely.

"You poor, needy little mess," he said softly, cruelly. "You pounced on me, expecting to be able to use me to satisfy yourself, hmm?"

"Please?" I begged, already knowing that was what he wanted. He loved hearing me beg. "Please, Rune?"

"What will you give me in return?" he asked. "Make it interesting, or you won't come for a week."

My eyes trailed down to his soft stroke of his cock. What could I offer Rune sexually that he'd find *interesting*? My mind spun, but none of my ideas seemed sufficient. And I was so *not* offering my unclaimed hole.

"You have thirty seconds."

I'd never hated anyone more.

"Remove the attitude from that pretty face or I'll paint it with my cum and refuse to let you clean it off for the rest of the day."

My eyes rounded. Rune appeared utterly delighted that he'd managed to shock the succubus. The irony was that he had always been far more demonic.

Frustration and panic clouded my mind. All I knew was the crushing weight of my own desire. Another beautiful irony.

He didn't say the offer needed to be sexual. My lips tugged down as I concentrated. What did Rune want from me? What lay unfulfilled, a lacking that, if met, was guaranteed to make him fall?

Realization struck, and I had my answer.

"I'll sing for you."

47

SCARLETT

Rune's mask of dominance dropped, and he pulled me to my feet. He smiled, brushing my messy hair behind my ears.

"Scarlett, baby, you've sold yourself short," he said softly. "You could've convinced me to trade my castle to hear your angelic voice one more time."

"I'll keep that in mind for future negotiations." My heart hammered, as if I'd offered him a limb instead. The prospect of singing for just one person sent a shock of stage fright through my system. Even if it was only Rune.

Or maybe *because* it was Rune.

"Then again, is that not what you already traded for my writing?" Rune asked, trailing his fingers across my collarbone and down my shoulder before dropping his hand.

I straightened. Oh, gods. He was right.

He chuckled. "Your poor little heart. Calm down, baby. You've still earned your reward."

I released the breath I'd been holding. He left me standing there for a moment as he grabbed a pillow and set it on the carpet below us. To my surprise, he was the one to lay down, resting his head on the red cushion as he looked up at me through dark lashes.

"Scarlett darling, be a good girl and sit on my face."

I nearly gasped. Do *what* now?

Rune chuckled, making a come-hither motion with his fingers that had my pussy aching. The scorch on my skin had nothing to do with the roaring fireplace.

My pace was slow as I approached him, and the stage fright anxiety was slow to dissipate. Rune was infuriatingly, devastatingly gorgeous as he tracked my every movement—his dark, nearly black hair brushing the top of his forehead, his smirk resting in the middle of brutally masculine edges and hollows. Everything about him was a trap. Enticing enough to catch even the most ruthless sex demon.

How the hell had I been the one to shoulder all the blame for our shared obsession when he looked like *that*?

When he looked *at me* like *that*?

"Now, Little Flame," he commanded, his voice gravelly as his eyes devoured my nude form. "Let your jealous God show you just how devotedly he worships you."

That was our dynamic, summarized in a sentence. Rune didn't demand my submission by breaking me or enforcing unearned respect and obedience. No, Rune earned the power I gave him. We worshipped *each other*. He demanded I gave him all of myself because he had already given me all of him.

I took a deep breath and straddled Rune. He grinned, his shadows coiling possessively around my legs. I shuddered at the way he looked at me, like he'd never cherished anything more. But also like he was *starving*. His eyes lowered from my face to my pussy.

"Ride my tongue until you come," he instructed. "Do not be shy, little demon. Close your eyes and imagine that violence and divine vengeance that got you so worked up. I want to taste your viciousness, your sweet, merciless wrath. I want my face wet with your darkness. I want to fucking drown in it."

He grabbed my thighs and forced me down, not even allowing me to think about my self-consciousness before he'd found my clit with his wicked tongue. I let out a raspy moan as he flitted against it, teasing before he began to lap me up. He slid his tongue across my folds before piercing my opening. He moaned like he was tasting the most luxurious dessert, pulling me closer as he slowly closed his mouth around my clit.

He sucked and pulsed, and flooded with his desire, I allowed myself to lightly grind against him. I closed my eyes, and I lost myself to pleasure.

How strange it was that an act that was meant to bring me pleasure, that was meant to show me Rune's devotion, was the one that had me tightly wound. Not the acts that degraded me, that hurt me. It was yet another victory to let go of this shame and claim these building waves of ecstasy instead.

I *deserved* pleasure. Reverence. Love. I deserved all of these aspects of my sexuality—from the painful to the sublime.

Rune consumed me. It was concerning how good he was with his tongue. His shadows held me captive above him as my eyes closed. He grabbed my ass, his fingers digging into my flesh.

I envisioned that divine violence as I rode peak after peak of rapture. I remembered my anger, my utter fury at being so fucking *used* by everyone, my whole life. Just a pawn, an object, a doll on a shelf. A sex toy.

A blood bag.

I imagined how it would feel to cut into Durian like he'd carved into me, over and over again. What would he look like kneeling before *me* begging for mercy? What would a fair punishment be for chipping away at my sanity, for beating me until I bled, for touching me and traumatizing me so he could get off to my pain and humiliation?

A severed head seemed far too lenient of a sentence.

I saw myself, powerful and healed, not a single mark on my skin save Rune's. This woman was a dark goddess, a being that didn't belong in this realm. The men who'd hurt her were bent at the knees, pleading for undeserved grace. They learned how it felt to see prayer after desperate prayer go unanswered.

How deeply, viscerally satisfying would it be to show the born elite that the human they enslaved in the name of Lillian was really her daughter and harbinger of their destruction?

They'd let a demon into the henhouse.

And they were so enamored with her that they were going to do it all over again.

My body was molten, my mind delirious with gratification. Fate was thunderous and melodic in my ears, my heartbeat a steady certainty.

My legs trembled, and Rune's grip on my ass tightened, his shadows coiling around my body. When his fangs lightly scraped against my most sensitive flesh, I cried out. The building tsunami crashed, and I rode Rune's tongue until I claimed every drop of my release.

∽

"Your stance is substantially less shitty," Uriah commented with a nod. "Remember what I said about your grip around the hilt."

I adjusted my fingers, facing down a dummy with the dagger Phillip gifted me in hand. A crowd roared at my back. The turned had gathered for a night of play fighting, tournament style. Uriah and I found a secluded nook for our nightly training session. Other than the stray lingering stare, we were left alone.

Snow was watching from a respectful distance, but Rune was nowhere to be found. I'd been right that it was best he didn't train me. There were too many emotions involved. Not to mention the violent lust.

It only took one attempted lesson between us to prove the hunch correct.

When my blade connected with the dummy, I imagined it was Durian.

"Good shit, Trouble," Uriah said with a beaming smile. "You hit the heart. Nearly guaranteed chance of vampire death. But remember, given the difficulty of hitting such a small target hidden by all those pesky bones—there's no shame in aiming for somewhere easier first. The blood onyx is going to weaken a vamp enough for you to recenter. The poison will be most effective where?"

"Major organs and arteries," I said, catching my breath.

Phillip's handcrafted weapons were forged with flecks of blood onyx, possessing magick that was paralytic and weakening to vampires. It was one of the many magickal ingredients Valentin supplied to Ravenia, the exports that were even more important during wartimes.

Uriah gave me a brief anatomy lesson.

We finished with strength training, my least favorite part of our sessions. Mostly because Uriah had no filter and routinely commented on how it seemed impossible for someone to be so physically weak.

By the time I'd collapsed on the dead grass next to Snow, I'd somehow stripped to thin layers, sweat beading along my forehead in the dead of winter.

She was sitting with her knees to her chest. She looked down at my sweaty, breathless form and laughed.

"Shut up," I snapped.

Uriah placed his hands on his hips, standing over us with a wide grin. "We all have our talents. I mean, your upper body might be comically feeble, but look what you did to the entire castle earlier..."

Snow flushed bright red, glaring at Uriah.

"Wait, what?" I asked between gulps of air. "What did I do to the castle?"

Uriah's jaw dropped. "No one told you?"

"Told me what?" I searched their faces for a hint of what they were talking about.

Snow made herself smaller, emitting a small groan of embarrassment as she avoided Uriah's amused gaze.

"Whatever the hell you and Rune were doing in the deliberation room had a, uh…" Uriah paused, as if searching for the right words, "…ripple effect."

Snow lay back, covering her face with her hand. Uriah laughed, delighting in her discomfort.

Oh, gods. I'd forgotten that aspect of my magick—the way it could leak out and influence everyone around me. That was how I'd inflamed the crowd of protesters, the elites in Durian's palace, and the patrons of Odessa. And this afternoon I'd been especially powerful, displaying not a single measure of restraint.

I glanced between Uriah and Snow.

"Who tackled whom?"

Uriah's guffaw was the only answer I needed.

"I thought we were supposed to be leaving shame out of sex, Snow?" I teased.

She sat up, her bright green eyes fiery. "It wasn't—I don't —ugh!"

Now Uriah and I were both lost in laughter.

I sat up. "Well… you're welcome." I winked at Snow.

I considered Uriah, assessing whether I could trust him with my friend's feelings. He was close to Rune, and that worked in his favor.

"How did you and Rune meet?" I asked.

Snow's smile faded, and Uriah's eyes flashed surprise. He shifted on his feet.

"Through Mason," he said. "Mason and I were old school vigilante vampire hunters, best in the city."

Why in the hell had I never asked this before? I had to pick my jaw up from the ground.

"You went from vampire hunter to vampire?"

Uriah shrugged. "Not as crazy of a leap as it sounds. There's only so much skill and strength you can amass as a human." He glanced back at the crowd of vampires betting and cheering on violent competitions. "We don't have to actively recruit humans to join our clan. They find *us*. We all have a similar story, you see."

Grief shone in Uriah's hazel-green eyes.

"We follow Rune because we owe him everything," Uriah said. "I know I do."

The way Snow regarded Uriah was nothing short of respectful now, compassionate. All of her playful irritation had melted away.

"I met him when he was still human," Uriah said. "Six months later, he was so much more. Mason and I took the leap soon after." He straightened. "But I would've followed Rune into battle after that first meeting, before he was the most powerful vampire in Valentin. Sometimes in this life, you just *know*."

48

SCARLETT

I tentatively knocked on Sadie's door. The weight of the notebook in my hand had my stomach twisting into knots. It felt like years had passed since I'd written in its sister's pages, sowing the seeds for my escape with Rosalind by my side. Fuck, I missed her. Grief and guilt were still a heavy mass in my throat.

Rune had left the notebook on the bed for me to find after my shower. I hadn't seen him since we'd left the deliberation room. I'd gone straight to a session with Belise, followed by time with Uriah and Snow. After Belise, I'd found a bowl of chocolate cookie dough ice cream sitting down the hall, still cold as if it had been left the moment I exited Belise's rooms.

It was as though Rune had reverted back to stalking me out of comfort, haunting me like a specter rather than talking to me directly.

Weirdly, it was a soothing coping mechanism for me too. The energy between us was volatile, explosive. We both needed to focus, now that Valentin was plagued with conflict from all directions.

I knew that when Rune finally did step out from his shadows, I'd be able to think of nothing and no one but him.

I heard footsteps approaching from the other side of Sadie's door. When I'd seen her on my way to the training field, she told me to wear something that made me feel powerful tonight.

Mental and physical exhaustion were clouding the corners of my focus. But I remembered my appearance facing the full-length mirror in the bedroom—long lashes, full waves of dark hair, piercing blue eyes, cheeks with a brush of contour and berry blush. A black dress with slits down either arm and both sides of my legs, shimmering golden vines threaded throughout. A tease of my thighs with every step, a bustier top that accentuated the curves of my breasts. My neck, bare, showcasing Rune's fading red bite marks.

Sadie greeted me at the door, her tall heels clicking as she led me inside. An herbal, woodsy scent permeated through the space, and candles flickered from every visible surface. They rose higher as Sadie passed them, and some flared black and deep red flames.

Furniture had been cleared in front of the fireplace to make space for a circle of salt and candles, a pentagram drawn in black in the center.

For the briefest moment, I thought of Durian and his demented sacrificial altar, and I shuddered.

"Is she here?" a voice squealed from an adjacent room, jolting me out of my memories.

A half-dressed Imogene hurtled out of the bedroom. She was beaming, her breasts exposed and lower half covered by a long blue skirt.

Sadie's other submissive, Cliff, trailed her sheepishly.

"Sorry, Mistress," he said, scratching his head. "She was excited."

Sadie, wearing a busty black leather top and matching pants, regarded her submissives with a raised brow and frowning lips.

"Kitten," she sighed. "Is exposing yourself to my guests appropriate or polite?"

Imogene's smile was nothing short of endearing. I imagined it was difficult to be too angry with her, even when you were a frightening, ancient witch domme. Imogene's shifter tattoo crawled up her bicep. She was a leopard shifter, and that made Sadie's pet name painfully adorable.

Imogene glanced down at her own chest, as if just now realizing she was topless. She giggled. "No, I'm sorry, Mistress." She looked at me next. "And I'm sorry Miss Scarlett."

"It's okay," I said with a small smile. "Hello again."

Imogene stared at me like I was some kind of celebrity. It was as disarming as it was discomforting.

"I'll be dealing with you later," Sadie said, her tone terse yet soft.

Again, I sensed nothing but love between all three of them. Cliff stared at Sadie like she was his only source of oxygen.

"Both of you need to find somewhere else to play for an hour. Cliff, make sure Kitten doesn't get into too much trouble."

He grinned. "Yes, Mistress, of course." He gently steered Imogene back to the bedroom, presumably to get her fully dressed before they went off on their adventure.

Sadie led me back into a small study, which was just as overrun by witchy materials as the main room. Lillian only knew what Sadie got up to in her free time. The power that leaked from the walls and rose up from the floors was deathly potent.

Sadie lifted a large circular mirror that was entirely black and opaque, clearing a space for us at a side table. We sat across from each other, and I tentatively placed the notebook and pen between us.

Her green eyes were sharp and intense, nearly reptilian. Her long dark hair was pulled back into a high ponytail.

"I wanted to make contact when you were ready to escape.

But it hadn't been viable, and Rune was being very *Rune* about everything," she said with a smirk. "And, as it turned out, you behaved exactly how I would've instructed to begin with."

I raised a brow, refusing to show her my instinctive intimidation at her powerful, assertive aura.

"I was going to tell you to pretend you were taken by force, to never let them know it was an escape," she explained with an amused glint in her eyes.

I lifted a shoulder, clasping my hands above the table. "It was a good play."

"You have no idea how rare you are, do you?"

I hesitated, unable to read her desires but detecting nothing but genuineness from her features.

"The average person, succubus or not, does not think and behave the way you do, my dear," she continued. "You possess a power that transcends magick or blood. It's the kind of power that makes history books. The same power I saw in Rune all those years ago."

She reached for the notebook, caressing its spine sensually as her eerie gaze went straight through me—as if she was gazing into some great beyond.

"You live long enough, and you begin to understand it, to look for it—that spark, the flame that burns in a select few. Most people, whether they're wealthy or poor, rich in magick or dreadfully barren, fade into oblivion without a trace. But then there are those few who burn, who can't help but make a name for themselves. It's not luck, that spark. It's a choice they make every day. Succumb or transcend. Fade away or become reborn."

I saw it now, as Sadie's words lit me up from the inside. Over and over, men told me that they owed Rune everything. Rune had done many great things, but behind Rune the Ruthless stood Sadie, the woman who'd started it all and claimed not an ounce of recognition in the eyes of the world.

"How does it feel to let men take all the credit for the world you've created?"

Sadie sat back in her chair, only the briefest lapse in those all-seeing eyes that told me I'd surprised her.

"That's what men do, darling," she said with a twirl of her hand. "Recognition is fickle. Power is forever. You survive a hell of a lot longer out of the spotlight. Besides, all the true fun is had behind the curtains."

I considered that for a moment, my lips turning down. "What does that say about Rune?"

Sadie's eyes burned into mine. She leaned forward. "It says that he is one hell of a fighter who has guarded himself with numbers and dispersed power. Rune may be public facing, but he's intelligent enough to remain as mysterious and unknowable as possible. He's not the type to burn out hard and fast. I made sure of it."

I thought about Rune's image, the way he'd forged himself as more myth than man, more god than vampire. No one knew his origins, and all they had was a single four-letter name.

The more I uncovered about Rune, his mentor, and his clan, the more I understood how outmatched Durian and the born had always been. I hadn't been entirely lying when I'd told Brennan that I'd always been drawn to powerful men. As a succubus, it was likely a part of my survival imperative. The power of this castle versus Durian's pitiful imitation was hardly a fair comparison.

"I'm ready to write to Kole," I said, lifting my chin. "And I'm grateful for any wisdom you could provide."

Sadie nodded, approval lightening her intense features. "What are your aims?"

"I have to preserve the story that I was taken against my will by Rune," I said. "Kole might suspect otherwise. Brennan might too. But that doesn't matter because both will blame Durian and the way he treated me. Durian's more of a wildcard, but he's at least already delusional and unhinged enough to be open to the warping of reality."

I paused, and Sadie again gave me a nod of praise.

I thought of that strange moment, when I'd been dozing off after Durian had saved me from his cruel visions of Rune. He'd laid next to me in bed, and I could've sworn his hand brushed across my face tenderly. Sociopath or not, Durian was under some kind of spell, too. I had to believe it would hold until the end.

I refocused.

"There's no safe way for me to write to Brennan and keep up my ruse except through Kole, right?"

Sadie considered this, her brow creasing as she tapped her red nails on the wood. "That's your most secure option," she affirmed. "We want as few moving pieces as possible now, the less complicated the better."

"Then my aims are to preserve my innocence, cater to each man's fantasy that they're the true object of my affection and the others are merely means to an end or obstacles, and to guide Kole to put me into contact with Brennan."

"What are your aims with Brennan?" Sadie asked curiously. "Besides encouraging his ambitions to overthrow Durian?"

I realized my brain had already jumped several moves ahead, and I needed to back up. "I need to ensure Brennan follows through with his coup. I'm going to play the part of his prize. Brennan is intelligent. He will have played his cards right in the aftermath of my rescue, taking full responsibility for the outing to Black Sapphire in order to preserve his new, lucrative relationship with Kole. Durian will assume that it was Kole's idea, given Kole's fondness of me. But Durian won't suspect either man of anything more than stupidity and disrespect of his ownership over me. Durian presumably exploded at Brennan, unable to show the same fury toward Kole given his own ambitions that involve the kingdom. Kole has remained safe, but wary. Brennan's resentment toward Durian is hurtling toward a breaking point, now that both men blame the other for my recapture, and Durian is likely icing Brennan out as a result. Or better yet, actively disparaging him."

Sadie's eyes flitted between both of mine, and the room swelled with dark feminine power. As heat crawled down my spine, I thought of Rune.

"I need to assess Brennan's position and see how close he is to leading a rebellion," I said. "If my hunches are correct, I have a feeling I might be the perfect peace offering for Brennan to offer Durian to get back into his good graces. He needs Durian as disarmed as possible before he goes in for the kill. He's likely already amassing supporters in that court of snakes as we speak. And stealing me from Rune will also make him appear powerful and effective, subtly undermining Durian. With me back in the palace, Brennan will have his shiny incentive to carry out what he started, lest he watch Durian ruin me all over again."

"Interesting," Sadie said. "You don't want to go straight through Durian?"

I shook my head. "Kole and Brennan need to each feel like white knights in their own respect, boosting their egos. Kole by connecting me to Brennan, and Brennan by saving me from Rune and then from Durian. Plus, Brennan will be sloppier in his execution, blinded by his infatuation and desperation for me. Durian's sociopathy makes him harder for me to work with and control. I also have an ulterior motive for wanting Brennan to be the one to save me."

Sadie grinned. "Do tell."

"He's going to sneak me back into the palace by revealing the secret tunnels underneath Hatham." I paused. "There are tunnels, right? I heard slaves talking about them, and then I thought about how Rune had smuggled me back to his castle from Odessa a *secret way*. There's a whole underground labyrinth beneath Aristelle, isn't there?"

Sadie appeared utterly enthralled as she leaned forward. She slid the notebook back toward me. "Correct."

"In his single-minded focus to have me back, under Durian's nose, Brennan is going to reveal a way for our forces to ambush the palace, too. It will be the perfect escape plan that Rune demands I have before he'll feel comfortable sending me back there."

I thumbed over the leather binding, slowly unfastening it.

"Rune will never be comfortable with any of this," Sadie said softly, releasing a long exhale. "Yet you must do it, anyway."

I nodded, my heart clenching. I knew he was going to be worried sick. He was already terrified. And I knew I wasn't nearly healed enough yet, still plagued by flashbacks and nightmares. It had only been a few weeks.

But I had to keep taking steps forward. I thought of Rosalind, and I lifted the pen.

The blank parchment paper asked me for the code in elegant script, and I ignored it. I began to write, and Sadie moved to stand next to me, reading over my shoulder.

> *Kole—it's Scarlett. I don't have much time. Gods, I hope this is the right journal. There were so many. I don't know when or if you'll ever see this message, but if you do, I wanted to tell you that I could write to you again at 9 p.m. tomorrow. I hope you can write me back, that we can talk properly. I miss you. I want to be back with you. I <u>will</u> be back with you as soon as possible.*

"Good," Sadie said. "If his heart still beats, his eyes will be glued to the pages tomorrow at nine sharp." My words slowly disappeared into the page. She closed the book before I could. "It doesn't matter if he's checking his correspondences right now. You want him to sit with the barest of scraps until you write him next. He's nothing but a puddle of denial under your boot."

I took a steadying breath, letting out a nervous burst of laughter as I stood. "It's strange to switch roles with Kole, yet it also feels more natural in this context. Because I *am* the one with all the power when I'm dealing with pathetic men. I do the most pretending when I'm playing the part of the innocent, subservient virgin who worships the ground men walk on."

Sadie placed her hands on my shoulders, her cruel red lips tilted up. "I can see clearly why Rune has been captured by you, Scarlett. He's always loved a challenge. And it would seem, so do you." She opened her mouth to say more and then halted, slowly moving her gaze to the corner of the room. "You know that shadow glamour shit doesn't work on me, pest."

Rune materialized seemingly out of thin air, a wall of shadow dissipating into smoke around his imposing form. His eyes narrowed on Sadie's hands on my shoulders.

"I do not recall saying you could touch my belongings when I agreed to allow you to mentor," Rune snapped.

Sadie removed her touch, her fingers softly caressing my shoulders as she pulled back.

I shot a look of irritation toward Rune. "Your *belongings?*" I hissed.

He only smirked. "And you," he said, amusement ripe in his eyes. "Don't you dare let all this domme energy go to your head. You're the one under my boot, Little Flame."

Sadie regarded Rune with a raised brow and piercing gaze, a look that made me remember how long they'd been friends, just how much they'd experienced by each other's side. I remembered that Sadie had technically topped Rune when she'd been eradicating him of bloodlust. It was strange to think of Rune in a position of servitude, but it made sense that Sadie had been the only person to manage such a feat.

Sadie chuckled, looking at the way my hands were on my hips, my spiteful mouth poised to strike.

She interjected. "You know what they say…"

Rune and I dragged our eyes away from each other to her.

"Doms are just brats with power," Sadie finished with a grin.

Rune laughed and shook his head at Sadie. He grabbed me roughly, pulling me to his chest as he kissed the top of my head. I squealed, his shadows crawling all over me.

"And Rune was the biggest brat of my career."

49

RUNE

"You have to tell her," Snow said, bursting into my private study with a nervous Uriah trailing her.

I set down the book I was reading, on revolutionary strategies and propaganda machines, before regarding the angry witch with a single raised brow.

"Before someone else does," she finished.

"Is that a threat?"

She threw up her hands. "No, it's not a *threat*." She brushed her wispy blonde hair behind her ears. "Are you really going to let her get all the way to Durian's palace before she finds out that he's been slaughtering mortals in her name? Don't you think that might make her vulnerable?"

I swallowed, every muscle tightening as my shadows trembled. "She's not going back to that place any time soon."

Snow searched my eyes, her anger melting an inch. "I know you're trying to protect her. I don't want her to go either." Pain engulfed her features, her eyes glassy. "But Scarlett came to Aristelle after being told by everyone in her village that she would die instantly upon arrival. She came when she still believed she was human and powerless. She had no training, no magick that she was aware of. She came here blind, driven by unfathomable courage and loyalty to her hateful, abusive sister. And, by the gods, she *accomplished what she set out to do.*" Snow threw up her hands. "Isabella is safe. Scarlett is alive. I mean, who else but her could've managed that? Who else could've believed in their reality so blindly and boldly that fate herself couldn't deny her?"

"No one," I said softly. "Fucking no one."

I didn't need the witch to remind me of Scarlett's impossibility.

"That's why I know she's going to go. And not only that, she's going to accomplish exactly what she sets out to do, no matter what's thrown in her way," Snow whispered. "We can't stay in denial. Not us nor her. No matter how badly we want to."

Snow and I mirrored each other's heartbreak, for the briefest of lapses. We wanted to stop Scarlett, just like her friend in Crescent Haven tried to do. We wanted to tell her it was a suicide mission, and she was far too vulnerable and breakable to survive.

But Scarlett had this obnoxious way of proving everyone wrong.

"Of course I will tell her," I said, rising from the chair. "Don't you understand?" I ran a hand through my hair, raw emotion threatening to spill over. "That the moment she finds out she will leave?"

Snow deflated even more, conflict in her features.

"Scarlett makes so many of her decisions out of guilt," I said, near angrily to cover up my devastation. "That's what childhood abuse and neglect does to us. It makes us fucking starving for attention, for validation, for love. And we get it all confused. We go looking for it in all the wrong places. We bear the weight of the world on our shoulders. Scarlett already carries so much guilt for what happened to her friend, to the human slaves, and even to Isabella. She blames herself for far too much. When she finds out that Durian's obsession with her has sentenced innocents to death…"

Wave after wave of sorrow washed over me, more than I'd allowed myself to feel in centuries. Everything I'd had to dam up and hide from Scarlett, so I could be strong for her, was now hemorrhaging. That someone so pure, so full of love, had to endure what Scarlett had—it broke me. It shattered me that I couldn't protect her from any of it.

I'd deluded myself into thinking that when I had her back, I'd be able to shield her from all pain and suffering for the rest of eternity.

But that wasn't how life worked. And it certainly wasn't how Scarlett operated. I felt my features moving to reflect my pain. My walls were slipping, and my shadows slowly bled.

"Rune," Snow said, tears falling from her soft green eyes. She walked to me and pulled me into a hug.

Uriah looked uncomfortably to the floor.

I leaned into Snow, remembering all the times she'd held space for me when Scarlett was with the born. She'd allowed me to be human, to be vulnerable.

"I'm grateful Scarlett has you," I whispered.

Snow sighed, as if her next words were reluctant. "I'm grateful she has you too, fascist prick."

I chuckled, pulling away from her. "Today's fascist prick is tomorrow's gods-blessed savior." I couldn't help but smirk. "Or vice versa."

Snow's eyes narrowed. "What does that mean? Spill."

I glanced over at Uriah, who was moving past his discomfort now that he wasn't forced to witness my emotions.

Uriah grinned. "The born civilian population isn't very happy, Blondie."

"In-fighting has begun," I illuminated. Then, I paused, glaring at Uriah. "How the hell have we been overrun by this many uninitiated women running around with top secret clearance and clan secrets?"

"Acting like they own the damn place, too," Uriah agreed, amusement coloring his eyes when Snow turned on him and glowered. "Won't listen to a single bloody order, ignore the chain of command and basic codes of conduct."

"God forbid you have to act like actual people every once in a while and flex some empathy muscles," Snow bit back.

It was more and more apparent every day why Scarlett loved her so much. Speaking of, my ears tingled, detecting the sound of approaching footsteps. I exchanged a glance with Uriah, making sure he knew that Scarlett was here, too.

"Rather than brainless soldiers controlled by Rune's hive mind," Snow muttered, continuing her little rant.

"You know, I actually quite like the sound of that," I said.

"You would," Scarlett said, surprising only Snow as she slipped into the study and looked around at all of us. "Given your pathological control freak tendencies."

I grinned, my shadows crawling along the floor to tease her ankles.

"I think there's some sexy roleplay potential in here somewhere," Uriah said, scratching his chin.

Snow fumed, her cheeks reddening.

"Leave me out of it, please," I drawled. I watched Scarlett, assessing her mental state.

She appeared tense, but present. I'd had her move her nightly session with Belise to earlier so I could take her out tonight before her communication with Kole.

It infuriated me that the reason she'd avoided leaving my castle had nothing to do with fear and everything to do with her schemes. She was paranoid about word getting back to Durian that she was, gods forbid, *happy* to be with me. She was intentionally keeping herself a slave, and it was a tragedy.

Scarlett deserved to experience the world with reckless

abandon. She deserved to live for herself, like she'd finally begun to before she was captured. To explore the nooks and crannies of the city, to travel to Valentin's coast and sleep surrounded by mountains, to get lost in the grit of existence, from the cavernous underbelly to life's greatest heights.

I had to take a page out of Scarlett's playbook. I had to believe her current state of denial was temporary, and I'd be able to give her the life of her dreams in due time. Then I'd give her another life, and another after that.

"You ready to go, baby?" I asked, leaving out all heavy emotion—all fear and grief and rage. I only left her with the sturdiest of branches to hold on to.

She nodded, concealing her own rich kaleidoscope of feeling. She wore a sky-blue dress embroidered with golden stars, falling just above her knees, with tan ankle boots.

"You're going to freeze," I admonished.

She crossed her arms. "No, I'm going to wear that big fur coat. I'll be fine."

The image of Scarlett in the long white coat that swallowed her petite body whole was adorable enough to relent.

∽

SCARLETT and I were on our way to Reggie's art gallery. Reggie had been one of Scarlett's most generous patrons at Odessa. She was fond of the silver fox, and the only reason Reggie still breathed was because he'd been nothing but respectful despite his infatuation. And, of course, he knew who Scarlett belonged to now.

Scarlett barely spoke to me as we walked. The plausibility of mortal spies around us reporting to Durian was near zero. Still, she looked downright pissed when I tried to make her laugh.

Naturally, I did so as often as possible.

To her credit, Scarlett played her part excellently, despite my sabotage attempts.

"Want me to treat you like a slave sexually?" I purred in her ear. "Right here, in the middle of the street? For the sake of your cover, obviously."

Scarlett blushed hard, staring up at me with those big blue eyes. Truly tragic for her that I could scent her blooming arousal, erasing all of her impressive efforts to feign disgust.

My hand found the back of her neck. I gripped her forcefully as we entered the charming gallery in River, close to the sprawling opera house and our grandest temple for Helia.

Inside, witch lights flickered, hovering near the ceiling and in the branches of crystalline, decorative trees.

A small crowd of exclusively turned men and women milled about the space, nodding with respect when I entered before all eyes moved to Scarlett. But preciously, Scarlett was staring slack-jawed at the gallery itself—hungrily devouring the nude marble sculptures, the paintings on the walls, the other pieces of art and décor meticulously placed.

I gently steered her forward with a hand on the small of her back. Our guards were scattered throughout the gallery, and several were standing watch outside.

Scarlett was blind to it all. When she finally tuned in to the array of prying, curious eyes, I assumed it was because the little demoness tasted their ripe desire.

My cock swelled in my pants. I fucking loved seeing Scarlett glow with amazement and appreciation, her features radiating that infectious, childlike awe. Just as I enjoyed seeing others burn with envy. Desired by all, my Scarlett breathed only for her vengeful God.

She peered up at me, unable to stop her eyes from glowing, her smile from spreading.

"That's a good girl," I whispered in her ear, delighting when she shuddered. "You're safe here. Let go and enjoy yourself or I'll force you to."

She laughed, and I drank the sound like a dying man. Then, her features turned genuine and unguarded—the most seductive version of Scarlett there was.

"I love when you threaten me to be good to myself, Rune," she said, her voice low as the vampire chatter resumed around us. "When I first met you, I wrongly assumed you were dominating me for domination's sake."

"Well, that's also hot," I said with a grin.

"But you never were, no matter how much you posture," she said. "Thank you for building me up when every other man I've known has made it their mission to tear me down."

I twirled her to face me, watching witch lights reflect in those perfect blue depths. "Always, Scarlett." I trailed a finger over her rosy cheek. Her skin was accented with shimmering powder, giving her an even more angelic appearance than usual. "I told you I would ruin all others for you. And that declaration had nothing to do with my cock."

She giggled, rolling her eyes. Then, she shrugged, eyeing me with a hooded gaze. "It could've."

I smiled and captured her lips with mine. "Wicked little demon." I kissed her temple. "The sexual obsession pales in comparison to the love, baby. No matter how much we like to pretend."

I guided Scarlett to the first set of pieces, and soon we were joined by a familiar face.

"Reggie!" Scarlett squealed. She hugged him, clearly taking the old vampire by surprise.

I could've sworn Reggie's fair skin reddened a shade. He smoothed his elegant navy suit, his silver hair artfully styled. He glanced at me and nodded in subservience, taking a respectful step back from Scarlett.

"You finally made it," Reggie said.

"I knew it would be incredible," Scarlett said. "You deserve to feel so proud."

Reggie shrugged. "It's a work in progress. Always will be. But thank you, Scarlett. Taste recognizes taste."

Reggie and I made small talk about the gallery while Scarlett appraised each piece. When she found an original Mellette, she spun toward us.

"That's the piece you were telling me about in Odessa—by the artist that paints about immortality as a prison," she said to Reggie, then nodded to me. "The same artist who did the painting in the castle library."

Reggie and I both nodded, and Scarlett turned back to the painting. It was bright pink with strokes of peach, light yellow, and orange—the brilliance of the clearest sunset. Yet its abstract, humanoid figures were folded in on themselves, hands on their heads in torment. Chains led to nowhere, looping around limbs and necks haphazardly. Everyone was utterly alone. Life's beautiful splendor expanded for an eternity.

"Does immortality have to be a sentence?" she asked.

My heart pulled. I knew she was asking for her own sake.

"No," Reggie said, before I could. "Mellette is a drama queen. Much like his devotees."

My lips curved at that assessment.

Scarlett threw a grin over her shoulder, her dangerous eyes ensnaring mine. "He must be Rune's favorite, then."

50

SCARLETT

I wrote at 9 p.m. sharp.

Kole?

I was still buzzing from the art gallery, my face sore from laughing with Reggie and Rune. I even connected with new turned I'd never met before, which may have been an ulterior motive of Rune's—to show me more of the clan I belonged to by virtue of belonging to him.

Rune and Sadie sat on either side of me in the deliberation room, and I forced them both to give me more breathing room after the initial cozy proximity.

I could hardly look at this damn table the same after Rune had bent me over it.

Kole wrote back immediately.

I'm going to give you ten seconds to describe the room I'm staying in.

I did as he asked, proving to him that it was at least me

writing—whether or not I had ulterior motives or a knife to my throat.

I'm happy to see proof of life.

I rolled my neck, remembering my aims. I allowed my succubus nature to take over. I squeezed out every last drop of shame. Which was more difficult with Rune next to me, making me self-conscious of my games with other men. But when his broad hand raked through my hair and then retreated, I relaxed deeper.

A familiar scorch coiled up my spine.

I'm alive. Just traded one prison for another.

I held my breath, waiting to see how Kole would react to this statement.

I have a feeling Durian's dungeon was far more dismal.

He was prying. I needed to feign trust, mimic openness, while revealing nothing of value.

True, being Durian's slave was unbearable. It would've killed me. But even still. I can't stop thinking about everything we talked about. Ravenia sounded like a dream, and I understand now what you meant about what the mainland calls "island madness." You're different from these vampires. They're running this place into the ground, and I want out.

Rune sighed, watching my face carefully, as if he wasn't sure whether to be impressed or terrified.

I'm sorry, Scarlett. My hands were tied when you were here. Do not think I didn't recognize your suffering, or the suffering of the other poor mortals. These vampires—

Kole stopped writing, as if debating whether to continue his thought. I focused my power on the notebook, imagining Kole on the other side of its magickally linked pages. Rosalind had confirmed that our magick still held over long distances, so long as the marks were still under our spell. Distance could even strengthen our influence when played correctly.

Still, it wasn't the same as being close. I couldn't use my body language or my beauty. I only had my words, my lofty promises, and his hazy memories. Fortunately, abstract fantasy and untethered potential were often infinitely more seductive than reality itself.

—are mad, Scarlett. They're bloody mad. I fear the current state of affairs in Valentin is worse than we ever could've imagined.

"It's playing out," I whispered.

"Don't get ahead of yourself," Sadie said tersely, earning a look from Rune. "Find out more before you jump to conclusions."

I fear the same. Kole, I hope I didn't get you or Brennan in trouble. He's one of the better ones. I can tell you respect him, and I defer to your judgment. I know that you have true wisdom when it comes to matters of power and leadership.

I made a face, annoyed that I had to pretend to base my thoughts off Kole's. As if I hadn't orchestrated Brennan's rise myself.

"Leave ego out of it," Sadie reminded me. "You don't need

recognition from these idiots. You need them to bend to your will by any means necessary."

Rune offered a hum of approval.

I'm afraid Brennan suffered more consequences than I did, my dear.

I grinned triumphantly, earning a pointed stare from both doms as they watched me.

"What? I can't celebrate my foresight?" Everything was going exactly according to plan, each person behaving as I knew they would.

"Focus, Little Flame," Rune snapped.

I slowly turned to Sadie, giggling at the way my stomach fluttered, getting double the attention from frightening, ancient beings who bled dark power.

Rune's shadows coiled around my neck, his glare downright menacing as he exchanged a glance with his amused mentor.

I focused back on Kole's writing.

But he will survive it. Don't worry on his behalf. He made his own choices. Just as I made mine. Choices I regret... choices such as letting a woman like yourself be treated the way you were. Or letting a woman like you go.

I sighed. Too easy. It was all far too easy.

Kole, I know how to make it all right again. I need you to be a good boy and put me into contact with Brennan. He's going to arrange my reacquisition to get back into Durian's good graces. From there, you will be able to negotiate taking me to Ravenia. You and I will make sure of it.

That had been Kole's hope all along, that he could potentially convince Durian to gift me to him as a bribe.

Even if Kole enjoyed pretending he was under my sharp heel, in the end, he objectified me the same as every other man. The prospect of rescuing me from vampires he saw as inferior was too juicy of a fantasy for him to resist.

I gave Kole ten more minutes of me, artfully avoiding getting into specifics that would ruin the illusion I'd spun. The illusion that Kole was special, that Brennan was a pawn on our board. That neither Rune nor Durian had captured my affections, which meant that I saw something so much more grand and noble in Kole than I saw in Valentin's most powerful vampires.

It all played into Kole's unique seduction profile and insecurities perfectly.

I closed the book, leaving Kole begging for more, frustrated beyond belief. Which was his main kink, in the end. He would do my bidding without a second thought.

I smiled.

Rune had been looking between the words on the page and my face for the past ten minutes, studying me as if for the sake of science.

Now, his gaze was glued to my curved lips. "You're fucking terrifying."

∼

It didn't take Kole long to link me with Brennan. They seemed to believe my cover story, which was that I was staying in Rune's chambers and knew he was guaranteed to be gone nightly at nine—to where, I had no idea. I emphasized the mystery of his strange behavior, embellishing details about how he dressed and acted when he left. All to distract from the implausibility of Rune leaving his correspondence journals vulnerable to me.

People believed what they wanted to believe when it came to matters of sex and love, far more often than one would imagine.

It was humorous to envision Brennan and Kole each taking turns writing to me in the same room, hiding their disappearing notes from each other as they did. Brennan couldn't let Kole know his feelings for me lest it risk his position with Durian. Kole could be more conspicuous, but he had reason to keep his cards close to his chest for his own plans. These men were vying for power over anything else, and they certainly couldn't be seen making decisions solely on behalf of a human woman.

It was all very hilarious.

I had to find humor in it all. Especially when I knew my days operating from a distance were numbered, and soon, my existence wasn't going to be all that funny anymore.

After tonight's chess matches, I sat in Rune's lap in the dining room, where he was forcing me to eat a late dinner.

"You can't skip meals, baby," Rune said. "I won't allow it."

I took a bite of buttery steak, sighing in contentment. Rune's chefs were the best in Aristelle.

"I'm sorry," I said. I tensed, a flashback of Durian entering my mind beyond my conscious awareness. Telling me to take care of his property or face the consequences.

"Hey, it's okay," Rune murmured. "I only want you strong and healthy."

I relaxed, taking another bite.

"Brennan is more obsessed with you than I'd ever imagined," Rune said, wrath in his tone that drove warmth to my core.

"And, more importantly, he *hates* Durian. Now more than ever."

"What if he stages a coup before you even arrive?" Rune asked.

I shook my head. "He won't. He might hate Durian right now, but he also still loves him, deep down. And he's terrified. He's not ready. He needs a push."

Rune was looking for any avenue to prevent me from leaving. Any loophole, any flaw in my logic.

I finished eating, relaxing into Rune's hold.

"I hate this," he whispered, his breath cool as it feathered across my neck. His shadows crawled up my legs, and when a tip brushed over the apex of my thighs, I squirmed.

Rune locked me still.

"I know," I whispered. "I'm yours, Rune. Forever."

"That's fucking right," he growled, lips grazing his old bite marks.

I moaned, anticipation building. I was radiating heat, desire thick in my blood.

He sucked on my sensitive skin. At the gentle brush of his fangs, I bucked.

Rune chuckled. "When this is all over, I'm taking you everywhere. I want to show you off in every major city in Ravenia. I want depictions of us drawn into every history book. I'm going to feed you the best food you've ever tasted, and you're going to sit in my lap, just like this, while I taste *you*."

I saw this vision of our future devastatingly clearly. It didn't matter that I knew Ravenia was at war, or that Rune would still be the clan leader after Durian was dead. I wanted to believe in a future where Rune finished his novel, and I studied music all over the realm. We would live out infinite lives, each richer with adventure and beauty than the last.

"Or perhaps you'll be under the table, servicing my cock while I drink your blood from a chalice," Rune said. "You'll have to earn the release of my saliva in your veins."

I gasped, the shadow doing more than teasing between my legs now. Rune shoved my thighs apart.

"With people watching?" I squeaked.

"I think a wicked demoness like yourself will come to enjoy a bit of exhibitionism," Rune purred. "Don't you want to show everyone what a good girl you are for me, baby?"

I sighed with pleasure. "Yes, Rune." The shadow continued to work my clit as Rune's fingers slipped underneath my skirt.

Two of them drove inside me, bending to hit a spot that had me crying out.

Rune's desire crested, and I fed from its power as he finally sunk his teeth into my neck.

His throaty groan vibrated through me. As the venom took over, I fell apart against Rune and his depraved shadows.

Over and over, until I couldn't remember my own name.

I melted into a vat of pleasure, so vast that I knew of nothing else—no pain, no grief, no heavy responsibilities or grand acts of sacrifice.

"That's it, Little Flame," Rune said, his voice the only thing tethering me to this realm. "Let go. Understand that you exist only as the perfect toy for my hands, my shadows, my cock, my fangs to play with and use to my satisfaction."

The place he'd bitten was a source of infinite ripples of pleasure. He spun me in his lap to straddle him. He tore off my black blouse, thumbing each nipple before squeezing and pulling.

At the sweet sting of pain, I made a cross between a moan and a cry.

My gaze was lost in Rune's dark eyes, staring so deeply inside of me that I feared he saw somewhere not even I could reach.

He freed his cock from his pants, letting it brush against my stomach. It was harder and more intimidating than ever.

I knew I'd soaked my blood with fear when a shadow gripped my throat. Rune lifted me and slowly lowered me onto him.

I felt the impossible stretch as my eyes rolled back.

"Shhh, don't pretend to be scared," Rune said darkly. "Your pretty pink pussy was begging for me. Don't you feel how soaking wet you are, my manipulative, duplicitous little demon?"

He bounced me up and down on his length, and I couldn't

help my accompanying screams. Rune delighted in them, watching me with eyes that burned, devoured.

"I hope the whole castle hears me ruining this needy cunt."

I exploded again the moment his fangs sunk into the sensitive flesh just above my nipple. My legs went from trembling to convulsing.

"Mm," Rune hummed against my skin as I fell apart. He was the only thing keeping me upright, stopping me from collapsing like a limp doll. His hand brushed through my hair tenderly. "Don't think passing out will save you, Little Flame. I'm going to use you until I've filled you with my cum and drunk your blood to my satisfaction. Losing consciousness will only make you more malleable."

To give further weight to his threat, the shadow around my throat was unrelenting, applying pressure to the sides of my neck until I saw stars.

Rune returned to drinking from me until I went quiet. His shadow released its hold on my throat and his tongue closed up my wound. He held me against his chest as he finished inside of me, his cock twitching as he spilled every last drop.

"Squeeze my hand if you're okay," Rune whispered.

His hand held mine, and I gave it a feeble squeeze.

"Good girl," he whispered into my hair, deeply inhaling. "Always so perfect for me. I've never loved anything more."

51

SCARLETT

My pen moved swiftly over the paper.

I'm tired of being a slave. I want to be someone's partner, Brennan. I want to be your partner.

Rune made a grunt of irritation, and Sadie rolled her eyes.

Once again, it was kind of hot to be sandwiched between the two of them.

Brennan wrote back quickly.

You know I want the same. Things are delicate right now, more than you even know. Matters a woman shouldn't have to be concerned about.

Now it was my turn to roll my eyes. "In other words, *don't worry your pretty little head.*"

"I'm the only one who should ever be allowed to condescend to you," Rune scoffed, making me laugh.

I know you're hesitant to return because of Durian. But I promise you, it would only be temporary. We're destined to be together, our union blessed by Lillian herself. Durian, he... well, it doesn't matter. Just know that soon you'll be <u>all mine.</u>

"The underlining was truly the confidence I needed to go all in," I joked. It was nice to be able to belittle these men with Sadie and Rune.

It was nice not to be alone anymore.

Brennan continued writing.

You can trust me, Scarlett. I'm already working on a way to bring you here safely, one that keeps you out of sight. Your addictive blood is an obstacle. I don't trust anyone around you but me, and there's too much discord in Hatham and on the border for you to wander back here blindly. But I think I have a way for you to come back to me with minimal risk, so long as you can make it to the border.

I wrote back to confirm things were going as I intended.

Wouldn't Durian be able to help? Are you going to tell him?

I watched his elegant writing manifest on the page.

No. I want to do this myself, and I want you to be a surprise. It doesn't matter... just trust me. No one will be able to track where you've gone. You'll be back at the palace unharmed.

I sat back in my chair arrogantly, looking between Sadie and Rune with an unabashed grin. They both lifted their brows, their expressions so similarly scolding that I giggled again at the sight of it.

"I told you," I said. "Tunnels!"

Rune sighed. "Sometimes I wish you were dumber."

I pretended extreme offense, gaping at him. "Why?"

"Easier to control," Sadie answered for him.

Rune angrily fucked my body with his eyes. "Precisely."

I lazily ended my conversation with Brennan, leaving him with the heavy lifting of securing my passage back to the castle via tunnels that would eventually spell his downfall.

"What's the kink for two doms staring at you?"

Rune glared at me, and Sadie smirked, her eyes trailing slowly down my form. My head was swimming with delirious pleasure from using my succubus magick.

"I dunno, but I have that kink too," a voice said from behind us, startling us all.

"Kitten," Sadie snapped. "What did I say about entering my chambers at this hour?"

I looked back at Imogene, her curvy form cloaked in a soft pink blouse and skirt. Her hand was halfway into a giant bowl of popcorn.

Her eyes widened. "Oh no, I'm sorry, Mistress, I must've misread the time," she hurried, her voice an octave higher than before. "I was distracted! And upside down!"

I couldn't even begin to imagine what she'd been up to that had her upside down. But with Mason's cagey behavior every time Imogene was mentioned, I hoped to the gods it involved her.

Maybe that was why the frightening vampire woman had been so much more personable lately...

I snorted, and all eyes returned to me.

"Sorry, was I... interrupting something?" Imogene asked while chewing on a mouthful of popcorn. She sounded hopeful.

And horny.

Rune stood, roughly manhandling me up and into his arms. "Bye, Sadie."

I winked over Rune's shoulder. Sadie laughed, Imogene squealed, and Rune's grip tightened.

"You're in so much trouble," he growled in my ear.

At first, I panicked. Then I remembered I was with Rune. I was safe.

But my days of safety were numbered.

~

THINGS WERE GOING AS WELL as they possibly could've been going. Rune's plants in born districts didn't need to do much pushing to rile the lower classes into a frenzy. Blood shortages had only gotten worse. And as fantastic as that was for our schemes against Durian, especially in showing Kole and the kingdom Durian's incompetence and lack of control over his own people, it was a disaster for mortals.

What was happening was unsustainable, and slaves were hurting most of all.

And no matter what Belise, Rune, Snow, Sadie, or anyone else said—it felt like it was all my fault. While I was healing, everyone else was suffering. And I had the power to end it all.

Kole wrote to me about how irritating it was that Brennan hogged the short time he had to write to me. Brennan wrote me poetry about the taste of my blood.

Rune enjoyed making fun of both men while filling me with his cock.

In Ravenia, the turned clans were giving Earle and his armies a run for their money, which also didn't bode well for Durian. It was becoming less and less likely that the kingdom was going to risk Valentin's exports or divert resources to deal with our conflict. Which meant that soon Rune and his clan would be free to make ballsier moves, no longer worried about the political ramifications of breaking the ceasefire.

Things were going so perfectly on all fronts, in fact, that I should've been expecting something to finally go wrong.

That was my first thought when I strode down the grand

hall on my way to the staircase, and I heard a familiar screeching.

Snow and Uriah crowded my vision. Snow's face twisted into a frightened warning. Cold air blew through the space, as if the front doors of the castle were ajar.

"*Scarlett!*"

A cold chill ran down my spine. I knew Snow was saying something, her mouth slowly moving in my periphery as my vision tunneled, but I didn't hear a word.

I walked past, barely glancing at the turned guards who were stock still and assessing the situation with sharp eyes and flaring shadow magick.

The door was in fact wide open, Rune's looming figure in the doorway with Mason and Percy at his side.

I glimpsed the tall blonde beyond them, standing on the front porch as her pointed finger moved wildly about in the cold air. She peeked around Rune's form, her light brown eyes narrowing on me. Her strong nose twisted in disgust, her thin lips curling.

"Oh, look whose legs work!" Isabella barked at me.

I nodded at Mason, and she begrudgingly stepped back, allowing me to stand next to Rune and face down Isabella.

"Let's step outside," I said hollowly, embarrassment flushing my body. "I don't want everyone to hear this."

Rune assessed me, thinly veiled anger in his features. "Are you sure? We can escort her back to the care center."

A vein in Isabella's forehead throbbed. "Where's my fucking money, huh? She's safe and sound. Where's my end of the bargain?"

I reared back, and Snow rested her hand on my shoulder.

"You don't have to do this right now," Snow said gently. "Or *ever.*"

I shook my head before stepping out onto the spacious

raised porch. Stone arches encased the area, offering a semblance of privacy from passersby.

Snow and Rune followed me, and I heard the booming sound of the door shutting behind us. Rune ordered the guards to step away.

"You found your perfect parasitic host to sink your teeth into and you don't give a shit about your sister?" Isabella seethed. "Can't even be bothered to pay me a visit while I heal from being used as a blood bag—the unspeakable horrors I endured because of *you!*"

Isabella shook with rage. And no matter how much I'd changed, how much I'd healed—my every instinct was to cower before her, to find a way to soothe her feelings and make myself small and apologetic.

My gaze flickered to Snow, anchoring myself to her reaction instead. I saw the way she was standing protectively close, pure fury and disbelief in her bright green eyes.

I looked up at Rune. "Can you please go get Isabella's belongings?" I whispered.

At first, Rune's brows drew together in confusion. Then he nodded. He exchanged a glance with Snow.

"I'll be right back," he assured the three of us.

"You mean the money that I'm owed?" she hissed at me. "For keeping your dirty little secret?"

Rune spun on her, and I grabbed his arm as Isabella flinched and took a step back. He towered over her with a snarl.

"I am not paying you to keep Scarlett's name out of your undeserving mouth," he said, eerily calm as his thorny shadows crawled across the ground. "You're going to do that so long as you want to live to see another day."

Isabella's survival instincts kicked in, finally exposing her fear.

"Is. That. Understood?"

Isabella nodded, and Rune turned, kissed my temple, and left without another word.

With Rune gone, Isabella went back to full cunt mode.

I took a steadying breath, moving quickly through an exercise to connect me back to my body. As I regained control, rooting myself to the present, I fundamentally understood that this was a test.

This was a pivotal chance to prove just how much I'd grown.

I straightened my back and lifted my chin. "Let's say I had gone to visit you," I said, my voice betraying me with a slight wobble. "How would you have treated me?"

Isabella looked at me like I was both crazy and stupid, as if the question had been spoken in an entirely different language.

"You owe me an apology," Isabella snapped. "You're not owed *anything*, Scarlett. How dare you speak to me like that!"

"You are the only one speaking to anyone disrespectfully," Snow interjected. "But I could understand how someone calmly questioning you would sound like an attack to you. Given that you're an emotionally immature, cruel narcissist without an ounce of self-awareness."

Isabella's nasty stare moved to Snow, looking her up and down and then ignoring her completely as if she was below even her acknowledgment.

Something was building inside of me, wrestling with the cloudy haze of my fight-or-flight ingrained trauma response.

All those excuses I'd made for Isabella rose from the abyss. That she'd only been a child, incapable of understanding the impact of her actions as her parents fell apart before her eyes.

We were adults now. And all those excuses dried up like sand on my tongue.

I worked every day to be better. For my own sake, for the sake of those who loved me, and for all of Valentin, my home.

I made every effort to heal myself, even when it broke my heart. Even when growth was so painful that I knew it would be easier to cling to resentment and self-pity instead. To wallow. To give up. To fill my heart with nothing but hatred, my veins with nothing but grief. I had more than enough justification to raise my fist against life itself.

And yet I chose to stay heedlessly in love with this messy, unfair world instead.

Isabella had gone the opposite way. Her choices had been her own.

She'd chosen to stay closed instead of open. She'd chosen to be cruel instead of loving, and she'd done so long before she knew I was a succubus.

Some people were addicted to suffering, and it not only made them weak, but it also left them painfully alone.

That was why I had an army ready to jump to my defense, and Isabella stood on this porch spewing hate with not a soul behind her.

"All my life, you have done everything in your power to make me hate myself the way you hate me," I said, tears burning my eyes. "You were born afraid. Of scarcity, of loneliness. You thought if our parents loved me, then they'd love you less. So you sabotaged my relationship with them at every turn. You told me they hated when I sang. You told them that I was a troublemaker. You isolated me from the other villagers, or worse, actively worked to turn them against me. You made sure I had no one. You hated Jaxon for defying you, for showing me I was worthy of love and friendship."

Snow was close, but I stood on my own two feet as I addressed Isabella. Even as she stared at me with an unchanging expression, her desires painfully, and predictably, set against listening to anything I had to say.

"I'm sorry you lost your parents young. I'm sorry you endured cruelty at the hands of vampires," I said. "But none of your suffering was *my fault*. Being raped wasn't my fault, no matter how many times you told me it was. You've allowed men to hurt me since I was a teenager, and you not only profited off my suffering, but you also kept me wounded enough to believe it was what I deserved."

I felt Rune at my back, but he made no further movement. He let me handle this myself, exactly how I needed to.

Isabella stammered, that vein still throbbing like it might burst. "You're a fucking—" She cut herself off before she said the word. "Well, you know what you are," she hissed.

"Why can't you hear anything I'm saying?" I asked, a sob building in my throat. "I still have feelings. I don't have a *dark void where my soul should be. I do have a soul, just like you.*" As I quoted Isabella's words she'd written in her diary, her eyes flashed.

"Allegedly," Snow said under her breath.

Isabella shot her a glare. "Her spell should've worn off if you know what she is. Yet you still defend her?" she asked Snow and Rune, completely ignoring me.

"Looks like someone is finally catching up," Rune muttered.

"You've never deserved Scarlett," Snow said. "And that's your loss."

Frustration bloomed in my chest, my fists clenching. I'd poured my heart out to Isabella, detailing years of severe abuse, and she hadn't responded to a word of it.

"I'm speaking to you," I spat at her, stupid tears finally rolling down my cheeks.

Isabella took a step back, disgust and a nearly bored-looking annoyance in her eyes as if she was facing down a diseased animal.

"I was still your family, adopted or not." My voice trembled with anger and grief, intensity rolling off me in powerful waves. "I was still a *person*. I did nothing to earn your hatred. I did nothing to earn anyone's hatred in that village. I see that now."

"Yeah, no," Isabella sneered. "That's just not true." Her voice was teeming with confidence from who-the-fuck-knew-where, considering Rune could obliterate her to ash and guts with one snap of his fingers. "You earned all of our hatred because you were an insufferable whore and man stealer who hurt people for sport. You teased and tormented men just to feed off their souls. You ruined women's lives with all your temptations and tricks. You—"

I was close to exploding, to fucking screaming until my throat was raw and bleeding. I cut her off, tired of hearing her twisted web of delusions, lies, and justifications. "I traveled all the way to Aristelle for *you*. Even after your own boyfriend told me not to go." I knew it was unnecessary, but I couldn't help the dig—to see the satisfying confusion in Isabella's eyes. "Everyone told me it was a deathtrap. I went anyway, all by myself. For *you*. I made a life for myself in a city I didn't understand, full of vampires who thirsted for my blood. Vampires who gave me even more trauma to work through with my healer than the heaping pile of bullshit you've been serving me my whole life. And, look!"

Isabella jolted at my raised voice.

"I found a way to save you from the trade that is famously fucking impossible to save people from."

I wiped away my tears before throwing my hands up.

"You're welcome!"

Isabella just stared at me. She offered me nothing. No apology, no murmur of gratitude. No recognition that she was wrong about me—that I was worthy of love, family, and friends, a home that was healing and warm.

I shook my head, reaching a breaking point. I turned to Rune and lifted a hand. He was quick to place Isabella's journal in my palm. I was blinded by hurt and rage when I tossed the diary to Isabella. She scrambled to catch it, recognition soon transforming to wrath.

"How dare you invade my privacy, you—"

One of Rune's shadows turned razor sharp, stopping a few inches in front of Isabella's face.

"Consider the invasion a matter of Valentin security," Rune said, his tone clipped. He pulled his shadow back.

"Oh? Like the slaughter of nuns this morning at one of Helia's temples?" Isabella snarled.

Snow and Rune both went utterly still, and my face contorted in confusion, shocked out of my heartache.

Isabella waved her diary around as she spoke. "Accompanied by a demand to return a certain *Miss Scarlett Hale, servant of Lillian, to her Master, Lillian's chosen one.*"

I heard the thunderous sound of my own heartbeat. I blinked. I thought reaching my limit would allow me to finally rage at Isabella the way she deserved. To hurl the same cruelty back at her that she'd spent years stabbing into my own heart.

Turned out, all reaching my limit did was send me sinking to the cool stone, my knees tucked beneath me. My body shut down, shouts fading to a dull hum. My vision became blurry, the cool air growing entirely unnoticeable.

I stayed there, in between life and death, until the emptiness transformed into conversations and events playing in my mind on repeat. What combination of words could I have spoken to get through to Isabella? To prove my worthiness? To receive her acknowledgment of my pain, her admission of guilt for causing so much of it?

I remembered every cruel word she'd ever told me, each sentence she'd scrawled about me in her diary.

Movement had my eyes refocusing. In front of me, a man in a bright magenta skirt and white blouse stood.

Belise met me on the ground, taking both my hands in his as his gold bracelets clinked together.

"She didn't—she *couldn't* hear me," I said. My cheeks were wet, my voice racked with sobs. "She had no interest in the truth. She had no interest in truly knowing or understanding who I am. For seeing how she'd hurt me, admitting she'd been wrong. Her only desires were to preserve herself and continue to tear me down."

"Hey, look at me," Belise said softly, his magick sending calming signals to my overworked nervous system. "You aren't ready to fully comprehend my next words, but let them absorb into your soul, anyway. They'll be there, waiting for you, when you're ready."

I met his eyes, yearning to hear some wisdom that might heal all parts of me all at once. Something that would take this pain away for good. I didn't want to feel this way anymore.

Like I was a plague, a deep pit of darkness that was destined to swallow everything and everyone I loved whole.

Belise took in a long breath, subconsciously guiding me to do the same. His warmth distracted me from my spiraling thoughts, my torn-open, primordial wound that wept and wept.

"You will never receive closure from other people. Closure is something that you give yourself."

52

RUNE

"Something isn't right," I said to Sadie on her patio, overlooking Aristelle.

Scarlett was with Belise, and I feared what she would say once she'd processed Isabella's cruel reveal. The witch had been right. It had only been a matter of time before someone told her. It could've easily been revealed in her correspondences with Kole and Brennan, though they'd been too consumed with themselves to cover other ground.

"It's nagging at me too," Sadie said.

"Scarlett is incredibly powerful. I don't doubt that," I said. "But in her blinding faith that she can smoothly stop this war before it begins, I worry she's ignoring vulnerabilities. I find it strange that Brennan would risk anyone knowing their current tunnel system." They would've already destroyed the tunnel we uncovered at Evangeline's mansion and rerouted. "It's too huge of a risk. I understand they underestimate Scarlett, but they shouldn't be underestimating *me*."

"It doesn't make sense," Sadie agreed. "Scarlett thinks Brennan wants to save her himself to be a white knight, and to surprise Durian as a grand gesture to make up for losing her.

But that's not completely adding up. It would be easier and less risky to bring Durian in on her rescue, to simply order soldiers at the border to escort her through. I understand Brennan wants to keep Scarlett all to himself, to limit her contact with others, especially Durian. But..."

"There's something we're missing," I finished.

"She won't want to hear it," Sadie said. "It's not going to change her mind. Now that she knows Durian won't stop killing mortals in her name, she will go to him. He needs to be eliminated for her to be free."

"Just like after Scarlett was taken, I'm infuriated by my own limitations. I know that without kingdom involvement, we could win a war against the born. I know I could annihilate all of Hatham if I wanted to."

Sadie sighed. "But it would only be kicking the can further down the road. You would radicalize survivors, lose kingdom support, and risk all of Valentin, including all of her innocents. You cannot base those kinds of decisions off this woman, no matter how special she is. She wouldn't want you to."

She smiled at me sadly, resting a hand on my shoulder as my whole body grew rigid and tight.

"I know," I said bitterly. "In waging war, burning this whole world to the ground for her—I would only end up losing her for good."

I'd once worried Scarlett's life would be ruined by war from afar. That conflict might prevent her from traveling, from living without the fear that she may brush up against violence that had nothing to do with her.

I never could've imagined that she'd root herself right in the middle of it all.

But perhaps I should've, because that was so very Scarlett of her.

"We will prevail because we are not like them." Sadie dropped her hand, looking out on the horizon as she sighed.

"We don't make irrational moves out of emotion. We don't flex our power heedlessly, making us vulnerable to a guaranteed assassination. We do what's right, for the greatest number of people, and we hope that the gods reward us for our effort."

"I won't lose her, Sadie," I whispered. "I won't risk the world, but I will risk *myself* for her. Always."

"I know, Rune."

∽

I FOUND Scarlett in the room of music, laying under the stars. She was wearing a navy blue gown, complete with a sweetheart neckline and silky fabric that accentuated her curves. She blended in with the cosmos, shining just as bright as any nebula.

The music she was listening to wasn't sad nor happy. Contemplative, moving, a rich alto woman's voice rising and falling with incredible, heart-stopping piano accompaniment. I'd set this recording aside for Scarlett, in a box of new acquisitions I knew she'd love.

She sat up when she saw me. Her face was puffy from crying, but her features were serene, as if she were at peace with it all.

Naturally, that scared the hell out of me.

"I'm ready to sing for you," she said. "I've been listening to this song for an hour. It's beautiful. Forgive me if I botch the words."

She smiled, and I sat down in front of her, pulling her trembling hand into mine.

"You sing whatever words you want, baby. They're hardly what I'm listening for."

"Close your eyes, please."

I obeyed. I gently stroked her hand, knowing she was mine, and I was hers. I pretended we lived in a world where that was all that mattered. Where I didn't fear opening my eyes and her not being there anymore.

Scarlett rose to start the recording over again. She sat back down and gave me her hand again as a piano melody softly trickled through.

When Scarlett began to sing, I worried perhaps I was dying, because my entire life flashed before my eyes. I was back in Crescent Haven, playing with my sisters out in the forest. I was laughing with them as we pointed up at the stars, making up stories about who we were going to be: the dragons we would one day slay, the castles we would live in, the strange and beautiful people we would know.

I was human, as human as I felt watching Scarlett sing that very first time. The day I'd returned to the forest my sisters had been slaughtered in, and I noticed that new life had formed from the ashes—a girl who dreamed as I once had, her feet digging into the same soil that had raised me.

As Scarlett's voice rose and fell, as multifaceted and complex as her dangerous mind, I saw that constellation of souls and life karma. I saw our etheric selves, intrinsically intertwined, with no hope of ever being free from each other.

I held her hand, grinning so wide my face hurt.

When she finally stopped, I wanted to bend her over my knee for it. I wanted to make her sing for me for an eternity.

"You can open your eyes," she said.

I opened them and immediately kissed her, holding her face in my hands. She tasted like hope.

I wondered if I tasted like grief to her perfect lips.

"It is a crime you were ever told to stop singing," I whispered as I pulled back. "A crime against existence itself."

"I feel the same way about your writing," she replied. "Promise me you'll finish that novel, Rune."

My grin was back, impossible to withhold. This precious girl was all mine, and I couldn't fathom how Lillian's bastard son could've gotten so lucky.

"I promise," I said, shifting under that weighted stare. She was the only being in this world capable of cracking me this uncomfortably open.

We spent the rest of the night pretending—pretending Scarlett wasn't about to leave me, pretending that she wasn't furious with me because of what I'd withheld from her about Durian's atrocities.

We laughed, making light of even the most egregious topics. I whispered secrets as the stars grew ever brighter amid the darkness, and Scarlett whispered hers right back. Our darkest thoughts lay bare. The moments we'd felt alone, the moments we'd feared we didn't belong in this world.

I showed her types of music she'd never heard before, and I told her about my travels all over Ravenia. I lost myself in the light in her eyes, the curve of her smile, her small hand wrapped around mine.

My soul was leaking out of me, and hers out of her, and there was no stopping any of it. Nor did I want to. We were fused at the heart.

She'd roused me from the deepest slumber, and now I couldn't remember how I'd breathed before her.

But one thing was certain—I wouldn't be able to breathe after.

"I want to record your voice," I whispered, when her head was on my chest.

"How does that work? The process of recording?" she asked.

"I have blank spheres. You recite a simple spell to begin recording, and you recite another to stop."

Scarlett paused, and I listened to her heart pick up a few paces. "Interesting."

53

SCARLETT

I spoke few words to Rune when we woke up the next morning. I'd barely slept, tossing and turning, processing what Isabella had told me.

What Rune had *withheld* from me.

I didn't write to Kole and Brennan last night. My absence would only work in my favor, preying on their fear and heightened emotions wondering what had happened to me.

In the deliberation room, Rune, Mason, Uriah, Sadie, and Snow sat around me as I sat at the head.

The first thing out of my mouth had the whole table falling silent.

"Isabella's reveal was what you all have been keeping from me, for weeks now," I said. "How many incidents like this have occurred? How long have you known they'd been carried out in my name?"

I watched as all eyes moved to Rune.

"Since a week after you were taken," Rune said. "Durian has been sending me letters."

"Letters?" I balked. "Saying *what?*"

"The same as all the others, Little Flame—that you're

destined to be with him," he said, face stony as he watched me. "He's just considerably more unstable than your other men."

Rune's anger twisted my heart, even if I knew it was in response to my imminent departure.

"Kole is terrified of him," I said, the lump of guilt only growing as all of Kole's messages about Durian's deteriorating mental state were given new light. My own anger arose as I glared at each person sitting here. "And you all just decided not to tell me? To keep allowing innocent mortals to die because you didn't want to hurt my fucking feelings?"

"You knowing wouldn't have stopped anything," Rune snapped.

"I thought you should know," Snow said softly. "But Rune is right. None of this is your fault. These were acts of terror carried out by unpredictable religious fanatics. And you're leaving now that you've heard the truth, right? You weren't ready before. I still don't think you're ready, but at least you're stronger now."

I bristled at her words, her lack of belief in me. It reminded me of Jaxon all over again.

"I'm so glad you all could come to a mutual decision on what's best for me," I said, bitterness coating my tongue.

I turned my attention to Sadie, choosing to be productive instead of stewing in anger. "You said you've been researching ways to see through Durian's illusions."

Her eyes had been flickering between me and Rune, assessing with all the sharpness of a wolf on the hunt.

"Yes," she said, leaning back in her chair. Her nails were painted black now, her hands resting confidently on the sleek wooden table. "The visions exist only in your senses, so removing your ability to perceive is, of course, an impractical option. Unless you're Rune and can remove senses by shadow." She sighed. "I can provide clarity spells that can aid, but in the end, Durian is powerful, and you must learn how to see through his illusions by maintaining complete control of your consciousness. Similar to a lucid dream, there will be tiny hints indicating what you're seeing isn't real. An extra finger here, the wrong shade of eye color there. Pay attention to detail *always*. Durian is not a seer, no matter what he'd deluded himself into believing. He's preying on our proclivity to accept what we perceive as reality, no matter the small inconsistencies. But he can't make his visions completely accurate, or see into your memories. He probably avoids having his visions speak for precisely that reason. They might say something completely out of character, breaking the illusion."

"My mind was cloudier when he was showing me that vision of you," Rune said. He'd artfully boarded himself back up, playing the part of the impassive vampire lord. "He was capitalizing off my desire to believe. You have to be extremely careful not to let your emotions distract you, not to see what you want to see. A cloudy mind is another sign he's priming you for manipulation, but as soon as you see through it, you'll become sharper again."

I watched the way Rune was avoiding my eyes, looking off into the distance instead.

"I should've noticed the way Millie, my shadowbird, had behaved. She's wary of strangers. She should've at least sniffed the air and appeared surprised. But she didn't react at all. She couldn't see you like I could."

Raw pain flashed in Rune's eyes, for the briefest of moments, before it was gone without a trace.

I nodded, letting this intel about Durian's magick sink in.

"I'm going to force Brennan to act," I said. "I'll be in Hatham by tomorrow night."

Rune's hand fisted against the table, the lights above flickering. "You cannot expect to accomplish anything by acting out of guilt and whim. You've barely trained, barely recovered, we still don't even—"

"I'm never going to be ready or strong enough for any of you," I said, cutting him off. "Now that I know what Durian has been doing, I cannot sit back and let him continue. Everything is going according to plan. The born are fighting each other, and public perception of Durian is turning. Kole's opinion of the born is lower than ever, and he's itching to jump ship. Brennan is *so close* to turning on Durian." I clasped my hands in front of me, burning with determination. "I'm going. Either you help me plan how best to accomplish that without getting myself killed…"

Rune winced, and Snow's face fell.

"…or I'll figure it out myself."

Rune's eyes locked on mine, his lip itching to curl. "Don't do that."

I didn't blink, holding his intensity.

"You know we're all sitting here to help you. If your mind is set, there's nothing we can do but prepare you the best we can," Rune said. He visibly fought the raw emotions underneath the surface that threatened his impassive leader persona.

"I'm sorry, Scarlett," Snow said. "I'm sorry you had to find out that way. I'm sorry you feel betrayed. We only wanted to protect you. Most of all, I'm sorry Durian has been doing any of it to begin with."

"He's punishing me," I said. Rosalind's face eclipsed my mind's eye, and I felt nothing but pure rage. "Even if he thinks I was taken against my will, he's punishing me, anyway. He wants me back, and he wants me broken, entirely dependent on him."

Rune's shadows crawled toward me, one of them wrapping around my wrist.

"I hate what you both kept from me," I said to Snow and Rune, given they were the ones I expected the most honesty from. "But I understand why you did it. I'm not going to leave angry." My rage melted, and my lip trembled. "I just want this all to be over."

Rune nodded, his shadow tightening around my wrist as if unconsciously. Snow's green eyes were watery.

It was time to focus on the task at hand. I steadied myself with a deep breath in. "I have new ideas."

∼

RUNE FORCED me to sit in his lap at dinner with everyone, and even though it was mildly embarrassing, I couldn't help but obey him. The humiliation was driving heat between my thighs, which only made my cheeks flush even brighter pink.

This delighted Rune, of course.

Several inner circle members joined us at the long dining table. Snow, Sadie, and I were the only non-turned other than the willing courtesans feeding guests.

Uriah was sitting extremely close to Snow at our right, shooting a feral glare at anyone who glanced at her seat at the table questioningly.

I looked up at Rune. He jolted when I lightly brushed my hand against his cheek.

"I need you to feed when I'm gone," I whispered.

His jaw ticked, his hard stare piercing straight through me.

"I need you to stay strong for me. I will never see it as a betrayal. You need to do what you need to do so that you can protect me when the time comes, okay?"

Rune nodded. "Yes, baby." He smiled sadly, brushing a strand of my hair behind my ear.

A turned man, Dev, entered the room. Rune's focus strayed to him.

"We've orchestrated a weak spot at the border, by all appearances," Dev said. He glanced at me for the briefest of seconds.

Rune's grip on me tightened. "Good, thank you, Dev."

Everyone pretended they hadn't heard a thing. My escape

was being carefully planned on both sides of the border, unbeknownst to the born.

Rune kissed my forehead. I gave him my wrist.

He stared into my eyes as he brushed his lips against my skin. At the flash of his fangs, my core turned molten.

He sunk down into my flesh, and I saw cosmos, heard music that sent pleasurable chills down my spine.

Someone cleared their throat.

"For the love of the gods," a male voice said.

Rune stopped feeding, homing in on the source of the comment—a turned man now staring down at his chalice of blood. The ire in Rune's eyes was downright murderous.

Uriah coughed, quickly rushing to his comrade's defense. "Look, you two stir up some intensity, you know..." His knuckles were white around his utensils, and Snow was staring at him like she was in heat.

I giggled, and Rune's possessive wrath was replaced with amusement.

Rune sunk his fangs back into my wrist, not caring the effect it had on the room. My eyes rolled back.

The calls to tone it down went ignored.

∽

"You're really leaving tomorrow?"

Snow and I sat out in the gardens, despite the cold. We'd put a blanket down, surrounded by shrubs and barren trees. I wished we could go somewhere out in the city, but I couldn't risk it. I'd thought I'd claimed freedom when I'd escaped Durian, but the truth was, I would never be free while he still breathed.

It was getting late, but I knew I wouldn't be able to do much sleeping, anyway.

"Yes," I said softly. "I told Kole and Brennan that my life is in danger here, that because of Durian's atrocities, everyone except Rune wants me dead or returned to the born. They think I've convinced two of Rune's guards to smuggle me out, because the guards want the violence to stop and think Rune is selfish for keeping me."

"They bought it?"

"Yes." My heart was beating too fast again, anxiety ripe in my body no matter how violently I tried to squash it down. "Brennan recommended a weak spot at the border, the one we created, and he's told me exactly where to go to meet his escort."

I was to make my way to a statue of Lillian inside an abandoned library. I'd learned that tunnel entrances were all marked by depictions of Lillian.

"You don't deserve any of this, Scar," Snow said.

Even underneath my gloves, my hands were starting to freeze. I lifted the mug of hot chocolate, warming my fingers as I took a sip. Though it seemed like we were alone in the frigid darkness, I knew at least three vampires were nearby keeping watch.

"*Deserve* is a strange concept," I murmured. "Do any of us truly deserve pain? Struggle? Loss?" I shook my head, glancing up at the clear sky of twinkling stars. "These things come for all of us, anyway. They're inescapable. I think measuring what life gives us against what we think we deserve causes a lot more suffering than necessary. Better to remember that it's all temporary, that a new season is right around the corner. I feel the most peaceful when I surrender."

Snow stared at me silently for a few beats before looking up at the stars, seeing what I saw.

"Mom calls it *the flow*. She says the flow is the natural course of the gods' will, inescapable and perfect. You can either move with it or fight it as it drags you along, but it keeps moving forward either way."

I thought of my own mom, my adoptive one. Did she believe

in the gods' will? I barely knew her, and that lodged a lump of heartbreak in my throat. I wondered if that was why these esoteric concepts came easily to me. I'd been made durable, insightful, by my trauma and upbringing. Just like Rune.

Maybe it all balanced out in the end.

I hoped so.

"I love you, Snow. Believe in me."

"Always, Scarlett."

54

SCARLETT

Rune's hand trembled slightly as he secured the lightweight holster around my waist, a dagger on each of my upper thighs. The belt was made from velvety black fabric, the entire contraption designed to be smooth and inconspicuous. The only point of bulkiness was the weapons themselves. Overtop, I would wear a skirt, blouse, and coat—an outfit that made me appear as vulnerable as possible.

They had no idea the vengeful demon they were welcoming back with open arms. And I was going to keep it that way until it was time to bite.

Rune pushed me up against the wall of his bedroom, looking down at my body clothed only in black underwear, a holster, and two deadly weapons.

"I can't even properly enjoy how fucking sexy and dangerous you look right now," Rune said with irritation. He lifted my chin. Scorching heat radiated from our bodies pressed together. "You are coming back to me, Little Flame."

"Yes, Rune, my God."

He chuckled darkly, his hand moving to squish my cheeks between his thumb and index finger.

"Good girl," he purred, kissing my forehead.

But underneath the dominance, I tasted the desperation in his desire. He wanted me to stay. He wanted to tie me to his bed and never let me go.

Rune the Ruthless was terrified, and the sight of it had my heart in a painfully tight squeeze.

He released my cheeks, and I instantly melted into him, putting my head on his chest. All of him held all of me—his arms and those creeping, sneaky shadows—and a part of me wanted to hide, to disappear into him rather than face this perilous destiny.

And that was why I loved Rune more than anyone had ever loved another. Because he would never allow me to lose myself in him. Rune wanted *Scarlett*, not a broken-down extension of himself.

"I love you so much it hurts," I said.

"Dramatic."

I laughed, breaking away to glare up at him. "Oh, are we ignoring the fact that you're the tortured writer and hopeless romantic here? Should I pull quotes from all those love letters?"

He smiled, his eyes sparking. "Did you memorize them?"

I shrugged. "Some of them. Others I copied down before they disappeared. I need you to never write to me in disappearing ink ever again. I want to drown in your words just as deeply as you wish to drown in my voice."

"Yes, Mistress Scarlett," he teased.

I wrinkled my nose. "Please don't. Gods."

His gaze moved slowly from my eyes over my face before he stepped back to appraise my body.

His shadows bled into the air, and if I were to dissociate for a moment, I might see just how terrifying Rune appeared to anyone else.

"I hate this," he said, his tone as sharp as my daggers.

"I know."

"Scarlett Hale, the trouble you will be in if you don't come home to me," he said, all the violence of the realm in his tone. "I will drag you back to this fucking plane of existence from anywhere in the cosmos. And I could say you wouldn't enjoy your punishment, but knowing you and your sick little desires, I'm not sure of that."

I rolled my eyes. "*My* sick little desires, huh?"

"Mm," he said. He grabbed my waist as he stunned me with a kiss that squeezed out my every last drop of oxygen. "Yes, my incorrigible slut."

I laughed. "Incorrigible slut," I repeated. I grinned and wished we could stay here, laughing, forever.

I went back in for Rune's lips, promising him with my body that we would have forever. I didn't know if fate gave much of a shit about what we *deserved,* but by the gods, I hoped the stars saw how much Rune and I were meant to spend eternity together.

∼

I DIDN'T WANT to dwell on goodbyes. Not only because they made me itchy and hot from discomfort, but also because I refused to make a huge production out of my departure.

I would be back soon. And then we'd all look silly and melodramatic.

I'd had one last session with Belise this morning, working through tools to soothe trauma responses and keep a clear head. Similarly, I'd met with Sadie, who'd burned bundles of herbs and twirled them in circles around my body for clarity. She'd also delivered one of her classic pep talks, going through scenarios with me that were more difficult to discuss with Rune.

I was as prepared as I'd ever be.

As I hugged Snow in the grand foyer, I wondered when the

shift had happened—the shift from victim to *powerful, dangerous woman*.

I thought perhaps it had happened slowly, over time.

"You don't need my faith, but I'll give it anyway," Snow said. She was in a casual black dress and platform boots, her trademark pentacle necklace around her neck. "You're the strongest person I've ever met."

"You're the wisest," I said.

Snow smiled, shaking her head. "Well, you don't know many people."

"The humblest too."

She laughed. Her eyes brimmed with tears. I whispered that I loved her and turned away.

"We're not hugging," I said to Mason, standing on the bottom steps with Uriah.

She offered the rarest of smiles. "Fuck no."

Rune stood by the door, watching me with those sharp, prying eyes.

"I want to keep my appendages intact, so I'll pass on that one too," Uriah said. "I'll see you soon, anyway, Trouble." He gave me a lazy salute, and when I returned it, he chuckled.

Sadie entered the hall, her heels clicking against marble. "One last thing, Scarlett dear." She was wearing a tight leather dress and chic cape that fell to her midriff. She walked all the way to me, towering over me in a way that had Rune tensing and moving closer. "From here on out, every doubt, every fall, every nightmare, every last drop of spilled blood is *fuel*. Don't bury any of it. *Use it all.*"

Her green eyes ensnared mine.

"Do you understand what I'm telling you?"

I thought of every terrible thing that had ever happened to me. They used to be hindrances—my every success won in spite of those horrors. But now, I saw that every traumatic event that had ever happened to me had made me who I was. They landed me right here, in a room of powerful men and women who were rooting for me.

"Yes," I answered, unflinching as I returned my own hardened stare.

Sadie was doing more than search my eyes. She was staring so deep inside of me that I wondered if she could see all the way to the beginning of time itself.

Her grin was nothing short of warlike. "You're ready." She stepped back.

Rune's features relaxed an inch at Sadie's words, a testament to how much he respected her. When I finally joined him on the porch, alone with him and my two escorts, he flickered between his stony demeanor as the vampire ruler of Aristelle and the vulnerable human man who loved me.

With a dagger on each hip, my succubus well of power overflowing, I'd never been more comfortable in my own skin.

I'd stood up to Isabella. It didn't matter how she'd reacted. Because the important part was that after years of being a doormat, a punching bag, a people pleasing victim, I finally told Isabella my truth. And I'd done it with grace, compassion, and tact.

Being proud of myself was a foreign sensation, but that was exactly what I felt right now, heading into battle to protect this island I loved and all of her most vulnerable citizens. I was damn proud of my excruciating, vulnerable healing. I was proud of my progress, my bravery, my resilience.

The guilt was still there, but at least now it was drowned out by all this love.

Rune's lips brushed my forehead.

"No more gooey words, please," I whispered. "Save it for when you're welcoming me home with fifteen more flavors of ice cream."

Rune's smile was strained, his eyes welling with raw

emotion. "Okay, baby, I won't give you any more of my beautiful sentences. You'll have to earn them."

I returned his smile. "Deal."

He pulled me into his arms, ignoring the man and woman awkwardly shifting on their feet—the underlings we'd tasked with smuggling me across the border.

I breathed in his crisp, woodsy scent.

"You made sure the pen worked?" he whispered.

I laughed. "Yes. That would be a funny mistake."

"It would absolutely *not* be funny."

I was taking in a single slip of paper and pen, hidden in a secret coat pocket, to communicate with Rune.

I pulled back, staring up into his dark eyes. "You want to say something gooey *sooo* bad."

He glared at me. "Get out of my sight."

I nodded. "Yes, Sir."

As I turned away from him, my lip wobbled, and Rune grabbed my arm and pulled me in for the deepest kiss of my life.

"I love you, my soul," he whispered against my lips.

"I love you too, my darkness."

55

SCARLETT

The general public didn't know what the infamous Scarlett Hale looked like, so we didn't exactly need to hide. We took a shadowbird to Talomon, and then we walked the rest of the way.

Race, the male turned, was a face I recognized. He'd guarded me a few times before I was taken. The woman, Kallie, was tall, lean, and muscular with a blonde buzz cut. She was supremely untalkative, and I could detect a great deal of magick beneath her skin.

I didn't really care to make small talk either, so we walked in a comfortable silence until we reached a camp of turned soldiers on a wide street.

A massive man with a shaved head eyed us suspiciously before nodding at Race and Kallie. His arms were crossed, leaning against a lamppost as he spoke to a group of uniformed turned. In the distance, I heard the unmistakable sound of stomping, yelling, and conflict—but it wasn't close.

Between looming buildings ahead, I could see magickal wards, a tinge of color that rippled out in both directions.

I wondered what these soldiers saw as we moved through

their camp. Did they see a human willingly crossing the border, perhaps to reunite with her family? Or could they tell from my face, the way I walked, that I was a fighter like them, even if my fight looked different from theirs?

Would they one day accept me as one of them? Let alone a ruler?

I dimmed my succubus powers just in case, boarding up my glamour the way Rosalind had taught me. I imagined myself as small and invisible, my aura opaque, my body uninteresting. I needed to be as inconspicuous as possible until I was back at the palace.

Race glanced over at me. "What was that?"

"What?" I asked.

He shook his head, staring back ahead. "I don't know, never mind."

Kallie glanced my way, but she didn't say anything.

I'd perhaps made the shift too violent, too jarring to vampires who'd grown accustomed to my energy. Looked like I was still learning new things about my magick every day.

"Hey," a loud voice boomed.

I couldn't help but jump at the sound, my heart hammering.

The buff bald man jogged to catch up to us. "There's increased activity on seventy-fifth street. I'd slip in using Stratford Alley."

"Understood, thanks, Thom."

I could taste Thom's ripe curiosity on his tongue as he looked at me, but his desire to be loyal and discreet was the prevailing force. The turned were an interesting bunch. I admired their commitment to each other. At first, I thought it was blind devotion to Rune, but now I understood that humans became turned because they wanted to be a part of something bigger than themselves. They found purpose in defending Valentin, in protecting the powerless. I knew that vampirism was a corrupting force, and many turned still succumbed to the less desirable traits of immortals. But they never lost their loyalty, and I found that noble.

"Grab drinks when you're back?" Thom asked, his gaze flickering between Race and Kallie.

"Pass," Kallie said dryly.

"Yeah, of course," Race said with a grin.

The absurdity of this kind of exchange, as the turned were unknowingly leading a succubus to Hatham to destroy the born from within, nearly made me snort with laughter.

When we reached Stratford Alley, my heart was in my throat. I could hear the boom of magick and conflict all around, even if it was distant. I knew the bulk of the fighting was on the other side of this flickering red ward.

It was translucent, and I could at least see that through this alley, the other side was clear. I was about to willingly cross over into Hatham.

"You understand where you're going?" Race asked. He looked uncomfortable, as if he were sending a lamb to slaughter and didn't truly understand why.

"Yes," I said.

"We would accompany you further, but we'd set off the wards," Race said.

"It's not far," I said softly, remembering every detail of Brennan's instructions and the map I'd studied for hours last night.

"Forces are distracted, you'll be fine," Kallie said confidently, one of the few times she'd spoken. She regarded me almost pityingly, and it pissed me off enough to get me moving.

"Thank you for all the help," I said.

They both nodded, staring at me curiously as I moved past them to the wavy red magick. I didn't hesitate. I was done being meek and fearful.

I was ready to show this world exactly how strong it had made me.

I stepped into Hatham, and my ears popped. The buildings on either side of me were abandoned, their off-white stone walls scorched and crumbling.

The conflict remained distant, most of the sound coming from my right. I took three deep breaths, reminding my body that I was safe, even when my mind plagued me with visions of Rosalind's lifeless body in the street.

This was the part of my journey Rune was most fearful of, but I'd been assured by Brennan that I wouldn't be alone for long. He planned to send his own escort, one that wouldn't raise suspicion.

I let the daggers at my waist flood me with confidence as I peeked around the corner, assessing the next street. No one but fighters dared venture to the border, so it was doubtful I'd casually stumble upon hungry vampires. Those were far more likely to be hanging around the mortal areas in the born districts. I shuddered at the reality those poor humans faced during a dire blood shortage.

Even so, I made sure my powers were as concealed as possible.

I spotted the tavern Brennan had described on the corner across the street, its sign reading *Timot n edge* when it should've read *Timothy and Hedge.*

I dreaded being underground. As helpful as the tunnels would be to my future escape, I wished it were possible to simply ride to the palace on a firebird instead. But vigilantes were shooting them down left and right, especially when they came from the palace. It was a vulnerable time to take to the sky in born districts. On the border most of all.

I crept past the tavern and turned down the next street. At the sound of movement, I froze, then quickly flattened myself to a nearby doorframe.

I peeked out left, then right. No one in sight, no more strange sounds.

My thumb brushed the hilt of one of my daggers underneath my long, black skirt.

Only one more block before the library. Less than five minutes before I was safe. Well, perhaps *safe* wasn't entirely accurate. But at least it was a milestone of my progress.

One step closer to carving into Durian's flesh, the same way he'd carved into mine.

The library had two columns out front, the stone structure mostly intact, though the door was busted through. My gaze darted all around before I entered.

The cobblestone streets were empty, only displaying evidence of past violence in the rubble and garbage strewn about.

As soon as I stepped inside, I felt sinister, cold magick that drove fear into the deepest parts of me.

Fuel. Use the fear as fuel. Do not dwell. Take another step forward, Sadie's resolute voice whispered.

Bookcases were knocked over, the cool air smelling of mildew and ancient paper. The fading sunlight barely penetrated the dim space.

"There's our lost lamb."

The voice sent shards of ice to my heart. I didn't stop walking, no matter how much I wanted to shut down. I kept moving toward the dark back room, where Lillian's statue stood.

I didn't stop, even when Aunt Carol stepped out from the darkness.

56

SCARLETT

Aunt Carol's gaze sharpened to my neck, no doubt seeing Rune's fang marks. "You disgust me."

"Hello again to you, too."

Her lip curled. At the sight of her palm twitching, I erased the fire from my eyes.

"We'll be touching that up before you're gifted back to your Master," she said, clicking her tongue. She snapped her fingers. A witch light appeared above us that moved as she did.

She led me back to the statue of the Dark Goddess, carved from onyx. My eyes trailed over her crown of black crystals and bones, the soft smile on her lips. The dress that accentuated her curves dipped low on her chest and had two slits in the skirt.

I said a soft prayer, one that was all my own, nothing like the ones Aunt Carol had forced us to recite.

I prayed for power.

"Our divine king deserves a nice surprise," Aunt Carol said, spinning around to glare at me. I intuited she was fighting every urge to hurt me, as if commanded against it. "We'll make sure you're as good as new for him."

She glared at me with utter disdain, her nose twisting. Her

long twists of hair were in a bun. Her black dress was modest and tarp-like.

Fanaticism and good taste didn't tend to mix.

"Your hand, whore," she bit out, removing a knife from her belt.

When the trauma response arose, I welcomed it, thanking my body for working so hard to protect me.

I'm safe. I'm the one with the upper hand.

"Why?"

She whispered a spell, and my body convulsed with freezing magick, penetrating all the way to my bones.

"You don't ask questions, you *obey*. I'd hoped you would remember your place, but it looks like we have a long road ahead to remind you," she hissed. She grabbed my arm and pulled me forward, making an incision in my palm as she held it over Lillian's bare feet.

I didn't make a single noise of pain, the adrenaline drowning it out.

"Lillian demands sacrifices of mortal blood to grant us safe passage."

I froze, my heart skidding to a stop.

Aunt Carol frowned, drop after drop of my blood falling to the ground. And nothing happened.

Because I was not mortal.

Aunt Carol blinked. Once. Twice. Three times.

She slowly gazed from Lillian's feet up to me. At first, she was merely confused, her mind spinning in circles.

I held my breath. My first instinct was terror. This might've been the end of the road.

As Aunt Carol's face shifted, I heard the words *obey, disgust,* and *whore* rattle around. That hissing, coiling snake unhinged its jaws, reminding me who and what the fuck I was.

Aunt Carol had the same realization.

"You—"

At the first sign of cresting magick, I didn't hesitate.

I reached for a dagger, and I slit Aunt Carol's throat.

Her arms fell back to her sides, and her blood sprayed out as I leaped back. She sunk to her knees, reaching for her throat futilely as she choked on her own blood. The hatred in her eyes transformed into fear.

The human side of me stared at her, slack-jawed and horrified, before my eyes snagged on the bloody dagger in my right palm.

The other half of me—the daughter of Lillian—stirred and came alive at the brutality of my actions. I looked down at Aunt Carol, and my lip curled.

"You disgust *me*," I whispered. "I hope Lillian eats you alive for using her as a scapegoat for your bullshit religion."

Aunt Carol couldn't retort, and I liked it better that way. I remembered all the times she'd hurt me, beat me, treated me as a sex and blood slave. I refused to feel guilty. Not on her behalf.

As she lay motionless, I cleaned my dagger on her ugly, tasteless dress. I wiped at my face with my jacket sleeve, pretending that I wasn't hopelessly drenched in crimson.

A river of blood swam toward Lillian's feet. More than enough of an offering.

The outline of a magickal door appeared in the wall next to the statue, as if it had been there all along. I didn't miss my chance. I stepped into the darkness, and I didn't look back.

Rune said my first kill would be the hardest. And it was a tad frightening how it hadn't been all too difficult at all. What did that say about my inherent ruthlessness? I imagined Rune's nod of approval, and it soothed my racing nerves.

Witch lights came to life above, illuminating a long, narrow hall of stone and earth. There was nothing glamorous about this secret underground.

It wasn't until the door disappeared behind me that I

realized my judgment may have been clouded by a layer of shock, after all.

Because I was now in the tunnels, all alone, without my assigned escort and therefore without a navigator.

The tunnel suddenly appeared far narrower, the walls so close I might be crushed between them. There wasn't enough light. Not enough space.

Not enough air.

I sucked in gasp after gasp, backing up against stone as my vision grew blotchy. Would I be trapped in here forever?

What had I *done*?

Snap the fuck out of it, Scarlett, my own inner voice commanded. *You had no choice. Time to adapt.*

I closed my eyes, practicing one of the breathing techniques Belise had taught me until I was no longer on the verge of a panic attack. My lungs expanded. My vision cleared.

My hand trembled slightly as I reached for the note and pen from my hidden jacket pocket.

I found the most even patch of stone I could find, and I placed the note on the wall. My eyes strained against the suboptimal light.

Rune, I had to kill my handler—Aunt Carol. She realized what I was because my blood couldn't open the tunnel. I don't know how to get to the castle.

Rune's linked page sent a small shock through his body whenever I wrote to him, so he could ensure he never missed it. He wrote back immediately.

Shit. Okay, don't worry. Take deep breaths. You did good, Little Flame, I'm proud of you. If you hadn't killed her, I would've at first sight.

His praise was a soothing caress, no matter how much distance was between us.

You'll have time to make up a solid cover story. I can guide you to the castle by following you on a map. Probably.

My eyes widened.

Probably???

He was slower to respond this time, and each second that ticked by increased my heart rate several beats per minute.

We can do this. It's a thirty-minute walk, tops. Just start moving, and each intersection you reach, give me your options in cardinal directions, and I'll make an educated guess. I was planning on mapping your route as you went, anyway.

Half of me was calmed by his words—his reminder that I was ensuring my escape by using the tunnels, providing Rune a safe and easy way to get to me in the palace. To even transport a whole group of specialized fighters through.

The other half of me was panicking all over again.

Cardinal directions? Who the hell knows their cardinal directions at any given moment, Rune?

His next words had me rolling my eyes.

I do. As would any decently trained, competent being. But, fine. Start moving, and I can figure that out too.

I wanted to sink my teeth into one of his tattooed forearms so damn bad right now.

Lowering my tense shoulders, I followed Rune's instructions. I walked until I came to my first branch of paths—an easy right or left.

Try left.

His use of the word *try* did not instill confidence.

Bright side to committing an unplanned murder? I didn't have to make small talk with Aunt Carol. Even if she hadn't learned what I was, I might've ended up killing her down here anyway, if only to rescue myself from her irritating piousness.

I glanced back down at the note every thirty seconds. Rune had made me backtrack a couple times now, and I wondered how much time I'd lost. Would Brennan eventually grow concerned and come for me himself? Or, more likely, send another aunt to come after me—likely the only being other than himself he trusted me with.

You're getting close.

It was strange for a victory to simultaneously feel like a nightmare, but that's exactly what returning to the palace would be.

The tunnels never improved. Their earthen, damp scent became more sulfuric. When I saw my first skeleton, I had to cover my mouth with my hand as I nearly jumped out of my skin. This underground labyrinth of horrors was far more fitting for the born than their façade of royalty and decorum aboveground.

I was breathing through my mouth by the time I reached the end of a hall and realized there was nowhere else to go.

I looked down at Rune's elegant script.

You're there.

My hand trembled as I pressed the paper against the wall, and I internally yelled at the limb to cut it out.

Thank you. I'll write to you as soon as I can.

He wrote back immediately.

You'd better. If I don't hear from you for too long, at any given stage, I will come for you without your approval. Don't write back to this. Stay safe. Put this note back in the secret pocket immediately. This is your world, Little Flame. Don't you fucking forget it.

I followed Rune's instructions, touching the smile on my lips as I steadied my racing heart. Adrenaline surged in waves, and I relaxed each muscle as I stood facing this dead-end wall.

Wait—how in the hell was I supposed to get out of here?

I pressed my palm against the wall, feeling for some invisible doorknob. At the sight of blood on my sleeve, I realized I was overthinking it.

I smeared some of Aunt Carol's blood on the wall and hoped for the best.

The wall rumbled slightly, another door manifesting. I whispered to the rising vengeance in my blood, asking it to replace my fear with strength in exchange for its next sacrifice.

I opened the door, only to be met with what appeared to be a wall of sleek wood on the other side.

Was it boarded up? Was I in the right place?

Terrified of the door disappearing and trapping me back down here, I shoved on the wood. It scooted forward, revealing dark floor beneath it. It was furniture. Ridiculously heavy furniture.

Uriah hadn't exactly made me buff, but I had to believe he'd improved my upper body strength enough to move a bookcase, or whatever the hell this was. Though you'd think that Brennan would've cleared the tunnel entrance in preparation for my arrival.

As the furniture slowly scooted, scraping against the floor thunderously, a sweat broke out on my brow.

When it started to move all on its own, I stepped inside and glanced at my palms. Could succubi develop telekinesis?

"What do we have here?"

My blood ran cold. The answer to my question was a resounding *no*. I could see that now, as I faced a smirking Liza and a creepy-as-ever Evangeline standing in the middle of a private drawing room.

57

SCARLETT

"Uhhh, have you all seen Brennan, by chance?" I asked. Their eyes scanned down my body, flashing with hunger.

Liza inhaled deeply. "Whose blood is that, little human? Because I can scent that it's not yours."

"How did you know about the tunnels?" Evangeline hissed.

They were both in front of me in a flash. Liza grabbed my wrist, and I attempted to jerk it back. Her grip tightened, and that same strange flicker of magick left her fingertips, just as it had when we first met in Odessa.

Yet, nothing happened.

She let go.

"Answer us freely, or you will not enjoy our methods of forcing an answer," Evangeline said.

I had no choice. The truth was my best option here. "Brennan helped me escape Rune," I said.

Both of their faces flashed with intrigue, their cold eyes narrowing with calculation.

"I'm supposed to be a surprise. For Durian."

"A surprise?" Evangeline asked, lifting a brow.

"People like surprises," I said, shrugging.

"Interesting," Liza said, catlike. She was obviously pleased to have uncovered valuable information. With the way the born men treated the born women, I had a hunch that secrets were their most lucrative form of currency around here.

But what did these women desire? Were they going to side with Durian, or with Brennan?

I searched their nauseating energy, finding all manner of sick and twisted urges to harm me. They were out for themselves, and it was clear they would side with whoever most benefited them.

"I assume I took the wrong passage," I whispered, refusing to cower in fear when Evangeline gave me a sickly smile and trailed her finger down my bloody jacket. "I had to guess, because a vampire in bloodlust killed Aunt Carol."

"Fascinating," Evangeline purred.

I wasn't sure if they believed me. It appeared as though they were simply giddy to have stumbled upon something interesting in a palace that relived the same night on repeat for an eternity. There were only so many ways vampires could torture and feast on human slaves.

"Well, we couldn't possibly stand in poor Brennan's way, not after such a catastrophic blunder," Liza said. "I'm feeling… exhausted." She grinned, putting a strange emphasis on the word that lit up Evangeline's eyes. "Evangeline, won't you see to it that Brennan finds his little *surprise*?"

All manner of warning bells were going off in a distracting cacophony. Both Evangeline and Liza were on my kill list, but it wasn't time for eliminations.

I played gloriously naive while simultaneously fearful as Liza stepped back and Evangeline moved closer. Both were dressed in long, silky gowns—Evangeline in emerald and Liza in blood-red. Evangeline's pearls were lopsided.

"Come with me," she said.

I quickly envisioned the golden threads that connected me to Brennan, and I *yanked*.

Find me, I whispered to his mind.

Evangeline led me out of the drawing room and into a long, empty hall. Her straight black hair barely moved as she walked. To our left hung an ugly painting of a vampire feeding on a nude human woman.

I'd only glanced at the painting for a moment before I was pushed up against the wall, my head hitting the stone with a *smack*.

I let out a soft noise of pain, and Evangeline's smile widened. She was feeding off my suffering, soaking in it.

"All this fuss over one pitiful little human," she said.

She placed her hand on my throat in warning, but she didn't yet apply pressure. She leaned into me, sniffing me like a wild animal. Her throaty groan made me want to vomit.

"Such a pity you weren't one of my girls," she said. "Durian never would've had to deal with your pesky acts of disobedience and attention-seeking. I would've made you into the most perfect, devoted little doll for him."

I remembered the girl with her mouth sewn shut, and I stayed perfectly still, even as my hand itched to grab that blood-onyx-infused dagger.

"I still envision that night we strapped you to the cross, the divine scent of your blood and cunt, drenched in fear—"

My fingers twitched. Just one move, and I could paralyze her. I could weaken her enough to aim for the heart.

She licked her dark red lips. She smelled of copper and overly-sweet perfume, perhaps to counteract her personality. "I can't wait to have my way with you. The time will come. Our king will see how much my skills are needed. Yes... I'll play with you until you're nothing but a pretty doll, ready to be used however her Master sees fit."

Her eyes grew crazed, and I kept a tight leash on my panic,

knowing it would only send her closer to bloodlust. She kept repeating herself, over and over, and all I could think of was Kole's voice saying *island madness.*

These vampires really were fucking nuts.

On her sixth ode to the breakability of my body and mind and her various plans to turn me into a human doll, I finally heard heavy footsteps down the hall.

Evangeline looked feral, her nostrils flaring.

"Get back," Brennan barked.

She let out a strangled noise, as if she were a cat in heat. Brennan had to peel her away, throwing her back against the opposite wall. Her lip curled, her chest rising and falling rapidly.

Brennan planted himself between us. "Go get yourself under control." His broad body was clothed in a black and burgundy uniform. His black boots were heavy against the marble.

At the flicker of power lighting up his palms, Evangeline finally slinked away.

Brennan turned back to me, and when he crushed his lips to mine, I became the best damn actress in all of Valentin.

I rewarded him for saving me, echoing back his own desire, melding my lips with his. I pretended his lips were Rune's, even if they were too soft, too desperate, too coated in saliva.

My golden web of influence wrapped around us both in a tight embrace.

We are destined. We are star-crossed lovers meant to be together. My blood was made for you.

Brennan's hands roamed my body, and I saved the anger and disgust for later. It was all fuel.

He pulled back, noticing the fang marks on my neck. "That bastard," he growled. "The thought of anyone else fucking touching you…"

Well, I hate to tell you this, champ, I joked to myself, using humor to distract myself from the trauma of unwanted groping.

He scanned the rest of my blood-soaked body, finally

coming back down to reality after his single-minded focus on finding me.

"Are you okay? What happened? Where is Aunt Carol?"

Rosalind's face entered my mind. I thought of her gleeful laughter when she was teaching me how to fake certain emotions for greater effect. I remembered the way she'd pouted her lips and summoned big tears, letting them roll down her cheeks before bursting into another infectious giggle.

I thought of her lying in the street. The way Brennan had barely glanced at her as she bled out, her light dimming for good.

Before he could ask another question, I cut in.

"There was this vampire man," I said, my voice shaking as manipulative tears clouded my eyes. I preyed on Brennan's jealousy and relief that I was alive to distract from the holes in my story. "He was going to kill me, and Aunt Carol saved me. He was going to—"

I pressed my head against Brennan's chest, sobbing.

He rubbed soothing circles on my back. "There, there. You're safe."

"I'm scared," I whispered, pulling back to stare up into his hazel eyes. "I don't want to be *his* surprise. I don't want to be his *anything*."

"I know, sweetheart," he said, his handsome features flickering from adoration to irritation. "Listen to me carefully."

Something inside me bristled at his tone.

"Do not tell a single soul about the tunnels. I'll clean up the mess with Evangeline and, presumably, Liza?"

I nodded in confirmation that Liza had been involved.

"But if you wish to be free, you mustn't tell anyone how I saved you. Not yet. Not even Durian. Is that understood?"

Confusion turned over in my gut, as well as more prickling at his vague threat. I was missing something. I nodded anyway, gazing at Brennan like he was my sole authority in this world, and I was blind in my subservience.

I could sense his ego expanding.

"There's power in accomplishing things with mysterious ease, you see," Brennan said. "You have no idea what plays I have up my sleeve."

I searched his web of desire with rising suspicion. I noticed that the seed I'd planted had not only grown and bloomed—but it had also shed new seeds, a whole new forest of ambitions rising in its wake.

Brennan was no longer courting his desire with treason, with assuming power.

It had become his greatest desire of all. I'd somehow misread his intentions through our letters, falsely assuming he was still loyal to Durian.

Not a single part of him was loyal. He was just waiting for the perfect moment to strike. And I was at the center of his plan, through means I didn't entirely understand.

My heart missed a beat, remembering all the times Rune and Sadie had chastised me for jumping to conclusions.

He must've read the real trepidation in my features.

"Trust in me, Scarlett. Just as we discussed," Brennan said. "You're safe. So long as you play your part, for only a little bit longer."

"I trust you," I lied, offering a demure smile.

His mind was all over the place, not even bothering to ask how in the hell I made it to the palace by myself. My dubious explanations remained tucked away.

"Durian is away for the night," Brennan said. "I would love nothing more than to sleep by your side, but we can't risk anything. Aunt Carol prepared your usual chambers before she left. You'll reside there until I present you to Durian. By the time he returns, the whole castle will have scented you in these halls. It'll be the most glorious of spectacles."

Doll. Toy. Pawn. Spectacle.

Wrong. Wrong. Wrong. Wrong.

Actually, I was a murderous, vengeful sex demon.

"You promise to stay put and lay low, and to keep everything that has happened between us from here on out?"

Brennan's paranoia had grown alongside his ambitions, as a natural consequence. I didn't show my instinctive fear at the erratic look in his eyes.

I only nodded and affirmed him again.

"It's late, but we'll take the private staircase," he murmured to himself. "I'll tell Kole. The silly fool thinks you're coming back for *him*."

He grinned, and I shook my head as if in pity, displaying a soft smile.

"He's been a huge help. I have a feeling he will only continue to be helpful in the days to come," I said softly.

Brennan sighed. "I love that you're not only pretty. You have intelligence, too. You're worthy of a great man, Scarlett."

58

SCARLETT

I wanted to set the pet bed in my chambers on fire. I glared at it, sitting at the foot of the real bed as I worked through several calming exercises.

Other than mild groping, Brennan had employed stellar self-control. He'd said I'd taste so much sweeter when I was finally his.

I laughed bitterly to myself before taking my hundredth deep breath. I'd seized my opportunity to stash one dagger away—underneath the pet bed, where no one but me would ever wander. The other was underneath my pillow, more accessible but also riskier. I could always play it off as self-defense, leftover from my escape from Rune.

It was a mindfuck to be back here, *of my own will*.

Stranger still was that while this room had remained unchanged and untouched, ready for my return, I was an entirely different woman.

I could hardly reconcile the heartbroken, traumatized girl who'd chosen to sleep on a glorified pillow meant for a dog rather than a real bed. The girl who'd been drowning in guilt and shame, mourning the loss of the first man who'd ever made her feel safe.

Yet she fought anyway. Without her resilience, I wouldn't be sitting here. I would never have learned that Rune still loved me, that I was still deserving of the life of my dreams.

I glared at that pet bed and everything it represented. My fists clenched and unclenched, my mind running around trying to figure out what the hell Brennan was planning.

My ears tingled, and my head jerked violently to the right to stare at the main door.

I was not surprised by Brennan's change of heart. I'd already mentally steeled myself for the possibility he might try to fuck me. I would do everything in my power to avoid it.

The door swung open.

It wasn't Brennan who entered my rooms.

I lifted from the bed and backed up, pretending to put a bed and distance between Liza and me out of fear. When in reality, I was moving closer to the pillow where my dagger was hidden.

Liza made no sudden movements. She stalked forward slowly, confidently, like a wolf cornering injured prey. She was cloaked in black now, not a strand of her short brunette hair out of place.

"You felt my magick, that night in Odessa. You remember that, Scarlett?" she asked. It might've been the first time she'd used my real name instead of calling me some variation of *little human*.

Her blood-red lips were shiny under the dim witch light above.

"Yes."

I was safe. She wouldn't hurt me, not in any lasting way. Brennan should've already threatened her, dissuaded her from sharing our secret about the tunnels. But why was she defying him to toy with me?

"Aw, look at that sharp little mind run in circles," she said, as if speaking to a child.

I was close enough to grab my dagger. I'd just need to be impossibly quick about it.

"Yet, not sharp enough to ever wonder how I uncovered Rune's obsession with you."

I had wondered, but honestly, I'd chalked it up to her seeing me with Uriah that one time when he was on bodyguard duty. I'd assumed she'd put together all the small hints and clues we'd been unable to conceal.

It hadn't really mattered how she'd found out. Or at least, I'd thought it hadn't.

"Do you remember what I'd asked for, when I touched your arm that night, and you felt my magick on your skin?"

My heart was hammering, caught between my survival imperative and my drive to understand Liza's motivations.

She was at the front of the bed now, caressing the bedpost as she stared me down. Only five paces away.

"You asked me for my secrets," I said, my voice raspy.

Liza grinned. "I told you I could sense one inside you that was bigger than all the rest. Silly me, when I dreamed of your connection to Rune, I assumed *that* was the big secret."

"Dreamed?" I echoed.

This talk of secrets had my guts twisting.

"You won't be alive for much longer, so I'll tell you *my* secret, little demon."

I went rigid, my heart banging so violently against my ribs I feared they'd bruise.

Liza watched my reaction with growing pleasure, relishing in my terror.

"If I touch you, I may see your deepest, darkest truth in a dream. Some secrets come quickly. Some are harder to decipher. But there are ways of speeding things along." She laughed, cocking her head and showing me faux concern.

"Don't look so glum! You had a spectacular run, truly. I've only begun to understand the influence you've had, now that I see you for what you truly are."

She took another step toward me, and my fingers twitched.

"Brennan is a whole new man. Your handiwork, I presume?" she said casually, picking at a cuticle before trailing her catlike amber eyes back up my body. "Durian is losing his mind, conveniently..." Her eyes narrowed. "Now that I think about it, ever since you entered the palace, all manner of chaos has been stirred up. Almost as if we've been infiltrated by a cunning demoness hellbent on sowing instability and destruction."

I mirrored her look of condescension. "Have you considered the possibility that you suffer from psychosis?"

Liza's lip curled. She leaped for me at the same time as I moved for my dagger.

Just as it had been during training, vampire speed was my biggest obstacle. Liza clawed my arm as she yanked me back, and I swung with my dagger where I thought her stomach was.

She was quicker. My dagger met air, and I was thrown to the ground. Where the fuck were my guards? Had she told them what I was?

Who else had she *told*?

This flurry of thoughts was background noise as I wildly swung again, nicking Liza in the arm. She hissed, fury in her eyes as she easily straddled me and pinned my arms down.

The blood onyx magick would enter her bloodstream and weaken her, but it wouldn't be nearly enough. I'd barely scratched her.

"They're not going to care what the fuck I do to you once I tell them what you are and what you've done," she said maniacally. "Not Brennan nor Durian. Not even pathetic Kole."

She flashed her fangs, grinding against me as my lips twisted in disgust.

At that, she spat on my face. I let out a gasp of surprise, shutting my eyes briefly to avoid the saliva.

"How dare you act like I repulse you, you good for nothing whore," she screeched. "You should be fucking pleading with me for your *life*."

My dagger was just out of reach, taunting me with its proximity. That was how little of a chance Liza thought I stood against her.

She suddenly lifted off me, stomping on my hand as soon as I reached for the hilt.

I screamed, and she laughed, kicking the dagger under the bed.

My hand throbbed, but still I tried to rise to my feet, only for Liza to pull me up by my hair. Tears brimmed my eyes from the sting.

She saw through my glamour. I was now weaponless and powerless. My only saving grace was that she wouldn't kill me before she exposed me.

Liza continued to drag me by the hair as I flailed, uselessly clawing for my freedom. She threw me down on the wood floor.

I was closer to the second dagger now, the pet bed a few feet away.

Stars shot across my vision, my head still aching from when Evangeline had smacked it against the wall. Everyone had it out for my poor skull today.

"Bet you fucking love it when vampires throw you around like the nasty slut that you are," she said, her eyes homing in on my jugular. "I can't wait to watch how they torture you, to listen to those sweet, useless screams."

Her tongue ran across her fangs. I used my bent knees to propel myself closer to the pet bed. Liza once again pounced to sit on my torso, and this time she went in for my neck, the same side as Rune's fading marks. She sunk into me, grinding against me again as my blood flowed into her vile mouth.

The venom was not going to help my already inferior reflexes. But at least Liza was too preoccupied and crazed by my blood to notice my hand slip underneath the pet bed.

I brushed the hilt. So close.

My skin was scorching, unwanted waves of sickly pleasure rolling from the puncture wound outward.

Thanks to Sadie's spells, I found it easier to fight the cloudiness. I extended my arm, shifting slightly and stretching as far as I could stretch. I struggled with the hilt, Liza moaning against my neck.

I pulled it toward me, and finally, I was able to find a grip. I had one shot. I inhaled, and I fought through the pain in my hand as I moved as fast as I could—straight for Liza's side.

The blade had barely plunged through skin before she'd unlocked from my throat, screamed in fury, and ripped the second dagger away from me.

"You fucking bitch!" she roared. This time her hands closed around my neck.

She was out of her mind with rage and bloodlust. There was no way in hell she was going to stop herself from killing me now. My eyes bulged as I choked, darkness eclipsing my vision.

I saw Rune's face, his wicked grin. I felt his steady heart under my ear, his arms and shadows holding me so tightly that I knew he'd never let me go.

My body stilled. And Rune's face was replaced by Liza's. Shifting from fury to confusion, her brows drew together. She coughed, and blood splattered on my face for the second time today.

When Liza collapsed on top of me, my first thought was that I'd been saved—I'd lived to see another day.

But then I realized death had come for me after all.

Because above me, holding a pretty pink and rose gold dagger, was Rosalind.

59

SCARLETT

I helped Rosalind push Liza's body off me. She offered me a hand and a pink scarf to wrap around my wounded neck. I secured the fabric in a daze. I found it hard to close my mouth, just staring up at her as I took her outstretched hand and rose to my feet.

Her blonde hair was as perfect and bouncy as ever, and she wore a classic Rosalind pink robe with a feather trim. Underneath was a matching silk and lace slip, and fuzzy slippers were placed on her feet. It was an objectively hilarious outfit to kill a vampire in.

The only imperfections I could find were a busted lip and black eye.

"You're dead," I croaked, unable to peel my wide eyes off her.

She looked down at herself then back up to my eyes. "Not since the last time I checked. Mother Dearest always did call me a cockroach. I'm unkillable, darling."

"No, I saw it," I said, my tone shifting in accusation. I took a step back, realization striking that if I was indeed alive, then Rosalind had to be a Durian vision.

I scanned her body, taking extra care with each hand.

"Are you *counting my fingers?*" Rosalind giggled.

My head was mostly clear, only slightly hazy with venom and blood loss. It didn't feel like the other times Durian had trapped me in his illusions.

And damn her, she had ten fingers and ten toes.

Her eyes were the same color. The small beauty mark above her lip was placed in the same spot. Everything about her was exactly the same as I remembered, right down to her mannerisms, voice, and speech.

"I'm an asset, Scar, remember? They wouldn't kill me unless absolutely necessary. But they sure as fuck weren't going to let enemies have me either."

I ran through the memory. "But, why did you fall?"

"I thought I'd been stabbed."

"But you hadn't been?"

She shook her head. "Just hit my head on the way down and passed out, I think. I'm not sure, honestly. It was like I was in a strange dream."

"You're real. He made us think you were dead, to protect you as an asset. But you're alive," I summarized. "I thought I'd gotten you killed, just as you feared I would."

My eyes welled, emotions slamming against me in violent, crashing waves. Rosalind's eyes were glassy, her lip trembling as she stared at me in similar disbelief. I wasted no more time before wrapping my arms around her.

"This is really sweet and all, and I totally missed you, too," Rosalind said, tense beneath my hold. "But you've now ruined my favorite robe and made our cleanup even more difficult, love."

Cleanup.

I pulled back from her. I looked down at Liza, my shock wearing off. "What do we do?"

Rosalind clapped her hands, her face resolute. "This isn't Auntie Rosalind's first murder cover-up. Don't you worry."

"Is it still murder if you had a *really* good reason?"

She snorted. "Our clothes and this body need to go, and this floor needs scrubbing. There's both a window and a pantry with cleaning supplies nearby."

"There could be people—vampires out there," I said, scrambling. "Plus, oh gods, what if she already told someone what I was? That was why she was attacking me, to catch you up to speed."

Rosalind shook her head. "The only person she would've told is Evangeline, and if she'd told her, then Miss Evil would've wanted to come join in on the fun. She definitely kept it to herself so she could fuck with you before she made the grand reveal."

I nodded. Okay, that made sense. "Can't we just tell people that she attacked me?"

"You don't need that heat on you, baby girl. You do not want Evangeline as an enemy."

Fuck, she was right. Especially after I showed up to the castle covered in blood and without Aunt Carol. There were only so many strange happenings and lies I could distract my men from before my web unraveled.

"Okay, so cleanup," I said, again staring at the dead vampire and pool of blood on my floor. "At least she's on hardwood."

∽

Rosalind returned with cleaning supplies and a rug she'd stolen from a drawing room.

It was late, even for partying vampires. Four in the morning, to be exact. The halls were sparse at this hour, but never guaranteed to be empty. So far, so good. Even though I found it strange and negligent that Brennan had left me with absolutely no protection.

"The coast was clear, and I've brought help." Rosalind said, setting her bag of goods and the rug down on the ground before heading back to the door.

Before I could ask what she meant, two people entered the room, each with slave collars around their necks.

Lana and Cassius.

"Rosalind!" I hissed.

She put a hand on her hip. "We needed help, and you're back to free them, aren't you?"

At that, Lana's eyes lit up, and Cassius searched my face almost desperately. They both seemed to be holding their breath.

"Yes," I whispered. "All the slaves will be freed soon. As long as I'm not exposed before then as a murderous traitor."

Or as a succubus, but I sure as hell didn't need anyone else knowing that secret. I prayed that knowledge had died with Liza.

Lana lifted her chin. "We're fucking elated that bitch is dead. We're not going to stand in your way. We want to help. All the slaves stand with Rosalind, and if she stands with you, then we're with you by extension."

I looked from Lana and Cassius to Rosalind, who was smiling like a mischievous child.

"Like I said at Black Sapphire, you needed an inside woman," she drawled. "You're not the only one who's made use of the last few weeks."

I let out a string of curses before waving them both over. I didn't even ask how they were here or what would happen if they were caught.

We were all in this shitstorm together now.

"You two would not have been able to lift a body and throw it out a window yourselves," Cassius pointed out as we scrubbed the floors.

"Rude," Rosalind and I both said at the same time.

We'd already wrapped up Liza in a rug, bandaging her chest first with more fabric to soak up the blood.

"I knew you were trying to distract them from us," Lana said suddenly, tucking her curly black hair behind her ears. She wrung out a sponge as she peered over at me. "That night they made us hurt you. I knew you were trying to help. When you were taken... something in my gut knew there was more to the story."

I nodded. I wasn't sure what to say.

"Rosalind told us we wouldn't have long to wait before we were freed," she said. "She said soon this place would be burned to the ground."

Cassius paused, wiping his forehead with his sleeve. "I always sensed there was something different about you. You were Rune's, before..." He stared into my eyes. "You're what we've been waiting for."

Whatever Lana and Cassius saw on my face must've been convincing, because the most beautiful hope sparked in their eyes.

"I don't—I can't say anything yet," I said, stumbling. It felt wrong to accept their vision of me as some kind of savior. I was only doing the bare minimum—the right thing. And claiming a decadent slice of vengeance on the side wasn't selfless in the least. "But I am here to help. You all just need to stay safe until it all goes down, okay?"

Tears brimmed Lana's eyes. "Whatever we can do, let us know. Forget the past—those slaves who had it out for you, they were hurting and misguided. Anything you need now, we can make happen."

Cassius nodded, and I smiled in return, despite my discomfort with their sudden adoration and faith in me.

The four of us developed a system, periodically emptying the bloody buckets of water into the shower. We also sprayed a fuck-ton of perfume and opened a window to rid the space of the lingering scents of Liza and her blood.

When the space was in working order, it was time for phase two.

Rosalind projected out her succubus magick, both searching for approaching vampires and also deterring them with a wall of repulsive, anti-seductive magick. I switched off my own power, following Rosalind's directions to board up my glamour and emit nothing but the most disgusting, unappetizing energy.

Rosalind beckoned us forward as Cassius and I hauled the rug full of dead body. Cassius very clearly lifted most of the weight, but I was fantastic at steering and providing morale by means of inappropriate corpse jokes.

Once we turned the corner, a tall window overlooking the city was a few paces ahead. It wasn't a hall that often garnered a lot of traffic, but there were plenty of residential chambers around, including Durian's. Thank all the gods he was gone tonight.

"Remember, toss her out, and then we need to disperse as quickly as possible," Rosalind whispered.

Lana stood watch at the far end of the hall, watching the staircase. Everyone nodded, and this beautiful, powerful energy flooded my veins—this feeling of being a part of something bigger than myself. It was thrilling, difficult to put into words.

I wondered if this was how the turned felt, united by loyalty and purpose in their fight against the born.

It was more than mere friendship. It was the surreal experience of sharing a vision, of fighting against common enemies and dreaming of the same brighter tomorrow.

We held each other's fates in our palms, and all we could do was trust each other and keep moving forward.

"Ready?" Cassius asked. His handsome features shone with exertion, a thin layer of sweat at his hairline.

He moved closer to the open window.

I nodded, and we hoisted Liza higher. Cassius pushed up on the front end, getting her onto the sill. Then, we shoved.

As soon as Liza was airborne, Cassius pulled the window shut, twisted the lock, and we all took off in different directions. I heard the crash as I sped away.

I took the corner and slipped into my room, launching immediately into my final round of cleaning and tidying. It was more than manageable now.

Gratitude swelled in my chest. I would be dead if it weren't for Rosalind. I would've likely been dead a second time if it weren't for Cassius and Lana.

My veins pumped with anxiety, knowing these two traumatized humans were now looped in to my master plan. Actually, it sounded like the whole horde of palace slaves were now in my web.

It was terrifying, this heavy responsibility weighing on my shoulders. The stakes had already been high, but now I had a growing pile of corpses in my metaphorical closet.

Exhausted, I somehow dozed off laying on top of my comforter. In and out of stressful dreams, only one thought woke me in the middle of the night.

I'd never asked Rosalind who gave her that busted lip and black eye.

60

SCARLETT

I'd updated Rune in a rush before I'd fallen asleep for a couple hours, and to say he and Sadie were *concerned* about the events that had unfolded was an understatement. But my job wasn't over yet, and I needed them both to stay calm and trust me.

Fate buzzed loudly in my ears as I dressed myself and covered my exhaustion and stress with makeup.

When an aunt entered my room, her eyes went to the open window first—perhaps admiring the pretty view of steel bars. I'd left it open as a precaution against the scent of Liza's death.

"It's winter," she said, her tone cold and mean. "This room is below freezing."

"I have a fireplace," I said, as if that was an excuse. "Fresh air is good for the soul."

She was all kinds of warm and fuzzy as she erased Rune's bite marks. I'd even gotten her to mend my wounded hand and bruises from Liza's attack.

It wasn't her place to ask questions, likely assuming all my injuries were from Rune.

My cleanup process was complete.

Relief was short-lived as Brennan entered my room soon after. He shooed the aunt away like she was nothing but a speck of dirt under his shoe.

"It's showtime, my love," he said. "Let's call this the opening act."

What in the gods did that mean?

I'd dressed myself in an actual dress, even if it was tiny and made of thin silk, because fuck these bloodsuckers for forcing me to walk around in lingerie. It was all black, in honor of Rune and his clan.

Brennan's eyes devoured my body only briefly, his mind clearly consumed with grander things.

He gripped my waist, staring down into my eyes as he revealed his fangs. "Remember what you promised me."

Trust. Fat fucking chance.

I smiled sweetly, masking my features with fear. The truth was, the more I was able to express my ruthlessness, to see myself as that viper in tall grass, the less terror coursed through my veins.

As we walked through the halls, vampires leered, gasped, and inhaled the air creepily.

All eyes were on me, as usual. But the collective energy was far more volatile than I remembered. Desire was ripe but conflicted, rivalries and strife evident in the tangled mess of competing goals and urges.

"Oh, by the way," Brennan whispered. "Liza was tossed out of a window last night. Dead."

I made no reaction, and Brennan didn't look for one until he spoke his next words.

"I personally will not miss the old bitch, and I doubt you will either, after the way she treated you," he said. "But I found it far stranger that your guard was missing, found drunk and fast asleep in his bed, with no recollection of how he got there. And that not a single witness can illuminate what happened to Liza."

I gasped. "I was... unguarded? With a murderer on the loose?" I searched his eyes, faux horrified.

Brennan swallowed. "I'm sorry, Scarlett. It feels like a failure on my end. I don't know how these things might be connected, or if they even are, but I'm glad you're safe."

"Strange," I echoed. "But you're right, Liza won't be missed."

As if on cue, Evangeline appeared at the end of the grand hall leading to the dining and throne rooms. She was too far away to have heard us, but her glare our way sent a chill to my very core.

"I worry she may need to be dealt with similarly," Brennan whispered. He glanced at me, then gave his head a slight shake. "Nothing for you to concern yourself with, my dear. I'll protect you."

I thought I'd been protecting myself just fine, thank you.

Vampires weren't concealing their shock and loud exclamations as they spotted me, turning to each other to gossip and wonder how I got here.

I heard someone say that Durian had landed and was on his way up.

Brennan couldn't hide his sly smile. He led me into the dining room, where powerful vampires were gathered around a long table. Born women were at tables off to the side, unworthy of breathing the same air as the lords.

Slaves milled about, cruel aunts watching them with sharp eyes. When the aunts saw me, I earned prying curiosity and disdain. I wondered if they had any idea what had happened to Aunt Carol. It was unlikely, as I presumed she'd been sworn to secrecy.

So many secrets, so many threads I couldn't quite wrangle together.

Audaciously, Brennan guided me without touch to join him in standing at the front of the room, directly in line with the empty head of the table. He pointed to the ground and snapped.

His eyes displayed a flicker of softness that was soon to disappear as he stepped into his confident, powerful role.

I sunk to my knees. A hush fell over the room. The lords were speechless, none more so than the ones entering the space for the first time. Some of them stopped walking entirely, looking back behind them as if waiting for someone.

It only took a few seconds for that man to appear in a rush of vampire speed.

My body trembled beyond my conscious control, and I couldn't remember a single breathing exercise as I quickly ran out of air.

Durian's fangs were bared, his cold, dark glare trained on me. His blond hair was perfectly straight, his burgundy attire meticulously ironed.

For a frightening moment, I regressed completely to who I was before my escape. Panic squeezed my heart, and I quickly averted my eyes. I wasn't allowed to look Master in the eyes so unabashedly. My every muscle tensed, and I heard the whoosh of air before a cane strike loud in my ears.

"I wanted her to be a surprise," Brennan said.

If I had to hear the word *surprise* one more time, I thought I might actually puncture my eardrums. That word would need to be retired from my vocabulary for the next several years.

At the relief of my sense of humor, I came back to myself. One foot firmly planted back inside my present reality.

I inhaled deeply, watching Durian's black boots slowly approach.

"I stole her back from Rune, with a meticulously orchestrated plan," Brennan said, and I realized he was speaking more to the lords now than he was to Durian. "Rune is furious."

Durian planted himself right in front of us, and I slowly lifted my gaze to see that his glare had moved to Brennan.

"You're the imbecile who lost her to Rune in the first place.

I'm not sure why you're begging for a victory medal for cleaning up your own shameful mess," Durian spat.

A single lord chuckled, and I could see that these men's desires were all over the place, too. They were all watching Brennan very, very closely. And I didn't miss that more than half of them were doing so with more than mere admiration.

But with *expectation*.

Brennan was unaffected, his smile teetering between cocky and peaceful. He knew something that Durian didn't, something huge. Brennan felt as though he'd already won.

I couldn't make sense of any of it.

Durian finally swept his gaze back to me, and I looked at the floor.

"I'm pleased to see my pet hasn't lost her manners," he said.

Though his tone was mostly even, there was this unsettling craze lurking beneath the surface. His breathing was rapid, his voice slightly raspy. His desires had only gotten colder, more erratic and frighteningly psychotic. Like a collar or a noose, a suffocating amount of his desire lassoed around my throat. The hairs on the back of my neck stood in warning.

Durian's obsession was so far off the edge of sanity that I feared I'd lost control completely.

"Although it would appear you've also been more than sufficiently *fed*," he said with disdain.

His words shocked me, my cheeks instantly heating with shame. When Rune had rescued me, I was a shell of what I'd once been—body and soul. I was unwell, gaunt.

Durian preferred me weak and sickly looking over healthy and strong.

My humiliation quickly transformed into dangerous anger, my palms itching to clench into fists.

Fuel, Sadie's voice reminded me.

"What are you still doing standing here? Take your seat, Brennan," Durian barked.

I glanced quickly at Brennan, who didn't for a moment show defeat or bashfulness. He turned and faced the lords with that same sly smile, unnoticed by Durian, who was in a state of frenzy as his eyes roamed over me.

He blinked. "Stand, pet. You may look at your Master."

I met his cold, black eyes, though I'd much preferred to avoid them. I stood, and Durian's welcome back gesture was to simply close his hand over my airways.

I gasped for oxygen, and he leaned in close, his breath reeking of bitter copper.

"You will not leave my fucking sight. You will sleep at my feet. You will offer every inch of your flesh to your Master to drink from and make beautiful art with. All in Lillian's honor."

Just like Liza had said, Brennan wasn't the only one who'd changed because of my influence.

Durian, who'd once been cold and calculating with a splash of insanity, now leaned far more heavily into his unruly psychopath side.

I choked for air, and Durian only squeezed harder, his eyes moving from lust to anger to lust and back again.

Not sexual lust, but lust for my brokenness, my utter degradation.

The mention of making art with my flesh had my stomach souring, bile threatening to rise.

Durian wasted no time sinking his fangs into my neck, so brutally I feared he might accidentally behead me.

I screamed, and he clamped down harder, my body slumping. He held me up, moaning into my throat.

I was fucked in many ways, but chief among them was that if I were to never leave Durian's sight, then I'd be unable to write to Rune. My piece of paper, pen, and daggers were all hidden in my slave accommodations.

Which meant Rune might come for me before I was ready—

before I knew what Brennan was playing at. Which pieces were set to fall, and when? Where did I fit in?

Why in the hell was Brennan so *smug*? So unfazed by Durian's dismissals and deteriorating mental stability?

As the venom overloaded my blood stream, my last coherent thought was utter panic.

All thoughts faded, and yet again, I found myself on the brink of certain death.

"Sorry, I don't mean to interrupt, Durian," a familiar voice cut through the haze of blood loss and venom cloudiness.

Kole.

Durian slowly pulled back, turning to glare at Kole, who'd taken a seat near the empty head of the table.

"Humans are quite breakable, and I think we can all hear how faint her heart is beating. I wouldn't want you to lose her again right after you got her back, by Lillian's grace." Kole was staring at me intently, and across from him, Brennan looked two seconds away from shattering the glass in his hand.

My head swam, flopping against Durian's chest as I lost the ability to keep it raised. I was barely conscious of my feet being dragged across marble, my body manhandled to rest in Durian's lap at the head of the table.

"So much interest in my *fucking pet!*" Durian yelled, the noise making me flinch even as my eyes fluttered, threatening to close for good. "She is mine! Lillian has given her to *me!*"

Lights and colors spun, and a euphoric emptiness clouded the edges of my consciousness.

"I don't give a fuck whose dick you sucked to get her back for me, you stupid piece of shit," Durian growled.

I was able to peek through my heavy eyelids, glimpsing the utter hatred in Brennan's eyes.

"You only fixed your own mistake, evidence of your deafening inadequacy," Durian continued. "You are nothing. The *Book of Lillian* doesn't even mention your existence."

"Where'd you find that last remaining copy of such a lost ancient book, Durian? I don't recall you ever saying," Brennan said coolly. "Strange there are no records of it in any library anywhere in the realm."

Durian vibrated with fury, the poison of it leaking from his skin to mine.

"But none of that is important, is it?" Brennan said. "Shouldn't we be discussing the uprisings among the poverty-stricken and hungry? The murder of a lady last night, with no leads or suspects? Or the growing problem of defecting soldiers?"

Durian gripped me so roughly I was scared he might actually break me.

"Have you lost the faith, brother?" Durian asked, his voice strange and high-pitched. "Leave my sight and come back when you've prayed your way back into Lillian's divine darkness." His grip on me loosened. "The Dark Mother and King Earle have blessed our war against blasphemy. Everything is going according to plan. We must see through the false prophets of Rune and his bastard brothers and sisters."

I couldn't do much with my magick, but I was still able to read the prevailing collective energy in this hall.

Everyone was listening, even the women. They heard the bizarre inflections in Durian's voice, the way he'd evaded Brennan's questioning and call to be practical in favor of religious fervor and delusion. The tides were turning, and they were not in the mad illusionist's favor.

He really *was* losing it.

My eyes drifted shut.

A hand gripped my face roughly.

"Why are you smiling, you stupid, useless cunt?"

I sleepily murmured my response.

"Because I'm back with my Master."

61

SCARLETT

I woke up on an altar.

Durian was staring down at me, his eyes nearly black.

When I screamed, he smiled, stroking my hair. "I've missed my favorite sound, terribly, pet."

This was my worst nightmare. I knew what I was walking into when I came back to this place, but I avoided thinking about the inevitable horrors as much as possible. And, naively, part of me hoped that I really could trust Brennan to protect me.

I would have to trust myself, instead.

Careening off the side of a rocky precipice, I scrambled for anything at all to grab hold of. If I fell all the way to the bottom, I wouldn't be able to be of use. To stand for something greater than myself.

Instead of imagining Durian carving into me, I imagined it was him on this altar.

I halted my fall into dissociation by imagining the look in his eyes when it was *he* who was restrained, unable to move.

I imagined those dark, beady irises the moment Durian

realized that this *stupid, useless cunt* had been turning his entire court against him.

My chest rose and fell rapidly, and I stared hard into Durian's eyes—watched them roam my body like he was admiring a fine cut of meat.

"Do you have a family, Master?" I asked, my voice raw from screaming.

Durian froze, and I'd possibly never seen him falter this noticeably. His brows furrowed, and his lips turned down.

"Obviously, pet," he said.

I watched his eyes flicker from confusion to paranoia to something more contemplative.

"I had to kill most of them," he said. "Such is the reality of a vampire destined for greatness. You live a life constantly threatened, and those closest to you are the biggest threats of all."

Durian raised a blade, twisting it around in his hand as if he were playing with a toy.

I showed fear, but underneath, I held on to that sturdy branch, heard fate's melody roar in my ears. I was laying with Rune under a field of stars, laughing and sharing secrets like we were young lovers.

I mumbled something quickly and softly under my breath.

Durian's confusion multiplied. "What did you just say?"

"Started everything," I said, praying it was close enough to what I really said to be believable. "I meant what I said when we were reunited. I've missed my Master. I admire him. When I was away from you, I was plagued by obsessions. I'd wished I'd been able to learn more about you and your powerful mind. I've never met someone more intelligent."

"You're far more talkative than usual," he growled, caught between basking in my ego-stroking and his drive to make sacrifices with my flesh for Lillian—his compulsion to reclaim me.

Even still, his eyes flashed at my declarations. He'd relaxed slightly, as if pleased the obsession had been mutual.

As if I *enjoyed* his grand romantic gestures of slaughtering innocents in my name and writing paragraphs upon paragraphs about the power of my blood and pain.

"It's an honor to serve the second most powerful vampire in the realm," I murmured.

Durian's eyes flashed, his blade suddenly pressed against my ribs. "What the fuck did you just say?"

"I'm sorry, Master," I said, wincing. "I meant second only to King Earle, the ruler of all vampires."

A tremor racked through his jaw. He gritted his teeth. He slowly withdrew the blade, taking a deep breath and rolling his neck.

"King Earle is on his way out, pet," Durian said. "I am his successor. Did your puny little brain fail to understand the meaning of *future king of all born vampires?*"

No. No, it hadn't.

I pretended to be the most vapid, mystified bimbo anyway. "What an honor, Master. To fill the shoes of someone you admire. Was he your inspiration growing up?"

Durian made a feral noise of rage, finally cutting into my stomach. I cried out, tears leaking from my eyes as blood trailed down my torso.

"I do not fill anyone's shoes, whore!" Durian spat, stray spit splattering across my face. "Earle is a failure. It is because of his own weak leadership that the mortals have risen against him, creating new races of bastard vampires. Lillian has sent me to make this whole world right again and restore her natural order. I do not *aspire* to be Earle. He should aspire to be *me*."

Durian licked the tears off my cheeks. He carved into my chest next as I screamed.

And I was thankful for the pain, welcomed it, even. Because without it, I might've let another smile slip.

When I'd reached my threshold and began to black out, Durian finally licked my wounds. And in my venom drunkenness, I slurred a series of whispered words together.

I ended them with *thank you, Master.*

Durian barely acknowledged me, too busy reciting prayers to Lillian and indulging in her daughter's addictive blood.

In my mind, I heard the song I'd performed for Rune. I remembered how it felt to sing in front of him, his warm eyes swimming with reverence, like I was a goddess in the flesh. My heart, once fast but slowing the deeper I fell into the music, rested in those broad hands.

I was held by our love, this understanding that no matter the leap or fall, I would be caught. Forever.

How beautiful it was to be free to soar, wings spread wide, after two decades of allowing myself to be shot down every time I brushed the clouds.

∼

I NEEDED out of these chambers. *Now.*

My collar was too tight, and I was desperate for air as I crawled in a futile attempt to escape Durian as he beat me with anything he could find. My thighs and ass were a rainbow of color, and not once had Durian allowed me to be healed.

Bruises decorated every part of my body, and my flesh was in various stages of healing from bites and slices.

"There's nowhere for you to run, pet," Durian said, his voice frighteningly crazed. "My lamb must repent for every day she spent away from her shepherd."

I had to write to Rune. If I didn't, he would come for me before all of my pieces were in place.

I'd slept at Durian's feet for two nights now. Sometimes he'd awoken in the middle of the night to hold me down and feed from me. He fed me blood replenishing potions only when I was close to death. When he had to leave, he chained me to his bed by my collar.

Brennan was nowhere to be found. No one was allowed to see me.

And Durian's obsessive need to isolate and punish me was putting a wrench in every single one of my schemes.

My work with Durian was finished. I'd gotten everything I'd needed. It was time for his destruction.

He grabbed my ankle, yanking me back as I collapsed against the floor.

If only I could get out of his damn rooms.

There was this deep, feminine rage filling the space inside of me that used to be a cold, dark void.

I wasn't drowning or regressing. All the new trauma Durian was forcing into my body was feeding a fire, strengthening a poison.

"What a beautiful masterpiece your body has become," he said.

My stomach rumbled. I hadn't been fed once, and my only source of water was a pet bowl by the bathroom that I had to drink from without using my hands.

Durian wanted me weak. He wanted me incapacitated. I couldn't think clearly through the venom on an empty stomach. My only hope of utilizing my succubus magick was in short moments of clarity between feeding sessions. And that was only if Durian wasn't conjuring nightmarish visions of monsters feeding on my flesh.

A window of opportunity finally opened. I wouldn't let it go to waste.

I turned to face him, staring deeply into those beady, crow eyes.

Those golden threads flickered with power, and I fought through the panic, the pain, the hunger.

I summoned from my deepest wells, and I forced my way

into Durian's mind. I breathed in his bitter paranoia, and I amplified it. I needed Durian to think it was his genius idea to let me out of his chambers.

You need to show off your masterpiece to the lords, especially to Kole—who clearly still wants to steal your pet away. Everyone needs to see she's yours and you can do with her whatever you wish.

"I wish I could show Rune the masterpiece I've created with your pristine, milky skin," Durian said, staring down at me as he placed a boot on my stomach.

My wounds seared with pain, and I gasped. The ceiling above was painted in ugly, bright colors—a depiction of Lillian's underworld.

I imagined Rune's ceiling instead. Me in that golden dress, surrounded by oceans and stars and the glittering lights of Aristelle.

"Does Rune fuck you, pet?"

My eyes snapped to his.

His boot pressed harder. "Answer me," he bellowed.

"Yes."

His eyes flashed, disdain curling his lip. "Disgusting pets don't deserve to be fucked. Powerful men don't succumb to base temptations."

If Durian's asexuality was preventing me from being raped, then all I could do was nod in agreement and keep feeding him a steady stream of magickal reinforcement.

"But I'm afraid a reclaiming is in order," he whispered.

No. I watched his hands, prepared for them to go for his belt.

He grabbed me by the collar. "After a trip to court, where you will get my cock hard by showing off your brutalized body to every man and woman there, I will take you back here to be fucked mercilessly. You will not enjoy a second of it. Your reclaiming will be a punishment for being a filthy slut and allowing a blasphemous bastard's cock inside you."

He let go, and I sucked in air after being deprived for so long. My stomach rumbled again, and Durian regarded me as if he were revulsed by the sound of my own starvation.

I wouldn't be returning to his chambers tonight. I didn't care what I had to do.

Durian's manhood would be cut from his body before it got anywhere close to what belonged to Rune—what belonged to *me*.

62

SCARLETT

Court was business as usual in the throne room. Witch lights floated about, illuminating the garish displays of wealth in rich crimson and shiny gold. Durian didn't take to the dais. He paraded me around, and I was clothed in nothing but a golden thong and a bra that pushed up but didn't actually cover my breasts. I was essentially nude.

I was allowed to walk, but Durian still led me on a collar and leash as he showed me off before his court.

When Kole saw me, his face paled, his eyes sweeping over my body in unconcealed horror and distaste.

I'd glimpsed myself in the mirror only once. My body was covered head to toe in constellations of marks, cuts, and bruises, and in a sick, twisted way—there was indeed a certain perverse artistry to Durian's cruelty.

That hadn't stopped me from dry heaving on the floor.

Durian had beaten me for that, too.

I'd still hadn't received a bite of food, and I thought perhaps my stomach was starting to eat itself. Every step hurt, my skin, muscles, and bones soaking in pain from my days of torture and abuse.

Brennan turned from his hushed conversation with a couple of lords, and as soon as he saw me, his face went utterly blank.

It was like he knew that if he allowed even a drop of his fury and disgust into his features, he might pull the trigger on his mysterious plans and blow up his coup before it began.

Instead, he merely moved his eyes to Durian. "Your pet is on the brink of death," he said dryly, lifting a brow.

I knew I must truly look like shit if even the cruel lords next to Brennan regarded me with something close to pity, or perhaps sadness for what had become of my once fuckable body.

"It would be quite ironic, if after all those attacks in the bastard districts—not to mention Brennan's reacquisition mission—you killed the girl anyway," Lord Nereus said.

Durian yanked me, and I choked, grasping the thick leather around my neck as I stumbled closer to him.

"Pet is fine," Durian hissed. "Her flesh is a conduit for the Dark Goddess's divine power."

While Durian fell inside his delusions, I was mildly irritated that Brennan and the lords kept talking up this special ops mission as if *I* hadn't been the one to orchestrate the entire thing.

Idiots.

Gods, I was hungry. I was flooded with shame at my exposed, destroyed body, exhausted from trying to keep myself from mentally shutting down, and still working through the puzzles of what Brennan was up to and how to escape my imminent rape...

Nope, I was going down.

I saw black as I collapsed.

"She needs fucking medical attention, Durian. She is not a toy; she is a human!" Brennan's voice reached me from my place on the floor, my limbs bent in very unsustainable positions.

Magick swelled. I saw a kaleidoscope of color behind my eyelids.

Kole's voice rose. "If you harm me, you harm King Earle. Stop this madness right this minute!"

"He is not in his right mind," Brennan said. "I think we can all see that."

"Durian has always had a taste for being rough with his slaves, Brennan. This is hardly irregular for our chosen, blessed by Lillian," a voice I didn't recognize said.

Collective desire for violence reached a peak, and I wished I could open my eyes.

Could someone please *stuff some food and potion in my mouth?* I didn't have the time for another bout of inconvenient unconsciousness. I needed to write to Rune.

"Liza was murdered, and none of you care!" a woman wailed with the high-pitched voice of a most grotesque ghoul. *Evangeline.* "You know Liza's gift, Durian. She was killed right after she touched that slave, right there, Scarlett fucking Hale!"

∼

"Wakey, wakey!"

I opened my eyes. Under me was a plush carpet. Above me were Rosalind and Kole. My stifling collar and its accompanying leash had been removed.

Everything ached. The ground beneath me vibrated as if by powerful magick. Rosalind swallowed, and Kole looked like he was about to piss himself.

"Sit up slowly, dear," Kole said.

When he handed me a sandwich, I lost all sense of shame. I took huge bites, ignoring them both as I stared lovingly at the most delicious food I'd ever tasted.

Rosalind handed me water, possibly seeing that without it, I would soon choke.

I washed down the food crammed in my throat, my memories returning. "What in the gods happened?"

"A fight broke out," Rosalind said. "That soon turned into some kind of hearing. No women allowed, obviously."

"Or non-Valentin born," Kole added.

I recognized that we were in Kole's living area. My room was in the opposite wing. Could I get there safely? Rune had likely sensed my heart nearly stop, and we hadn't communicated for three days. Not to mention, the last he heard was that I'd just committed a second murder. Or, at least, had aided in one.

"Durian was out of his mind," Rosalind said. "The walls were bleeding. People were hallucinating. I showed up after you were out cold."

"And I took it upon myself to get you out of there," Kole said, puffing up his chest.

"Does he know where I am?" I asked, remembering what Durian had threatened me with tonight.

Rosalind shook her head. "I don't think he saw us, but he could find you pretty easily. However, you should be the least of his concerns right now."

They'd covered me with a blanket. Whether it was for my sake or theirs was uncertain. Likely both. I was not currently pleasant to look at.

"We need to get out of here," Kole said. "I've seen enough. I can only trust my king will believe what I tell him about the state of Valentin's affairs and cut ties with this lot immediately."

I thumbed my earlobes, tracing the crystal orbs that had been fashioned into simple earrings. By his use of the word *we*, it was clear that he wanted to take Rosalind and me with him.

"Kole, it's time we speak plainly," I said.

His eyes darted to mine. He nodded, shifting on his feet as he nervously babbled. "I agree. We have an opportunity right now—we could leave this island behind. You both would—"

"Hey!" I cut in, slowly rising to my feet as I kept the blanket wrapped around my battered form. I embodied Sadie, her fierce dominance that was unquestionable and respected.

Kole's attention snapped to me, and he visibly calmed. I removed my earrings, my eyes never leaving his as I held my hand out.

He stared down at the crystal balls encased in delicate gold.

"These are disguised recording crystals," I said. "My first night back with Durian, I recorded him saying that he was Earle's successor, that Earle was a failure whom he held no respect for, among other damning comments."

The memory of that night flitted through my mind, my successful subterfuge filling me with satisfaction. The words I'd mumbled before and after Durian had fed from me were *start recording* and *stop recording*. Who knew spellcasting could be so intuitive?

Kole absorbed my words, anger flashing in his eyes. "Treasonous prick."

It was clear that Kole respected his king, just as Sadie had confirmed. Kole was a true loyalist, and he was going to advocate for what was best for the kingdom's interests. It was now time to show him that those interests aligned with Rune's.

"Brennan almost had me convinced, but I'm afraid I can no longer speak highly of anyone in this palace." He paused. "Save the two of you."

His features were genuine, his eyes lighting with the fire of righteousness.

"Let alone back them politically," he continued. He shook his head, looking down at the orbs once more before lowering his hand and meeting my eyes. "You are an incredible woman, Scarlett. You will be rewarded handsomely for your service to the crown."

"My service was for Valentin and her innocents, too," I said. I dropped the blanket, forcing Kole to witness what Durian had done to me. "Give one orb to the council, another to Earle, to ensure the state of the born here is understood by as many reasonable minds as possible. I want you to take all the credit, Kole. Tell them you were the one pulling the strings, following a hunch."

Kole's mouth opened then closed, his light brown brows furrowing.

"You deserve the recognition," I said. "You deserve to be seen as a protector of the crown."

At this, Kole's ears perked up. His deepest desires were stoked, his need for approval and respect. He enjoyed the idea of being seen as someone skilled in espionage, and I was more than willing to step out of the spotlight when it came to the kingdom.

"Durian's religion is spreading through Ravenia, and you can help stop it before it sows even more chaos." I looked down at my body, nausea churning in my guts as I did. "Before it leads to even more slaves treated the way I have been. Even more mortals poisoned against your kind. Vampires need *us*, not the other way around."

Kole's mind churned. After a minute of silence, he bent to pick up the second half of my sandwich and water and handed them both to me.

"Good boy," I murmured.

His lips quirked up, sudden amusement in his eyes as he raked a hand through his hair. He glanced away for a moment before sighing. "You stand with Rune. You're here on behalf of the turned."

"No," I said, my tone sharp. "I stand with the turned, because I believe they are best suited to rule, as you should understand by now as well. Just as you should understand that it's your duty to ensure the kingdom recognizes that fact for a second time. But I am here for *me*."

Once Kole delivered these recordings, with the help of

personal accounts of what had happened inside this palace and in born districts, the kingdom would understand Durian's psychotic treason and the necessity of Rune's rule to ensure stability and the steady flow of exports for their war. At that point, any moves the turned made would be justified, the ceasefire null. Valentin would live to see another day as an autonomous entity with a once-human ruler.

Kole's lips quirked up, his gaze sweeping from me to Rosalind and back again. He sighed. "Funny how beautiful women always seem to be lurking in the shadows of every man's vie for power in Valentin."

I smirked.

Rosalind shrugged as she admired her pink nails. "I'm just a sex demon, Kole," she drawled. "You're giving me far too much credit."

"How's Sadie?" Kole asked me, searching my face for clues he wouldn't find.

My smile was unchanging. "Who?"

"Hm." Kole slipped the orbs into his pocket as the palace trembled again with dark power. "We need to leave now, ladies."

Rosalind spoke first. "I'm not leaving the slaves," she said. "Unless you can bring them to safety, too?"

Kole frowned. "I'm afraid I do not have that capacity, as sympathetic as I am—"

"Then I'm staying," she said, cutting him off. "Though the door will remain open for a future venture to Ravenia. If you should return when things are more stable."

Kole nodded in resignation before his eyes flitted to mine. He might've been under my spell, but like I'd read at that first meeting, Kole was always going to be most interested in Kole.

I'd also been careful not to stir up too much obsession in him. Kole wanted me, but it was different from the way Brennan and Durian did. He was far more level-headed and intelligent, with centuries of life experience under his belt. Not to mention he enjoyed being dominated and denied, an entirely different power dynamic than I had with the others. As long as I let him down easy, I knew there was little risk of total collapse.

"I have a responsibility to my fellow slaves, too, Kole," I said gently. "I want you to return to Earle's court and demand the recognition you deserve, and I will write to you and help in any way I can. And if you return to Valentin, come see me."

Rune would sooner behead him than let him think he had a shot with me, but that was next month's problem.

"I wish I could do more to help," Kole said, disappointment bleeding in his eyes as my true intentions sunk in. "I worry for you both. It's no longer safe here, and Scarlett, there's something you should know."

I swallowed my last bite of sandwich and sipped water. I was still in excruciating pain, but at least I was no longer on the brink of fainting again.

Kole's apologetic features had dread pooling in my guts.

"I'm afraid whatever escape plan you were counting on may no longer be viable."

63

SCARLETT

I held my breath, terrified of Kole's next words. That nagging image of Brennan's sly smile assailed my focus, along with his cryptic hints of some master plan.

"Brennan is convinced that he is about to have Rune in his clutches. He didn't specify how, but he was confident. One of the many reasons I find it prudent to leave this place as soon as possible."

Rosalind stared at me. I was forced to breathe again, to steady myself.

"I don't disagree that despite my personal feelings, the turned clan's rule seems to be in the best interest of all parties involved. At least for now," Kole said. "I don't believe Rune would be stupid enough to walk into a trap, but Brennan's conviction was strong, and I would be remiss if I didn't warn you."

Trap.

I couldn't hear anything else Kole was saying. I was suddenly livid that he'd waited this long to say something, that he'd cared more about taking me back to live as a courtesan princess than ensuring Valentin's stability and the freedom of all slaves.

"Leave, Kole," I said sternly, attempting to keep the depths of my wrath from my voice. "You wouldn't want to miss your opportunity."

Kole studied my features, understanding washing over him. "Good luck, Scarlett. I apologize." He scanned my body one last time. "For all of it."

I pointed with my head toward the door, and Rosalind came to my side.

Before we left, Kole spoke one final time.

"This world was built by beautiful, deadly women, as much as we men would rather believe otherwise," he called. "Give them hell, ladies."

I wanted to throw an obscene gesture over my shoulder at his patronizing display of allyship, but I resisted the urge.

"Stay safe, Kole," I managed to bite out.

As soon as we left Kole's room, I hissed to Rosalind, "We need to get to my chambers *now*."

I had to stop Rune and his fighters from walking straight into a trap—a trap Brennan had set from the very beginning and one I'd been too blinded by my own arrogance to consider. I thought I'd led Brennan to make a stupid mistake with the tunnels, but it had been the other way around.

Brennan was the one who'd played us.

∼

WITCH LIGHTS WERE GOING in and out of power as we moved. Rosalind knew this place like the back of her hand, guiding us to my wing through back halls. We hadn't encountered anyone yet.

Palace vampires were a little busy currently.

I was nearly sprinting now, passing the window we'd thrown Liza out of, and beelining for my room.

Rosalind screamed, and I turned with my hand on the

doorknob just in time to see a river of blood rushing for us. The deep crimson roared, sloshing up against the sides of the halls.

I flung open the door. The wave of blood crashed up against the other side as I pulled it shut behind us.

"Visions," I said.

Rosalind gasped for air. "Durian is plaguing the whole castle with them."

I rushed to the vanity, opening my makeup drawer and finding the tin of pressed powder where I'd stashed my note. Then I opened an empty tube of eyeliner to retrieve my pen.

"I like Scarlett the spy. She's a badass," Rosalind murmured.

My heart was pounding, my legs aching from running when they were this badly bruised. I unfolded the note.

Rune, it's a trap. Don't use the tunnels.

I stared so intensely at the paper I feared my rage and terror might somehow set it aflame.

Minutes passed. All of me was tightly wound. It was hard to swallow. My palms were slick.

No response.

I wasn't sure how long it had been when Rosalind placed a hand on my shaking shoulder.

"You've done all you can do. I'm sorry, Scar, but we really need to keep moving," she said.

The blank piece of paper stared back. And I couldn't say the words out loud—the reality that if Rune wasn't answering me, that meant he *couldn't* answer me. Because there was no way in Helia's green earth that he would've felt that shock through his system, for the first time in three days, and not drop everything to read my note.

I felt so stupid. Of course, Brennan would assume that Rune had dosed me with his blood after everything, that Rune would only let me go if he thought he could get me back.

Brennan *wanted* me to reveal the tunnels to Rune.

I ran through our conversations, squashing down my panic so I could concentrate. Brennan didn't think that I was working with Rune. He thought I was oblivious to everything, only leading Rune into a trap inadvertently.

The secrets of my true nature and allegiance were all I had left.

I put the note and pen back in their hiding spots in silence. The thought of something happening to Rune, to Uriah or Mason or anyone he'd brought with him, had a lump lodged in my throat.

It would be all my fault.

Keep taking the next right step, Rune commanded inside my mind.

The voices of everyone who was rooting for me were my lifelines as I put on the only garment of clothing I could find that covered my daggers.

Rosalind watched me in a respectful silence as I slipped on a black skirt and a jeweled bra that actually covered my breasts.

"Can you see my daggers?" I asked her. I did a little twirl.

"No, but they won't be hard to feel. And vampires tend to want to undress you."

I shrugged. "All we can do is try," I said, my voice trembling.

Rosalind straightened and smirked. "Get it together, *Scarlett fucking Hale*," she said, making fun of what Evangeline had said right before I blacked out. "You once asked me if I wanted my life to mean something. I hated you for it. Because once you hear something, you can't *unhear* it. I'd spent so many years living as a slave—a slave to *fear*—that I'd forgotten what it was like to live for anything else."

I took a long, deep breath.

"You came into this place like a violent storm," she continued. "I was so irritated by it at first, because I knew you were about to make my life exasperatingly harder. And you did," she said with a snort. "But I'm fucking grateful for it. For you. I don't want to go back to who I was before. And I don't want you to either, because I've seen you go from an imprecise storm to a lethal, tactful demon of perfect control. One that I would follow into battle any day of the week."

"I'm proud of you too, Rosalind." I straightened, already feeling steadier. I'd needed that metaphorical slap to the face.

"I'm going to fulfill my end of our plans and get these slaves out of here," she said, lifting her chin. "The aunts herded them away from the fray, and the castle is in the perfect state of chaos to strike. I've been hiding weapons in their quarters, studying each aunt's powers, habits, and weaknesses. I can move them out in batches starting now, so the turned can do whatever the fuck they want to this place without worrying about harming innocents. I have friends in the city who will help hide them."

I was terrified for her. I suddenly understood how Snow and everyone who loved me must've felt, watching me vow to bring down an entire regime, facing beings infinitely more powerful than myself.

Rosalind wouldn't be alone, and all we could do was believe in each other now.

"If I have to mourn you again, I'm going to be *pissed*."

Rosalind winked. "Cockroach, darling. Remember?" She took my hands in hers. "Close your eyes."

Behind my eyelids was that beautiful darkness, where I belonged.

"Dark Mother," Rosalind whispered. "We pray that you watch over your daughters, that you help us destroy those who have used your name in vain—these weak, mediocre men who disgrace you. Let us bring glory to your mysterious, chaotic, alluring power. Let us remind this world that it was designed to worship women."

"Amen."

That was a prayer I could wholeheartedly believe in. And as

we spoke, I felt a kind of religiosity infect my blood. I remembered when Snow and I had been attacked and I'd nearly died. I'd seen Lillian's beautiful, ruthless face, whispering the words *not yet*. I held fast to that vision—her smile, her flowing black hair, her crown of bones and onyx.

She'd known me long before I knew her.

It was her power that had always lived inside me—the power to humble men and bring them to their undeserving knees.

"I'll see you when it's all over," I whispered, dropping Rosalind's hands after giving them a squeeze.

We didn't say another word as we each departed, going in opposite directions.

I was going back to the den of mad vampires, praying futilely that Rune hadn't walked into the trap I'd left.

Even though I knew in my heart that he had.

64

SCARLETT

I'd seen multiple vampires on my way to the main hall that led to the throne room and dining room. None had done more than leer or say vile things to me. Most were women and guards, and just about everyone was in a state of panic, more wrapped up in self-preservation than accosting Durian's slave.

My brutalized body might've been as much a deterrent as my property status. These vampires may have been cruel, but a slave covered head to toe in gashes, marks, and a rainbow of bruises wasn't exactly appetizing.

No one wanted a peach that was soft and damaged all over.

I hardly felt the pain of movement as adrenaline steadily pumped through my system. When I turned the final corner, into the wide-open space with windows flanking either side that led to the grand rooms, a woman screeched.

"There she is!" Evangeline said, surrounded by a group of born women. They all turned toward me.

But before any of them could question me about their dead bitch friend, a searing heat erupted on my neck.

I wasn't the only one who froze in place, turning to look at the imposing marble staircase leading to the main palace entrance on the first floor.

Doors were shoved open from the dining room. I was caught between two sets of commotion—bodies moving up the stairs, the sound of heavy boots and shouts, and then Brennan and several lords walking from the opposite side of the space. Born men flowed out into the hall behind them, watching in anticipation.

"Brennan!" Durian bellowed, feral and crazed.

The walls were warping, bleeding darkness and crimson. The marble trembled, and dark cracks exploded across the floor. I stumbled back before I understood they were more illusions.

Brennan spotted me. "Scarlett, thank Lillian," he said, though his eyes flashed disgust when they roamed my skin. "I'm glad you're here for the closing act, my love."

At those last two words, the lords eyed me and then Brennan in surprise. Durian appeared positively aghast.

All of our attention was soon diverted back to the staircase.

That lump in my throat melted into abject terror.

A group of born soldiers marched up the steps, surrounding two men dragging along a prisoner.

Rune.

He was alone. My heart shattered. Did that mean—oh gods, did that mean whoever was with him didn't survive? How many had I sentenced to death?

Around Rune's neck and wrists were spiked shackles, and I realized with certainty that they were forged with flecks of blood onyx. That was the only reason Rune wasn't using his shadow magick to rot this palace to the ground.

I'd never seen Rune powerless before. I wasn't sure anyone had.

The sight of it chilled me to my bones, along with the knowledge that I'd been the one to lead him here.

A hush fell over the hall as the soldiers brought Rune forward. Even Durian had stilled, his mind driven to the depths of insanity suddenly going quiet.

All eyes moved to Brennan. Brennan's focus glued on Rune, shackled and thrown to his knees at Brennan's feet. Rune struggled to raise his head, but his gaze went straight to me.

I couldn't react. I couldn't crumble at the sight of those dark eyes reaching for me, the way his muscles strained as if attempting to fight poison itself.

"My army has captured Lillian's bastard son," Durian boomed, raising his arms into the air like a demented holy man as illusory ashes fell from the ceiling.

"No," Brennan snarled, addressing the crowd of lords and ladies. "*I* have captured Rune, and I alone." He followed Rune's line of sight to me. "With a special thanks to Valentin's most desired human for serving as such delicious bait."

My stomach dropped. I avoided looking at Rune at all costs now, desperate to hide any emotion that might ruin the last trick we had left.

"You lords have seen the way Durian has failed even the most basic tests of competency during our hearing. If you still stand with him, you will fall with him," Brennan hissed.

I tasted a small trickle of anger from a few lords, but the prevailing desire was to back the most powerful man in the room.

And that was no longer Durian.

"Durian served a useful purpose in uniting the born against our new guest," he said, kicking Rune in the ribs.

Rune made absolutely no reaction as he absorbed the impact, only glaring up at Brennan in a silent promise.

Brennan made a gesture to the group of soldiers, and half

the lords moved in tandem, surrounding Durian in a rush of vampiric speed.

The lords who hadn't moved didn't intervene.

Durian shouted orders that fell on deaf ears, and for a moment, the room went pitch black. All I could feel was my own heart beating hard and fast in the emptiness.

Demonic whispers assailed my eardrums, speaking of Lillian's divine will, her wrath for anyone who opposed her chosen.

It didn't take long for the darkness and voices to cease, thrusting us all back into the bright reality of the palace.

I blinked multiple times, almost wondering if I was still trapped in a vision or a dream.

Because Durian now joined Rune in bondage. The aggressors of this coup surrounded their ex-leader as he struggled against the spiked shackles around his wrists and ankles. They didn't humiliate him with a spiked collar, much to my disappointment.

The harder Durian fought and writhed, the quicker the poison entered his system. Rune, on the other hand, knelt perfectly still. He was meditative, almost like a monk. It was fucking eerie how much power he could retain even when he'd been captured by enemies.

"As I was saying," Brennan continued. "Durian can no longer be trusted to rule. He is not of his right mind. If we still hope for kingdom support, let alone to reunite our own people and army, then we need a capable, fit leader. Someone who gets results." He lifted his chin, pointing down at Rune. "I have proven my effectiveness, and I've done it for years, despite the credit Durian has stolen from me."

I did this. All of it. I rewrote history, altered the course of an entire people. I changed the terms of a war that had once seemed inevitable, destined to tear apart the island I loved and condemn thousands of mortals to death.

I killed for this. I got my soulmate captured for this.

And by the gods, I would see this through.

Rune vibrated with rage. He ground his teeth as his eyes traced over my exposed skin—Durian's psychopathic art—my body as a canvas, and whips, blades, canes, and hands as his divine instruments.

"Durian is not a prophesier," Brennan said. "He is not a man of the goddess. He is not chosen; he is a vampire just like the rest of us. He is nothing more than an ambitious illusionist and propagandist who comes from a long line of men destined for insanity. There is a reason his family line fell out of power. And there is a reason I'm the one with royal blood in my veins."

I took step after step toward Brennan, and he tracked me as he spoke.

"I am destined to rule, not because of some fabricated book. But because I am the man who will clean up all of Durian's blunders and lead the born into our new epoch of prosperity and power."

I reached Brennan's side, Rune now only two feet away. He stared forward, eyes unfocused, jaw set.

Brennan looped his arm around me, and I winced. Brennan glared at Durian, his lips curving in manly bravado and triumph.

I had to admit, it was satisfying to hear Durian screech, writhing violently against his bondage until the poison pushed him into a catatonic state.

Brennan looked down at me, and I mirrored his smile.

"I told you that you could trust me," he said softly.

Another respected lord began to speak, fervently in favor of maintaining order and backing Brennan. There were more than a few vampires that stared at their disgraced leader in mourning, unsettled by his state of incapacitation.

But no one moved to free him.

I filled my eyes with admiration as I held Brennan's gaze. "I always knew this was your destiny, since I first laid eyes on you."

Brennan's strong hands gripped my face. He smiled like a general who'd just won the most important battle of his career.

With Rune at our feet, Brennan crushed his lips to mine. And as his tongue explored my mouth, I forced my lips to cooperate.

I reached for Brennan, deepening our kiss, using every pair of eyes on us to fuel the bursting, vengeful, mysterious darkness poised to strike.

When he pulled back, a soldier approached, carrying two sets of keys. Brennan stashed them smoothly in his pockets, his arm looping around me again as he faced the stunned crowd of vampires.

I caught more than a few glares of distrust directed at me. I was no mind reader, but I could surmise the prevailing sentiment was something along the lines of: *whore.*

I made a point to smile and meet the eyes of each vampire who watched me with cold hatred. They could despise me until they bled bitterness, but they couldn't touch me.

Brennan's men, on the other hand, viewed me hungrily—recognizing me as the prize, the masculine marker of success. To them, I was a symbol of power, of status.

To this entire crowd, I was a convincing reason to stand behind Brennan. Because whether they hated me or trusted me, I clearly always found myself on the arm of the most powerful man in the room.

And as I watched several lords mark me with their eyes, felt their desire to plant their own flags in my flesh to prove their worthiness—I imagined this tasteless palace rotting away by shadow and crumbling by tall, spitting flames.

I wasted no time whispering to Brennan's mind, which was now entirely beholden to my every influence. I had never had someone wrapped so tightly around my finger. Beyond his conscious awareness, Brennan's psyche recognized me as the granter of his every last wish.

Scarlett needs a healer. Tonight, she will be mine, and I need her strong enough to take me.

"Take Durian and Rune to the dungeons, and set them up facing each other," Brennan commanded the nearby soldier. He whispered to me, "Poetic, no?"

I laughed, but we weren't laughing for the same reason.

"Who wants to deliberate how we will torture and maim Lillian's bastard son beyond recognition?" Brennan asked. "Women permitted," he added.

How progressive of him.

The crowd cheered.

A soldier yanked Rune to his feet, and with Brennan's eyes back on me, I couldn't meet Rune's intense gaze. Even with spikes of magickal poison in his veins, he radiated power, the kind that couldn't be killed. The kind that would live on forever.

Rune and Durian were dragged away, both half-paralyzed. And I wasn't the only one staring at their backs in stunned silence, hardly able to believe my eyes. These were the two most influential vampires in Valentin, sworn enemies who'd been on the brink of leading armies against each other, now immobile and forced to inhabit the same prison.

"Elaine," Brennan snapped at a witch gathered with the born women. "Fetch a healer witch. Tell them to meet us in the throne room."

The witch nodded, although I could sense a level of trepidation in her desires. That was something that Brennan *would've* needed to grapple with. The fact that these witches had been fully indoctrinated into Durian's religion, and they wouldn't be so quick to accept Brennan's decree that the *Book of Lillian* was a sham.

He *would've* needed to deal with that problem—if the end

goal of his puppet master had been to place him in a position of power.

Unfortunately for him, her plans would leave him dead by the end of the night.

Brennan suddenly stiffened, peering around the opulent hall. "Someone go find Kole," he barked.

65

RUNE

"It's a trap," I said, facing a group of my most trusted clan members with Sadie, Uriah, and Mason at my side. We stood in front of the windows in the deliberation room, a few feet from where I'd bent Scarlett over the hard table and fucked her while she'd envisioned the borns' destruction.

"Brennan's men will surround me as soon as I make it to the end of the tunnels," I said with certainty. "I will take a vial of mortal blood, and I will be going alone."

I'd already told the friends who stood at my side, but they still stared at me as if this was the first they'd heard of my plan. Sadie was furious, though she'd long accepted I would willingly sacrifice myself for my Little Flame no matter the consequences, forever.

Scarlett was dying. I could feel it through the blood bond. She was wasting away at a rapid pace. The sound of her poor heart revving up before beating fatally slow was a twisted melody that followed me everywhere I went, impossible to tune out.

I knew this would happen, but Scarlett hadn't wanted to hear a word of it. Durian had lost the plot, irreversibly. I didn't need to see the future to know that his obsession with her was too unrestrained and volatile for him to resist squeezing the life out of her.

"When I cross the border, we will spread the information that the palace is in upheaval and Brennan has removed Durian from power," I said. "I am Brennan's final play, his evidence that he deserves to rule."

My men and women were loyal and well-trained, but I could still see the nervousness in their micro-expressions, the fear in their eyes hearing that I would be taken prisoner.

"I trust Scarlett like I trust any of you," I continued. My heart shattered, yearning to be closer to hers—now beating laboriously and strained. "I trust her to be effective in what she was sent to do, which is to crumble the born from within. I will be safe in her hands."

My clan was flabbergasted, not understanding that Scarlett was more than a seductress and a spy, a human double agent. They didn't know she was a succubus, and I doubted that would even help their faith if they did know.

"The kingdom is no longer a concern of ours. An hour after I'm taken, we will break the ceasefire and begin the process of reassimilation."

∼

Everything occurred exactly as I'd predicted.

My shadows strained against the poison. My mind fought to stay lucid and sharp.

I couldn't look away from her. Scarlett's half nude form, every inch of her covered in bruises and injuries of varying severity.

I glared at Durian's marks of brutality until I could no longer breathe, and I was forced to stare back down at the marble floor.

As my cunning little demon's plans unfolded exactly as she'd devised, I burned with pride, with endless devotion. I wished I could focus on that feeling, but it was her abused body that plagued my mind instead, overtaking all else.

This court would burn for what it had allowed to happen to her. Brennan was already at the top of my fucking list. But when he kissed the other half of my soul, the rage that consumed me guaranteed his end was as violent and gruesome as what he'd allowed Durian to do to Scarlett.

How dare he act like her white knight, offering her body as collateral damage to secure his position of power. He was no valiant, honorable soldier. He wasn't even a man.

He was simply *dead*.

I couldn't fight the soldiers as they lifted me. I looked only to Scarlett, to the places on her body Brennan currently touched. She couldn't meet my eyes. It was too dangerous.

Good girl. My perfect, ruthless, spiteful Little Flame. I would reward her for years, for centuries for her beautiful artistry.

For her strength that she'd claimed from gods knew where. Her ability not only to endure, but also to transform her suffering into pure power, was unlike anything I'd seen in my lifetimes of existence.

She was the eternal fire that refused to die. She was violent storms and summer rain, sex and yearning, the sweetest dessert and the most wicked dagger to the heart.

And she was mine.

～

I WASN'T sure how much time had passed. Durian and I were facing each other in a dank, gray room of stone and chains. We each watched the blood trickle from the other's flesh with satisfaction.

Before Scarlett left, never in a million years could I have

predicted I'd be incapacitated by blood onyx in a born dungeon, my cellmate none other than *Durian*.

Durian had finally stopped futilely writhing about like a captured animal. We were both perfectly still, preserving the little strength we had left.

He stared at me, his blond hair slick and tangled, his nearly black eyes crazed while his lip curled.

"My devotees will kill the betrayer and free Lillian's chosen," he said, half drooling as his eyes focused and unfocused. "And when they do, *pet* is going to be broken beyond recognition for disrespecting her Master."

Either he was merely speaking his mind, or Durian was attempting to provoke me. I stayed rigid, my face blank. My wrath bubbled beneath the surface, lying in wait.

"I made her a promise, you see," he continued, his lips forming a smirk as his eyes grew crazed. "To reclaim her with my cock. Painfully, savagely. I will destroy her cunt until it weeps blood for me. I won't let a single drop go to waste."

If my body wasn't currently held in stasis by blood onyx, Durian's tongue would have already been removed from his vile mouth.

Soon.

He would reap no satisfaction from my reaction. I kept my voice bored, my eyes utterly dull, as I regarded Durian.

"I wonder, how will you accomplish such an act without a head?"

66

SCARLETT

I was sitting on a cushion of pillows and blankets on the dais, left of the throne. I was a pet who'd traded one master for another.

The healer watched me take a blood replenishing potion as she prepared a salve. She barked at me to lie down.

I realized my mistake halfway through the potion.

I'd forgotten about my daggers.

I couldn't let her remove my skirt or touch my thighs.

She started working on the cuts across my chest and stomach, the injuries bared to her, with a mixture of energy work and touch with her hands coated in salve.

Brennan was loudly speaking to his comrades, clinking chalices. He'd not sat on Durian's throne yet, but he'd clearly taken his place on all accounts. Court was stiff, not quite knowing how to behave in the aftermath of a coup, but keenly understanding that they were to do their damn best at feigning normalcy.

After all, capturing Rune was cause for uproarious celebration no matter which psychopath reigned supreme.

I yanked on a cord of magick, and Brennan met my eyes. I forced big tears to form, my lip trembling.

She's traumatized. She doesn't want to be touched by anyone but you.

This thought clearly perplexed Brennan, as if he had absolutely no concept of trauma or its effects. It took more power than necessary to root the thought deep before he acted on his desire to protect me.

"Don't touch her," Brennan ordered the healer. "Do what can be done without touching her."

The witch halted, hiding her irritation poorly with her back turned to Brennan. She lifted her hands and continued to heal me with energy, working on the deeper internal bruising.

When she was wrapping up, I let out a sigh of relief. I was still armed. And I was stronger too, no longer on the brink of fainting with every sudden movement. I still ached all over, but the pain was substantially lessened. She let me rub salve myself over the rest of my visible bruises, and they began to fade at an accelerated pace.

"Come, Scarlett," Brennan said, his tone impatient. His ego had never been grander as he beckoned me to the group of powerful, gloating men, all discussing the various ways they would parade Rune's desecrated corpse around the born districts.

An underling approached the group as I did, dropping his eyes in respect. "We can't find Kole. His firebird is missing from the stables. And the aunts are complaining of missing slaves," he said quickly.

Go Rosalind. I prayed she was staying safe. Kole too, so he could deliver my messages to the kingdom.

Brennan straightened, pulling me against him so that I rested against his chest, overlooking the gathered lords.

"Kole was spooked by the violence. He's a skittish little man," Brennan joked boldly, and the lords laughed, feeling safe now that Kole had left. "We will write to him. He backs me wholeheartedly."

Funny, and also false.

"As for the aunts..." he glanced around, likely ensuring my healer had departed. "We must be prepared for all manner of falsities that will cast doubt on my rule. They are loyal to Durian through shared delusion. We will need to reconsider their place in our new order if they can't find a religious justification to fall in line."

The lords eyed me, curiosity, distrust, and lust screeching in a loud cacophony of desire.

"Fascinating," Lord Nereus said, his light blue eyes narrowed on me. "This little human's uncanny ability to survive regime changes no matter which side of the aisle she currently resides."

I returned his stare. I no longer needed to play the same game I had played under Durian. With my back to Brennan's chest, all I needed to do was continue to uplift and soothe his masculinity.

"My heart has only ever belonged to one man," I said, earning chuckles and sneers of condescension from several ancient vampires. Like I was a poor, lovesick child. "But a silly little human with a very breakable body needs to survive. I don't have as many options to that end, which I know is a difficult experience for men like yourselves to imagine. Does that help illuminate my actions?"

The men were silent for a moment, and several vampires looked taken aback. It was as though they were seeing me for the first time. In a way, they were. I'd never been able to speak freely in front of any of them but Brennan, unless it was to answer orders, ever the demure and faithful slave.

I smiled as I eyed them all dangerously. Seductively.

Cocks hardened, each man envisioning how it would feel to put me back in my place. To fill my too confident mouth with their manhood until I no longer had a voice.

"I love her fire," Brennan groaned, his own cock swelling as it pressed up against my back. "Credit where credit is due, gentleman. Without her, we wouldn't have Rune the Ruthless chained to a wall in our dungeons. She's elated to be free of both weaker men."

I nodded, twisting to look up at Brennan like he was the only man in the room I saw.

"Now excuse me while I have a victory drink," Brennan said with a smirk, enjoying that finally, after weeks of jealousy, *he* was the one showing me off to a crowd.

I was nothing but a prize. He perched me in his lap on the throne. His fangs poised to strike as the room of partying vampires watched in anticipation. His fingers trailed over my skin, his length hard and ready beneath me.

He didn't trail his fingers down my outer thighs, so he had yet to notice my daggers. The silky strips of fabric of the holster were soft enough not to be noticed. I focused intently on the parts of my body I wanted him to touch, imagining them basking in golden desire, while I made the area my daggers rested black and impenetrable.

"Do you want to fuck me, my lord?" I asked him, imbuing my voice with innocence and nervousness.

"Terribly," he growled, throaty and desperate.

"In front of all of them?" I asked, continuing to boost that ego run rampant. Encouraging him to look out over his people celebrating the capture of an ancient, powerful enemy.

You've done the impossible. You won, I whispered softly to his mind. *You're invincible.*

"Yes," he groaned, now slightly grinding against my ass as he breathed into my neck.

"I have a better idea," I whispered with a giggle. "But it's naughty."

Brennan peered down at me as I twisted to look at him, his lips curving into a crooked smile. "Tell me."

I allowed my cheeks to redden, my heart to pick up its pace. "Do you swear you won't think less of me? It's filthy... oh gods, now I'm embarrassed."

Brennan gripped my chin. "Well, now I demand you tell me."

I paused, teasing out the suspense until Brennan was nearing a breaking point.

"I think we should have some fun in the dungeons," I whispered.

Brennan inhaled sharply, his cock impossibly hard. "Oh?"

"You see, I've never been wetter and more aching with need than when you had both of my kidnappers on their knees before you. Rune and Durian, in shackles and powerless. When you'd shown everyone in the palace who the true ruler of Valentin has always been," I said, letting my voice get raspy with my alleged desire. "I want to see them like that again, while you're driving inside me."

The desire was real, my thighs pressing together with want. But instead of envisioning the picture my words painted, I imagined the walls of this palace painted with blood. *Real* blood.

Born blood.

"Fuck, Scarlett," Brennan rasped. "You wicked, wicked creature."

He lifted me at the waist, and I slid to the floor. He twirled me around so that his lips could consume mine again, and I giggled into his mouth.

The laughter was real, too. As real as my smile, as real as the wetness gathering in my thong. The hidden daggers at arm's reach filled my stomach with warmth.

Fate was a melody, a rush as powerful as oceans, its certainty as bright as a field of stars. My veins pumped deep darkness, and sex oozed from my every pore.

I was addictive. I couldn't be denied.

Brennan tongued my lower lip, biting roughly before pulling back. "Let's. Go. *Now.*"

67

SCARLETT

Brennan was so drunk off me that he was ordering guards away left and right, ensuring I had enough privacy to be the naughtiest little slut for him.

This part of the dungeons was far less opulent than the side devoted to sex and debauchery, but they still had a surprising amount in common. Pain, pleasure, denial, and release swept through this vast underground, fueling the power I'd been building since before I knew what I was.

Since before I was *proud* of what I was.

We slipped into a hallway of stone and dim lighting, and Brennan ordered the group of soldiers posted outside a heavy wooden door to leave. They took one look at my wide pupils, flushed cheeks, and Brennan's hand gripping my ass before taking off in unison.

The heat on my neck was a comfort, distracting me from the devastation of what I saw when I entered the dungeon cell.

Rune, blood streaming down puncture wounds in his neck and wrists, his heavy shackles attached to a hard point on the wall above his head. The sight of him impaled, hurting, and slumped against the stone, tore me open inside. I felt his wounds in my own skin, and now I understood just a fraction of what he must've felt knowing I was suffering for weeks at Durian's hand.

My eyes swept to Durian.

The door boomed shut at my back, the sound of it reverberating through my bones.

Durian was staring back, a dribble of spit pouring from the corner of his mouth as if his lips were partially paralyzed. He was in a similar predicament as Rune, without the spiked collar. Still shackled to the wall in a catatonic heap, his blood dripping down to the floor.

"How does it feel to be unable to move and fight, *Durian?*" I asked, using my anger to distract from seeing Rune in pain. I emphasized Durian's name, my refusal to call him *Master* or any other undeserved honorific.

Brennan watched me with a hooded gaze, high off power and delayed gratification.

"I had always wondered—all those times you had me bound to that demented altar—how satisfying it would be to finally see *you* shackled and immobile." I stepped toward Durian, cocking my head as if considering my own question. "I'd say it's exceeded my expectations."

Brennan had little interest in my moment of vengeance and catharsis, already pawing at me, his warm lips on my collarbone.

Durian's eyes went wild, his muscles trembling. "You vile—"

I cut him off. "Whore? Slut? Cunt? Bitch?" My fists clenched, irritated by Brennan ruining my moment with his unwanted advances. I rolled my eyes. "Boring."

"Mm," Brennan groaned. "Keep insulting him while I fuck you, my love."

Brennan cupped my breasts in a way that had me as dry as a desert wasteland.

In a flash of movement, my skirt was on the floor.

My eyes blew wide. Durian had a similar reaction, in direct view of the pretty black belt and dagger on each outer thigh.

Brennan stiffened. I held my breath. Durian laughed.

Rune remained silent.

"Scarlett, dear?" Brennan asked, slowly spinning me to face him instead of Durian. I caught a glimpse of Rune behind him, staring at me fiercely, his tattoos straining against their magickal bondage.

Brennan's gaze raked over my form, homing in on my weapons. "I thought I'd felt something, before…"

For the first time, I sensed a strange quivering in the threads connecting me to Brennan. As if my glamour was slipping.

I smiled, remembering everything Rosalind had taught me. I had to stay calm.

"You think I'd come to this place unarmed?" I asked, counteracting my heightened dangerousness with big, innocent eyes and a slight smile. "The palace was in chaos earlier today, so I came back to court prepared for anything."

I placed both my hands on Brennan's chest. I wasn't fast enough to stab a vampire if his guard was up. I'd learned that lesson by now. I kept my hands far away from my weapons, making him think that the thought of harming him was far from my mind.

"Where were you, during the hearing?" Brennan asked. "I was distracted, after you collapsed, and the fight broke out."

"The succubus and the male submissive dragged her away," Durian hissed.

Rune's gaze was so intense now that it was hard not to meet his dark eyes. He was as still as a statue, as if holding his breath.

I nodded, hoping I hadn't let any of my mounting panic slip into my features. "Yes, Kole and Rosalind took me back to my room and brought me food. Then they left me alone, at my request. So I could arm myself in secret. Evangeline seemed like she had it out for me, after all."

Brennan's grip on my waist was firm. I trailed a finger across his chest, pretending to be utterly oblivious to the knock against my image as an innocent, helpless human.

"You were with Kole," he said, looking away from me as his forehead creased. "Do you know why he left?"

I frowned. "He kept saying something about island madness, but I was pretty out of it and weak. Considering I'd only just regained consciousness and had been starved nearly to death for days."

I let Brennan connect the dots on his own. I needed to get him to stop thinking—to go back to his haze of lust. Rune's eyes burned with rage in my periphery.

"Evangeline said Liza touched you, when you emerged from the tunnels," Brennan said, an accusation he hid behind a casual tone.

"Um, I don't know," I said. "They did have me cornered. I only remember Evangeline touching me." I shuddered as I allowed that memory to resurface.

Brennan's eyes finally softened.

"Secrets, secrets," Durian slurred behind us before laughing like a madman.

The cadence of it made me wince, and Brennan sighed, cupping my face.

"I'm sorry, Brennan. Did I do something wrong?" I asked, putting my hands over his.

He had more unanswered questions. My glamour still hung in the balance, racked by political instability and powerful emotions. But I was stronger. I maintained perfect control, flooding the room with my power.

There's an explanation for all of it. She is everything you've ever wanted. She chose you. You love her flare of danger, and it does not contradict her sexy human innocence. Durian is attempting to get inside your head—don't let him.

Brennan inhaled deeply, his eyes filling with both violence and lust.

"No, Scarlett," Brennan said. "You've done nothing wrong, I'm sure."

My smile faltered. "Why didn't you tell me Rosalind was alive?"

Brennan lifted a brow. "I didn't think you'd care."

"She was my friend," I said. "I mourned her. I thought it was my fault she was killed."

Brennan let out an exasperated sigh. "The thought truly never crossed my mind," he said, his voice dripping with annoyance. "Can we let all of that go now, please?"

Without waiting for my response, he tore off my bra. He hungrily gazed at the peaks of my breasts, a familiar frenzy in his eyes.

Brennan turned back to Rune now with an arrogant smirk. "You should be thanking me, Rune the Ruthless, for allowing you to see these perky tits one last time." Brennan grabbed the back of my neck roughly and pushed me forward to face Rune, gesturing to my body as if I was a sculpture he was auctioning off. "Take a good look. It's all you're ever going to get."

Brennan laughed, tearing off my golden thong next. He dragged his eyes slowly from the space between my thighs to Rune.

"Have a final look at this sweet pussy too," he said. "You should be *praising* me for my generosity."

Anger boiled in my blood. Brennan loved to act like he was the better man, a bastion of chivalry and nobility.

I was as much an object to him as I was to Durian.

I welcomed the divine feminine rage that rose like specters from Crescent Haven's graves, the cemetery where mine and Rune's parents were buried. The place drunk men had torn open my dress and stolen parts of me that didn't belong to them.

None of me had ever belonged to any man.

Though I'd freely given myself to Rune.

We locked eyes—two halves of the same soul, two beings of wrath and darkness. Lillian's divine serpent coiled up my spine, and my eternal flame rose into the night sky, reaching for the cosmos.

The tips of Rune's lips curved ever so slightly, as if he saw what was building inside me.

"How tight is your pretty pussy, Scarlett dear?" Brennan asked, playing with my nipples as he taunted Rune.

"Really fucking tight," I purred. "According to Rune."

Rune made no comment, much to Brennan's growing agitation.

Brennan suddenly fell over the edge of an emotional peak, turning back toward me and slapping me hard across the cheekbone.

I gasped, caught off guard. My eyes stung with tears. My face seared with heat.

"Do not remind me of your impurity, please, sweetheart," Brennan said with a heavy exhale. "I do not want to hear about the men who came before me." Then he stared at me pointedly, waiting for something.

"I'm sorry," I lied.

He kissed my forehead. "Now, where were we?"

He didn't even look at me when his hand slipped between my thighs, his fingers parting my lips. He was only looking at Rune.

He didn't see where my own hands went. My left hand wrapped around his forearm, and my right moved to my outer thigh.

Brennan assaulted me at the same moment I impaled him.

I lodged my dagger into his side, an area home to organs that tended to fare poorly when met with magickal poison.

Brennan dropped to his knees in shock. I took the

opportunity to shove the second dagger in his chest, intentionally missing his heart. The panic in his eyes was so satisfying that I made a throaty groan.

I shoved him, letting him fall back and slam his head against the stone. Blood poured steadily from his skull and his wounds.

He couldn't fight me as I dug into his pants pockets, pulling out two sets of keys.

"Scarlett?" Brennan managed to mumble, searching my face.

I didn't answer him. I didn't even meet his heartbroken eyes.

"Leave the dagger in his chest where it is and take the one in his stomach back, just in case," Rune drawled from behind me, his voice slurred with poison.

I followed his helpful advice, letting Rune keep watch over Brennan's paralyzed form as I approached him.

Rune was grinning, even as blood continued to leak down his neck and chest, his power straining.

I started with the gruesome shackle around his neck. My hands shook as I tried various keys in the lock, glancing back at Brennan periodically.

"Baby, I'm watching him," Rune said gently. "Take a breath. You're okay."

A tear fell down my cheek at the warmth in his voice. I finally found the right key, dropping the incorrect set to the floor before wrestling with the heavy metal. It made my stomach turn over to carefully dislodge the spikes from Rune's neck.

And like he was made of steel himself, Rune made not a single noise as I lifted the heavy collar and tossed it to the ground. Blood poured from his neck in steady streams, and Rune merely sucked in shallow gulps, his eyes glassing over.

"Don't worry," he bit out, "about me. Just remove the cuffs, so I'm free of the blood onyx."

"Won't you still be weak?" I whispered, panic rising in my

guts—cutting through the delirious head high of a successful seduction.

"I will need to feed," Rune said. "To regain my strength."

The wrist cuffs fell to the ground next, leaving Rune free even as he remained slumped against the wall. His vampire healing could kick in now that he was no longer impaled by the blood onyx.

"Oh, duh," I murmured. My head was filled with adrenaline and euphoric compounds from my succubus magick, leaving my senses sharp even as my mind floated.

I straddled Rune, and he managed to chuckle. "Don't think you can have your way with me just because I'm restrained," he growled. When I grinned, he sighed. "Give me your wrist, sweet girl."

"Ask nicely," I said.

Rune's smile broadened, his eyes darkening. "You're going to pay for that."

"Promise?"

I gave him my wrist, and Rune wasted no time sinking his fangs into my flesh. My eyes rolled back.

Durian cackled. I glanced back at him, the way his eyes darted from me to Rune to a motionless Brennan on the floor. Brennan's hands twitched wildly as he grunted unintelligible nonsense.

Durian's demonic, hateful eyes locked on mine. I winked.

"She's a fucking succubus."

68

SCARLETT

I could feel the moment my glamour shattered irreversibly for both born men, Durian's revelation the final crack before total collapse.

"No," Brennan mumbled.

"Yes," I responded, nearly a moan. My lips tipped up, Rune's venom going straight to that bundle of nerves between my thighs.

When Rune's hands finally gripped my waist, I sighed in relief. He was no longer paralyzed. His vampire healing had kicked in, closing each of his wounds.

His power thrummed through the air as he drank my blood, staring hard into my eyes.

The moment his irises flashed in warning, he lifted me off his lap. Rune had Brennan bound to the wall with his thorny shadows before I had time to blink.

The dagger I'd lodged in his chest clattered to the ground.

Rune grinned, walking back to me to help me to my feet and to close the wound on my wrist with a kiss. Then he casually collected the wrist cuffs from the ground and stepped to Brennan, who was writhing and spitting insults my way.

Rune tsked. "One more cruel word about my soul and your tongue is gone."

He only placed one cuff on Brennan, on his left wrist. Brennan stupidly yanked against his bondage to the stone wall as more poison infected his system. His free arm swung wildly. It wasn't long before he fell on his ass.

"You know why I left your right arm unbound?" Rune stood at my side, his fingers slowly running through my hair. I shuddered, leaning against him, finding comfort in his swelling darkness.

Brennan refused to answer.

"Because that was the hand you used to hurt Scarlett."

I knew what was coming. I offered Rune the dagger I'd replaced in my holster, and he kissed my temple before crouching in front of Brennan.

"I don't want to take this from you, baby, if you'd rather do the honors?" Rune asked politely.

"That's sweet of you," I said. "But I don't think I have the stomach for severing limbs yet."

Rune nodded. "We'll work on it."

He slammed Brennan's forearm on the stone, holding it still so his hand was flat.

Though I didn't want to do it myself, I also didn't look away when Rune brought the dagger down in a rush of vampire speed. He cut straight through flesh and bone, blood squirting out.

Brennan screamed. Rune tossed his hand to the side like it was a piece of trash.

He stood, and he walked straight to me, pulling me flush against him as he locked his lips with mine.

I'd never been kissed like this before. Rune's lips consumed mine, his tongue reclaiming the mouth that had only ever belonged to him. Death pushed up against us from all sides, and

I could taste the perilousness of existence, the brutality of love and war that held us in its tight grip.

He gripped my throat without applying pressure. My skin was on fire. My nipples and clit were sensitive as they rubbed against Rune's blood-soaked black uniform.

I pulled back, giggling. "I subdued the enemy wearing nothing but a belt with daggers strapped to my thighs. I stabbed a man, *nakedly*."

Rune laughed. We ignored the screaming, hissing, and spitting from the enemies at each of our backs.

"Yes, you did, baby," he groaned, teasing my neck with the graze of his fangs before lightly sucking. He raised back up. "And it was the sexiest thing I've ever seen. I will be replaying that image in my head for the next several centuries. Possibly forever, because how could anything else compare?"

"I looked hot while I did it?"

Rune raised his brows. "To put it mildly."

"Good. That was all that mattered to me, anyway." I turned and glared at Durian.

Rune followed my gaze, cleaning the dagger I'd given on his pants leg before handing it back to me. "Your turn."

Now this was true love.

"You really are my soulmate, you know that?"

Rune rolled his eyes. "I've known it since that night I watched you work Noel's. But I'm glad you've finally caught up."

We both crouched in front of a crazed and immobile Durian. He glared at me with a hatred that reminded me of every drop of derision men and women had forced down my throat. In those beady black depths, I saw every rape, every assault, every cruel word, every act of emotional or physical abuse. I saw a lifetime of objectification.

A lifetime of underestimation.

"How does it feel, Durian?" I asked again, my voice nearly unrecognizable as I burned with the rage of two decades of trauma. "To have been defeated by the woman you called stupid, useless, weak, pitiful, and worthless?"

I cut open his shirt, revealing a pasty white stomach.

"An ugly canvas, but it will do," I said with a twist of my nose.

"You're not a woman, you're a *mistake*," Durian spat.

I hesitated, seeing a vision of a faceless human leaving me at Helia's temple in Crescent Haven. A helpless baby, unwanted and alone.

"You're a freak of nature that will never belong on this plane. One day you will be put out of your misery, and you will die a nobody whore."

Rune placed a hand on my shoulder.

I looked up at him. "Remove his tongue."

Rune didn't hesitate, yanking Durian's tongue with his fingers before a tendril of razor-sharp shadow squeezed it clean off.

More blood flew through the air, and I squeezed my eyes shut as specks landed on my face.

Rune waited patiently as I sucked in air through my clenched jaw, finally bringing the tip of the dagger to Durian's stomach. In deep slashes, I dug an S into his flesh.

It wasn't very pretty.

The H was a lot better. The straight lines were made for initial carving.

"Marked by Scarlett Hale," I said, my hands no longer trembling. "The woman you brutalized, assaulted, and threatened with rape. The woman who destroyed everything you built. The woman who will ensure you're recorded in history as nothing more than a footnote—remembered only as a madman, a *failure*."

Durian's mouth was full of blood. All he could do was gurgle now.

It was better that way.

"Whoever said vengeance wasn't as sweet as you imagine it in your head was full of shit," I declared.

I rose to my feet, staring down at my abuser as he choked on his own blood. My initials were dug into his skin, his blood was splattered on my naked body.

Rune followed me, his eyes trailing over my form. "Something about you nude, armed, and covered in blood has my obsession with you driven to new peaks, Scarlett darling."

"Do something about it, then," I said, breathless. I was caught in a whirlwind of power—mine and Rune's, forever intertwined by blood and stardust.

Rune's smirk did terrible, wicked things to my body. By the time he'd freed his cock from his pants, I was a mess of desire and need.

He glanced from Brennan to Durian. "Pay attention, boys. Maybe you'll get it right next life." He tongued his fangs, shrugging. "Or not. In my religion, the gods are punishing. Lillian saw what you did to her daughter."

I licked my lips, staring at Rune's imposing length.

He grabbed my chin and forced my eyes back up. "And unfortunately for you, in this life and all the rest, *I* am Scarlett's God."

He lifted me, slowly lowering me onto him, stretching me with his impossible thickness. I cried out, and Rune thrust deep. He pushed me up against the wall opposite the door, giving both Durian and Brennan a side view of him driving into me.

The stone was not very comfortable, but I hardly noticed. All I felt was a tsunami of pent-up emotions crash over me, chief among them, utter fucking relief to be back in Rune's arms where I belonged. I was drowning in dark, depraved magick, all of me yearning for the ultimate heights of release.

Rune angled deep, and I moaned as his lips brushed mine.

"How about you show these lesser men what a perfect, good

girl you are for me," Rune said softly, his voice tickling my ear. "Ass in the air, Scarlett baby."

He lowered me to my feet. We moved to the center of the room where I used my discarded skirt as cushioning, and I arched my back on my hands and knees.

Rune took me from behind, and Brennan made a feral screech. The sound of Rune's accompanying laughter did something to me that had me barreling for the edge of that steep precipice.

"Good girl, good fucking girl," Rune praised. "Now show them those adorable little noises you make when you come on my cock."

He wrapped an arm around my torso and held my back to his chest as he continued to drive deep, his other hand reaching for my clit and moving in circles.

"Look at them," Rune instructed.

It was entirely unhinged, so dirty and sinful that my entire body flushed with heat. I turned my head toward Durian first. I soaked up his hatred before admiring the cruelty I'd shown his body that was only a fraction of what he'd done to mine. My lips curved, feeling Rune stretch me, hold me close against him as my thighs trembled and an orgasm crested.

Then I looked at Brennan, focusing on the sting that still lingered on my cheek from when he'd struck me. He watched me with a fury I'd never seen in his once-handsome features. His handless stump continued to ooze crimson.

My smile and focus were soon to disappear as Rune sunk his fangs into my neck and I finally exploded, my thighs shaking violently now. My scream transformed into contented moans, riding an everlasting orgasm I never wanted to end.

Rune withdrew his fangs. His dark chuckle vibrated through my limp body. "Those were exactly the noises I was talking about. What a good little demon, milking my cock as you find your release." He flipped me over on my back, and now neither of us seemed to care about the hard stone floor. His hips rocked, and my eyes rolled back.

His fingers entered my mouth. His shadows crawled all over me, one of them forming a thorny collar. Others tormented my breasts. I moaned and sucked on Rune's fingers for comfort.

My blood mixed with Brennan's and Durian's. I was drunk off it all—the river of crimson on my pale skin, the sweet retribution, the filthy acts of exhibitionism, the violence and unanswered cries from our prisoners.

Rune stopped to have another drink from my wrist as I writhed with pleasure beneath him. He played with my sensitive clit, and by the time he was back to filling me with his cock, I was exploding all over again.

"To answer Brennan's insightful question from earlier," Rune said, still chuckling as I convulsed beneath him. "Yes, her sweet pussy is impossibly tight." He stroked my cheek. "It's also *mine*."

I saw stars and crimson, heard soft melodies and the sound of blades piercing flesh.

"Forever." Rune licked the trails of my blood his thorny shadow collar had left on my chest. "Isn't that right, baby?"

"Yes," I breathed. "Yours, forever."

"You're going to be marked by your God and dripping with his cum as this palace crumbles," Rune growled.

"By Lillian's grace," I said.

Durian gurgled. Brennan's yells were becoming less and less frequent. Either the poison was overtaking him, or he'd been sufficiently cucked into submission.

I was satisfied by either explanation.

Rune had one last, long drink from my throat and squeezed a third orgasm out of me. I was shattered and boneless as my body was racked with wave after wave. I clung to Rune—the only thing keeping me from drowning in my own pleasure.

With a primal, possessive growl, Rune emptied himself inside of me.

"Those fucking eyes," he hissed through a clenched jaw. "They're a spell of their own."

He slipped out of me and lifted me like I weighed nothing, placing me on my feet and watching me while he pulled up his pants.

"Now look at that beautiful sight," Rune said.

My cheeks flushed, following his gaze to the cum dripping down my thigh.

Rune removed his sleek outer uniform jacket and pulled off his black undershirt. He made a motion for me to raise my arms. I was mesmerized by his bare chest, the whorls and thorns of shadow, his beautiful muscles.

Rune chuckled. "I'm sorry I can't provide aftercare at this very moment, but I swear I'll make it up to you when we're home." He pulled the shirt over my body, so oversized on me that it hung like a dress. "That's better. My eyes are up here, baby."

I slowly found his dark irises again.

"I know you're riding all kinds of highs right now, but I need you to touch back down to earth until we're out of here," Rune said softly, his tone a mix of dominant and warm. "Can you do that for me?"

I tuned back in to the sounds of Durian choking on blood and Brennan spitting cruel insults. I wiggled my toes, reconnected myself to my five senses. I tasted salt from Rune's fingers on my tongue, smelled his comforting, woodsy scent mixed with musk and blood.

Lillian's dark power continued to slither under my skin, reminding me that we weren't finished yet.

I remembered Sadie's clarity spells, the smell of smoke from her bundles of herbs.

"I'm back," I declared, fighting the floaty feeling of Rune's venom in my system.

Rune searched my eyes with a smirk. "Good enough."

As my brain came back online, so, too, did my anxiety. "Wait, who did you come with? Who did I kill?" I asked, grabbing Rune's arm.

He shook his head, his features twisting into confusion before realization dawned. He placed hands on either side of my face to steady me. "I knew it was a trap, Scarlett."

I only stared at him, his words not quite reaching me yet.

"I came alone. I knew they'd barricade me with too many strong fighters to take down in an enclosed space." He dropped his hands back to his sides.

"You knew?" I squeaked. "And you still came?"

Rune smiled, shrugging a shoulder. "Of course, I came. You needed me."

69

RUNE

"I made you a promise," I said, meeting Scarlett's big blue eyes as she stared up at me. "Both of these men have fed from you, no?"

She nodded. "Yes, Rune."

I melted. She was adorably subby right now, fucked into submission while covered in the blood of her enemies. The wicked temptress was riding the greatest high of her life. Yet she looked at me like I was her sun, her only source of life. She was such a good girl.

I stared possessively at her body, now marked with my cum and cloaked in my clothing. It wasn't enough—it wasn't even close. Heads needed to roll.

"Who first?" I asked her.

She pointed.

"Final words?"

Scarlett walked to Brennan. She looked down at his slumped form, the way he shook with rage and humiliation.

"You kiss like a dog," she said, making me both chuckle and see red at the same time. "You're no better than Durian. You were easy to manipulate, and even easier to bring to slaughter.

You couldn't see me through your own overinflated ego, and your blindness to my strength spelled your downfall." She took a breath. "You disgust me."

Brennan was quick to start speaking over her. "You filthy fucking demon," he spat. "You—"

My shadows made short work of his tongue.

Scarlett took a step back and crossed her arms, glancing up at me. "I'm done speaking to either of them. Closure doesn't come from words."

I nodded. "No, it comes from within. It comes from our actions." I tilted her chin up, filling my eyes with warmth as I gave her the praise she deserved. "Your closure came from showing them your strength, your cunning. It came from your rejection of shame, your reclamation of sex and pleasure. It came from the resilience in your bones that humbles me, unlike anything I've seen in all my centuries. Let the flame that refuses to die be your closure, Scarlett."

Her eyes welled with those feelings as vast and deep as the sea. She nodded, and I saw unrestrained fire in their place.

∽

"ARE YOU HUMMING, RIGHT NOW?" Scarlett loudly whispered, throwing me a side-eye.

"Is that not allowed?"

Dead guards lay in a river of blood behind us.

When we rose from the depths of the dungeons, we were greeted by another batch of them at the top of the stairs.

My hands were occupied, so I used my shadows to slit each throat.

I continued to hum the song that Scarlett had sung for me as we stepped over the pile of writhing, dying bodies.

Scarlett shook her head, shuddering as she did every time she glimpsed what I was carrying in each fist.

The floor rumbled, and it wasn't from my power. I could sense a great deal of magick emanating from the heart of the palace, exactly where we were headed.

"Between the energy I was channeling and projecting outward from the dungeons, and the divisions at court... my guess is that more in-fighting has commenced," Scarlett said. "Not everyone was happy with the regime change."

I grinned at the image of the born crumbling from within, without a clue that Scarlett had been the one who'd orchestrated it all. "Naturally." My smile fell, and I paused by a window.

"The main hall is just through here," Scarlett murmured, turning to see why I'd stopped.

She followed my gaze to the crowd of born swarming the palace, soldiers and guards attempting to keep them back as magick flew through the air.

"It would appear that word of Durian's fall from grace has landed with the masses," I said.

"Or they don't give a fuck who's sitting on the throne, and they're most concerned about going hungry and mummifying."

I lifted a shoulder. "Not great for our escape plans, but on a macro level..."

Scarlett smiled. "Mission accomplished."

At the sound of shouts and a loud crash, she nearly jumped out of her skin.

I needed to get Scarlett out of here.

But, first, I had gifts to bestow.

"Scarlett," a woman whispered.

I whipped around, and a blonde woman leaped back. She raised her arms nonthreateningly, swallowing hard.

"Rune, meet Rosalind," Scarlett said.

Rosalind looked better than she had when I last saw her, when she'd been dying in the street. I gave her a nod of respect.

She took notice of what I was carrying, and her mouth fell open, her eyes wide as saucers.

"Okay, cool, cool, cool," she said, stumbling to regain her graceful nonchalance. "I've already gotten out half the slaves. My top secret Rosalind road to safety remains clear, despite the peasant uprising out there." She took a deep breath. "Please, eliminate any aunt you see. I have a feeling you two will serve as the perfect distraction so I can pull the rest of the slaves away from court."

"My shifters say you've maintained contact," I said. I'd received word of their allyship after Scarlett had already left and discovered Rosalind was alive. "Are they being helpful?"

Rosalind grinned, her gaze sultry as she threw a wink Scarlett's way. "In more ways than one."

"Stay safe, please," Scarlett said.

I echoed the sentiment. "Get this last batch out and don't look back. If we can help, we will."

Rosalind reached for Scarlett's hand and gave it a squeeze. Scarlett appeared surprised by the gesture, her features melting.

Rosalind smiled. "See you on the other side."

∽

THE DOORS to the throne room were wide open. Inside, brawling vampires had gone silent, frozen in place. My shadows returned to me, more dead vampires lying in heaps at our backs.

A boom from outside racked the palace's foundations.

I was one step ahead of Scarlett, and we stopped a foot past the doorway. I glanced up at the dais—the empty throne, the floor littered with dead vampires, and the born who'd been engaged in fights but had halted as soon as they'd laid eyes on me.

Then I regarded the mass of bodies on the main floor. I

caught a glimpse of blonde curls in a far corner, a woman in a poofy pink dress ushering humans her way.

But the born stared at me, Scarlett by my side.

After they got a good look, I tossed what I'd been carrying into the space.

Durian and Brennan's heads made a rather unappetizing cracking noise when they met the marble dais.

Before the born could react, I bathed the room in darkness.

I was the only one who could see, and I watched with satisfaction as the slaves linked arms, and Rosalind led them out the back entrance.

"Baby," I whispered. "I'm going to have some fun, now. Stay close."

"Yes, Rune," she answered like a good girl.

I scented her reawakened arousal at the sheer magnitude of my power.

I let it fuel me, the same as her powerful succubus blood in my veins. My gaze narrowed, my senses heightened. I was merely a predator homing in on prey.

The born had already been driven to madness by a cunning succubus who'd entered their ranks. But with their most powerful men's heads on the floor while they bathed in the shadows of Lillian's bastard son—their sanity was obliterated for good.

Scarlett broadcasted her power, and a wave of bloodlust consumed the born scrambling like beheaded chickens.

Some of them managed to resume the fights they were already involved in, doing my job for me as they finished off their rivals. I made short work of the closest group of born, letting my shadows reduce them to mangled body parts.

Toward the far end of the room, where the slaves had escaped, I sent a hellish cyclone of rot and decay. The walls and floor blackened where my magick touched, and hordes of born fell in piles of ash and bones.

Someone wielded light, illuminating where Scarlett and I stood.

I beheaded him next, deftly lifting Scarlett and dodging the blades thrown our way. I flattened us against a wall, my shadows feasting on flesh as I let every last buried emotion and desire burst free from my careful control.

When I'd been captured, I'd been forced to watch Brennan touch Scarlett. I'd been forced to study her poor body covered in bruises and gashes, unable to lift a finger. I'd kept all that rage, horror, and heartbreak carefully tucked behind my guarded armor.

All the while, I'd known this moment would come. When I could finally let my true impulses roam free.

I sensed Scarlett's magick aiding mine, amplifying the room's chaos and hiding us behind a wall of glamour.

Now this was true love.

I stole a quick kiss, her lips melding with mine for too brief a moment.

"Shh," I soothed, her little heart ramping up as she shifted her thighs together.

I spun my web of destruction, wielding magick with a ruthlessness I hadn't been able to use in years. I killed a born for every bruise I'd counted on Scarlett's body the first time she was here, and then I killed a born for each mark I'd seen today.

At a certain point, I found myself laughing at the way their magick and weapons sought me uselessly, the way they fell pitifully to the gaudy rugs and marble. Their shitty art was eaten up by shadow, their tasteless sculptures and furniture shriveling and crumbling to rubble.

By the time a fire had started, I'd already gotten more than enough of my fill of violence.

I wasn't sure who'd lit the match, but at the sight of leaping flames licking up the side of the wall opposite us, I pulled back my straining veil of shadow magick.

"Might be the work of the uprising outside," Scarlett said. She searched my face. "Do you need to feed again?"

Few living born remained. A bold idiot raced toward me, and I took him out with my bare hands, plunging a dagger into his neck. I caught sight of others fleeing through the second set of main doors down from the ones we entered through. I obliterated any I could reach.

I replaced Scarlett's dagger in her holster.

"No, baby, you've given enough. I need you lucid for what's next," I said, answering her previous question.

No one else dared come near us. Scarlett surveyed the damage, the room piled with corpses and decay.

"Okay, so villagers weren't exaggerating about what you were capable of, then," she said with wide eyes. She coughed, the flames rapidly spreading now.

"Are you frightened, Little Flame?" I drawled. My cock twitched, already yearning for her again.

Her gaze became hooded. Her breathing was shallow as she stared at me and my dark power. When she coughed again, I snapped out of my lust.

Before she could answer me, I pulled her into my arms and concealed us with shadow as I took off with vampire speed.

She covered us with her own invisible glamour, making us as energetically uninteresting as possible.

An impressive feat considering we were two of the most interesting beings to grace this realm.

"Do you have a plan?" Scarlett asked, clutching me tight.

"Sort of."

"That's very reassuring."

Someone must've started a fire in multiple places, because I didn't understand how the flames were spreading so rapidly.

I took the grand staircase but ducked around the corner, avoiding the main entrance where bodies were tangled in a vicious battle. Guards were fighting back the growing crowd of dissenters, and at the same time, the remaining born were attempting to escape. My shadow glamour was already wearing thin. I struggled to see through the smoke.

Scarlett coughed. Her heart fluttered. She needed blood replenishing potion. She'd given me more of herself than I would've taken under normal circumstances, but I knew it was what was best for her in the long run.

"We need to take the west exit," someone hissed.

Through the haze, I saw a group of born women slipping through a side hall.

I followed them at a distance as my glamour flickered and Scarlett continued to struggle to breathe.

Between monitoring behind us for trouble and keeping careful notice of my proximity to the women ahead, I fell into a rhythm. Scarlett was breathing easier again as we headed toward clearer air.

It was only when the exit was in sight, doors wide open and fresh air pouring in from the palace grounds, that I sensed the unmistakable prickle of warning raise the hairs on the back of my neck.

"There she is," Evangeline Naya purred, her sickly-sweet voice recognizable to anyone who'd ever heard it.

It was the last thing I heard before Scarlett was ripped from my arms and a heavy chain was pulled tight against my throat.

70

RUNE

"What did Liza see?" Evangeline screamed at Scarlett like a banshee. She'd thrown her up against the wall, mere feet from the doors to our freedom.

I strained against the hexed chain at my throat. I watched Scarlett crumple to the floor, her waves of brunette hair wild, those big blue eyes wide with fear and anger. She moved for a dagger, but Evangeline was quicker.

Evangeline bent her wrist at an unnatural angle, and I heard my Little Flame's bones snap with a crunch that had my stomach turning over.

"What did she *see!*" Evangeline wailed. "You killed her. We know you killed her."

Scarlett screamed, and the sound of it shattered me. She managed to grab the other dagger with her non-dominant hand and surprise Evangeline with a gash to her calf.

My power had been sufficiently depleted. But seeing someone harm Scarlett, for the thousandth time, while I watched helplessly, triggered the deepest rage in my blood.

The primal need to protect what was mine.

I forced the shadows on my skin to leap in search of the

woman at my back. At the sound of blood gurgling, a body went limp behind me. The chain fell to the ground, allowing me to breathe and access what was left of my strength.

Two more women rushed at me, their own sharp weapons raised.

Scarlett had slowed Evangeline down, but she'd also deeply angered her. Evangeline entered bloodlust immediately, crawling on top of Scarlett as she sunk her teeth into her neck.

I fought the remaining two born women as my heart thundered.

Distracting me during battle was a feat only Scarlett could pull off. The truth of the situation was slamming into me, making it difficult to remain calm.

My Little Flame's heart was too slow. She was already drained from my intensive feeding from earlier. And Evangeline was a beast gone rabid, not caring that Scarlett was running out of blood to give, that she'd torn open her delicate neck too roughly. The space between life and death for someone low on blood was a matter of seconds.

It took me three seconds to wrap my shadow vines around the two women, their blood spraying the walls as they fell in heaps of flesh.

It took me two more to yank Evangeline off Scarlett's limp body, to snap her neck and kill her instantly.

Only five seconds.

It had taken five seconds for Scarlett's heart to stop.

~

Time was no longer a concept I understood.

I'd clotted Scarlett's torn open throat with my own saliva and exited the palace.

Scarlett was bathed in blood as I cradled her lifeless body to my chest. When I found an aunt hiding in the gardens, I set Scarlett down gently next to a bed of red roses—her favorite.

I tore open the witch's throat just as Evangeline had done to Scarlett, pulling the woman's essence into my body until she fell, pale and bloodless.

With Scarlett back in my arms, I kissed her forehead, brushing the hair from her own too-pale skin.

"We'll be home soon," I said, unable to recognize my own voice.

I annihilated anyone in my way, now replenished with vile witch blood. I ran with Scarlett down a route I'd studied before I left. I ascended the sloping side streets of Hatham, avoiding the heavy traffic of crowds of born watching the palace burn.

During key moments, I hid us in shadow rather than risk further exertion. Other times I let my shadows feast.

I heard Millie's call before I saw her. My shadowbird soared for us. She would get us the rest of the way home.

In Hatham's grandest park, I had a stunning view of Aristelle. The nighttime cityscape, one of Scarlett's favorite things in this world. The world that had betrayed her, that had shown her cruelty and hatred and endless violence. The world she was hopelessly in love with despite it all.

The wolves had taken Scarlett through here during her first escape. I wondered what she'd been thinking in those moments, what she'd been feeling in that big, beautiful heart of hers.

I looked down at her serene, peaceful features, her body impossibly small and still under my black shirt. It clung to her now, drenched in her blood.

The scent didn't even reach me. I'd gone numb to it.

From my vantage point, I could see a battle on the border. It wouldn't be long before the born realized there was nothing left to fight for except preservation. Scarlett had made sure of it.

Millie landed, causing the ground to tremble. Three more

shadowbirds circled overhead, carrying Uriah, Sadie, and Mason.

Millie's eyes were glassy, her demeanor hesitant as I approached.

"Why do you look so sad?" I asked her. "What pain have you seen? Have the stable workers not given you enough treats lately?"

Millie huffed, her black nostrils flaring. She slowly moved her head toward me, nudging Scarlett gently before staring into my eyes. I swallowed, the onyx of Millie's irises seeing too much of me.

My beast lowered, her webbed wings tucking in as she helped me mount her.

"I don't know why you love this damn city, baby," I whispered to Scarlett as Millie began her ascent. "I've had enough. Take one last look. We're escaping to the countryside for a century or two."

The looks on Mason, Sadie, and Uriah's faces were not ones I wished to dwell on. They stared at Scarlett and me then at each other before going utterly silent. I wanted to tell them they could go back to the victory calls, the laughter and the widest grins.

Instead, I blocked their shock and alarm out completely. I focused on the rushing of wind, the sensation of soaring. I imagined this ride through Scarlett's eyes. What song would be playing in her mind? Which dreams would she be envisioning?

Perhaps she'd be thinking of the ocean she'd yet to see. The one in the painting her mother had hung in the upstairs bathroom of the family cottage. She'd once asked me if the waters could really be that mesmerizing, electric shade of blue.

She'd asked if it was magick, or if it was the beauty of nature.

"It's all magick, baby," I said, kissing her hair.

I CRADLED Scarlett in the room of music. I heard voices outside, soft and hushed and growing steadily louder. I was studying the colors of the galaxies, thinking about how tiny we were in comparison.

I'd put on *Frida and Friends* for Scarlett.

"Blondie, please, just give him a minute," Uriah said.

The witch entered anyway, her green eyes going straight to the blood-soaked girl in my arms.

She was silent for several seconds. Underneath her blonde bangs, her brows creased.

"She needs blood replenishing potion," Snow said. She wiped at her tears, her features shifting from grief to calm resoluteness.

I nodded, gesturing for her to approach with a bottle.

"Gods above," Uriah muttered, coming in after her. Sadie joined him, but Mason stayed outside.

Sadie was staring at Snow, her head cocked, her lips in a deep frown.

"Snow—she's *gone*," Uriah said in horror.

Uncorking the top, Snow knelt in front of me and handed over the bottle. The greenish liquid sloshed, smelling of crisp apples.

"No, she's not," Snow said angrily over a sob.

Uriah's irritation melted into heartbreak, joining Snow on the ground.

"Blondie," he rasped. "Please."

I lifted Scarlett's head.

"This needs to stop—" Sadie started, her eyes wide and her power flaring. Smoky shadows circled her feet.

Snow reached for Scarlett's hand. "No," she said, her voice fierce and level now. "You don't understand."

She locked eyes with me.

"Scarlett isn't dead."

71

SCARLETT

I am not dead!

It felt like I was shouting, but my lips weren't moving. My eyes weren't opening.

"She's possuming," Snow said.

"She's fucking—what?" Uriah asked.

I could hear their voices clearly, but my body was completely shut down. My glamour was locked in place, like a thick black film I couldn't clear.

"I can see her aura," Snow said. "She's alive."

"Sadie?" Uriah asked.

"Auras aren't in my wheelhouse," Sadie retorted. "Explain yourself, please, witch."

"My coven has this ancient text with a chapter on succubi and incubi," Snow said. "My high priestess allowed me to read it, but I couldn't take it or replicate any of its contents. It was part of my research, when I first learned what Scarlett was and wanted to help. There was the briefest mention of what they called possuming. You know, like the animal. Because sex demons are so prone to, well, *being murdered,* some of them develop an ability to fake death when real death is imminent.

It's a defense mechanism, in the hopes that their aggressors relent and they can escape. It's a death glamour, basically. It can last for hours."

"Can she hear us?" Uriah asked.

Yes! I yelled, to no avail.

"I'm not sure. I don't know a lot about it," Snow admitted.

"Knock it off, Trouble," Uriah muttered, hope in his voice. "The attention-seeking has gotten out of hand."

Liquid poured down my throat, and I didn't have the ability to swallow or cough.

"You're safe," Rune said, clutching me tight. "You're safe."

My once-faint heart was thunderous now, the potion working instantly. All of my bodily systems were coming back alive, and I could once again feel pain.

Like the stabbing, stinging bundle of nerves that was screaming in my neck. Or the excruciating throb in the wrist Evangeline had snapped.

I finally coughed, and it was violent. I heaved in air, my vision filling with patchy darkness.

"No, no, no," Mason said, seeming to burst into the room. "She was fucking *dead*."

I wasn't sure if I was hearing laughter or sobs anymore. Maybe a blend of both.

"I'll get a healer," Mason said, softer now.

"I can't see," I croaked.

"Give it a minute," Snow said. I felt her hand on my arm, grounding me.

Rune just held me. I could hear the way his heart had started up again in tune with mine, his breathing matching the rise and fall of my own chest.

He gasped. My vision returned, and I locked on his dark eyes, watery and filled with emotion deeper than the sea.

"I thought that had been the end," I rasped. "I would've been so fucking *pissed*. If Evangeline had been the last thing I saw."

Rune snorted. "Me too, Little Flame. I don't think *pissed* adequately describes what I would have felt. What I—what I *did* feel."

He trembled, a muscle in his jaw feathering as a shudder rolled through him. His shadows crawled all over me.

A single tear fell down Rune's face.

I lifted up even as my entire body protested against it.

I caught the tear on my tongue, following its trail up his cheek.

"You're demented," Rune whispered, his lips curving.

I smiled. "Thank you, Rune."

∼

"How's the wrist?" Snow asked.

I lifted my right hand and wiggled all five fingers. "All better."

We descended the stairs. Snow was in a long lavender gown, and I was in deep burgundy. The fabric was silky against my skin, teasing a hint of cleavage with a side slit to show off the thigh that Rune had possessively marked with a bite.

The castle was full of celebrating vampires and mortals, attendees pouring out the doors and onto the grounds. Laughter floated lazily through the air.

Rune and Uriah tracked us all the way down, as did everyone in the grand foyer. Though the turned knew better than to stare at me for too long, especially with Rune around.

Before, the turned had regarded me with curiosity, the occasional low level of distrust. Now, they looked at me with respect. Though my succubus identity was still confidential, Rune didn't hide the fact that I'd brought down Durian and Brennan from within. In fact, he bragged about me to anyone who would listen, enjoying the way it made my cheeks flush.

He still stared at me with glowing pride, and more than that, with the utmost gratitude I was alive.

Rune lifted my hand to his lips, those dark eyes never failing to rid my mind of all thought but him.

"Beautiful beyond words, as always," he said, his voice low as he bent to kiss my forehead. "Are you sure that you—"

"*Rune*," I warned.

He nodded, his hand falling to rest low on my back.

He'd been nervous to host a celebration in the wake of everything that had happened. He wanted me to understand that the castle was my home now, too, and that my own healing and well-being mattered more than a party.

But he had a duty to his clan, and now, so did I. I *wanted* to celebrate our victory. It belonged to all of us.

"How's the assimilation going?" I asked as we walked down the hall.

Snow and Uriah were arguing behind us in that lighthearted way they did. At this point, I was convinced it was their foreplay.

"We're working with several born and mortal dissenters to finalize plans for the born districts," he said. "Surviving nobility and aunts have gone into hiding. If the born want mortals to move back into their districts, blood cafés to be rebuilt, and feeding clubs to be running normally, then the slave trade needs to end. A hunt has begun for anyone connected to Durian, who has now been rightfully blamed for the blood shortage by the majority of born citizens. It's not perfect, but reasonable people on all sides see that negotiation and rebuilding is the only path forward, as difficult of a path as it will be."

"And the kingdom?" I asked.

We stopped several times as we spoke. Rune introduced me to generals, eyes, and others of his broader circle. Each time they acknowledged my *service*, I hardly knew what to say. It felt strange to accept so much respect when sex and desire were my weapons. But in the end, my weapons were what had ended the war before it began. I'd taken down born leadership and dismantled the entire court.

And I deserved to feel as proud of myself as Rune did.

"Kole delivered the recordings," Rune said. "Earle went into a blind rage hearing his *friend's* unfiltered thoughts about him. He's more paranoid and erratic than ever. But that's no longer our concern, as the kingdom has stepped out of Valentin's affairs for the foreseeable future. So long as we continue to supply their weapons."

"Rune!" a woman exclaimed with a grin. Her face fell when she noticed me, and she eyed me with slight irritation.

I recognized her as the blonde Rune had used to make me jealous in Odessa's dungeons. I held Rune's arm a tad tighter, and Rune chuckled.

The woman sipped blood from a silver chalice as she introduced herself, attempting to conceal her envy. Rune barely glanced at her as he exchanged pleasantries, mostly just staring at my lips.

"I'm not the only one in high demand," I murmured as we walked deeper into the castle.

Rune played dumb, shrugging a broad, chiseled shoulder.

"Are you content with this unspoken alliance with the kingdom?" I asked. The turned clans of Ravenia were putting up a hell of a fight, and I knew that Rune and his clan were sympathetic to their cause.

"No." Rune sighed. "But I have a duty to Valentin. We need to act with care until we're more stable."

I frowned, and Rune spun me around to face him. He dipped me, following to lock his lips with mine as his hands and shadows gripped me tight.

Then his lips went lower, gently sucking on the sensitive flesh of my throat.

When he pulled me back up, I was breathless. Vampires were

all around us, pretending not to watch Rune's uncharacteristic display.

"Any more political inquiries, baby?" He grinned devilishly.

I shook my head. "I know everything is going to work out for us. I'm ready to celebrate."

"Yes it will," Rune agreed. "This is your world, Scarlett. You've proven that. And I intend to help you keep it that way by any means necessary."

"You give me far too much credit," I said incredulously.

Rune was the one who'd waged a war and ruled an entire island for centuries.

"And you give yourself far too little," Rune countered.

He led me out back, where witch lights floated above and people in lavish attire danced to live music. A haze of warmth magick countered the chill of winter.

I caught a glimpse of Reggie in a light pink suit that only he could pull off. He danced with Maize, one of the friendlier human courtesans from Odessa. They both waved at me with smiles.

Rune pulled me close, and I rested my head on his chest as we moved to the sound of beautiful string instruments cascading over us.

Snow danced with Uriah, and I winked at her. She rolled her eyes, still pretending not to be hopelessly in love with her brutish blond vampire.

Uriah was looking down at her like she was the most perfect thing he'd ever seen. His honey blond hair was pulled back into a bun, and he was in a black suit with a lavender pocket square.

Sadie approached from the gardens, and Rune and I exchanged an amused look before laughing to ourselves. She was wearing a shiny black dress and matching gloves that came to her elbows. Her long brunette waves fell down her exposed back. Her heels were so tall, I wasn't sure how she was standing. The dress pushed up her breasts, and she radiated such intense dominant energy that it was hard to look away.

She scanned the crowd, eyes narrowing on Imogene as she approached a stagnant Mason standing by the doors.

"I have never seen Mason *nervous*," I gossiped to Rune, tilting my head in that direction.

He tactfully repositioned to give us a better view. Imogene was blinking up at Mason, her eyes trailing over Mason's bulging muscles in her all-black pantsuit. Imogene's curves were cloaked in a navy blue silk gown.

Mason stared down at her, both of them speaking in hushed whispers. Mason rolled her eyes, hard.

My mouth fell open. Rune chuckled.

"Baby, you are not being covert at all," he whispered.

I watched as Imogene led a painfully stiff Mason into the crowd of dancers, Mason's hands falling to Imogene's waist as they began to move to the music.

"Mason is dancing!" Uriah blurted.

Snow elbowed him.

Mason shot us all glares that might've been laced with real poison.

I laughed, and Rune kissed the top of my head and pulled me close.

The witch lights sparkled above, and the air smelled of pine and firewood. I was surrounded by more love than I knew what to do with.

I relaxed into Rune's hold and fell into the beautiful melody of the current song. I knew that just like Valentin, I had a long road of healing ahead. But surrounded by shadows and loyalty, I'd never been safer.

Rune gently peeled me off him, and I was drunk with happiness when I stared up into his eyes.

He smiled, stroking my cheek. "The first of many surprises and grand romantic gestures has arrived."

I lifted a brow, biting down on a smile. "Oh?"

"Mmhmm," he rumbled. "Get used to it now, Little Flame. You're going to be showered with my obsessive, all-consuming brand of love until you're sick of me."

"Never," I whispered. "I will never be sick of our love."

We were lost in each other's eyes until Rune looked over my shoulder, his smile turning mischievous.

"Scarlett?" a man asked.

I stiffened. My whole body flooded with recognition.

72

SCARLETT

"Jaxon?" I squealed, leaving Rune's arms to run to my childhood best friend. He was dressed in navy and black. His curly brown hair was cut shorter than when I'd last see him, but that familiar silver stud still pierced his right ear.

Jaxon laughed as I nearly tackled him. His arms wrapped around me. He smelled exactly as I remembered, like summer, his favorite bar of soap, and everything wild and untamed.

"Hi, baby girl," Jaxon said.

He stiffened slightly.

"Tell your man I'm not into women," he whispered. "That glare was deadly."

"Noted," Rune said from behind me, joining us with a hand on my lower back.

Jaxon pulled away, and we both grinned as we stared at each other in disbelief.

"Pleasure to meet you," Rune said, offering Jaxon a hand.

Jaxon shook it, giving Rune a polite nod. "When I asked Scarlett if she was going to knock on your door and demand you end the slave trade, I should've known she'd take me seriously." He shifted nervously even as he joked, clearly out of his element.

"Yes, you should've. I'll leave you two to talk," Rune said, amping up the intensity of his power in a silent warning to Jaxon and a comfort to me.

I threw him a pointed look to show him the move was unnecessary.

"About that day," Jaxon began, blowing out a sigh as he scratched his head. "Scarlett, I can't apologize enough. I regretted what I did—how I left things—as soon as I was airborne."

"I think we both felt betrayed in that moment," I said, remembering our conversation in the kitchen.

Jaxon and I had planned our escape for months. We'd dreamed of it for years. And I'd stubbornly refused to abandon my abusive sister, no matter how little she cared for me. I'd thrown all of our adventures away to come to Aristelle—for what appeared on the surface to be a suicide mission. In return, Jaxon had given me the cold shoulder and left without so much as a goodbye.

"Yes, I did feel betrayed," he said. "But I should've told you I loved you, too. I left you hanging, and it was cruel. I was frustrated that you couldn't see Isabella for what she was, and I spoke to you in a way I deeply regret. And even if Isabella didn't deserve your efforts, I shouldn't have been so quick to underestimate you, either." He glanced around, a small smile on his lips. "Because I was clearly, fucking humiliatingly, wrong. And I've thanked Helia for it every day since Rune reached out, and I learned you were alive."

Jaxon and I had never been very touchy-feely, so these were uncharted waters for me. I hesitated only a second before hugging him again.

"I forgive you, Jaxon," I said, pulling back and offering him a smile. It looked like sometimes closure *could* come from words.

But I still had to claim that sense of completion and forgiveness myself, in my own heart. "I'm so happy you're here."

"Where's your bitch sister?"

I laughed, and he finally broke out into that impish grin I adored.

"Heading back to dearest Phillip with her pockets lined with what she loves most," I said, lifting a brow.

Jaxon rolled his eyes knowingly. He made a cunty remark under his breath that had me giggling like old times.

I had no interest in seeing Isabella again, nor her me. I was learning to accept that no one was entitled to my energy, my time, or my sanity. I didn't owe anyone my love or devotion. I gave myself only to those who gave the same in return.

"I'm free of her, or at least, I'm getting there," I continued. "Freedom from Isabella has never been about the physical distance between us. It's a process of cutting the invisible cords she'd wrapped around me when I wasn't looking." I tapped on my temple. "Freedom is in here."

"You sound so wise," Jaxon teased with a crooked grin.

I glimpsed Snow covertly leading Uriah into my line of sight to check on me. I gave her a nod, a ritual we'd been practicing since I first started working at Odessa.

"I like this Scarlett," he said. "You have a radiance in your eyes that burns brighter than I've ever seen. You look strong. Powerful, really." He grinned. "That's all I've ever wanted for you."

"You too, Jaxon," I said. "You seem healthy. Happy."

Releasing the tension between us had lifted both of our shoulders, an air of nostalgic euphoria binding us together. Forgiveness was a powerful thing. Perhaps in time, I would find that same release with Isabella. Not that she would ever hear of it.

It would be a secret serenity I'd claim only for myself.

Because I deserved to live without a drop of resentment

poisoning my heart—my heart that was too full of blinding love to hold anything else.

"Did you see the ocean?" I asked.

Jaxon's eyes lit up.

"Tell me everything."

My second surprise of the night was wearing a shimmering pink gown with white fur draped around her shoulders.

Rosalind had not one, but *two* shifter men on her arms. As soon as she spotted me, she abandoned the men where they stood.

I rose from the couch and embraced her. "Thank the gods."

"We both know which goddess to thank," Rosalind said with a wink.

We shared smiles of comradery, my unspoken secret binding us together forever.

"How did things go for you?" I asked. I'd heard she was safe, thanks to Rune's network of mortals loyal to him in the born districts.

"Things didn't go completely according to plan," she said, a flicker of grief in her warm brown irises. "I saved as many as I could. And I'm going to use my born connections to keep fighting the good fight."

I squeezed her hand. I smiled, overcome with pride at how far she'd come. How far we had *both* come.

"Sit with us," I said.

We'd dragged chairs and couches together in a back drawing room where things were more private. I was sitting in Rune's lap. Next to us were Jaxon and Sadie. Snow was perched on Uriah in a chair, and Imogene and Mason shared a love seat, Mason hilariously bashful as Imogene fawned over her.

Rosalind took a plush black chair across from the couch. She was looking around at the furnishings, the tasteful, classical beauty of Rune's castle.

"This place is lovely," Rosalind said.

"Thank you, Rosalind. I'm glad you could make it," Rune said. He relaxed as soon as I was back in his lap, where I belonged. His smoky shadows crawled across my legs. "And thank you for protecting Scarlett in the castle."

Uriah looked Rosalind's way with a grin. "Heard you killed Liza." He raised his glass.

"Did you really throw her out a window?" Mason asked, her lips tipping up.

Rosalind pointed my way with her own glass. "Scar was partially responsible for the window toss. She got a stab in, too. But, yes, Auntie Rosalind delivered the final blow. A highly coveted kill, I'm sure."

Rune's chest vibrated with a chuckle. "I'd say this whole castle is seething with jealousy."

"Good," Rosalind purred. "Just how I like it."

I shot her a warning look, not entirely enjoying the way she was eyeing Rune. She tilted her head back with playful laughter. It was hard to stay mad at her.

"How many people did you end up stabbing, Trouble?" Uriah drawled.

"Um," I said slowly. The whole circle erupted in laughter as I performed my mental calculations. "Five? I think?"

Snow's eyes widened.

Uriah clutched his heart. "You've made your instructor proud."

Sadie smiled. "You've made us all proud, Scarlett. You claimed your own kind of vengeance. It was a privilege and honor to witness."

Emotion welled in my heart as my gaze flitted around the circle. My friends, my allies. These beings who believed in me, not in spite of who I was, but *because of it*.

"You all did more than witness me step into my power," I said to them. "You each helped me make that leap, in your own way. And I will never forget to be grateful for your patience and your generosity."

Rune's hand rubbed soothingly on my upper thigh. He kissed my ear, and I leaned into his touch.

"None of us make it through this life without help," Sadie said, her power flooding the room. Her darkness teased mine and Rune's, forever intertwined. "The weak fall alone and the powerful rise together."

"I am grateful to have met you, Scarlett fucking Hale," Rosalind said.

Everyone echoed the sentiment, making my cheeks flush with heat. Rune felt my face with his cool fingers, chuckling at my embarrassment. I attempted to elbow him but was immediately restrained by shadow.

I met Snow's eyes—that soft green that had comforted me in my darkest moments inside the palace. Her wisdom that had broken through my walls of shame and fear. The voice that had taught me how to finally accept the love always dangled just a touch out of reach.

Love for myself, the greatest love of my life.

She smiled. "You used to clip your own wings when you flew too high. Now, you can't help but soar."

73

RUNE

I watched early morning sunlight fall across Scarlett's fair skin, illuminating the slight rosiness of her cheeks, the long, dark lashes that softly fluttered as she dreamed.

I was sitting up, resting against the headboard.

It was comforting and familiar to watch her while she was unconscious and unaware of my obsession. I got to admire her exposed, nude body in peace, without her sharp tongue and bratty banter.

I loved it all.

I loved her silent and vulnerable, and I loved her wicked and unrestrained. I loved her wild and covered in enemy blood, and I loved her docile, on her knees, staring up at me with the recognition that I was her one and only God.

She breathed deep and slow. When her hand twitched, I wanted to kiss every finger.

I tried not to think about when Scarlett's heart had stopped beating. In that space of lost time, my body and brain had been operating, but my soul had left in search of hers.

I'd only experienced that kind of cavernous, obliterating

terror once in my life. And that was the day I'd found my sisters' bodies in Crescent Haven's woods in early autumn.

Scarlett still didn't know anything about her birth parents or why she was left at Helia's temple in some nowhere village. She wanted answers, and I would support her in that endeavor.

But, personally, I enjoyed the serendipitous mystery of it all. She was new life that had sprouted in a decayed wasteland, the spring that followed winter. I'd been powerless to save my sisters, and now Scarlett was mine to protect forever.

Early autumn had once been a time for mourning. Not only my sisters, but my humanity too. Now autumn was a time for gratitude. Because of all the places to leave a vampire-human baby, Scarlett's savior had put her in my path.

I wanted to believe it was all magick, all karma and soul connections, and who was I to rob myself of this humanlike devotion to the ethereal?

Scarlett stirred, and my gaze jumped to her features, assessing them for signs she was trapped in a nightmare.

They remained peaceful.

I slowly trailed my fingers through her long, dark hair. She only relaxed deeper; her soul knew it was safe with mine.

"Thank you," I whispered to her, my heart clenching. "You were well worth the wait."

I lowered, brushing my lips to her forehead as I lay next to her. I watched as my shadows moved from smoke to solid form, one of them coiling around her throat. Their thorns stayed tucked in.

I moved on top of her, hovering without placing my weight. One of her hands was up near her head, the other resting on her stomach. I kissed each of her breasts, her skin warm beneath my touch.

My lips continued their trail lower until I found my target. I eased between her thighs, gently shifting them. This perfect pussy belonged to me for an eternity. I refused to let a day go by without showing my appreciation.

As soon as my tongue found her clit, Scarlett's breathing changed. I loved playing with her when she was trapped between sleep and consciousness, adorably confused and surrendered to pleasure.

As soon as I heard her first groggy moan, my gentleness shifted to hunger. I devoured her, her legs already beginning to tense and tremble.

"Good girl," I purred, my voice humming against her sensitive flesh.

"Rune," she mumbled, another moan escaping her.

She deserved to be rewarded for moaning my name like that, knowing how much it drove me insane.

I sucked, pulsing over her clit as I angled two fingers inside her.

She clenched around me, her legs moving together as she came closer to the edge.

"I'm so sleepy," she whined, her voice a soft rasp.

I chuckled. "No whining. Be a good girl and come for me, little demon."

At this, her flame sparked to life. But her desire to come was far more powerful than her desire to be disobedient, evidenced by the way she began to gently grind against my mouth.

When she moaned my name again, I knew she was desperate for release.

I angled my fingers, pumping them inside of her as I sucked her clit with the exact speed and pressure she needed.

Scarlett fell easily, exploding on my tongue as her body went slack.

I kissed her sensitive flesh before easing back up her body. I stared into those bright blue eyes, deep enough to drown in while searching for a bottom that didn't exist.

"Good morning."

She smiled dreamily. "You wake up too early."

"You would spend your life asleep without me. I'm not sure how you survived this long on your own."

That sharp tongue poised to strike, and I captured it with a kiss before it could.

Scarlett relented easily, beautifully submissive before she'd had a chance to fully awaken.

She paused, and I heard her heart stutter. I raised up, my eyes tracking the way her hand had shot to the shadow around her throat.

"Sorry," she mumbled, giving her head a little shake.

I pulled back my shadow.

"No," she said quickly. "It's okay, I just got confused."

I pulled her hand into mine, shifting onto my side to face her. I trailed my fingers gently down her shoulder.

"Ever since you were first rescued, I've seen you reach for your neck hundreds of times. Sometimes, you panic, as if you've forgotten something," I said slowly, watching her body stiffen as I continued to feed her soothing touch. "He made you wear a slave collar, didn't he?"

I'd never seen her in it, but I remembered seeing imprints on her neck at the meeting with Kole and assumed that was the case.

"Yes," Scarlett said.

"He was not a master, Scarlett. He was a piece of shit misogynist. Durian *wished* he was man enough to earn true respect and submission, but he died a lowlife cuck driven to insanity by his own grandiose delusions."

Seeing Durian's head fall to the ground was a memory I would live inside every time Scarlett flinched. Every time she woke in the middle of the night screaming. Every time she left Belise and immediately crawled in my arms to cry until she felt safe again.

She nodded, her tension easing a touch. "I know it was

nothing like when you collared me," she said. "Nothing he did was anything like what happens between you and me."

It warmed my heart to hear her say that, to reassure me that I had made her feel cherished even during our roughest play sessions. Scarlett deserved to experience every ounce of pleasure, even the kind that came from pain and degradation. I was immeasurably proud that she'd learned how to accept her darkness even through her years of trauma.

"Collaring isn't about the dominant, even in the strictest master and slave relationship. In a consensual dynamic, everything is for the benefit and pleasure of the sub. Rules, protocol, and limits are entirely dictated by the person who voluntarily relents their power. It's all theater, a game, for both parties. I collared you because *I* am devoted to *you*." I kissed her forehead. "Because you are mine to protect, mine to cherish, mine to take care of—mind, body, and radiant soul. You will choose to serve me only if you deem *me* worthy of that honor."

Scarlett traced my jaw, and I captured her hand to brush my lips against her knuckles.

"Rune, you have earned my respect a thousand times over. You have held me and nourished me during my lowest moments. You have fought for me when I didn't know how to fight for myself. You have allowed me to be my own person, make my own decisions, even if you disagree. You've never taken away my agency, and you have only ever made me feel heard and respected, even in a room full of vampires far older and more powerful than me."

Her lower lip trembled, and I traced it with my thumb. "I wouldn't be so quick to say others are more powerful than you, baby."

She smiled. "You see me for exactly who I am. It used to frighten me, the way you've always been able to penetrate straight through to my core. But now, I feel safest when I'm spread bare before you."

At this, I smirked.

"You worship even the darkest parts of me. You always have," she continued. "I thought soulmate love was for other people. But you proved me wrong." Her eyes welled. "You are my home, Rune."

"And you are mine." I kissed her slowly, drinking her vulnerability like it was the most powerful drug. "You know I love when you manage to spin such sweet, beautiful words with that spiteful mouth of yours."

We stared into each other's eyes as my shadows pulled her close.

"I *want* to give you all of myself the same way you have done for me," she said. "I want to explore everything in this world with you, even the things my abusers attempted to steal." Her eyes burned into mine, those full lips curling into something beautifully defiant. "I want to reclaim it all."

"If that's what you desire, then that's what we will do," I assured her. "I only ask that you take it slow. Don't let me push boundaries before you're ready. I don't want to re-traumatize you."

She absorbed my words, her mind churning with consideration. "No implements yet, but bare-handed spanking is no longer a limit."

I smiled. "Is this your way of asking to be put over my knee?"

Scarlett blushed hard. "No!"

"Don't think I haven't been silently adding to your list of offenses."

"There is no list," she said. "I am a perfect angel. It is you who is evil."

Scarlett was over my lap before she understood what was happening. She flailed wildly, and I laughed at her pitiful attempts to crawl away.

She huffed, turning her head to the side and glaring angrily.

I massaged her perfect ass. She kicked her legs.

My shadows made quick work of a leg bind.

"It might be hard to punish someone so cute," I drawled.

She relaxed. Scarlett was intelligent enough to know the truth: There was nowhere to run where I wouldn't find her.

"Sorry, I meant it might be hard for *others*. But like you said," I caressed her cheekbone, moving her hair behind her ear, "I am evil."

I delivered a slap to her ass. It was enough to make her gasp in surprise, but it wasn't intended to cause more than a sting.

After the second spank, I slipped a finger inside her. "Baby, why are you already so wet?"

"I have my reasons." Her voice was slightly muffled against the comforter. She clenched her jaw as my hand came down again. I pushed her head further into the bed before twisting her hair into my fist.

"You might be good at spinning those beautiful lies and half-truths for lesser men, but you know I demand your absolute honesty," I said, enjoying the way I'd left red handprints on her ass.

My perfect, fuckable ass.

I went easy on her, the impact far more pleasurable than painful. I watched her face and her body, checking in every once in a while with words.

When I was finished playing with her, she curled up in my arms. She trailed her fingers along my muscles, her heart slowing.

"I've never felt safer," she whispered with a contented smile. "Thank you, Rune. You were worth the wait and more."

74

RUNE

I entered the deliberation room, flanked by Uriah and Mason. Our guest followed close behind.

Kylo, the Hekate clan's leader. One of the groups of turned vampires in Ravenia seeking to overthrow Earle and establish a new council.

He was one of the few men I did not tower over, as he matched my height. He was tattooed, but I wasn't sure if the constellation of dark markings were ornamental, clan-related, or of magickal origins.

I could sense strong magick, but he kept its nature carefully concealed. His hair was black, his eyes a deep blue.

I gestured for him to take a seat at the end of the table, Mason at my side and Uriah at his. No one sat at the head. I preferred to keep the air casual, encouraging Kylo to feel as comfortable as possible until we had a better understanding of him and his clan's aims.

He was young, likely turned in his midtwenties. When and by whom was uncertain, but I could sense he wasn't anywhere near a century old. Immortality had ways of showing up in a vampire's mannerisms and demeanors even if their youth remained changeless.

"Will your better half be joining us?" Kylo asked casually. He rested his hands on the sleek wood, watching my face with careful attention.

Though his tone and smile were polite and lighthearted, a tendril of darkness coiled up my spine at his interest in Scarlett.

"My apologies," he said. "Word is spreading quickly, you see. Of Rune's mysterious human partner in crime who destroyed the born from within."

I smiled at this summary of events, but that smile was quick to fade. Scarlett's part in Durian's downfall wasn't common knowledge, especially given its recency. Aristelle was run rampant by rumor and speculation about Scarlett's time on both sides of the border. Her role wasn't entirely understood by anyone but my inner circle, considering few born had lived to tell the tale.

How a clan leader from Ravenia knew that she was directly responsible was a perplexing question indeed.

"I'd prefer to keep her a mystery to unknown powers, as I'm sure you can understand," I said curtly.

"I understand more than you know." His gaze unfocused for the briefest lapse, as if remembering something.

An interesting slip of the tongue, but not my main concern. "You want exports. Blood onyx, blood replenishing potions..."

His eyes lit up at each magickal good and weapon listed, confirming the obvious. "I know the timing isn't optimal. I understand the hold that the kingdom still has over Valentin, its military power wielded as an ever-present threat should you choose to cut financial ties."

I nodded. At least he was lucid about the impossibility of his ask, when we'd only just narrowly escaped our own war.

Uriah watched Kylo thoughtfully, and I could sense his excitement bubbling under the surface. Ever the idealist, Uriah had been anticipating this meeting for weeks, hoping it might sway me into some form of allyship.

Mason shared my guarded vigilance.

"I came myself, during a time my clan needs my presence and leadership more than ever," Kylo said. "I knew the risk I faced taking to the sky, and the increased risk upon my return. But I believe in the value of putting a face to a name. I am doing this for my people—turned vampires and innocent mortals alike." His demeanor remained respectful even as he spoke with increasing authority. "Though we haven't met, I grew up on stories about you. I've studied your moves during Valentin's civil war, read everything in our libraries about you, however sparse. I believe in showing respect when respect is due and learning from those who came before."

"You make me sound ancient," I said, my lips turning up.

There was a charming genuineness to Kylo's little speech. Whether it was calculated flattery, I had to admit it was convincing. From what little I'd heard about his personality from my eyes, he'd been described as arrogant, ambitious, and cold.

But I knew that those were also words that the world had used to describe *me*.

He laughed. "You don't look it."

"Hey, only I'm allowed to flirt with Rune," Uriah said, leaning back in his chair. He glanced between Mason and me with a sigh. "Is there anything we can do on the down low?" He quickly added, "After further vetting, of course."

I rolled my eyes at Uriah's over-excited transparency.

"On the surface, I think it's obvious where my clan stands idealistically," I said to Kylo. "And it is not with the kingdom. But I will not jeopardize my clan's rule nor Valentin's mortal populations. Without the mortals, we wouldn't have access to the goods you seek, anyway." I paused. "You may state your case. And, if convincing, we can discuss options."

"That's all I can ask for," Kylo said softly.

By the time he was finished, I already knew where I stood.

I cursed the dickhead for making my life more complicated.

When all I wanted was to escape to some nowhere village and continue to scientifically test if I could impregnate my succubus soulmate.

It wasn't remotely possible, according to Sadie.

But a man could try.

EPILOGUE

SCARLETT

Rune carried me in his arms. My eyes were open, but all I saw was darkness. The only noise I could discern was the rapid beat of my own heart.

Then I was moving. I squealed the moment my feet touched something like dirt, but softer. My toes dug into the damp grittiness, and I felt Rune's lips on mine.

He unveiled his shadows.

I gasped, my senses returning all at once. Crashing assailed my eardrums, and I nearly raised my hands to cover my ears. They adjusted to the sound slowly.

Besides, I was too overcome with the vision before me to care about hearing loss.

Ocean waves rose and fell with a power I felt in my bones. The sun was ascending over the vast blue, painting the sky in hues of pink and orange that shimmered in the sea's reflection.

Rune laughed at me softly, but I didn't care about that either.

All I could do was walk forward, lips parted and eyes wide. I didn't want to miss a thing. I looked down at the sand, the way it rose around my submerged feet the closer I got to the sea.

The cool water was up to my ankles, and when a tall wave crashed and moved toward me, I squealed and backed right up into Rune's chest.

He wrapped his arms around me, bending to kiss my temple. "Look what you would've missed out on if you hadn't woken up when I told you to." He trailed a finger down my arm, and I shivered. "Bet all that whining and begging feels silly now, huh?"

"It was like, four in the morning!" I protested. "How was I supposed to know your surprise was worth it?"

Rune tsked. "Bad girl. When have any of my surprises ever failed to exceed your expectations?"

It appeared we'd already reclaimed the word *surprise*. We'd been reclaiming a lot of things lately.

At those glorious mental images of submitting to Rune in increasingly depraved ways, my core tightened. I became hyperaware of Rune's hold over me, physical and mental.

"Never," I admitted. I stared at the bright blue waters, unable to hold back a grin.

"Mm," Rune hummed his approval.

I saw a giant rock in the distance, heard the calls of birds above. I peered over Rune's shoulder to the sloping hills of sand, rocks, and green plants with blooming pink flowers. The tops of homes and buildings lay beyond.

"Can we swim?" I asked, nearly bouncing with excitement.

Rune laughed. "Do you know how?"

"Uhhh…"

Rune laughed harder, and I glared up at him.

"I'll teach you, Little Flame. You're a quick learner," he murmured, tilting my chin up. "You might want to take off your clothes first."

I looked down at the bottom of my cornflower blue gown billowing in the water. "Right."

"There's more," Rune said.

"How could there possibly be more?" I gestured to the vast

landscape of shimmering blue touched by Helia's radiance. "Than *this*?"

"I brought you the next two chapters," he said. "To read on the beach, when you inevitably tire yourself out learning to swim."

At the adorable hesitation in his usually assured features, I melted.

Now I really did jump up and down, making Rune roll his eyes as water splashed.

"I can't wait to read them."

"Don't get too excited," he said. "You know what happens when I finish the book."

My stomach dropped at that reminder. I crossed my arms. "I'm not ready yet."

Rune chuckled. "I'll make sure you're ready." He tucked strands of my hair behind my ears—a futile effort, considering the wind would undo his work with the next gust. "You've already sung in front of a crowd, remember? Three times now."

"The first time was a succubus oopsie accident," I said quickly, remembering when I'd accidentally seduced a crowd of witches and shifters with my voice in Lumina's park. "The other two... they were small crowds, and you had to literally dominate the fright out of me."

Rune had forced me to sing in a couple small venues around Aristelle, in front of *strangers*. I'd only ever been an opening act, just for a song or two.

It had been horrible. And exhilarating. And I'd hated it. But I'd also loved it.

Besides, I'd been rewarded with ice cream.

"And I look forward to the domination required to get your bright red ass out onto the opera house's stage," Rune said.

That was our deal. Rune finished his novel, and I performed before hundreds, just like he'd always dreamed.

Just like *I* had always dreamed. Before, I thought I'd have to wait for my next incarnation. Now, Rune was stubbornly insisting I live out my every last fantasy, no matter how grand or unachievable they each seemed.

"You have a long way to go," I said, in an effort to soothe my racing nerves at the mere prospect of standing on that enormous stage.

Rune shrugged. "Maybe it's a novella."

"No. No way. No cheating."

He laughed. He flipped me around, undressing me himself. "You're keeping your underwear on. I don't want to have to murder the locals."

When he left to place my dress with our belongings on dry sand, I turned and gazed out at the rising sun. I remembered how I'd felt right before I left Crescent Haven, imagining great adventures and even greater loves.

What the gods had given me was infinitely more magickal than anything I could've conceived of myself.

"I'd do it all over again," I said softly when Rune returned.

The waves were as magnitudinous as our intertwined power, his thorny shadows and my deceptive, beautiful webs of desire.

Rune placed his hands on my waist as the tide rolled in and water rose up around us.

"All of it—the heartbreak, the loss, the betrayals and the sacrifices. I would live every moment all over again. Just to stand here in the sand with you."

The ocean roared, and I realized it wasn't unlike the steady hum of fate that had been guiding me through this life, as if by an invisible thread.

"You were always the destination, the tomorrow I sought on the horizon."

"You mind if I steal that?" Rune whispered with a wicked grin. "It would go great in a novel."

"Take whatever you need."

He lifted me into his arms, his lips an inch from mine as we sunk into the vast sublime, the great unknown. Together.

"Always."

ALSO BY MAGGIE SUNSERI

ETERNAL OBSESSION DUET
Stalked by Seduction and Shadows
Taken by Touch and Torment

THE LOST WITCHES OF ARADIA
The Discovered
The Coveted
The Illuminated
The Hunted
The Scorned
The Claimed
The Redeemed

ABOUT MAGGIE SUNSERI

Maggie Sunseri is the author of fantasy romance books by day and a witch, tarot card reader, and succubus by night. She has a bachelor's degree in Anthropology/Sociology. When she's not traveling the world, you'll find her curled up with a good book and a hot cup of tea, pretending it's autumn no matter the season.

She also writes a Substack about spirituality and witchcraft, critical theory, sexuality, holistic health, community building, and addiction and trauma recovery.

Connect with Maggie:
maggiesunseri.com

Made in the USA
Columbia, SC
10 February 2025